DATE DUE			

DINOSAURS

DINOSAURS

STORIES BY RAY BRADBURY,
ARTHUR C. CLARKE, ISAAC ASIMOV
AND MANY OTHERS

Edited By

MARTIN H. GREENBERG

DONALD I. FINE BOOKS
NEW YORK

DONALD I. FINE BOOKS
Published by the Penguin Group
Penguin Books USA Inc., 375 Hudson Street,
New York, New York 10014, U.S.A.
Penguin Books Ltd, 27 Wrights Lane,
London W8 5TZ, England
Penguin Books Australia Ltd, Ringwood,
Victoria, Australia
Penguin Books Canada Ltd, 10 Alcorn Avenue,
Toronto, Ontario, Canada M4V 3B2
Penguin Books (N.Z.) Ltd, 182–190 Wairau Road,
Auckland 10, New Zealand

Penguin Books Ltd, Registered Offices:
Harmondsworth, Middlesex, England

Published in 1996 by DONALD I. FINE BOOKS
an imprint of Penguin USA, Inc.
1 3 5 7 9 10 8 6 4 2

PUBLISHER'S NOTE
This is a work of fiction. Names, characters, places, and incidents either are the product
of the authors imagination or are used fictiously, and any resemblance to actual
persons, living or dead, events, or locales is entirely coincidental.

ISBN 1-55611-482-6
CIP data available

This book is printed on acid-free paper,

∞

Printed in the United States of America

AUTHOR NOTES

RAY BRADBURY made his first professional fiction sale in 1941 and contributed fantasy, mystery and science fiction to pulp magazines including *Weird Tales, Thrilling Wonder Stories, Planet Stories*, and *Dime Mystery*. His first book, the collection *Dark Carnival* (1947), is a seminal work of modern fantasy, and his first two novels, *The Martian Chronicles* (1950) and *Fahrenheit 451* (1951) are milestones in postwar science fiction. Much of Bradbury's fiction is suffused with nostalgia for childhood and his small-town past, glimpses of which can be found in his five semi-autobiographical novels *Dandelion Wine* (1957), *Something Wicked This Way Comes* (1962), *Death is a Lonely Business* (1985), *A Graveyard for Lunatics* (1990), and *Green Shadows, White Whale* (1992). Bradbury has also edited two collections of modern fantasy, adapted his stories for the comics, written several volumes of plays and poetry, and turned out screenplays for several movies, including John Huston's "Moby Dick." "The Foghorn" was adapted in 1953 as the film "The Beast from 20,000 Fathoms."

With over 400 hundred books to his name, ISAAC ASIMOV is one of the most prolific writers of all time. He sold his first science fiction story in 1939 to *Amazing Stories*, and quickly became one of the leading writers of science fiction's "Golden Age." *Astounding Science-Fiction* published many of the robot stories in which he evolved the now-classic "Three Laws of Robotics," and in 1941 "Nightfall," considered by many the single best science fiction story ever written. In 1942 Asimov wrote his first "Foundation" tale, about a future galactic empire loosely modeled on the Roman empire, and for the next 50 years developed its history through a series of novels including *Foundation* (1951), *Foundation and Empire* (1952), *Second Foundation* (1953), *Foundation's Edge* (1982), *Robot's and Empire* (1985), *Foundation and Earth* (1986), and *Prelude to Foundation* (1988). He is also the author of the Black Widower mystery series, the Lucky Star science fiction juveniles (under the pseudonym Paul French), and numerous books and columns of popular science. He is a recipient of the Nebula Award and a multiple Hugo award winner, most recently for *I, Asimov* (1994), a posthumously assembled collection of reminiscences.

PAT CADIGAN's first contribution to science fiction and fantasy was the acclaimed semi-professional magazine *Shayol*, which she co-edited with her husband Arnie Fenner between 1977 and 1985. Her first short story appeared in 1978, and her first novel, *Mindplayers*, in 1987. Her second novel, *Synners* (1989), is considered one of the major works of cyberpunk fiction. Cadigan is a distinguished writer of short fiction, and her collections *Patterns* (1989) and *Dirty Work* (1993) collect most of her fantasy and science fiction stories to date, including the Nebula Award-nominated "Angel" and "Pretty Boy Crossover." Her most recent novel is *Fools* (1992).

ARTHUR C. CLARKE is probably best known for his collaboration on the screenplay for the 1968 film "2001: A Space Odyssey," which grew out of his story "The Sentinel" (1951) and novel *Childhood's End* (1953), and resulted in his novelization of the film and two sequels, *2010: Odyssey Two* (1982) and *2061: Odyssey Three* (1988).

The blend of hard science and metaphysics that distinguishes this series can also be found in Clarke's novels *Against the Fall of Night* (1953), *The City and the Stars* (1956), and *Rendezvous with Rama* (1973), which won the Hugo, Nebula, John W. Campbell, and British Science Fiction Awards. He has written many books of popular science, most notably *The Exploration of Space* (1951), and much of his best short fiction has been collected into *More Than One Universe: The Collected Stories of Arthur C. Clarke* (1991). Although British by birth, Clarke has lived since 1956 in Sri Lanka. His two most recent books are his autobiography, *Astounding Days* (1989), and the novel *The Ghost from the Grand Banks* (1990).

KRISTINE KATHRYN RUSCH has compiled enviable publishing credits since she began writing professionally in 1987, including the science fiction novella *The Gallery of His Dreams* (1991), the fantasy novels *The White Mists of Power* (1991) and *Heart Readers* (1993), and the horror novels *Facade* (1992) and *Sins of the Blood* (1994). She received the John W. Campbell Award for Best New Writer in 1990, and has appeared in numerous magazines and anthologies, including the *Full Spectrum* and *Year's Best Fantasy and Horror* series. With Dean Wesley Smith she founded the specialty press Pulphouse and edited twelve issues of *Pulphouse: The Hardcover Magazine* between 1988 and 1994, as well as *The Best of Pulphouse* (1991). In 1991, she became the editor of *The Magazine of Fantasy and Science Fiction*.

MICHELLE SAGARA is the author of "The Sundered" saga, a fantasy epic of the struggle between good and evil that currently includes the novels *Into the Dark Lands* (1991), *Children of the Blood* (1992), *Lady of Mercy* (1993), and *Chains of Darkness, Chains of Light* (1994). A John W. Campbell Award nominee, Sagara has also written short fiction that has appeared in *Dinosaurfantastic!* and other anthologies. When not writing, she runs Bakka Books, Canada's premiere science fiction bookstore.

EDWARD BRYANT is that rare writer who has distinguished himself in fantasy, horror *and* science fiction, and done so almost exclusively in the short-story form. He is the author of *Cinnabar* (1976), a collection of dark stories set in a future California, and the novella *Fetish* (1991), a tale of modern witch craft. Bryant collaborated with Harlan Ellison on *Phoenix Without Ashes,* a novelization of the teleplay for the pilot "Starlost." His story collections include *Among the Dead and Other Events Leading Up to the Apocalypse* (1974), *Particle Theory* (1981), *Neon Twilight* (1990), and the forthcoming *Flirting with Death.* For the last five years, he has worked as a book reviewer for *Locus* and the annual compiler of "Horror and Fantasy in the Media" for *The Year's Best Fantasy and Horror* collections.

HOWARD WALDROP's renown as a writer of some of the most audacious and offbeat short science fiction of the last two decades is reflected in the titles of his story collections: *Howard Who?* (1986), *All About Strange Monsters of the Recent Past* (1987), and *Night of the Cooters* (1990). His characteristic extrapolation of fanciful adventure from solid historical fact can be found in the alternate history novel *Them Bones* (1984), and *A Dozen Tough Jobs* (1989), which reconceives the legend of the twelve labors of Hercules for a heroic saga set in the depression-era American South. Waldrop won the Nebula Award for his 1980 story "The Ugly Chickens."

In his nearly fifty years as a writer of fantasy and science fiction, POUL ANDERSON has won six Hugo Awards and two Nebula Awards for his short fiction. His scores of novels include *Brain Wave* (1954), *The High Crusade* (1960), *Three Hearts and Three Lions* (1961), *Tau Zero* (1967), and *The Boat of a Million Years* (1989). Anderson is probably best-known for the many novels and short stories of Nicholas van Rijn and Ensign Dominic Flandry, which comprise a future galactic history loosely fashioned from the social and political undercurrents of Europe's golden age of exploration, and include *The Day of Their Return* (1973), *A Knight of Ghosts and Shad-*

ows (1974), and *The Earth Book of Stormgate* (1978). His Hoka stories, which were written in collaboration with Gordon R. Dickson and collected in *Earthman's Burden* (1957), *Star Prince Charlie* (1975), and *Hoka!* (1984), rank as one of science fiction's few successful comic series.

Canadian author ROBERT J. SAWYER began writing science fiction professionally in 1981. He published his first novel, *Golden Fleece*, in 1990, and has since become known for his Quintaglio Trilogy—*Far-Seer* (1992), *Fossil Hunter* (1993), *Foreigner* (1994)—which imagines a world not unlike our own, save that dinosaurs have emerged as the dominant intelligent species. Sawyer has also written *End of An Era* (1994), about time travel to Earth's Creataceous period, and *Terminal Experiment* (1995), a science fiction suspense novel. He has twice won Canada's Aurora Award for science fiction, and is a recipient of the Crime Writers of Canada Arthur Ellis Award.

Over the last twenty years, SHARON FARBER has written dozens of short science fiction and fantasy stories for *Whispers, Isaac Asimov's Science Fiction Magazine, Amazing Stories*, and *Omni*. Her work has been anthologized in *Sherlock Holmes Through Time and Space, Blood is Not Enough*, and *The Orbit Science Fiction Yearbook*. Farber's tales range in tone from the whimsical "Space Aliens Saved My Marriage" and "Dr. Sharon N. Farber's Science Fiction Weight Loss Diet" to the poignant "Return of the Dust Vampires," a World Fantasy Award nominee. She practices medicine in Tennessee.

HARRY TURTLEDOVE's first two novels, *Wereblood* and *Werenight*, appeared under the pseudonym Eric Iverson in 1979. Since then, he has written six novels in his acclaimed Videssos Cycle, which begins with *The Misplaced Legion* (1987) and tells of Roman legion that finds itself transported to a kingdom where magic works. Turtledove's training as a history professor informs much of his science fiction, including the alternate histories *A World of Difference* (1990), *The Guns of the South* (1992), and *Worldwar: In the Balance* (1993). His short fiction has been collected in *Kaleidoscope* (1990) and *Departures* (1993).

L. SPRAGUE DE CAMP is one of the best known writers from science fiction's "Golden Age," and the author of numerous stories and non-fiction articles for *Astounding Science-Fiction* and other pulp magazines. He began writing humorous fantasy for *Unknown*, which published his first novel, the classic alternate history *Lest Darkness Fall* (1939), and "The Incomplete Enchanter" series co-written with Fletcher Pratt. His vast body of work includes *Rogue Queen* (1951), *The Hand of Zei* (1982), and further space operas in his Viagens Interplanetarieas series, and his compilations and completions of Robert E. Howard stories which led to a revival of interest in the sword-and-sorcery hero Conan the Barbarian. De Camp's distinguished nonfiction includes *Lovecraft: A Biography* (1975), the profiles collected as *Literary Swordsmen and Sorcerors* (1976), and with his wife Catherine *The Science Fiction Handbook* (1953) and *Dark Valley Destiny: The Life of Robert E. Howard* (1983). He is a recipient of the Nebula Grand Master Award, and has written his autobiography, *Time and Chance.*

ROBERT SILVERBERG enters his fifth decade as a professional science fiction writer with two Hugo Awards, five Nebula Awards, and over a hundred books of fiction to his credit. Following a prolific career as a writer of short fiction for the science fiction digests of the postwar years, he emerged in the late 1960s as one of science fiction's most insightful commentators on the human condition in *Thorns* (1967), *Downward to Earth* (1970), *Dying Inside* (1972), *The Book of Skulls* (1971), *Shadrach in the Furnace* (1975), and other novels of loss and alienation set in future societies. In recent years, he has devoted much of his writing to the heroic fantasy of his Majipoor series, and historical novels that include *Lord of Darkness*

(1983) and *Gilgamesh the King* (1984). He is the author of more than 60 nonfiction books. Alone and in collaboration, he has edited scores of anthologies, including the prestigious Alpha, New Dimensions, and Universe series of all-original stories.

CONTENTS

DINOSAURS

INTRODUCTION

The dinosaurs have been gone from the world for sixty-five million years. But they live on with mythic power in our imaginations. Even in our secular and skeptical age they seem like magical creatures, looming like dragons in our minds—bizarre nightmarish beasts, titanic and mysterious, whose bellowing cries across the abyss of eternity resound with strange and irresistible fascination in our ears. We never tire of peering at their monstrous bones in our museums—nor, as the overwhelming success of the movie *Jurassic Park* showed a few years ago, do we grow weary of fantastic tales that pretend to bring these vanished giants back to life.

Dragons and monsters, of course, have been the stock in trade of storytellers since the beginning of human history, and probably well before that. The Mesopotamian bard who composed the Gilgamesh mythos nearly five thousand years ago sent that earliest of known human heroes into battle against the terrifying creature Humbaba; Homer, a couple of thousand years later, subjected the voyagers of the *Odyssey* to the ferocities of Scylla and Charybdis; dragons rise up out of the Egyptian papyri; dragons abound in Chinese art and legend; Apollo did battle with a dragon at the shrine of Delphi. We have not yet found a dragon on the walls of one of the decorated caves of Cro-Magnon times, but it would not

1

surprise me if further explorations in those caves were to turn one up.

And, indeed, when workmen excavating for the foundations of Renaissance palaces began uncovering giant bones in Europe, they were thought to be the relics of ancient dragons that had been drowned by Noah's flood. Not until the nineteenth century, when fossil-hunting became an intense preoccupation, did it become clear that those huge remains were in fact vestiges of giant reptilian creatures that once had thundered across the face of the earth, unthinkable millions of years ago. When reassembled and placed on display, these extraordinary souvenirs of a vanished world came immediately to exert a powerful impact on our minds. What child has not stared in awe and wonder at the monsters in the museums? Who is not familiar with the names *Tyrannosaurus* and *Brontosaurus* and *Stegosaurus* and *Triceratops*? Here were dragons indeed, real ones, whose all too solid bones, released from the earth's captivity, rose before us in undeniable actuality.

Inevitably, modern-day mythmakers seized upon the dinosaurs as material for the modern-day myths that we call science fiction. Jules Verne, in *A Journey to the Center of the Earth* (1864), was, as usual, the first to turn his characters loose in a hidden corner of the world where the dinosaurs still thrived. Sir Arthur Conan Doyle's *The Lost World* (1912) amplified and intensified that theme. John Taine's *Before the Dawn* (1934) looked backward in time to show us the dinosaurs at work and play in their own era. Such motion pictures as *King Kong, One Million B.C.*, and the various adaptations of *The Lost World* made dinosaurs even more vivid as popular mythology, long before Spielberg's *Jurassic Park* gave a new generation of children the velociraptor horrors. And so forth.

But there is more, of course, to the appeal of the dinosaurs than the great size and menace of the most familiar species and the fantastic strangeness of their form. The enormous intellectual puzzles posed by the existence and sustained survival of these extraordinary beasts are some of the most stimulating and challenging scientific mysteries of the twentieth century.

How, for example, did they manage to dominate their world for so phenomenally long a span of time? We know that the earliest dinosaurlike creatures were present on Earth at least 170 million years ago, inaugurating a reign that would endure for some 100 million years. We can barely comprehend an era so lengthy—we who can trace our own ancestry back a paltry few million years to the protohuman primates of the late Pliocene, and who did not reach something approximating our present evolutionary form until just a few hundred thousand years ago. The whole period of mankind's existence is just a tick of the clock compared with the length of the dinosaurs' stay on Earth.

And if the riddle of their extraordinary durability is a mystifying one, what about the enigma of their extinction? After having ruled the world so long, they appear to have vanished totally, some sixty-five to seventy million years ago, within a period of no more than a million years. That is in itself no brief moment, of course; but on the geological scale of things it is an incredibly short time for the wiping out of a race as hardy as the dinosaurs. So not only the problem of their extended survival but also the mystery of their relatively swift disappearance has been a major concern of the scientists.

More recently, with the development of modern analytic techniques, speculations of the most startling sort have been put forth concerning the nature of dinosaur metabolism and intelligence. Were they, as has long been thought, mere sluggish dull-witted behemoths, helpless prisoners of their environments like all cold-blooded creatures? Or is it possible that they were intelligent and adaptable warm-blooded animals far more capable of coping with life's challenges than the early paleontologists ever suspected? This astonishing theory—elaborately buttressed with convincing scientific evidence—has touched off one of the liveliest scientific controversies of recent times.

3

Today's best science-fiction writers take into account not only the mythographic mysteries of dinosaurs and their downright scary aspects, but also the full range of scientific speculation that has made them so interesting a focus for our thoughts on the evolution and development of life on this planet. In this book Martin H. Greenberg has brought together an assortment of modern s-f classics that once again bring the dinosaurs back to life in all their gaudy roaring glory, while at the same time offering a few tentative answers to the huge questions posed by this most extraordinary tribe of vanished monsters.

—ROBERT SILVERBERG

THE FOG HORN

RAY BRADBURY

Out there in the cold water, far from land, we waited every night for the coming of the fog, and it came, and we oiled the brass machinery and lit the fog light up in the stone tower. Feeling like two birds in the gray sky, McDunn and I sent the light touching out, red, then white, then red again, to eye the lonely ships. And if they did not see our light, then there was always our Voice, the great deep cry of our Fog Horn shuddering through the rags of mist to startle the gulls away like decks of scattered cards and make the waves turn high and foam.

"It's a lonely life, but you're used to it now, aren't you?" asked McDunn.

"Yes," I said. "You're a good talker, thank the Lord."

"Well, it's your turn on land tomorrow," he said, smiling, "to dance the ladies and drink gin."

"What do you think, McDunn, when I leave you out here alone?"

"On the mysteries of the sea." McDunn lit his pipe. It was a quarter past seven on a cold November evening, the heat on, the light switching its tail in two hundred directions, the Fog Horn bumbling in the high throat of the tower. There wasn't a town for a hundred miles down the coast, just a road which came lonely through dead country to the sea, with few cars on it, a stretch of two miles of cold water out to our rock, and rare few ships.

"The mysteries of the sea," said McDunn thoughtfully. "You know, the ocean's the biggest damned snowflake ever? It rolls and swells a thousand shapes and colors, no two alike. Strange. One night, years ago, I was here alone, when all of the fish of the sea surfaced out there. Something made them swim in and lie in the bay, sort of trembling and staring up at the tower light going red, white, red, white across them so I could see their funny eyes. I turned cold. They were like a big peacock's tail, moving out there until midnight. Then, without so much as a sound, they slipped away, the million of them was gone. I kind of think maybe, in some sort of way, they came all those miles to worship. Strange. But think how the tower must look to them, standing seventy feet above the water, the God-light flashing out from it, and the tower declaring itself with a monster voice. They never came back, those fish, but don't you think for a while they thought they were in the Presence?"

I shivered. I looked out at the long gray lawn of the sea stretching away into nothing and nowhere.

"Oh, the sea's full." McDunn puffed his pipe nervously, blinking. He had been nervous all day and hadn't said why. "For all our engines and so-called submarines, it'll be ten thousand centuries before we set foot on the real bottom of the sunken lands, in the fairy kingdoms there, and know *real* terror. Think of it, it's still the year 300,000 Before Christ down under there. While we've paraded around with trumpets, lopping off each other's countries and heads, they have been living beneath the sea twelve miles deep and cold in a time as old as the beard of a comet."

"Yes, it's an old world."

"Come on. I got something special I been saving up to tell you." We ascended the eighty steps, talking and taking our time. At the top, McDunn switched off the room lights so there'd be no reflection in the plate glass. The great eye of the light was humming, turning easily in its oiled socket. The Fog Horn was blowing steadily, once every fifteen seconds.

"Sounds like an animal, don't it?" McDunn nodded to himself. "A big lonely animal crying in the night. Sitting here on the edge of ten billion years calling out to the Deeps. I'm here, I'm here, I'm here. And the Deeps *do* answer, yes, they do. You been here now for three months, Johnny, so I better prepare you. About this time of year," he said, studying the murk and fog, "something comes to visit the lighthouse."

"The swarms of fish like you said?"

"No, this is something else. I've put off telling you because you might think I'm daft. But tonight's the latest I can put it off, for if my calendar's marked right from last year, tonight's the night it comes. I won't go into detail, you'll have to see it yourself. Just sit down there. If you want, tomorrow you can pack your duffel and take the motorboat in to land and get your car parked there at the dinghy pier on the cape and drive on back to some little inland town and keep your lights burning nights, I won't question or blame you. It's happened three years now, and this is the only time anyone's been here with me to verify it. You wait and watch."

Half an hour passed with only a few whispers between us. When we grew tired waiting, McDunn began describing some of his ideas to me. He had some theories about the Fog Horn itself.

"One day many years ago a man walked along and stood in the sound of the ocean on a cold sunless shore and said, 'We need a voice to call across the water, to warn ships; I'll make one. I'll make a voice like all of time and all of the fog that ever was; I'll make a voice that is like an empty bed beside you all night long, and like an empty house when you open the door, and like trees in autumn with no leaves. A sound like the birds flying south, crying, and a sound like November wind and the sea on the hard, cold shore. I'll make a sound that's so alone that no one can miss it, that whoever hears it will weep in their souls, and hearths will seem warmer, and being inside will seem better to all who hear it in the distant towns. I'll make me a sound and an apparatus and they'll call it a Fog Horn and whoever hears it will know the sadness of eternity and the briefness of life.' "

The Fog Horn blew.

"I made up that story," said McDunn quietly, "to try to explain why this thing keeps coming back to the lighthouse every year. The Fog Horn calls it, I think, and it comes. . . ."

"But—" I said.

"Sssst!" said McDunn. "There!" He nodded out to the Deeps.

Something was swimming toward the lighthouse tower.

It was a cold night, as I have said; the high tower was cold, the light coming and going, and the Fog Horn calling and calling through the raveling mist. You couldn't see far and you couldn't see plain, but there was the deep sea moving on its way about the night earth, flat and quiet, the color of gray mud, and here were the two of us alone in the high tower, and there, far out at first, was a ripple, followed by a wave, a rising, a bubble, a bit of froth. And then, from the surface of the cold sea came a head, a large head, dark-colored, with immense eyes, and then a neck. And then—not a body—but more neck and more! The head rose a full forty feet above the water on a slender and beautiful dark neck. Only then did the body, like a little island of black coral and shells and crayfish, drip up from the subterranean. There was a flicker of tail. In all, from head to tip of tail, I estimated the monster at ninety or a hundred feet.

I don't know what I said. I said something.

"Steady, boy, steady," whispered McDunn.

"It's impossible!" I said.

"No, Johnny, *we're* impossible. *It's* like it always was ten million years ago. *It* hasn't changed. It's *us* and the land that have changed, become impossible. *Us!*"

It swam slowly and with a great dark majesty out in the icy waters, far away. The fog came and went about it, momentarily erasing its shape. One of the monster eyes caught and held and flashed back our immense light, red, white, red, white, like a disk held high and sending a message in primeval code. It was as silent as the fog through which it swam.

"It's a dinosaur of some sort!" I crouched down, holding to the stair rail.

"Yes, one of the tribe."

"But they died out!"

"No, only hid away in the Deeps. Deep, deep down in the deepest Deeps. Isn't *that* a word now, Johnny, a real word, it says so much: the Deeps. There's all the coldness and darkness and deepness in the world in a word like that."

"What'll we do?"

"Do? We got our job, we can't leave. Besides, we're safer here than in any boat trying to get to land. That thing's as big as a destroyer and almost as swift."

"But here, why does it come *here?*"

The next moment I had my answer.

The Fog Horn blew.

And the monster answered.

A cry came across a million years of water and mist. A cry so anguished and alone that it shuddered in my head and my body. The monster cried out at the tower. The Fog Horn blew. The monster roared again. The Fog Horn blew. The monster opened its great toothed mouth and the sound that came from it was the sound of the Fog Horn itself. Lonely and vast and far away. The sound of isolation, a viewless sea, a cold night, apartness. That was the sound.

"Now," whispered McDunn, "do you know why it comes here?"

9

I nodded.

"All year long, Johnny, that poor monster there lying far out, a thousand miles at sea, and twenty miles deep maybe, biding its time, perhaps it's a million years old, this one creature. Think of it, waiting a million years; could *you* wait that long? Maybe it's the last of its kind. I sort of think that's true. Anyway, here come men on land and build this lighthouse, five years ago. And set up their Fog Horn and sound it and sound it, out toward the place where you bury yourself in sleep and sea memories of a world where there were thousands like yourself, but now you're alone, all alone in a world not made for you, a world where you have to hide.

"But the sound of the Fog Horn comes and goes, comes and goes, and you stir from the muddy bottom of the Deeps, and your eyes open like the lenses of two-foot cameras and you move, slow, slow, for you have the ocean sea on your shoulders, heavy. But that Fog Horn comes through a thousand miles of water, faint and familiar, and the furnace in your belly stokes up, and you begin to rise, slow, slow. You feed yourself on great slakes of cod and minnow, on rivers of jellyfish, and you rise slow through the autumn months, through September when the fogs started, through October with more fog and the horn still calling you on, and then, late in November, after pressurizing yourself day by day, a few feet higher every hour, you are near the surface and still alive. You've got to go slow; if you surfaced all at once you'd explode. So it takes you all of three months to surface, and then a number of days to swim through the cold waters to the lighthouse. And there you are, out there, in the night, Johnny, the biggest damn monster in creation. And here's the lighthouse calling to you, with a long neck like your neck sticking way up out of the water, and a body like your body, and, most important of all, a voice like your voice. Do you understand now, Johnny, do you understand?"

The Fog Horn blew.

10

The monster answered.

I saw it all, I knew it all—the million years of waiting alone, for someone to come back who never came back. The million years of isolation at the bottom of the sea, the insanity of time there, while the skies cleared of reptile-birds, the swamps dried on the continental lands, the sloths and saber-tooths had their day and sank in tar pits, and men ran like white ants upon the hills.

The Fog Horn blew.

"Last year," said McDunn, "that creature swam round and round, round and round, all night. Not coming too near, puzzled, I'd say. Afraid, maybe. And a bit angry after coming all this way. But the next day, unexpectedly, the fog lifted, the sun came out fresh, the sky was as blue as a painting. And the monster swam off away from the heat and the silence and didn't come back. I suppose it's been brooding on it for a year now, thinking it over from every which way."

The monster was only a hundred yards off now, it and the Fog Horn crying at each other. As the lights hit them, the monster's eyes were fire and ice, fire and ice.

"That's life for you," said McDunn. "Someone always waiting for someone who never comes home. Always someone loving some thing more than that thing loves them. And after a while you want to destroy whatever that thing is, so it can't hurt you no more."

The monster was rushing at the lighthouse.

The Fog Horn blew.

"Let's see what happens," said McDunn.

He switched the Fog Horn off.

The ensuing minute of silence was so intense that we could hear our hearts pounding in the glassed area of the tower, could hear the slow greased turn of the light.

The monster stopped and froze. Its great lantern eyes blinked. Its mouth gaped. It gave a sort of rumble, like a volcano. It twitched its head this way and that, as if to seek the sounds now dwindled off into the fog. It peered at the lighthouse. It rumbled again. Then its eyes caught fire. It reared up, threshed the water, and rushed at the tower, its eyes filled with angry torment.

"McDunn!" I cried. "Switch on the horn!"

McDunn fumbled with the switch. But even as he flicked it on, the monster was rearing up. I had a glimpse of its gigantic paws, fishskin glittering in webs between the fingerlike projections, clawing at the tower. The huge eye on the right side of its anguished head glittered before me like a caldron into which I might drop, screaming. The tower shook. The Fog Horn cried; the monster cried. It seized the tower and gnashed at the glass, which shattered in upon us.

McDunn seized my arm. "Downstairs!"

The tower rocked, trembled, and started to give. The Fog Horn and the monster roared. We stumbled and half fell down the stairs. "Quick!"

We reached the bottom as the tower buckled down toward us. We ducked under the stairs into the small stone cellar. There were a thousand concussions as the rocks rained down; the Fog Horn stopped abruptly. The monster crashed upon the tower. The tower fell. We knelt together, McDunn and I, holding tight, while our world exploded.

Then it was over, and there was nothing but darkness and the wash of the sea on the raw stones.

That and the other sound.

"Listen," said McDunn quietly. "Listen."

We waited a moment. And then I began to hear it. First a great vacuumed sucking of air, and then the lament, the bewilderment, the loneliness of the great monster, folded over and upon us, above us, so that the sickening reek of its body filled the air, a stone's thickness away from our cellar. The monster gasped and cried. The tower was gone. The light was gone. The thing that had called to it across a million years was gone. And the monster was opening its mouth and sending out great sounds. The sounds of a Fog Horn, again and again. And ships far at sea, not finding the light, not seeing anything, but passing and hearing late that night, must've thought: There it is, the lonely sound, the Lonesome Bay horn. All's well. We've rounded the cape.

And so it went for the rest of that night.

The sun was hot and yellow the next afternoon when the rescuers came out to dig us from our stoned-under cellar.

"It fell apart, is all," said Mr. McDunn gravely. "We had a few bad knocks from the waves and it just crumbled." He pinched my arm.

There was nothing to see. The ocean was calm, the sky blue. The only thing was a great algaic stink from the green matter that covered the fallen tower stones and the shore rocks. Flies buzzed about. The ocean washed empty on the shore.

The next year they built a new lighthouse, but by that time I had a job in the little town and a wife and a good small warm house that glowed yellow on autumn nights, the doors locked, the chimney puffing smoke. As for McDunn, he was master of the new lighthouse, built to his own specifications, out of steel-reinforced concrete. "Just in case," he said.

The new lighthouse was ready in November. I drove down alone one evening late and parked my car and looked across the gray waters and listened to the new horn sounding, once, twice, three, four times a minute far out there, by itself.

The monster?

It never came back.

"It's gone away," said McDunn. "It's gone back to the Deeps. It's learned you can't love anything too much in this world. It's gone into the deepest Deeps to wait another million years. Ah, the poor thing! Waiting out there, and waiting out there, while man comes and goes on this pitiful little planet. Waiting and waiting."

I sat in my car, listening. I couldn't see the lighthouse or the light standing out in Lonesome Bay. I could only hear the Horn, the Horn, the Horn. It sounded like the monster calling.

I sat there wishing there was something I could say.

DAY OF THE HUNTERS

ISAAC ASIMOV

It began the same night it ended. It wasn't much. It just bothered me; it still bothers me.

You see, Joe Bloch, Ray Manning, and I were squatting around our favorite table in the corner bar with an evening on our hands and a mess of chatter to throw it away with. That's the beginning.

Joe Bloch started it by talking about the atomic bomb, and what he thought ought to be done with it, and how who would have thought it five years ago. And I said lots of guys thought it five years ago and wrote stories about it and it was going to be tough on them trying to keep ahead of the newspapers now. Which led to a general palaver on how lots of screwy things might come true and a lot of for-instances were thrown about.

Ray said he heard from somebody that some big-shot scientist had sent a block of lead back in time for about two seconds or two minutes or two thousandths of a second—he didn't know which. He said the scientist wasn't saying anything to anybody because he didn't think anyone would believe him.

So I asked, pretty sarcastic, how *he* came to know about it.— Ray may have lots of friends but I have the same lot and none of them know any big-shot scientists. But he said never mind how he heard, take it or leave it.

And then there wasn't anything to do but talk about time machines, and how supposing you went back and killed your own grandfather or why didn't somebody from the future come back and tell us who was going to win the next war, or if there was going to be a next war, or if there'd be anywhere on Earth you could live after it, regardless of who wins.

Ray thought just knowing the winner in the seventh race while the sixth was being run would be something.

But Joe decided different. He said, "The trouble with you guys is you got wars and races on the mind. Me, I got curiosity. Know what I'd do if I had a time machine?"

So right away we wanted to know, all ready to give him the old snicker whatever it was.

He said, "If I had one, I'd go back in time about a couple or five or fifty million years and find out what happened to the dinosaurs."

Which was too bad for Joe, because Ray and I both thought there was just about no sense to that at all. Ray said who cared about a lot of dinosaurs and I said the only thing they were good for was to make a mess of skeletons for guys who were dopy enough to wear out the floors in museums; and it was a good thing they did get out of the way to make room for human beings. Of course Joe said that with *some* human beings he knew, and he gives us a hard look, we should've stuck to dinosaurs, but we pay no attention to that.

"You dumb squirts can laugh and make like you know something, but that's because you don't ever have any imagination," he says. "Those dinosaurs were big stuff. Millions of all kinds—big as houses, and dumb as houses, too—all over the place. And then, all of a sudden, like that," and he snaps his fingers, "there aren't any anymore."

How come, we wanted to know.

But he was just finishing a beer and waving at Charlie for another with a coin to prove he wanted to pay for it and he just shrugged his shoulders. "I don't know. That's what I'd find out, though."

That's all. That would have finished it. I would've said something and Ray would've made a crack, and we all would've had another beer and maybe swapped some talk about the weather and the Brooklyn Dodgers and then said so long, and never think of dinosaurs again.

Only we didn't, and now I never have anything on my mind but dinosaurs, and I feel sick.

Because the rummy at the next table looks up and hollers, "Hey!"

We hadn't seen him. As a general rule, we don't go around looking at rummies we don't know in bars. I got plenty to do keeping track of the rummies I do know. This fellow had a bottle before him that was half empty, and a glass in his hand that was half full.

He said, "Hey," and we all looked at him, and Ray said, "Ask him what he wants, Joe."

Joe was nearest. He tipped his chair backward and said, "What do you want?"

The rummy said, "Did I hear you gentlemen mention dinosaurs?"

He was just a little weavy, and his eyes looked like they were bleeding, and you could only tell his shirt was once white by guessing, but it must've been the way he talked. It didn't *sound* rummy, if you know what I mean.

Anyway, Joe sort of eased up and said, "Sure. Something you want to know?"

He sort of smiled at us. It was a funny smile; it started at the mouth and ended just before it touched the eyes. He said, "Did you want to build a time machine and go back to find out what happened to the dinosaurs?"

I could see Joe was figuring that some kind of confidence game

17

was coming up. I was figuring the same thing. Joe said, "Why? You aiming to offer to build one for me?"

The rummy showed a mess of teeth and said, "No, sir. I could but I won't. You know why? Because I built a time machine for myself a couple of years ago and went back to the Mesozoic Era and found out what happened to the dinosaurs."

Later on, I looked up how to spell "Mesozoic," which is why I got it right, in case you're wondering, and I found out that the Mesozoic Era is when all the dinosaurs were doing whatever dinosaurs do. But of course at the time this is just so much double-talk to me, and mostly I was thinking we had a lunatic talking to us. Joe claimed afterward that he knew about this Mesozoic thing, but he'll have to talk lots longer and louder before Ray and I believe him.

But that did it just the same. We said to the rummy to come over to our table. I guess I figured we could listen to him for a while and maybe get some of the bottle, and the others must have figured the same. But he held his bottle tight in his right hand when he sat down and that's where he kept it.

Ray said, "Where'd you build a time machine?"

"At Midwestern University. My daughter and I worked on it together."

He sounded like a college guy at that.

I said, "Where is it now? In your pocket?"

He didn't blink; he never jumped at us no matter how wise we cracked. Just kept talking to himself out loud, as if the whiskey had limbered up his tongue and he didn't care if we stayed or not.

He said, "I broke it up. Didn't want it. Had enough of it."

We didn't believe him. We didn't believe him worth a darn. You better get that straight. It stands to reason, because if a guy invented a time machine, he could clean up millions—he could

18

clean up all the money in the world, just knowing what would happen to the stock market and the races and elections. He wouldn't throw all that away, I don't care what reasons he had.— Besides, none of us were going to believe in time travel anyway, because what if you *did* kill your own grandfather.

Well, never mind.

Joe said, "Yeah, you broke it up. Sure you did. What's your name?"

But he didn't answer that one, ever. We asked him a few more times, and then we ended up calling him "Professor."

He finished off his glass and filled it again very slow. He didn't offer us any, and we all sucked at our beers.

So I said, "Well, go ahead. What happened to the dinosaurs?"

But he didn't tell us right away. He stared right at the middle of the table and talked to it.

"I don't know how many times Carol sent me back—just a few minutes or hours—before I made the big jump. I didn't care about the dinosaurs; I just wanted to see how far the machine would take me on the supply of power I had available. I suppose it was dangerous, but is life so wonderful? The war was on then—One more life?"

He sort of coddled his glass as if he was thinking about things in general, then he seemed to skip a part in his mind and keep right on going.

"It was sunny," he said, "sunny and bright; dry and hard. There were no swamps, no ferns. None of the accoutrements of the Cretaceous we associate with dinosaurs,"—anyway, I think that's what he said. I didn't always catch the big words, so later on I'll just stick in what I can remember. I checked all the spellings, and I must say that for all the liquor he put away, he pronounced them without stutters.

That's maybe what bothered us. He sounded so familiar with everything, and it all just rolled off his tongue like nothing.

He went on, "It was a late age, certainly the Cretaceous. The dinosaurs were already on the way out—all except those little ones, with their metal belts and their guns."

I guess Joe practically dropped his nose into the beer altogether. He skidded halfway around the glass, when the professor let loose that statement sort of sadlike.

Joe sounded mad. "*What* little ones, with whose metal belts and which guns?"

The professor looked at him for just a second and then let his eyes slide back to nowhere. "They were little reptiles, standing four feet high. They stood on their hind legs with a thick tail behind, and they had little forearms with fingers. Around their waists were strapped wide metal belts, and from these hung guns.—And they weren't guns that shot pellets either; they were energy projectors."

"They were what?" I asked. "Say, when was this? Millions of years ago?"

"That's right," he said. "They were reptiles. They had scales and no eyelids and they probably laid eggs. But they used energy guns. There were five of them. They were on me as soon as I got out of the machine. There must have been millions of them all over Earth—millions. Scattered all over. They must have been the Lords of Creation then."

I guess it was then that Ray thought he had him, because he developed that wise look in his eyes that makes you feel like conking him with an empty beer mug, because a full one would waste beer. He said, "Look P'fessor, millions of them, huh? Aren't there guys who don't do anything but find old bones and mess around with them till they figure out what some dinosaur looked like? The museums are full of these here skeletons, aren't they?

Well, where's there one with a metal belt on him. If there were millions, what's become of them? Where are the bones?"

The professor sighed. It was a real, sad sigh. Maybe he realized for the first time he was just speaking to three guys in overalls in a barroom. Or maybe he didn't care.

He said, "You don't find many fossils. Think how many animals lived on Earth altogether. Think how many billions and trillions. And then think how few fossils we find.—And these lizards were intelligent. Remember that. They're not going to get caught in snowdrifts or mud, or fall into lava, except by big accident. Think how few fossil men there are—even of these subintelligent apemen of a million years ago."

He looked at his half-full glass and turned it round and round.

He said, "What would fossils show anyway? Metal belts rust away and leave nothing. Those little lizards were warm-blooded. I *know* that, but you couldn't prove it from petrified bones. What the devil? A million years from now could you tell what New York looks like from a human skeleton? Could you tell a human from a gorilla by the bones and figure out which one built an atomic bomb and which one ate bananas in a zoo?"

"Hey," said Joe, plenty objecting, "any simple bum can tell a gorilla skeleton from a man's. A man's got a larger brain. Any fool can tell which one was intelligent."

"Really?" The professor laughed to himself, as if all this was so simple and obvious, it was just a crying shame to waste time on it. "You judge everything from the type of brain human beings have managed to develop. Evolution has different ways of doing things. Birds fly one way; bats fly another way. Life has plenty of tricks for everything.—How much of your brain do you think you use? About a fifth. That's what the psychologists say. As far as they know, as far as anybody knows, eighty per cent of your brain has no use at all. Everybody just works on way-low gear, except maybe a few in history. Leonardo da Vinci, for instance. Archimedes, Aristotle, Gauss, Galois, Einstein—"

21

I never heard of any of them except Einstein, but I didn't let on. He mentioned a few more, but I've put in all I can remember. Then he said, "Those little reptiles had tiny brains, maybe quarter-size, maybe even less, but they used it all—every bit of it. Their bones might not show it, but they were intelligent; intelligent as humans. And they were boss of all Earth."

And then Joe came up with something that was really good. For a while I was sure that he had the professor and I was awfully glad he came out with it. He said, "Look, P'fessor, if those lizards were so damned hot, why didn't they leave something behind? Where are their cities and their buildings and all the sort of stuff we keep finding of the cavemen, stone knives and things. Hell, if human beings got the heck off of Earth, think of the stuff *we'd* leave behind us. You couldn't walk a mile without falling over a city. And roads and things."

But the professor just couldn't be stopped. He wasn't even shaken up. He just came right back with, "You're still judging other forms of life by human standards. We build cities and roads and airports and the rest that goes with us—but they didn't. They were built on a different plan. Their whole way of life was different from the ground up. They didn't live in cities. They didn't have our kind of art. I'm not sure what they did have because it was so alien I couldn't grasp it—except for their guns. Those *would* be the same. Funny, isn't it.—For all I know, maybe we stumble over their relics every day and don't even know that's what they are."

I was pretty sick of it by that time. You just *couldn't* get him. The cuter you'd be, the cuter he'd be.

I said, "Look here. How do you know so much about those things? What did you do; live with them? Or did they speak English? Or maybe you speak lizard talk. Give us a few words of lizard talk."

I guess I was getting mad, too. You know how it is. A guy tells you something you don't believe because it's all cockeyed, and you can't get him to admit he's lying.

But the professor wasn't mad. He was just filling the glass again, very slowly. "No," he said, "I didn't talk and they didn't talk. They just looked at me with their cold, hard, staring eyes—snake's eyes—and I knew what they were thinking, and I could see that they knew what I was thinking. Don't ask me how it happened. It just did. Everything. I knew that they were out on a hunting expedition and I knew they weren't going to let me go."

And we stopped asking questions. We just looked at him, then Ray said, "What happened? How did you get away?"

"That was easy. An animal scurried past on the hilltop. It was long—maybe ten feet—and narrow and ran close to the ground. The lizards got excited. I could feel the excitement in waves. It was as if they forgot about me in a single hot flash of blood lust— and off they went. I got back in the machine, returned, and broke it up."

It was the flattest sort of ending you ever heard. Joe made a noise in his throat. "Well, what happened to the dinosaurs?"

"Oh, you don't see? I thought it was plain enough.—It was those little intelligent lizards that did it. They were hunters—by instinct and by choice. It was their hobby in life. It wasn't for food; it was for fun."

"And they just wiped out all the dinosaurs on the Earth?"

"All that lived at the time, anyway; all the contemporary species. Don't you think it's possible? How long did it take us to wipe out bison herds by the hundred million? What happened to the dodo in a few years? Supposing we really put our minds to it, how long would the lions and the tigers and the giraffes last? Why, by the time I saw those lizards there wasn't any big game left—no reptile more than fifteen feet maybe. All gone. Those little demons were chasing the little, scurrying ones, and probably crying their hearts out for the good old days."

And we all kept quiet and looked at our empty beer bottles and thought about it. All those dinosaurs—big as houses—killed by little lizards with guns. Killed for fun.

Then Joe leaned over and put his hand on the professor's shoulder, easylike, and shook it. He said, "Hey P'fessor, but if that's so, what happened to the little lizards with the guns? Huh?—Did you ever go back to find out?"

The professor looked up with the kind of look in his eyes that he'd have if he were lost.

"You still don't see! It was already beginning to happen to them. I saw it in their eyes. They were running out of big game—the fun was going out of it. So what did you expect them to do? They turned to other game—the biggest and most dangerous of all— and really had fun. They hunted that game to the end."

"What game?" asked Ray. He didn't get it, but Joe and I did.

"Themselves," said the professor in a loud voice. "They finished off all the others and began on themselves—till not one was left."

And again we stopped and thought about those dinosaurs—big as houses—all finished off by little lizards with guns. Then we thought about the little lizards and how they had to keep the guns going even when there was nothing to use them on but themselves.

Joe said, "Poor dumb lizards."

"Yeah," said Ray, "poor crackpot lizards."

And then what happened really scared us. Because the professor jumped up with eyes that looked as if they were trying to climb right out of their sockets and leap at us. He shouted, "You damned fools. Why do you sit there slobbering over reptiles dead a hundred million years? That was the first intelligence on Earth and that's how it ended. That's *done*. But we're the second intelligence—and how the devil do you think *we're* going to end?"

He pushed the chair over and headed for the door. But then he stood there just before leaving altogether and said: "*Poor dumb humanity*! Go ahead and cry about that."

DINO TREND

PAT CADIGAN

"The tyrannosaurus body is so popular, the cultural elite's scurrying to look up other, less vulgarized varieties," Marcia Durant said to her partner, Randall Quinn.

"What, already?" said Randall.

"Sure. It's the Age of the Nanosecond as well as the Age of Nanotechnology. Every time we get something that works fast, our attention spans get shorter."

"Huh?" said Randall, looking up from the jar of Bronto-Cream she had brought home. They were sitting in their living room which was currently in flux as it became the bedroom; Randall was feeling affectionate. These days, they could have afforded to annex another room, but they had both agreed: why bother? Why bother changing location when the location could simply change for them? Then they didn't have to interrupt whatever they were doing or saying. One room was very time-efficient, and the nano-transformers changed it often enough to keep it from getting too boring. And they could use the money to buy better nano-transformers. It was a policy that fell in line with their general agreed-upon philosophy, *Do only things that make sense.*

"Do you really want us to be brontosauruses?" Randall asked her. His magenta face acquired hazard-yellow stripes along his cheekbones; doubt indicators. Color semaphore also made sense to them. They had, in fact, met through a color semaphore group. "Won't the tails kind of get in the way dragging along behind us, maybe knocking stuff over whenever we turn around?"

"It's just a free sample. They were handing the jars out downtown and I took one," Marcia said, shifting to her left as the carpet rose like yeast and absorbed the chair she was sitting in to become the bed. Randall had placed himself a little better and was already leaning against the headboard while his clothes dematerialized. Marcia's silver face took on a row of concentric orange circles across her forehead, for frowning.

"I thought you got rid of the nanostim elements. You know that made me uncomfortable. There are some things I'd rather tend to myself."

Randall's yellow stripes disappeared as the deep purple spots of embarrassment appeared all over his face. "I did get rid of them. I'm afraid it's a reflex now. As soon as my clothes go, *ba-da-bing!*"

A red lightning bolt of displeasure cut from Marcia's left temple to the right corner of her mouth. "Where *do* you pick up those antiquated expressions? Have you been on the tiresome computer net again?"

"No," he lied, handing the jar of Bronto-Cream to the nightstand as he reached for her.

She looked down and flinched. "Jesus, I'm just *never* going to get used to that."

"It works fairly well for a lot of the animal kingdom," he said, rather smugly.

"For *dogs*," she insisted. "*Dogs* have ones that—telescope." Wavy blue lines of distaste appeared around her mouth, disappearing almost immediately, but not too quickly that Randall didn't see.

"When are you going to give me a break?" he demanded, falling back against the pillows, white curlicues swimming down his face. "You know it wouldn't have happened if you hadn't insisted on us trying the nano-ticklers. I know, I know—" he put up a hand as she started to protest "—there was no way *you* could have known they were defective any more than *I* could have. But I *still* say I'm lucky to be alive. They could have eaten the rest of me away, too. As it was, I had a bad time with the trauma, and I expected *a lot* more understanding from *you*—"

"Hey, I was traumatized, too, you know," Marcia said. "I'll never forget the sight of you laying there while your—"

"All right, all *right*!" Randall pulled the sheet over himself.

"What," Marcia said, looking pointedly at the covered lower half of his body.

"It's customary to cover the dead, excuse me very much." He stared away from her. "You had to *insist* that I get rid of the 'stims. And worse, *I* had to listen to you."

"Fine," Marcia said tonelessly, and took the Bronto-Cream from the nightstand.

The cream had been loaded with pixie dust, which glittered a lot for the sake of special effects but was otherwise inert. Marcia's body was transformed within ten minutes. She made a rather small brontosaurus, of course, but she was an exquisite jewel-tone green.

"Nice tail," Randall said, impressed in spite of everything. He picked the open jar up off the bed where Marcia had left it. She couldn't pick anything up herself now. "Boy, not much left here. I guess I'll have to just watch tonight."

She gazed at him with her flat, reptilian eyes and wiggled her toes.

"Well, what?" he said. "Do you want to go out now or something?" He laughed. "Remember, it's just a body. If you have a craving to wade in muddy water and eat seaweed off the bottom, it's strictly psychosomatic."

"I *know* that," she growled, her voice sounding slightly muffled and slurred. "I guess I'll go out to one of the new dino clubs. Unless you have some objection." He didn't; she plodded toward the front door. It dematerialized, parting for her like a curtain, and then resolidified as soon as the tip of her tail disappeared.

"I don't know," Randall sighed. "I just don't know anything any more." He looked over at her side of the bed.

"You were supposed to beg her not to go," said Marcia's side of the mattress, a little chidingly. "Either that or say you wanted to go with her, and stop on the way and get a dino body."

"Oh, shut up." Randall drew the blanket up on her side. "Everything's so easy for a mattress. You ought to try it walking around out here where you actually have to put it all on the line every day. I bet it wouldn't seem so simple then."

"Any time you want to switch, say so," came the mattress' voice faintly from beneath the sheet. "I bet you wouldn't think my job was any picnic either."

"Don't be ridiculous, you're not even intelligent. You're a goddamn answering machine that fell into the bed one day and got lost. In case you've forgotten. *I* haven't. It cost enough to get a new one."

"A *much* better model, however," said the new answering machine from the nightstand.

"Shut up, shut *up!*" Randall said, irritated. He jumped out of bed and threw a handful of clothing matter at himself. Two minutes later, he was covered in a suit that seemed to be made of dinosaur hide. "Now look at that. A trend already. Don't answer that!" he added quickly, addressing both the mattress and the new answering machine. "There was a time when people didn't have to engage in stupid conversations with their possessions. The dinosaurs, too, were thusly blessed."

He headed for the door, expecting it to dematerialize and hit the woodlike surface nose first. "Oh, come *on*." He glared at the bed. "You didn't slip into the door, too, did you?"

The mattress sat up. "No, it just has strong feelings for Marcia."

Randall turned back to the door. "I'll get an *axe*."

The door promptly dematerialized for him and he stomped out. The streets were filled with a mixture of fancied-up people and dino-people. The sight of the dinos mixed in with everything else wasn't unexpected, but he found it depressing just the same. Maybe it was because those reptilian heads all had a built-in snobby air, with those strange flat eyes and strangely placed nostrils, or maybe it was because he couldn't tell whether any of the brontosauruses were Marcia, if indeed *any* of them were.

She couldn't have gotten very far very fast, he reasoned, since she didn't seem able to move too quickly as a brontosaurus. None of the brontosauruses he could see were in a hurry, but maybe that was because she knew he wouldn't be able to pick her out. Maybe this was her way of breaking up with him. Declaring their relationship extinct, so to speak.

Well, that *was fast*, he thought unhappily. One moment they had been getting ready to make love, the next she was starting a new life as a plant-eating reptile.

Age of the Nanosecond. Every time we get something that works fast, our attention spans get shorter.

As if to underscore Marcia's remembered words, the pavement under his feet changed from a toasty-golden color to a shiny black, the change sweeping along like a chromatic tidal wave.

"Well, that's *terrible*," complained a nearby allosaurus in a strained and slightly muffled female voice. She lifted one mighty-looking hind leg and then another. "It makes the whole street look like a *tar pit*. Why on Earth would anyone think we all wanted to walk in a *tar pit?*" Her foreclaws opened and closed in distaste. Randall blinked at her, then rubbed his eyes. Horrible as it was to contemplate, the allosaurus looked good to him. So Marcia had been more correct than she knew, he thought; he was going along with the trend in a slightly different way. Or rather, the trend was hijacking him. No, *hacking* him—it had found an access to him and entered there, working a few subtle alterations in his *Weltanschau-*

ung. He sighed, but that didn't make the allosaurus look any less good to him.

Maybe it's because she's a flesh-eater and that association appeals to me more than a plant-eater, he thought, sidling closer to the allosaurus. It was strange, since he and Marcia had both been vegetarians. But then, the allosaurus also had limbs that would serve as hands, whereas Marcia was now limited to going around on all fours. Why hadn't Marcia thought of that?

Or had she?

Now he was getting on his own nerves with his paranoia. He looked at the allosaurus, who was regarding him with what appeared to him to be speculation. Or . . . hunger?

"Um?" he said. The allosaurus wasn't actually any bigger than he was but it *felt* bigger. *Stronger.* Well, it *looked* stronger.

"Excuse me, miz." A hadrosaur with navy blue accents and a badly fitting Sam Browne belt materialized at Randall's side, pointedly looking only at her. "Is this biped bothering you?"

"I was just going," Randall said and hurried down the sidewalk, weaving between the dinos and the still-recognizably-humans. When he dared to turn around and look back, he couldn't really see anything except the top of the allosaurus' head, and even then, he couldn't have sworn it was the same one.

"Tyrannosaurus cream?" someone said close to his ear. He turned and found himself looking at a man who might have been the result of a crocodile-human liaison.

"Were you giving out brontosaurus cream a while ago?" Randall asked suspiciously.

"All gone," said the man apologetically and licked his chops. "After this runs out, I think they'll give me some stegosaurus ointment. Bronto-Cream will probably be going on sale at the nearest nano-boutique any minute now—"

Randall resisted the urge to lunge for his neck with both hands. It was a thick neck and there were entirely too many teeth in the man's smile. Instead, he walked on, feeling so morose and frustrated that even his semaphore had subsided.

Maybe he should just follow Marcia into whatever dino club she was frequenting these days. Except he was pretty sure that if he wanted to be any kind of dinosaur, he'd choose one with hands—or whatever—so perhaps their relationship had been doomed after all.

"Everything comes to an end," he said, sighing.

"Pardon?" said a passing iguanodon, looking at him suspiciously. Or just looking at him—the reptilian face looked suspicious as a matter of course.

"Nothing," Randall said, "I was just talking to myself."

"For god's sake, *why?*" asked the iguanodon, gesturing with its claws.

"Boy, you know, people as dinosaurs are a lot nosier than they were as people," he said.

The iguanodon motioned at itself. "It's like a full-body mask. Both liberating and concealing." The voice was so strained, Randall couldn't say for sure whether it was a man or a woman, and he couldn't bring himself to look closely at the physiognomy to find out. Dinosaur throats weren't made for talking, he thought. *What if people stop talking, what will they do?* he wondered. *Perhaps they'll take up sign language—those that have the right kinds of forelimbs . . .* He thought of Marcia; what about her species and those like it?

The dinosaur population on the street seemed to be increasing as he stood there and, as Marcia had mentioned, an awful lot of them were tyrannosauruses. Nanotechnology and the nanosecond. Marcia had always had a lot of insight to offer about modern life; he was going to miss her.

And what was he doing out on the street anyway? If he wasn't going to get to a nano-boutique for the latest in makeover trends, he might as well go home and wait it out. Even if there wasn't anyone to wait it out with anymore.

*　　*　　*

When the door dematerialized and let him back in, he found himself hip-deep in swamp water. Whether it was a swamp from the Jurassic or the Cretaceous, he didn't know, but he knew the brontosaurus standing in the middle of the room where the bed had been.

"I thought you were going to a dino club," he said, taking a step toward her.

"Was," Marcia said with some difficulty. "Then I decided it was no fun without you." She swung her head from side to side. "I redecorated. I know, I know, it's psychosomatic, but it makes me feel better. If you really hate it, we can change it, or even switch it back later."

"Actually, I could get used to it," he said, looking down at the water. "It's nice and quiet without the answering machines jabbering and interrupting the way they used to. But I feel a little out of place."

Marcia swung her long neck toward something that looked like an antediluvian rubber plant. There was a jar on top of it. Randall picked it up.

" '*Camptosaurus*,' " he read. " '*One of the first of the bird-hipped dinos, herbivorous, bipedal.*' " He looked up at her, touched. "It's got *hands*."

Marcia's head bobbed up and down slowly. "Even when I'm a dinosaur, I understand you. And—well—certain features have more appeal for me now. You know, some things just seem more appropriate on a reptile."

"Yeah. I know." He sighed, thinking of the allosaurus. "Well, okay. But later, do you think we could switch to meat-eaters?"

The brontosaurus looked hesitant. Or maybe it had no expression at all. The color semaphore had not survived the transformation and he wasn't used to it yet. "We can talk about it, but frankly, I don't think the apartment is big enough."

33

"We could add another room now," he said. "Doesn't that make sense?"

"Let me give it some thought," she said.

He considered asking if they could reinstate their color semaphore as well and decided against pushing things for the time being. He would wait until they became carnivorous. But the trend was extinct before they got that far, and when they became mammals again, they broke up after all.

TIME'S ARROW

ARTHUR C. CLARKE

The river was dead and the lake already dying when the monster had come down the dried-up watercourse and turned onto the desolate mudflats. There were not many places where it was safe to walk, and even where the ground was hardest the great pistons of its feet sank a foot or more beneath the weight they carried. Sometimes it had paused, surveying the landscape with quick, birdlike movements of its head. Then it had sunk even deeper into the yielding soil, so that fifty million years later men could judge with some accuracy the duration of its halts.

For the waters had never returned, and the blazing sun had baked the mud to rock. Later still the desert had poured over all this land, sealing it beneath protecting layers of sand. And later— very much later—had come Man.

"Do you think," shouted Barton above the din, "that Professor Fowler became a paleontologist because he likes playing with pneumatic drills? Or did he acquire the taste afterward?"

"Can't hear you!" yelled Davis, leaning on his shovel in a most professional manner. He glanced hopefully at his watch.

"Shall I tell him it's dinnertime? He can't wear a watch while he's drilling, so he won't know any better."

"I doubt if it will work," Barton shrieked. "He's got wise to us now and always adds an extra ten minutes. But it will make a change from this infernal digging."

With noticeable enthusiasm the two geologists downed tools and started to walk toward their chief. As they approached, he shut off the drill and relative silence descended, broken only by the throbbing of the compressor in the background.

"About time we went back to camp, Professor," said Davis, wristwatch held casually behind his back. "You know what cook says if we're late."

Professor Fowler, M.A., F.R.S., F.G.S., mopped some, but by no means all, of the ocher dust from his forehead. He would have passed anywhere as a typical navvy, and the occasional visitors to the site seldom recognized the Vice-President of the Geological Society in the brawny, half-naked workman crouching over his beloved pneumatic drill.

It had taken nearly a month to clear the sandstone down to the surface of the petrified mudflats. In that time several hundred square feet had been exposed, revealing a frozen snapshot of the past that was probably the finest yet discovered by paleontology. Some scores of birds and reptiles had come here in search of the receding water, and left their footsteps as a perpetual monument eons after their bodies had perished. Most of the prints had been identified, but one—the largest of them all—was new to science. It belonged to a beast which must have weighed twenty or thirty tons, and Professor Fowler was following the fifty-million-year-old spoor with all the emotions of a big-game hunter tracking his prey. There was even a hope that he might yet overtake it, for the ground must have been treacherous when the unknown monster went this way and its bones might still be near at hand, marking the place where it had been trapped like so many creatures of its time.

Despite the mechanical aids available, the work was very tedious. Only the upper layers could be removed by the power tools, and the final uncovering had to be done by hand with the utmost care. Professor Fowler had good reason for his insistence that he alone should do the preliminary drilling, for a single slip might cause irreparable harm.

The three men were halfway back to the main camp, jolting over the rough road in the expedition's battered jeep, when Davis raised the question that had been intriguing the younger men ever since the work had begun.

"I'm getting a distinct impression," he said, "that our neighbors down the valley don't like us, though I can't imagine why. We're not interfering with them, and they might at least have the decency to invite us over."

"Unless, of course, it *is* a war research plant," added Barton, voicing a generally accepted theory.

"I don't think so," said Professor Fowler mildly. "Because it so happens that I've just had an invitation myself. I'm going there tomorrow."

If his bombshell failed to have the expected result, it was thanks to his staff's efficient espionage system. For a moment Davis pondered over this confirmation of his suspicions; then he continued with a slight cough:

"No one else has been invited, then?"

The professor smiled at his pointed hint. "No," he said. "It's a strictly personal invitation. I know you boys are dying of curiosity but, frankly, I don't know any more about the place than you do. If I learn anything tomorrow, I'll tell you all about it. But at least we've found out who's running the establishment."

His assistants pricked up their ears. "Who is it?" asked Barton. "My guess was the Atomic Development Authority."

"You may be right," said the professor. "At any rate, Henderson and Barnes are in charge."

This time the bomb exploded effectively; so much so that Davis nearly drove the jeep off the road—not that that made much difference, the road being what it was.

"Henderson and Barnes? In *this* godforsaken hole?"

"That's right," said the professor gaily. "The invitation was actually from Barnes. He apologized for not contacting us before, made the usual excuses, and wondered if I could drop in for a chat."

"Did he say what they are doing?"

"No; not a hint."

"Barnes and Henderson?" said Barton thoughtfully. "I don't know much about them except that they're physicists. What's their particular racket?"

"They're *the* experts on low-temperature physics," answered Davis. "Henderson was Director of the Cavendish for years. He wrote a lot of letters to *Nature* not so long ago. If I remember rightly, they were all about Helium II."

Barton, who didn't like physicists and said so whenever possible, was not impressed. "I don't even know what Helium II is," he said smugly. "What's more, I'm not at all sure that I want to."

This was intended for Davis, who had once taken a physics degree in, as he explained, a moment of weakness. The "moment" had lasted for several years before he had drifted into geology by rather devious routes, and he was always harking back to his first love.

"It's a form of liquid helium that only exists at a few degrees above absolute zero. It's got the most extraordinary properties—but, as far as I can see, none of them can explain the presence of two leading physicists in this corner of the globe."

They had now arrived at the camp, and Davis brought the jeep to its normal crash-halt in the parking space. He shook his head in annoyance as he bumped into the truck ahead with slightly more violence than usual.

"These tires are nearly through. Have the new ones come yet?"

"Arrived in the 'copter this morning, with a despairing note from Andrews hoping that you'd make them last a full fortnight this time."

"Good! I'll get them fitted this evening."

The professor had been walking a little ahead; now he dropped back to join his assistants.

"You needn't have hurried, Jim," he said glumly. "It's corned beef again."

It would be most unfair to say that Barton and Davis did less work because the professor was away. They probably worked a good deal harder than usual, since the native laborers required twice as much supervision in the chief's absence. But there was no doubt that they managed to find time for a considerable amount of extra talking.

Ever since they had joined Professor Fowler, the two young geologists had been intrigued by the strange establishment five miles away down the valley. It was clearly a research organization of some type, and Davis had identified the tall stacks of an atomic-power unit. That, of course, gave no clue to the work that was proceeding, but it did indicate its importance. There were still only a few thousand turbo-piles in the world, and they were all reserved for major projects.

There were dozens of reasons why two great scientists might have hidden themselves in this place: most of the more hazardous atomic research was carried out as far as possible from civilization, and some had been abandoned altogether until laboratories in space could be set up. Yet it seemed odd that this work, whatever it was, should be carried out so close to what had now become the most important center of geological research in the world. It might, of course, be no more than a coincidence; certainly the physicists had never shown any interest in their compatriots near at hand.

Davis was carefully chipping round one of the great footprints, while Barton was pouring liquid perspex into those already uncovered so that they would be preserved from harm in the transparent plastic. They were working in a somewhat absentminded manner, for each was unconsciously listening for the sound of the jeep. Professor Fowler had promised to collect them when he returned from his visit, for the other vehicles were in use elsewhere and they did not relish a two-mile walk back to camp in the broiling sun. Moreover, they wanted to have any news as soon as possible.

"How many people," said Barton suddenly, "do you think they have over there?"

Davis straightened himself up. "Judging from the buildings, not more than a dozen or so."

"Then it might be a private affair, not an ADA project at all."

"Perhaps, though it must have pretty considerable backing. Of course, Henderson and Barnes could get that on their reputations alone."

"That's where the physicists score," said Barton. "They've only got to convince some war department that they're on the track of a new weapon, and they can get a couple of million without any trouble."

He spoke with some bitterness; for, like most scientists, he had strong views on this subject. Barton's views, indeed, were even more definite than usual, for he was a Quaker and had spent the last year of the War arguing with not-unsympathetic tribunals.

The conversation was interrupted by the roar and clatter of the jeep, and the two men ran over to meet the professor.

"Well?" they cried simultaneously.

Professor Fowler looked at them thoughtfully, his expression giving no hint of what was in his mind. "Had a good day?" he said at last.

"Come off it, Chief!" protested Davis. "Tell us what you've found out."

The professor climbed out of the seat and dusted himself down.

"I'm sorry, boys," he said with some embarrassment, "I can't tell you a thing, and that's flat."

There were two united wails of protest, but he waved them aside. "I've had a very interesting day, but I've had to promise not to say anything about it. Even now I don't know exactly what's going on, but it's something pretty revolutionary—as revolutionary, perhaps, as atomic power. But Dr. Henderson is coming over tomorrow; see what you can get out of him."

For a moment, both Barton and Davis were so overwhelmed by the sense of anticlimax that neither spoke. Barton was the first to recover. "Well, surely there's a reason for this sudden interest in our activities?"

The professor thought this over for a moment. "Yes; it wasn't entirely a social call," he admitted. "They think I may be able to help them. Now, no more questions, unless you want to walk back to camp!"

Dr. Henderson arrived on the site in the middle of the afternoon. He was a stout, elderly man, dressed rather incongruously in a dazzling white laboratory smock and very little else. Though the garb was eccentric, it was eminently practical in so hot a climate.

Davis and Barton were somewhat distant when Professor Fowler introduced them; they still felt that they had been snubbed and were determined that their visitor should understand their feelings. But Henderson was so obviously interested in their work that they soon thawed, and the professor left them to show him round the excavations while he went to supervise the natives.

The physicist was greatly impressed by the picture of the world's remote past that lay exposed before his eyes. For almost an hour the two geologists took him over the workings yard by yard, talking of the creatures who had gone this way and speculating about future discoveries. The track which Professor Fowler was following now lay in a wide trench running away from the main excavation, for he had dropped all other work to investigate it. At its end the trench was no longer continuous: to save time, the professor had begun to sink pits along the line of the footprints. The last sounding had missed altogether, and further digging had shown that the great reptile had made a sudden change of course.

"This is the most interesting bit," said Barton to the slightly wilting physicist. "You remember those earlier places where it had stopped for a moment to have a look around? Well, here it seems to have spotted something and has gone off in a new direction at a run, as you can see from the spacing."

"I shouldn't have thought such a brute *could* run."

"Well, it was probably a pretty clumsy effort, but you can cover quite a bit of ground with a fifteen-foot stride. We're going to follow it as far as we can. We may even find what it was chasing. I think the professor has hopes of discovering a trampled battlefield with the bones of the victim still around. That would make everyone sit up."

Dr. Henderson smiled. "Thanks to Walt Disney, I can picture the scene rather well."

Davis was not very encouraging. "It was probably only the missus banging the dinner gong," he said. "The most infuriating part of our work is the way everything can peter out when it gets most exciting. The strata have been washed away, or there's been an earthquake—or, worse still, some silly fool has smashed up the evidence because he didn't recognize its value."

Henderson nodded in agreement. "I can sympathize with you," he said. "That's where the physicist has the advantage. He knows he'll get the answer eventually, if there is one."

He paused rather diffidently, as if weighing his words with great care. "It would save you a lot of trouble, wouldn't it, if you could actually *see* what took place in the past, without having to infer it by these laborious and uncertain methods. You've been a couple of months following these footsteps for a hundred yards, and they may lead nowhere for all your trouble."

There was a long silence. Then Barton spoke in a very thoughtful voice.

"Naturally, Doctor, we're rather curious about your work," he began. "Since Professor Fowler won't tell us anything, we've done a good deal of speculating. Do you really mean to say that—"

The physicist interrupted him rather hastily. "Don't give it any more thought," he said. "I was only daydreaming. As for our work, it's a very long way from completion, but you'll hear all about it in due course. We're not secretive—but, like everyone working in a new field, we don't want to say anything until we're sure of our ground. Why, if any other paleontologists came near this place, I bet Professor Fowler would chase them away with a pick-axe!"

"That's not quite true," smiled Davis. "He'd be much more likely to set them to work. But I see your point of view; let's hope we don't have to wait too long."

That night, much midnight oil was burned at the main camp. Barton was frankly skeptical, but Davis had already built up an elaborate superstructure of theory around their visitor's remarks.

"It would explain so many things," he said. "First of all, their presence in this place, which otherwise doesn't make sense at all. We know the ground level here to within an inch for the last hundred million years, and we can date any event with an accuracy of better than one per cent. There's not a spot on Earth that's had its past worked out in such detail—it's the obvious place for an experiment like this!"

"But do you think it's even theoretically possible to build a machine that can see into the past?"

"I can't imagine how it could be done. But I daren't say it's impossible—especially to men like Henderson and Barnes."

"Hmmm. Not a very convincing argument. Is there any way we can hope to test it? What about those letters to *Nature?*"

"I've sent to the College Library; we should have them by the end of the week. There's always some continuity in a scientist's work, and they may give us some valuable clues."

But at first they were disappointed; indeed, Henderson's letters only increased the confusion. As Davis had remembered, most of them had been about the extraordinary properties of Helium II.

"It's really fantastic stuff," said Davis. "If a liquid behaved like this at normal temperatures, everyone would go mad. In the first place, it hasn't any viscosity at all. Sir George Darwin once said that if you had an ocean of Helium II, ships could sail in it without any engines. You'd give them a push at the beginning of their voyage and let them run into buffers on the other side. There'd be one snag, though; long before that happened the stuff would have climbed straight up the hull and the whole outfit would have sunk—gurgle, gurgle, gurgle . . ."

"Very amusing," said Barton, "but what the heck has this to do with your precious theory?"

"Not much," admitted Davis. "However, there's more to come. It's possible to have two streams of Helium II flowing in opposite directions *in the same tube*—one stream going through the other, as it were."

"That must take a bit of explaining; it's almost as bad as an object moving in two directions at once. I suppose there *is* an explanation, something to do with relativity, I bet."

Davis was reading carefully. "The explanation," he said slowly, "is very complicated and I don't pretend to understand it fully. But it depends on the fact that liquid helium can have *negative* entropy under certain conditions."

"As I never understood what positive entropy is, I'm not much wiser."

"Entropy is a measure of the heat distribution of the Universe. At the beginning of time, when all energy was concentrated in the suns, entropy was a minimum. It will reach its maximum when everything's at a uniform temperature and the Universe is dead. There will still be plenty of heat around, but it won't be usable."

"Whyever not?"

"Well, all the water in a perfectly flat ocean won't run a hydro-electric plant—but quite a little lake up in the hills will do the trick. You must have a difference in level."

"I get the idea. Now I come to think of it, didn't someone once call entropy 'Time's Arrow'?"

"Yes—Eddington, I believe. Any kind of clock you care to mention—a pendulum, for instance—might just as easily run forward as backward. But entropy is a strictly one-way affair—it's always increasing with the passage of time. Hence the expression, 'Time's Arrow.' "

"Then *negative* entropy—my gosh!"

For a moment the two men looked at each other. Then Barton asked in a rather subdued voice: "What does Henderson say about it?"

"I'll quote from his last letter: 'The discovery of negative entropy introduces quite new and revolutionary conceptions into our picture of the physical world. Some of these will be examined in a further communication.' "

"And are they?"

"That's the snag: there's not 'further communication.' From that you can guess two alternatives. First, the editor of *Nature* may have declined to publish the letter. I think we can rule that one out. Second, the consequences may have been *so* revolutionary that Henderson never did write a further report."

"Negative entropy—negative time," mused Barton. "It seems fantastic; yet it might be theoretically possible to build some sort of device that could see into the past . . ."

"I know what we'll do," said Davis suddenly. "We'll tackle the professor about it and watch his reactions. Now I'm going to bed before I get brain fever."

That night Davis did not sleep well. He dreamed that he was walking along a road that stretched in both directions as far as the eye could see. He had been walking for miles before he came to the signpost, and when he reached it he found that it was broken and the two arms were revolving idly in the wind. As they turned, he could read the words they carried. One said simply: To the Future; the other: To the Past.

They learned nothing from Professor Fowler, which was not surprising; next to the dean, he was the best poker player in the college. He regarded his slightly fretful assistants with no trace of emotion while Davis trotted out his theory.

When the young man had finished, he said quietly, "I'm going over again tomorrow, and I'll tell Henderson about your detective work. Maybe he'll take pity on you; maybe he'll tell me a bit more, for that matter. Now let's go to work."

Davis and Barton found it increasingly difficult to take a great deal of interest in their own work while their minds were filled with the enigma so near at hand. Nevertheless they continued conscientiously, though ever and again they paused to wonder if all their labor might not be in vain. If it were, they would be the first to rejoice. Supposing one could see into the past and watch history unfolding itself, back to the dawn of time! All the great secrets of the past would be revealed: one could watch the coming of life on the Earth, and the whole story of evolution from amoeba to man.

No; it was too good to be true. Having decided this, they would go back to their digging and scraping for another half-hour until the thought would come: but what if it *were* true? And then the whole cycle would begin all over again.

When Professor Fowler returned from his second visit, he was a subdued and obviously shaken man. The only satisfaction his assistants could get from him was the statement that Henderson had listened to their theory and complimented them on their powers of deduction.

That was all; but in Davis's eyes it clinched the matter, though Barton was still doubtful. In the weeks that followed, he too began to waver, until at last they were both convinced that the theory was correct. For Professor Fowler was spending more and more of his time with Henderson and Barnes; so much so that they sometimes did not see him for days. He had almost lost interest in the excavations, and had delegated all responsibility to Barton, who was now able to use the big pneumatic drill to his heart's content.

They were uncovering several yards of footprints a day, and the spacing showed that the monster had now reached its utmost speed and was advancing in great leaps as if nearing its victim. In a few days they might reveal the evidence of some eon-old tragedy, preserved by a miracle and brought down the ages for the observation of man. Yet all this seemed very unimportant now; for it was clear from the professor's hints and his general air of abstraction that the secret research was nearing its climax. He had told them as much, promising that in a very few days, if all went well, their wait would be ended. But beyond that he would say nothing.

Once or twice Henderson had paid them a visit, and they could see that he was now laboring under a considerable strain. He obviously wanted to talk about his work, but was not going to do so until the final tests had been completed. They could only admire his self-control and wish that it would break down. Davis had a distant impression that the elusive Barnes was mainly responsible for his secrecy; he had something of a reputation for not publishing work until it had been checked and double-checked. If these experiments were as important as they believed, his caution was understandable, however infuriating.

Henderson had come over early that morning to collect the professor, and as luck would have it, his car had broken down on the primitive road. This was unfortunate for Davis and Barton, who would have to walk to camp for lunch, since Professor Fowler was driving Henderson back in the jeep. They were quite prepared to put up with this if their wait was indeed coming to an end, as the others had more than half-hinted.

They had stood talking by the side of the jeep for some time before the two older scientists had driven away. It was a rather strained parting, for each side knew what the other was thinking. Finally Barton, as usual the most outspoken, remarked:

"Well, Doc, if this *is* Der Tag, I hope everything works properly. I'd like a photograph of a brontosaurus as a souvenir."

This sort of banter had been thrown at Henderson so often that he now took it for granted. He smiled without much mirth and replied, "I don't promise anything. It may be the biggest flop ever."

Davis moodily checked the tire pressure with the toe of his boot. It was a new set, he noticed, with an odd zigzag pattern he hadn't seen before.

"Whatever happens, we hope you'll tell us. Otherwise, we're going to break in one night and find out just what you're up to."

Henderson laughed. "You'll be a pair of geniuses if you can learn anything from our present lash-up. But, if all goes well, we may be having a little celebration by nightfall."

"What time do you expect to be back, Chief?"

"Somewhere around four. I don't want you to have to walk back for tea."

"O.K.—here's hoping!"

The machine disappeared in a cloud of dust, leaving two very thoughtful geologists standing by the roadside. Then Barton shrugged his shoulders.

"The harder we work," he said, "the quicker the time will go. Come along!"

* * *

The end of the trench, where Barton was working with the power drill, was now more than a hundred yards from the main excavation. Davis was putting the final touches to the last prints to be uncovered. They were now very deep and widely spaced, and looking along them, one could see quite clearly where the great reptile had changed its course and started, first to run, and then to hop like an enormous kangaroo. Barton wondered what it must have felt like to see such a creature bearing down upon one with the speed of an express; then he realized that if their guess was true this was exactly what they might soon be seeing.

By mid-afternoon they had uncovered a record length of track. The ground had become softer, and Barton was roaring ahead so rapidly that he had almost forgotten his other preoccupations. He had left Davis yards behind, and both men were so busy that only the pangs of hunger reminded them when it was time to finish. Davis was the first to notice that it was later than they had expected, and he walked over to speak to his friend.

"It's nearly half-past four!" he said when the noise of the drill had died away. "The Chief's late—I'll be mad if he's had tea before collecting us."

"Give him another half-hour," said Barton. "I can guess what's happened. They've blown a fuse or something and it's upset their schedule."

Davis refused to be placated. "I'll be darned annoyed if we've got to walk back to camp again. Anyway, I'm going up the hill to see if there's any sign of him."

He left Barton blasting his way through the soft rock, and climbed the low hill at the side of the old riverbed. From here one could see far down the valley, and the twin stacks of the Henderson-Barnes laboratory were clearly visible against the drab landscape. But there was no sign of the moving dust-cloud that would be following the jeep: the professor had not yet started for home.

Davis gave a snort of disgust. There was a two-mile walk ahead of them, after a particularly tiring day, and to make matters worse they'd now be late for tea. He decided not to wait any longer, and was already walking down the hill to rejoin Barton when something caught his eye and he stopped to look down the valley.

Around the two stacks, which were all he could see of the laboratory, a curious haze not unlike a heat tremor was playing. They must be hot, he knew, but surely not *that* hot. He looked more carefully, and saw to his amazement that the haze covered a hemisphere that must be almost a quarter of a mile across.

And, quite suddenly, it exploded. There was no light, no blinding flash; only a ripple that spread abruptly across the sky and then was gone. The haze had vanished—and so had the two great stacks of the power-house.

Feeling as though his legs had turned suddenly to water, Davis slumped down upon the hilltop and stared openmouthed along the valley. A sense of overwhelming disaster swept into his mind; as in a dream, he waited for the explosion to reach his ears.

It was not impressive when it came; only a dull, long-drawn-out whooooooosh! that died away swiftly in the still air. Half unconsciously, Davis noticed that the chatter of the drill had also stopped; the explosion must have been louder than he thought for Barton to have heard it too.

The silence was complete. Nothing moved anywhere as far as his eye could see in the whole of that empty, barren landscape. He waited until his strength returned; then, half running, he went unsteadily down the hill to rejoin his friend.

Barton was half sitting in the trench with his head buried in his hands. He looked up as Davis approached; and although his features were obscured by dust and sand, the other was shocked at the expression in his eyes.

"So you heard it too!" Davis said. "I think the whole lab's blown up. Come along, for heaven's sake!"

"Heard what?" said Barton dully.

Davis stared at him in amazement. Then he realized that Barton could not possibly have heard any sound while he was working with the drill. The sense of disaster deepened with a rush; he felt like a character in some Greek tragedy, helpless before an implacable doom.

Barton rose to his feet. His face was working strangely, and Davis saw that he was on the verge of breakdown. Yet, when he spoke, his words were surprisingly calm.

"What fools we were!" he said. "How Henderson must have laughed at us when we told him that he was trying to *see* into the past!"

Mechanically, Davis moved to the trench and stared at the rock that was seeing the light of day for the first time in fifty million years. Without much emotion, now, he traced again the zigzag pattern he had first noticed a few hours before. It had sunk only a little way into the mud, as if when it was formed the jeep had been traveling at its utmost speed.

No doubt it had been; for in one place the shallow tire marks had been completely obliterated by the monster's footprints. They were now very deep indeed, as if the great reptile was about to make the final leap upon its desperately fleeing prey.

CHAMELEON

KRISTINE KATHRYN RUSCH

Wilhelmina crept inside Mrs. Anderson's room, and sat there, with the lights off. Outside the windows, snow fell in big white flakes, faster and faster, so fast that Willi couldn't see the teacher's parking lot just across the sidewalk. The chameleon paced in its little cage. The mama gerbil had her back to the cold, and the papa gerbil, in his own glass world, watched the snow as Willi did. The snake cage was open—the boa constrictor was still missing—and the mice were crowding their own cage in its absence. The rabbit sat on a table up front, nibbling on a carrot and staring at Willi with beady eyes.

Willi didn't mind. She felt safe here, in the humidity, with the smell of too many furry bodies. Even with the boa constrictor on the loose, popping out of the duct work, and scaring the principal as it had done the day before.

Everyone else was waiting out the storm in the auditorium. Willi hated the auditorium. She would rather wait here, with the animals.

The snow had started that morning, after gym. The principal made an announcement, saying it was too dangerous to drive. The radios had already announced that the parents should *not* try to pick up their kids. Everyone would spend the night at school, if they had to, and Mrs. Bates, the cook, would make them something extra special. Lucky she did at lunch, because the electricity went out just before math. The clock behind Willi's head still read 1:15.

Willi wasn't scared. She knew her mom would come anyway. A storm would never stop her mother.

The animals didn't seem frightened either. They liked the quiet, just like Willi did. She was glad to get away from stinky old Greg Matson, and weird Dougy Spencer. The kids hadn't stopped picking on her since she had come to school two months ago, just after Thanksgiving. They made fun of her clothes, and when she went into the bathroom and zapped herself into new ones, the kids stopped laughing and no longer even looked at her. Sometimes they called her a witch, and she couldn't even tell them to stop because that was what she was.

She brought her knees up against her chest. When she had told her mom about it all, her mom had said that Willi shouldn't want to be like the other kids. Willi didn't agree until a week later, when the teacher took them to the natural history museum, in the history of science building attached to the grade school. (Her mom had enrolled her in a university lab school, thinking that smart kids would be kinder than the dumb ones Willi had studied with in Kentucky.) The kids laughed and pointed at all the dead animals, stuffed and frozen in their glass cages. The bobcat had moth holes in its fur, and just beneath the surface, Willi could hear a faint whisper of memory, begging to go free. She wasn't powerful enough to free the bobcat, so she sat in front of the cage and cried.

And had been called Crybaby Witch ever since.

Outside the wind howled, and a bit of cold seeped in through the windowpanes. The rabbit's fur ruffled. Willi whispered a protect spell and blew it at all the animals. They looked up at her, as if in gratitude, and she blew them a kiss.

She wished she knew where the boa constrictor was. It had always been her favorite. She liked its long slimy length, the power in its straight body, the alien coldness in its black eyes. Maybe, if she used dust magic, she could find it.

She whipped the dust into little particles, and sent them searching, but the snake wasn't in Mrs. Anderson's room. Willi slipped out into the hall. Maybe the snake did travel the duct work like the principal said, and she would find it in someone else's classroom.

The hallway was dark, darker than she had ever seen it. The lockers stood like soldiers at the Air Force Base where she had lived with her daddy just before he died and her mother decided to stay for good. The window displays beside each classroom's door had lights glowing on the contents. The hearts Willi had painstakingly cut with scissors because her mom told her not to show her powers glowed redly. Something moved in the fifth grade's display case, and as she walked by, she saw the boa constrictor, its body flaking and dry, wrapped around a Peek-a-Boo doll.

It hadn't been eating school mice as Mrs. Anderson had said. It had gotten itself trapped. And it was dying.

Willi glanced up and down the hall. She didn't see anyone. In the distance, she could hear singing coming from the auditorium. They had been singing all afternoon in the fake generator lights, away from the storm. Willi thought that everyone would be hoarse by now. She saw someone cross the hall and disappear into the boys' room. She was as alone as she could be.

She ran back into Mrs. Anderson's room and got two mice, begging their forgiveness. She wasn't too fond of mice—they ate their babies, just like the papa gerbil did—and that made her mad, but she wasn't sure she wanted to kill them. But, as her mom would say, creatures ate each other. That was the way of the world.

Willi hurried back into the hall with the mice trapped in her pockets. She sat on the floor and raised her fingers, making a small turning motion. The thin silver lock guarding the display case clicked and the door swung open. The snake nearly fell out. Willi flattened her hands like a bed, and let the air carry the snake to her. She eased the snake down and put the mice in front of it. She made an invisible barrier so that the mice couldn't run away. The snake looked up at her, its cold cold eyes actually seeing her for the first time, and then it snapped a mouse between its oversized jaws.

Willi stood. She couldn't watch this.

Greg Matson stood behind her, his face white as the bunny's fur. "You *are* a witch," he whispered. "And I'm going to tell everybody that you stole the snake and you're killing mice."

"I did not!" she said. "It was dying!"

But he had already taken off, running down the hall, his Nikes slapping against the tile floor. She couldn't let him tell. She couldn't. The kids hated her bad enough. But if the teachers thought she'd messed with the snake, she would never go into Mrs. Anderson's room again.

Never see the rabbit again, never hold the chameleon and watch its personal magic. Never be safe.

Without thinking, she raised her hand and bid the air to tie Greg's feet. He tripped and skidded along the tile, finally landing outside the auditorium. He sat up and flopped his legs like a fish. Then he started screaming.

The principal burst out of the auditorium door, his short rotund frame crouching over Greg. Willi put a hand over her mouth. She had made it worse.

The snake had swallowed the second mouse and was slithering against the wall, trying to hide. Willi glanced around. The principal would see her. Anywhere she went, he would see her, and she had already used her magic quota for the day. She was trapped.

She turned and ran down the hall, past the doors to the gym, past the music room and into the narrow hallway where the grad students had their tiny offices. All the doors were shut and locked. They must have gone home before the snow hit.

The end of the hallway smelled of paint and formaldehyde. Willi burst through the double doors leading to the natural sciences building. She spun around the corner, and found herself face to face with a stuffed bear. She stifled a scream. The bear was so old, its fur had no whisperings at all. She ran past it and all the other dead animals, until she found the hall of the dinosaurs.

Her teacher, Mr. Hayes, hadn't taken them in there. He had pointed at the dinosaurs and laughed. "Those models," he had said, "were made in the 1950s, before I was born. They're out of date and wrong." But they had looked great to her, tall majestic beasts, with green skin and eyes as cold as the snake's.

She didn't hear anyone behind her. Her heart was pounding in her chest, and her breathing was coming hard. She hurried into the dinosaur room, and snuck around the big green dinosaur in the middle. The dinosaur had a long neck and a tiny head that was staring at the door. She touched its flank. The dinosaur was made of plaster of Paris. It was cold and hard.

She sank on her knees and leaned against the dinosaur's leg, waiting for the principal to find her.

She didn't know how long she sat there, in the dust and the dry-smelling heat. No one had walked on this side of the dinosaur in a long time. Her tennis shoes had left patterned footprints on the floor. Her jeans were covered with a white and green powder. It took a moment before she realized that the dinosaur's legs were peeling.

Willi touched it, and more dust dropped onto her hand. She couldn't imagine being so old and out of date that no one even tended her. Poor dinosaur. She leaned her head on the plaster of Paris, and listened, but heard no whisperings, no hope, no feeling of being trapped like she had gotten from the bobcat.

The dinosaur wasn't dead. It had never been alive.

Somehow that made her very sad. She brought her knees up to her chest and tucked her chin against them. Ice pelted the side of the building, sounding like rocks thrown against a concrete wall. No one had come after her yet. Maybe they hadn't seen where she had gone. She was used to her mother, whom no one could ever hide from.

Willi got up and dusted off her jeans. She wandered to the back of the dinosaur room. Other dinosaurs stood against the wall. A rounded one, with a big head, and an armor-plated back, had lost all its covering on one side, revealing a mesh frame. The pterodactyl (her favorite and the only kind she had heard of) was missing one wing. Maybe Mr. Hayes hadn't brought them here because the dinosaurs were in such bad condition, not because they weren't up to date.

Maybe she would stay here forever. The dinosaurs didn't care who she was. They were different from all the dead animals, just like she was different from all the other children. Her mom said she had to blend in, learn how to get along with humans. But Willi didn't want to blend in. She wanted to save a snake without Greg Matson telling on her, and she wanted to talk to the rabbit without people thinking her crazy. She wanted to free what little life she had found in the bobcat, if she could only find a way.

Her mom made it look so easy. Everyone thought her mom was normal. They didn't know that she made dinner by pulling out the groceries they had bought for appearance's sake, snapping her fingers, and setting out serving trays. They didn't know that she changed her hair color without going to a beautician. They didn't know that she didn't work for a living because she had all the money she had earned on horse races since gambling became a craze in Atlantic City.

No one could put anything past her mom, but her mom could put stuff past them. That, her mother had said, was what Willi had to learn.

What Willi had failed to do this afternoon.

She sighed, and coughed as dust got into her lungs. No one

would come for her. She would rot in this back room with all the non-dead dinosaurs. Half of her wanted to get found. Half of her wanted the principal to kick her out.

The other half wondered who would take care of the animals if he did.

She wandered back to her hiding spot and touched the side of the dinosaur. This time she did hear whisperings, but like nothing she had ever heard before. Voices. Voices were trapped inside the dinosaur.

. . . is too. They get really big and they stomp all over everything and eat people . . .

. . . I'm going to get on its back and it'll take me away, like Danny and the Dinosaur *. . .*

. . . If only I was as big as you. Then they wouldn't hit me any more . . .

The voices were small, light. Children's voices.

. . . It is too real. You just can't see it. It comes out at night and watches us while we sleep . . .

. . . and it was really hot, and all they got to do was eat and sleep, and hunt . . .

. . . I don't know why I like 'em. I just think dinosaurs are cool . . .

Willi moved her hand away. The dinosaur's head had turned just a little. It seemed to be smiling at her. What lived inside it were fantasies, beliefs, fears, and it held them dear. She leaned her head against its side.

"I'm sorry that you're flaking," she whispered. "If they let me come back tomorrow, I'll have enough magic to fix you."

The dinosaur's smile grew, and the voices swirled around her, almost too fast to catch. It took a few minutes for her to realize that some of the voices she was hearing were coming from the hall.

She let go of the dinosaur. The children's voices disappeared. Only two adult voices remained.

". . . saw her in the middle of the hallway, feeding the snake.

We don't tolerate theft in this school, Mrs. Ramsey." The principal's nasal voice echoed. Willi ducked against the dinosaur's leg.

"Of course she fed it." The voice was her mother's. The tone was one of exasperation at a stupid human being. "The snake was dying. It must have been a hard choice for her. My daughter loves animals. She had to sacrifice mice to keep the snake alive."

"We don't know that the snake was dying, any more than we know that your daughter ran this far. This area is forbidden to children—"

"Mr. Caldwell, I have had just about enough of your prattle," her mother said. "I know my daughter's mind. If she's going to hide, she's going to hide well. And what I said about the snake is pure logic. You said it's been loose for a long time—a fact I find appalling—and I assume there are no mice or rats in this building, except for the ones in cages. Now, I don't know how long a boa constrictor can go without a meal, but it stands to reason that the thing would not be in good health."

They stopped outside the door. Willi saw their feet swirl the dust. Her mother was wearing her black cowboy boots with their four-inch heels. The principal had on his good leather shoes, the ones without the scuffs.

"I must be frank with you, Mrs. Ramsey. Ever since Willi came here, she has not fit in. She spooks the other children and she does strange things like she did this afternoon. I don't know what she said to Greg Matson, but he was so frightened that he couldn't move his legs for the longest time—"

"Mr. Caldwell, my daughter is brilliant and talented and unusual. I thought an experimental school like this one would be a haven for her, but you're like the other teachers in this country. You only care about making her normal. Well, she's not normal and she never will be. Perhaps you should concentrate on making the children better individuals instead of better clones." Her mother took a step into the room. "Willi?"

The yell was for show. Willi's mother knew where Willi was, and Willi knew better than to stay hidden. She snuck out around the side of the dinosaur, wishing it could protect her. But it could only listen and absorb her hopes and fears.

Her mother's hair frizzed in all directions, and her leather coat hadn't a speck of snow on it. The principal looked rumpled in his black suit.

Her mother said, "Willi, are you all right?"

Willi's hands were clenched in small fists. "I didn't mean to do anything wrong. The snake was just trapped, and I was trying to help it, and Greg Matson is so mean!"

"It's all right, honey. You're not coming back here." Her mother held out a leather-gloved hand. "Let's go."

"I must protest," the principal said. "There's a blizzard out there. You may have made it here safely, Mrs. Ramsey, but you'll never make it home, not with the child."

"Try me," Willi's mother said. They started down the hall, Willi's hand tightly wrapped in her mother's. "By the way, you might want to catch that snake. It's stalking Willi's favorite rabbit."

"How—?"

"No!" Willi shouted. She broke free. "Stop it, Mom. You've got to stop it." She ran down the hall, around the corners, past the bear, past the offices, past the rooms, until she reached Mrs. Anderson's. The snake had made its way under the desks to the table in the front. The rabbit was washing its face, all unaware. Willi scooped it up and hugged it to her chest, burying her face in its warm, musky fur.

"It won't get you," she whispered. "It won't."

She whirled and climbed on the table, leaning against the windows, against the swirl of depthless white. The rabbit trembled in her arms.

Her mother and the principal appeared at the door. The principal saw the snake, turned and hurried down the hall. "Willi," her mother said. "You're being silly."

"No, I'm not," she said. "This rabbit's just like me. Nobody likes it and nobody protects it."

"You protect it," her mother said as she came into the room, gingerly stepping over the snake. She stopped by the window and tapped the chameleon's cage. "You would do a better job if you became like this little fellow. Blending into your environment, but never losing track of who you are."

"That's what you yelled at him about."

"Mr. Caldwell?" Her mother smiled, making her entire face look no older than Willi's. "No, honey. He wants all children to goose-step in place, to be the same creature. In the real world, snakes, rabbits, and mice all share the same plot of ground, but they have to be careful of each other." Her mother glanced around. "You're right. This is a very safe room. No wonder you like it here."

Willi leaned against the window. The glass was like ice against her back.

"Here, let's put that snake back so your rabbit is safe." Her mother clapped her fingers and the snake floated across the air. The lid on the cage came open, and the snake lowered into it, gently. Then the lid went back on.

Slowly Willi set the rabbit down. The rabbit scampered a few feet away, then huddled, as if it still wasn't over its fright.

"Let's go home, honey."

"No," Willi said. "They'll wonder how we did it."

"It's all right. You're not coming back."

This would be the fourth school she'd left in the past year, and the only one with animals. Willi glanced at her rabbit, at the chameleon, at the snake. The dinosaur in the next room needed her help, and the animals needed her protection. She didn't want to leave them, no matter how mean Greg Matson was.

When the snake had run away, it had nearly died.

"No," Willi said. "I want to stay."

"I thought you didn't like it here."

"I like some things," Willi said. She liked Mrs. Anderson and the animals. She even liked that back room, filled with dust and dinosaurs. She especially wanted to see the dinosaur again. "Maybe I've been too much like the rabbit. Maybe it's time to see what the chameleon can do."

Her mother smiled and hugged her. "Fitting in isn't what matters. Being true to yourself is. You're not a rabbit, honey."

She knew that. But she wasn't a chameleon either. She was a big green dinosaur, the kind that didn't exist by human standards, made of strange materials, and filled with fantasies, beliefs, and fears.

She put her arm around her mother, and they headed to the auditorium. They would stay. They would suffer through the singing and the cold food, and maybe Willi wouldn't fit in, maybe she wouldn't be normal, but maybe for a short time, in the dark, in the storm, the other kids would think she was one of them.

SHADOW OF A CHANGE

MICHELLE M. SAGARA

She didn't know when it started.

One morning, she had simply been April Stephens, part of the typing pool at a large, sedate computer firm. She caught the same bus every morning at 7:30, arrived at work every morning at 8:15 (give or take a few minutes for traffic), and made her way to her desk, coffee in hand, at exactly 8:30. She wore neutral colors, neutral styles, and a very conservative bob; she wore sensible shoes, ate healthy food, and lived a very quiet life.

Sometimes, on the bus on the way home, when traffic stalled in the misnamed rush hour, she would gaze out the window and try to remember if this was what she had wanted out of life. Eavesdropping on the fluttering conversations that changed daily, she would catch a spark of something bright and shiny and new in the hushed whispers or excited chattering that made her yearn, for a moment, for someone else's youth.

Home was a simple affair; she lived in the two story, two bedroom home that she had inherited when her mother had passed away. Her father, long gone from even memory, had not survived her second year, but his picture hung over the mantle of the fake fireplace. She dusted that mantle, oiling its dark, rich wood, with a particular care to detail; it was one of the few things in the house that she thought beautiful.

Certainly she did not consider herself so.

She had one or two friends, made in grade school, whom she had anchored a part of herself to, and she kept in contact with them by the use of the phone and a judicious letter here and there, although they all lived in the same city. She rarely went out, and rarely invited anyone in; it was stressful, not to know how to behave, what to say, or how to entertain. Easier was simply this: to enter in through the side door of her home, lock it behind her back, drop her bags by the side of the umbrella rack, and sag against the wall. She added tea to her daily routine; she watched television. She did not live an unhappy life.

She should have known something was wrong when she missed the bus on a Monday morning in early spring. The snow had started its second melt of the season, and her rubbers, filthy with mud and crusted with dried salt, made squishy, awful protests as she ran, briefcase tailing her like exhaust, to the bus stop in time to see the great, red rectangle pull away.

In six years of work, she had not once missed the bus. Unsettled, she clutched her briefcase to her chest and held it there, as if it were a shield. The next bus came, and she caught that easily enough; fumbled in her pocket for her bus pass, and then stumbled to a seat.

The drive to work, across the muddied water left by melting snow, was not restful either; she rocked back and forth, against the lurch and halt of the bus's motion, while she tried to remember the dream that had anchored her so thoroughly to sleep that she had slept late, missed breakfast, and then been late for the first event of her morning.

She missed her morning coffee, but made it to her desk in time for an orderly 8:30. But the day had an edge to it that even a large lunch and a whole pot of tea at its end couldn't dull. When she went to bed that evening, she made certain that the alarm was set just a little early; made certain that it was across the room, rather than beside her bed.

But the darkness held her in. When she managed to open her eyes in the morning, the light through the sheers told her that the claxon of the alarm had been going on for at least fifteen minutes. She struggled with blankets, tossed them off, and then tried to stand.

I'm sick, she thought, as the room spun. Her knees hurt, and her elbows; her focus came strangely, as if she were looking through convex glass. Holding the side of the bed, she stood. She had to shut off the alarm clock before the bells shattered the insides of her skull.

She made it, although her fingers felt thick and wide and she had to struggle—every movement came at some effort, as if movement itself were foreign—to hit the small switch that would stall the bells.

They stopped, and the silence that descended, rich with sunbeams and the blue of a clear, morning sky, felt hollow. She barely noticed the time. Breakfast. Food. She stumbled out the door and down the stairs, clinging to the banister.

That morning, she was also late for work.

April half-walked, half-crawled, through the side door of her house at the end of the day. She dropped her bag in the wrong spot, left her coat on, and plunked herself down on the couch. She wanted to sleep, but the light in the room was too bright; with an exhausted snarl, she stood up, yanked the blinds closed, shut off the lights, and then returned to the couch.

There, in the silence and the blessed shadow, she listened to the heavy rasp of her breath. Wondering what she was sick with. Wondering where she had got it, and how long it would take to go away.

That night, when she finally managed to leave the couch and the living room, she dreamed of shadows and darkness and hunger.

"April, are you all right?" Susan Lundstrom, the oldest member of the typing pool and therefore the one with the unspoken seniority, made a place for herself at the cafeteria table, settling down with her tray, her purse, and the ashtray that she'd moved from the smoking section.

April nodded, distracted.

"Well, if you don't mind my saying so, you look a little green. Are you sure you're okay?" When April failed to hear her, Susan leaned forward, casting a shadow over the wood veneer surface.

"I'm fine," April said. She straightened out her shoulders and picked up her sandwich. "I just didn't sleep well last night."

"Have it your way," was the cheerful reply. But the voice lost some of its lightness. "April? April?"

April Stephens was staring at the two slices of white bread and the tomato, cheese, and lettuce between them as if they were asphalt. She tried to bite it all, even tried to chew it, and at last stood up, muttering her apologies around a mouthful of food that she could not swallow.

She found the washroom, trying to tuck the food beneath her tongue so that no one would notice, and quickly swung into a cubicle. There, she got rid of it. And the soup that had preceded it.

Shuddering, her stomach rolling beneath her flesh, she wiped her mouth with the back of her hand, stood, and made her way to the sink. The mirror, with someone's fingerprints at the lower edge, showed her the tired and strained face of a very upset woman. She breathed deeply, breathed again, and then straightened out her glasses.

Come on, April. It's not like you've never been sick before.

But it was like she'd never been sick.

Coming home by bus, with a stop at the supermarket, became a fog of dizziness, hunger, and nausea. She wasn't certain when she got off the bus; wasn't certain when she entered the supermarket; couldn't remember what she'd bought there. All she remembered was the *now* of the moment; the past and the future faded around her as if the present were the only island on which she could stand.

The only time she panicked was when she couldn't remember having paid, but a quick count of her money assured her that she'd certainly spent some of it.

Dinner was quickly prepared; she turned on the television, settled uncomfortably back against the couch, propped her legs up on the coffee table and started to eat. She tried to keep track of what was on the television—she thought it was the news—but the picture kept rotating like a warped record. Annoyed, she played with the remote, but it brought no relief—only a surge of new colors, different distortions.

Snarling, she turned her full attention to her food.

Which she didn't remember cooking, because she hadn't. She stopped chewing as she realized that her mouth was full of something cold and wet; looked down to see that her fingers had all but disappeared into what was left of a slab of beef. Blood and warming fat greased her nails as she dropped the meat. She ran to the sink, bent over it, and spit out everything that she hadn't already swallowed.

Then, choking, she slid down the side of the cupboard in front of the sink, curled her knees up under her chin, and began to cry.

She didn't notice that as she did, she was licking her fingers clean.

She knew her work wasn't up to standard in the following week. Susan knew it. Alexis knew it. Kelly knew it. None of them said a word, although Susan continued to ask after her health. Susan even did her best to see that the workload was less evenly distributed than usual; if April hadn't felt too ashamed, she would have been grateful.

But she did have to do typing work, and the work that she did get assigned was expected to have a certain quality to it. Until now, April had always been certain that everything that left her desk with her initials on it was as perfect as anyone could make it. That was gone. Her fingers felt sluggish and heavy; the keypad of the word processor was suddenly tiny and incomprehensible. She had to *look* at the keys; her fingers had forgotten years of instinctive movement.

Stephen Hawthorne was the first person to bring back a complaint. He didn't, of course, carry it directly to her; he had to go to the head of the typing pool to let his displeasure be known. But April heard him shouting in his high, nasal voice. She hated it; had she not been afraid of drawing more attention to herself, she'd have plugged her ears.

He came back three times that day, and at the end of the day, Susan was exhausted enough to call April to the front of the room, where Stephen Hawthorne stood, angrily tapping the floor with his perfect black shoes.

"Ms. Stephens?" he asked, in that clipped, nasal voice.

"Yes?" She kept her own as steady and as low as possible.

"What is your excuse for *this*? I need this report for a *client*; this is not a normal interoffice scribble. Look at *this*—did you even run it through a spellchecker?"

She nodded obsequiously, hoping that it would be enough to

send him away. But he kept on and on and on until at last she grabbed the report and curled it in trembling hands. She couldn't—wouldn't—listen to another word.

"I'll fix the goddamned report and have it on your desk in the morning. Is there anything else or do you expect me to sit here and listen to you whine for the rest of the day?"

She had the satisfaction of watching all of the blood rush to his face before she turned and marched smartly back to her desk. She half-expected him to follow her, but he didn't. Which was a pity.

At the end of the day, only this memory stayed with her; all others vanished into the haze of her encroaching disease. Perhaps tomorrow she would do the unthinkable. Perhaps tomorrow she would miss her first day of work.

When she got home, she walked into the kitchen, turned the oven on, pulled her dinner out of the little Safeway bag, and walked into the living room. The windows remained shuttered against the end of the day; the television remained dull, faceless glass. She didn't want the noise, or the mix of noises. She felt nauseated, but beneath the nausea was hunger. She ate.

This time she paid careful attention to what she was eating, fascinated by it, detached from its reality. The meat in her mouth was cold and grisly; it tasted slightly rank, too old. But it was food; real food; she could chew it slowly and then swallow it. It was almost good. Only when she had finished eating did she remember to turn off the oven.

In bed, the lights dimmed, the clock set, she cried; the tears silent and bewildered, with no force and no anger behind them.

In the morning she saw the first clear sign, the whisper of a real change. Her skin was darker, harder. She thought at first that her fingertips themselves were somehow callused; nothing felt right to the touch—not the bedsheets, not her clothing, not the meat that she ate in the morning.

She looked at herself, carefully, in the mirror. Her face was the same shape, but it, too, was darker. She opened her mouth and her teeth were sharp.

The doctor. She had to call the doctor.

She ran back to her bedroom, leafed through the phone book, found the number and then picked up the phone. Jabbing awkwardly at the impossibly small buttons, she managed to hit the right sequence of numbers—on the ninth try.

"Dr. Kennedy's office, may I help you?"

"I'd like to make an appointment to see Dr. Kennedy," April said, her voice throaty and deep with the early morning. "It's an— an emergency." She wasn't used to making this much of a fuss, and her voice broke on the last word.

The sound of flapping pages could be heard before the receptionist's voice returned to the receiver. "There's an appointment for tomorrow at 11:30, if you're available then."

Tomorrow. April Stephens shook her head.

"Hello?"

"I'll—it's not important."

She lied, of course. It was important; she knew it. So important, in fact, that she phoned Susan to carefully explain that she would be coming in later in the day. She dressed carelessly and grabbed a purse—not her briefcase—before she flew out of the house in search of a bus.

The bus, hot and crowded, was oppressive. She was aware of every stranger's gaze, and wondered if they were looking at her because she looked like a circus freak. She covered her teeth more prominently with her lips, pressing them into a tight, whitened line. She also pulled up the collar of her long jacket, and tried skulking beneath its line. It wasn't comfortable.

Transferring helped somewhat; the air, cool and crisp, refreshed her. For a moment she felt almost human. Then the second bus came, and once again she was crushed into a tiny, rectangular space with far too many people and far too little air. She wanted to scream, bit her lip instead, and instantly regretted it.

But the hospital, thankfully, loomed up ahead with its twin smokestacks. She could leave this bus, and these people, and find solace in the emergency room there. They could tell her what was happening. They could help.

Before she crossed the street, she was hit by a wave of nausea. Her knees bent; her arms stiffened and drew up. Everything twisted, converging and separating in a mindless, dizzying pattern.

She managed to remember where she was; where she had to go. Forcing herself to her feet, she crossed the street. She couldn't understand why the cars screeched out in wide circles around her; couldn't understand why they were honking so loudly. Someone rolled down a window and waved a fist in the air; his words were lost to her comprehension, but his meaning was perfectly clear.

April Stephens opened her mouth and *roared*.

The roar lengthened into a terrified scream. With halting, awkward steps, she loped up the long stretch of road toward the emergency ward of the hospital.

It shouldn't have been crowded at this time in the morning; she was certain it shouldn't be so crowded. But she hadn't been to a hospital since she was eight years old and skateboards were a necessity of life, and she didn't remember clearly.

"Miss? May I help you?"

It took a minute to realize that the person sitting behind the desk was talking to her, and another minute to realize that he expected her to come to him. She walked across the floor, once again too aware of the eyes of the people in the waiting room. Her hesitance grew as she awkwardly took the chair in front of the young man and his computer terminal.

He asked her questions. Had she been here before. Did she have her Health Card with her. Did she know her family doctor. She answered them curtly, impatiently. Finally, after filling out line by line of trivial information, he actually *looked* at her.

"What exactly is the nature of your problem?"

She blinked, confused.

"What's wrong?"

"I'm—I'm changing," she replied.

The young man raised a pale brow. "Changing, ma'am?"

"My skin is harder and my teeth are funny and I can't eat properly."

If he noticed that her voice was going up an octave, his expression didn't give him away. He carefully and neatly input all of her information and then watched the computer screen for a minute. "That'll be all, Ms. Stephens. If you'd care to take a seat, a doctor will be with you as soon as possible."

"When? When is that?"

"Just as soon as possible," came the firm reply. It did not allow for any other question.

The chair that she chose was as far away from anyone else as she could possibly make it. She wanted to curl her legs up beneath her chin, but they felt awkward and heavy, and she wasn't sure they would fit on the small edge of the chair. There were magazines, all at least a month old, in messy piles on a small table beside her. She picked one up. Politics.

But politics was better than change. She forced herself to read article after article while she tried to remember who all the names and faces in the little pictures belonged to.

At last, they called her name. They had to call it three times, as if her conscious mind, slumbering in an uneasy state, refused to recognize it as her own. She rose stiffly, kept her lips firmly shut, and followed the young man in the green nightshirt. He pushed his way out of the waiting room, through a thick, wide door which creaked as it swung on its hinges. He was obviously used to patients who walked slowly, for his step was measured, and he glanced over his shoulder often.

She followed him, glancing from side to side in bewilderment. Within this new set of rooms and curtained vestibules was another set of chairs, another wait. Still, the chemical, medicinal smell of the inner room reassured her; she was close to help now, she was certain of it. She sat.

Five minutes passed, at least it felt like five minutes; she was certain that that's what the round clock on the wall said. Big hand, little hand, hand that moved quickly. Her head hurt; her stomach rumbled and twisted painfully. She doubled over, clutching her sides. Crying, or trying not to cry. After a while, there was no difference.

Someone was ushered into the room with great care. They put him beside her. She knew this because there was something about his *smell* that was familiar, almost tantalizing. Out of the corner of her eye, she glanced in his direction, hoping that he wouldn't notice, half-embarrassed.

She forgot it, though. His arm, bandaged somehow, was a deep, bright red. His face was white, but his forehead was cut, and a little rivulet of blood ran, like a tiny brook, between the crevices of his wrinkled forehead.

"I'm all right, miss," the man said, as he drew back from her probing fingers. "Just had a little disagreement, s'all."

April nodded, hypnotized. She looked at her fingers, at the blood on their tips, and then raised them slowly to her mouth. She didn't notice when the patient blanched and moved four seats away.

"Well, then, what seems to be the problem, Ms. Stephens?"

She opened her mouth suddenly, pulling her lips over her pronounced teeth.

73

"Throat problem, is it?" He reached for a wooden stick. "Let me see it, then." He reached for her chin, and then frowned as she pulled away. "Feels like you've got yourself a case of eczema there, ma'am." He paused, ran his hands over his eyes, and then blinked. It had been a long shift, and he was almost, thank God, off. Interning was a rite of passage so stressful it was impossible to imagine it from the relative safety of medical school.

She watched him with her wide, unblinking eyes. He could see the fear in them, but their intensity made him uncomfortable. "I'm changing, Doctor," she whispered, and her voice was a rasp. "I don't know what's wrong."

He could tell, from the thick puffiness of her lids, that she'd probably been crying. Now, now, he thought, glancing furtively at his watch. Two cardiac arrests, two very serious knife wounds and a host of stitches on three hours of sleep left him very little room for sympathy, very little strength to comfort.

"It's nothing," he said brusquely. "You're probably under some sort of stress, and you're obviously eating or wearing something you're allergic to. Here, I'll give you a shot of Atarax, and I'll give you a prescription for the skin itself." She started to speak, and he held up his hand to ward off the words. "Don't worry about it, Ms. Stephens. Happens all the time." Standing, and trying very hard not to yawn or show his fatigue, the young intern went in search of the section nurse.

April Stephens sat alone in the curtained vestibule, with the little lights flashing in her eyes. All of the words she wanted to say backed up in her throat; she choked on them, shaking. She wanted to believe the doctor—doctors knew what they were doing, didn't they?—she did her best. She took deep breaths.

She was almost relieved to see the nurse, who proved to be a matronly woman, not a young, almost teenaged-faced girl. "You're Ms. April Stephens?" the nurse asked, as she set aside a clipboard. "Good. Here, then. You might want to bend over—this is a muscle shot, and it'll hurt your arm like hell."

April shook her head mutely, but offered her left arm instead of her right one. The nurse shrugged, took the offered arm, and readied the needle.

Just a single shot, April thought, repeating the words like a mantra, a prayer. Just a single shot. It happens to everyone.

She was heartbroken, but not at all surprised, when the needle snapped before it penetrated her skin. The nurse, flustered now, disappeared, but April Stephens didn't wait for her return. There were too many odd smells in this hospital now, and chief among them was the lingering scent of blood beneath her nails.

She didn't go to work; she couldn't. When she got home, the mirror showed her that her skin was indeed of the consistency to break—snap, really—the thin, hard spine of a doctor's needle. Her head hurt, her stomach ached, and the taste of a wounded man's blood lingered in her mouth. She stumbled to the kitchen, yanked the fridge door open, and watched it fall off its hinges with a crash.

Her hands were clumsy as they pulled the packages out of the fridge. Molding lettuce and cucumbers that had almost liquified she tossed to the side and forgot; she didn't even spare them more than an instinctive shudder of disgust. She ate what she could, but it wasn't enough; she knew it.

She knew what she wanted. She bit her tongue, and her tongue bled; she growled and whimpered.

This isn't happening. This can't be happening.

But she had never been in control of her life and its changes, and although she felt despair and horror, she felt no surprise.

That night, she woke up in the open drive of her house, the upturned throat of a limp cat between her jaws. She felt good for at least two seconds, and then her mind caught up with her body and she began to choke. She was changed, she knew it; she could see, in the soothing moonlight, the shadow of a thick tail at her back.

*   *   *

She didn't bury the cat; indeed, until she got into the house, she would have sworn that she had thrown it aside in either fear or disgust. But she hadn't; its warm, sticky body remained with her, as if it were steel and she, a strong magnet. In the dim light of the inner house, she recognized the slack face of the cat—it was Duffy, from two houses down. A young cat.

She had killed it. She was eating it. She couldn't make herself stop.

No. No, she wasn't this. She wasn't doing this, it wasn't real. Bones snapped against the second row of her sharp teeth.

With a cry that was feral, worse than feral, she threw the cat away and ran down, down into the darkness. The steps were hard to take, too close together and too tiny for her feet. Gravity started what determination had finished; she felt the ground shake as she hit it with her full weight. Standing, she could just make out the large, round metal dome of her ancient furnace. Wooden joists scraped against her head; she heard the unpleasant, hard sound of something meeting wood.

She thought she must be crying, and opened her lips to moan; instead, she growled, a sound so low and so gravelly it reminded her of a car tearing down an unpaved drive. Silence descended as she clamped her jaw shut. Her teeth clicked sharply.

She would stay in the darkness, in the cool damp shadows. Wait here, without light to show her the changes, without a mirror to reflect how out of control she had become. There were no living things, there were no other people; if she could be still and sleep, everything would pass into dream.

Her lids grew heavy. Her forehead fell forward slightly, although she had no desire to do anything but stand as sleep began to wash over her.

This was fine. This was what she wanted. Just sleep. Escape. A place where the changing didn't matter.

*   *   *

"Hello?"

In the darkness, the word was hard and sharp and clear. It was followed by light, something that, like the word, was almost crystalline in its clarity.

"Hello? I'm here to read the gas meter. Door was open, and I thought I'd come in. Hello?"

Sound and light were followed by scent, the moving of shadow, the presence of warmth.

"Hello?" The light stopped bouncing, and suddenly became a spear, a straight beam shearing into the unwary eye.

She *roared* in anger, and the sound of her voice killed the little words completely. Joists creaked as she stood; she lifted her head and felt them snap against the column of her spine. Her tail hit poured cement, her claws left a trail in the ground. In the darkness, she could not see herself, could barely see the thing that made noise and light.

And she knew what she wanted. Her nostrils were full of the scent of fear and life. The fear was no longer hers. She had slept, she knew, and in waking, the dream of ages was pulled from her mind, the sight of smallness lifted from her vision. This was what she was, what she had been, what she would be.

Hungry, she took one step, and then another. The little creature turned to flee, moving quickly, breathing loudly. She liked it, this sudden spurt of movement. It felt natural to follow it; felt natural to take it out of the world with a crunch of jaws and a swing of the head.

In the darkness, April Stephens fed, tearing flesh off bone with a tongue that would grate against metal. Then, not quite satisfied, she reared up again, pushing past thick layers of plaster and old wood. She had had enough of the darkness; now it was time for the jungle, the light, and the hunt to follow.

April Stephens had never been in control of her life or the things that changed it and shaped it. But she had never been so free as this: She neither knew that she had no control, nor cared. She strode out, primitive, great, old—a thing of memory, a dream of children, a walking death.

Her roar filled a slumbering suburbia with its life and its breath. Soon, all of the dreamers would wake to her call, and she would hunt again.

STRATA

EDWARD BRYANT

Six hundred million years in thirty-two miles. Six hundred million years in fifty-one minutes. Steve Mavrakis traveled in time—courtesy of the Wyoming Highway Department. The epochs raveled between Thermopolis and Shoshoni. The Wind River rambled down its canyon with the Burlington Northern tracks cut into the west walls, and the two-lane blacktop, U.S. 20, sliced into the east. Official signs driven into the verge of the highway proclaimed the traveler's progress:

DINWOODY FORMATION
TRIASSIC
185–225 MILLION YEARS

BIG HORN FORMATION
ORDOVICIAN
440–500 MILLION YEARS

FLATHEAD FORMATION
CAMBRIAN
500–600 MILLION YEARS

The mileposts might have been staked into the canyon rock under the pressure of millennia. They were there for those who could not read the stone.

Tonight Steve ignored the signs. He had made this run many times before. Darkness hemmed him. November clawed when he cracked the window to exhaust Camel smoke from the Chevy's cab. The CB crackled occasionally and picked up exactly nothing.

The wind blew—that was nothing unusual. Steve felt himself hypnotized by the skiff of snow skating across the pavement in the glare of his brights. The snow swirled only inches above the blacktop, rushing across like surf sliding over the black packed sand of a beach.

Time's predator hunts.

Years scatter before her like a school of minnows surprised. The rush of her passage causes eons to eddy. Wind sweeps down the canyon with the roar of combers breaking on the sand. The moon, full and newly risen, exerts its tidal force.

Moonlight flashes on the slash of teeth.

And Steve snapped alert, realized he had traversed the thirty-two miles, crossed the flats leading into Shoshoni, and was approaching the junction with U.S. 26. Road hypnosis? he thought. Safe in Shoshoni, but it was scary. He didn't remember a god-damned minute of the trip through the canyon! Steve rubbed his eyes with his left hand and looked for an open cafe with coffee.

It hadn't been the first time.

All those years before, the four of them had thought they were beating the odds. On a chill night in June, high on a mountain edge in the Wind River Range, high on more than mountain air, the four of them celebrated graduation. They were young and clear-eyed: ready for the world. That night they knew there were no other people for miles. Having learned in class that there were

3.8 human beings per square mile in Wyoming, and as *four*, they thought the odds outnumbered.

Paul Onoda, eighteen. He was Sansei—third-generation Japanese-American. In 1942, before he was conceived, his parents were removed with eleven thousand other Japanese-Americans from California to the Heart Mountain Relocation Center in northern Wyoming. Twelve members and three generations of the Onodas shared one of four hundred and sixty-five crowded, tar-papered barracks for the next four years. Two died. Three more were born. With their fellows, the Onodas helped farm eighteen hundred acres of virgin agricultural land. Not all of them had been Japanese gardeners or truck farmers in California, so the pharmacists and the teachers and the carpenters learned agriculture. They used irrigation to bring in water. The crops flourished. The Nisei not directly involved with farming were dispatched from camp to be seasonal farm laborers. A historian later laconically noted that "Wyoming benefited by their presence."

Paul remembered the Heart Mountain camps only through the memories of his elders, but those recollections were vivid. After the war, most of the Onodas stayed on in Wyoming. With some difficulty, they bought farms. The family invested thrice the effort of their neighbors, and prospered.

Paul Onoda excelled in the classrooms and starred on the football field of Fremont High School. Once he overheard the president of the school board tell the coach, "By God, but that little Nip can run!" He thought about that and kept on running ever faster.

More than a few of his classmates secretly thought he had it all. When prom time came in his senior year, it did not go unnoticed that Paul had an extraordinarily handsome appearance to go with his brains and athlete's body. In and around Fremont, a great many concerned parents admonished their white daughters to find a good excuse if Paul asked them to the prom.

Carroll Dale, eighteen. It became second nature early on to explain to people first hearing her given name that it had two *r*'s and two *l*'s. Both sides of her family went back four generations in this part of the country and one of her bequests had been a proud mother. Cordelia Carroll had pride, one daughter, and the desire to see the Hereford Carrolls retain *some* parity with the Angus Dales. After all, the Carrolls had been ranching on Bad Water Creek before John Broderick Okie illuminated his Lost Cabin castle with carbide lights. That was when Teddy Roosevelt had been president and it was when all the rest of the cattlemen in Wyoming, including the Dales, had been doing their accounts at night by kerosene lanterns.

Carroll grew up to be a good roper and a better rider. Her apprenticeship intensified after her older brother, her only brother, fatally shot himself during deer season. She wounded her parents when she neither married a man who would take over the ranch nor decided to take over the ranch herself.

She grew up slim and tall, with ebony hair and large, dark, slightly oblique eyes. Her father's father, at family Christmas dinners, would overdo the whiskey in the eggnog and make jokes about Indians in the woodpile until her paternal grandmother would tell him to shut the hell up before she gave him a goodnight the hard way, with a rusty sickle and knitting needles. It was years before Carroll knew what her grandmother meant.

In junior high, Carroll was positive she was eight feet tall in Lilliput. The jokes hurt. But her mother told her to be patient, that the other girls would catch up. Most of the girls didn't; but in high school the boys did, though they tended to be tongue-tied in the extreme when they talked to her.

She was the first girl president of her school's National Honor Society. She was a cheerleader. She was the valedictorian of her class and earnestly quoted John F. Kennedy in her graduation address. Within weeks of graduation, she eloped with the captain of the football team.

It nearly caused a lynching.

Steve Mavrakis, eighteen. Courtesy allowed him to be called a native despite his birth eighteen hundred miles to the east. His parents, on the other hand, had settled in the state after the war when he was less than a year old. Given another decade, the younger native-born might grudgingly concede their adopted roots; the old-timers, never.

Steve's parents had read Zane Grey and *The Virginian*, and had spent many summers on dude ranches in upstate New York. So they found a perfect ranch on the Big Horn River and started a herd of registered Hereford. They went broke. They refinanced and aimed at a breed of inferior beef cattle. The snows of '49 killed those. Steve's father determined that sheep were the way to go—all those double and triple births. Very investment-effective. The sheep sickened, or stumbled and fell into creeks where they drowned, or panicked like turkeys and smothered in heaps in fenced corners. It occurred then to the Mavrakis family that wheat doesn't stampede. All the fields were promptly hailed out before what looked to be a bounty harvest. Steve's father gave up and moved into town where he put his Columbia degree to work by getting a job managing the district office for the Bureau of Land Management.

All of that taught Steve to be wary of sure things.

And occasionally he wondered at the dreams. He had been very young when the blizzards killed the cattle. But though he didn't remember the National Guard dropping hay bales from silver C-47s to cattle in twelve-foot-deep snow, he did recall, for years after, the nightmares of herds of nonplused animals futilely grazing barren ground before towering, slowly grinding bluffs of ice.

The night after the crop-duster terrified the sheep and seventeen had expired in paroxysms, Steve dreamed of brown men shrilling and shaking sticks and stampeding tusked, hairy monsters off a precipice and down hundreds of feet to a shallow stream.

Summer nights Steve woke sweating, having dreamed of reptiles slithering and warm waves beating on a ragged beach in the lower pasture. He sat straight, staring out the bedroom window, watching the giant ferns waver and solidify back into cottonwood and box elder.

The dreams came less frequently and vividly as he grew older. He willed that. They altered when the family moved into Fremont. After a while Steve still remembered he had had the dreams, but most of the details were forgotten.

At first the teachers in Fremont High School thought he was stupid. Steve was administered tests and thereafter was labeled an underachiever. He did what he had to do to get by. He barely qualified for the college-bound program, but then his normally easygoing father made threats. People asked him what he wanted to do, to be, and he answered honestly that he didn't know. Then he took a speech class. Drama fascinated him and he developed a passion for what theater the school offered. He played well in *Our Town* and *Arsenic and Old Lace* and *Harvey*. The drama coach looked at Steve's average height and average looks and average brown hair and eyes, and suggested at a hilarious cast party that he become either a character actor or an FBI agent.

By this time, the only dreams Steve remembered were sexual fantasies about girls he didn't dare ask on dates.

Ginger McClelland, seventeen. Who could blame her for feeling out of place? Having been born on the cusp of the school district's regulations, she was very nearly a year younger than her classmates. She was short. She thought of herself as a dwarf in a world of Snow Whites. It didn't help that her mother studiously offered words like "petite" and submitted that the most gorgeous clothes would fit a wearer under five feet two inches. Secretly she hoped that in one mysterious night she would bloom and grow great, long legs like Carroll Dale. That never happened.

Being an exile in an alien land didn't help either. Though Carroll had befriended her, she had listened to the president of the pep club, the queen of Job's Daughters, and half the girls in her math class refer to her as "the foreign-exchange student." Except that she would never be repatriated home; at least not until she graduated. Her parents had tired of living in Cupertino, California, and thought that running a coast-to-coast hardware franchise in Fremont would be an adventurous change of pace. They loved the open spaces, the mountains and free-flowing streams. Ginger wasn't so sure. Every day she felt she had stepped into a time machine. All the music on the radio was old. The movies that turned up at the town's one theater—forget it. The dancing at the hops was grotesque.

Ginger McClelland was the first person in Fremont—and perhaps in all of Wyoming—to use the adjective "bitchin'." It got her sent home from study hall and caused a bemused and confusing interview between her parents and the principal.

Ginger learned not to trust most of the boys who invited her out on dates. They all seemed to feel some sort of perverse mystique about California girls. But she did accept Steve Mavrakis's last-minute invitation to the prom. He seemed safe enough.

Because Carroll and Ginger were friends, the four of them ended up double-dating in Paul's father's old maroon DeSoto that was customarily used for hauling fence posts and wire out to the pastures. After the dance, when nearly everyone else was heading to one of the sanctioned after-prom parties, Steve affably obtained from an older intermediary an entire case of chilled Hamms. Ginger and Carroll had brought along jeans and Pendleton shirts in their overnight bags and changed in the restroom at the Chevron station. Paul and Steve took off their white jackets and donned windbreakers. Then they all drove up into the Wind River Range. After they ran out of road, they hiked. It was very late and very dark. But they found a high mountain place where they huddled and drank beer and talked and necked.

They heard the voice of the wind and nothing else beyond that.

They saw no lights of cars or outlying cabins. The isolation exhilarated them. They *knew* there was no one else for miles.

That was correct so far as it went.

Foam hissed and sprayed as Paul applied the church key to the cans. Above and below them, the wind broke like waves on the rocks.

"Mavrakis, you're going to the university, right?" said Paul.

Steve nodded in the dim moonlight, added, "I guess so."

"What're you going to take?" said Ginger, snuggling close and burping slightly on her beer.

"I don't know; engineering, I guess. If you're a guy and in the college-bound program, you end up taking engineering. So I figure that's it."

Paul said, "What kind?"

"Don't know. Maybe aerospace. I'll move to Seattle and make spaceships."

"That's neat," said Ginger. "Like in *The Outer Limits*. I wish we could get that here."

"You ought to be getting into hydraulic engineering," said Paul. "Water's going to be really big business not too long from now."

"I don't think I want to stick around Wyoming."

Carroll had been silently staring out over the valley. She turned back toward Steve and her eyes were pools of darkness. "You really going to leave?"

"Yeah."

"And never come back?"

"Why should I?" said Steve. "I've had all the fresh air and wide-open spaces I can use for a lifetime. You know something? I've never even seen the ocean." *And yet he had* felt *the ocean.* He blinked. "I'm getting out."

"Me too," said Ginger. "I'm going to stay with my aunt and

uncle in L.A. I think I can probably get into the University of Southern California journalism school."

"Got the money?" said Paul.

"I'll get a scholarship."

"Aren't you leaving?" Steve said to Carroll.

"Maybe," she said. "Sometimes I think so, and then I'm not so sure."

"You'll come back even if you do leave," said Paul. "All of you'll come back."

"Says who?" Steve and Ginger said it almost simultaneously.

"The land gets into you," said Carroll. "Paul's dad says so."

"That's what he says." They all heard anger in Paul's voice. He opened another round of cans. Ginger tossed her empty away and it clattered down the rocks, a noise jarringly out of place.

"Don't," said Carroll. "We'll take the empties down in the sack."

"What's wrong?" said Ginger. "I mean, I . . ." Her voice trailed off and everyone was silent for a minute, two minutes, three.

"What about you, Paul?" said Carroll. "Where do you want to go? What do you want to do?"

"We talked about—" His voice sounded suddenly tightly controlled. "Damn it, I don't know now. If I come back, it'll be with an atomic bomb—"

"What?" said Ginger.

Paul smiled. At least Steve could see white teeth gleaming in the night. "As for what I want to do—" He leaned forward and whispered in Carroll's ear.

She said, "Jesus, Paul! We've got witnesses."

"What?" Ginger said again.

"Don't even ask you don't want to know." She made it one continuous sentence. Her teeth also were visible in the near-darkness. "Try that and I've got a mind to goodnight you the hard way."

"What're you talking about?" said Ginger.

Paul laughed. "Her grandmother."

"Charlie Goodnight was a big rancher around the end of the

century," Carroll said. "He trailed a lot of cattle up from Texas. Trouble was, a lot of his expensive bulls weren't making out so well. Their testicles—"

"Balls," said Paul.

"—kept dragging on the ground," she continued. "The bulls got torn up and infected. So Charlie Goodnight started getting his bulls ready for the overland trip with some amateur surgery. He'd cut into the scrotum and shove the balls up into the bull. Then he'd stitch up the sack and there'd be no problem with high-centering. That's called goodnighting."

"See," said Paul. "There are ways to beat the land."

Carroll said, " 'You do what you've got to.' That's a quote from my father. Good pioneer stock."

"But not to me." Paul pulled her close and kissed her.

"Maybe we ought to explore the mountain a little," said Ginger to Steve. "You want to come with me?" She stared at Steve, who was gawking at the sky as the moonlight suddenly vanished like a light switching off.

"Oh, my God."

"What's wrong?" she said to the shrouded figure.

"I don't know—I mean, nothing, I guess." The moon appeared again. "Was that a cloud?"

"I don't see a cloud," said Paul, gesturing at the broad belt of stars. "The night's clear."

"Maybe you saw a UFO," said Carroll, her voice light.

"You okay?" Ginger touched his face. "Jesus, you're shivering." She held him tightly.

Steve's words were almost too low to hear. "It swam across the moon."

"What did?"

"I'm cold too," said Carroll. "Let's go back down." Nobody argued. Ginger remembered to put the metal cans into a paper sack and tied it to her belt with a hair ribbon. Steve didn't say anything more for a while, but the others all could hear his teeth chatter. When they were halfway down, the moon finally set beyond the valley rim. Farther on, Paul stepped on a loose patch of shale, slipped, cursed, began to slide beyond the lip of the sheer rock face. Carroll grabbed his arm and pulled him back.

"Thanks, Irene." His voice shook slightly, belying the tone of the words.

"Funny," she said.

"I don't get it," said Ginger.

Paul whistled a few bars of the song.

"Good night," said Carroll. "You do what you've got to."

"And I'm grateful for that." Paul took a deep breath. "Let's get down to the car."

When they were on the winding road and driving back toward Fremont, Ginger said, "What did you see up there, Steve?"

"Nothing. I guess I just remembered a dream."

"Some dream." She touched his shoulder. "You're still cold."

Carroll said, "So am I."

Paul took his right hand off the wheel to cover her hand. "We all are."

"I feel all right." Ginger sounded puzzled.

All the way into town, Steve felt he had drowned.

The Amble Inn in Thermopolis was built in the shadow of Round Top Mountain. On the slope above the inn, huge letters formed from whitewashed stones proclaimed: WORLD'S LARGEST MINERAL HOT SPRING. Whether at night or noon, the inscription invariably reminded Steve of the Hollywood Sign. Early in his return from California, he realized the futility of jumping off the second letter *O*. The stones were laid flush with the steep pitch of the ground. Would-be-suicides could only roll down the hill until they collided with the log side of the inn.

On Friday and Saturday nights, the parking lot of the Amble

Inn was filled almost exclusively with four-wheel-drive vehicles and conventional pickups. Most of them had black-enameled gun racks up in the rear window behind the seat. Steve's Chevy had a rack, but that was because he had bought the truck used. He had considered buying a toy rifle, one that shot caps or rubber darts, at a Penney's Christmas catalogue sale. But like so many other projects, he never seemed to get around to it.

Tonight was the first Saturday night in June and Steve had money in his pocket from the paycheck he had cashed at Safeway. He had no reason to celebrate; but then he had no reason not to celebrate. So a little after nine he went to the Amble Inn to drink tequila hookers and listen to the music.

The inn was uncharacteristically crowded for so early in the evening, but Steve secured a small table close to the dance floor when a guy threw up and his girl had to take him home. Dancing couples covered the floor though the headline act, Mountain Flyer, wouldn't be on until eleven. The warmup group was a Montana band called the Great Falls Dead. They had more enthusiasm than talent, but they had the crowd dancing.

Steve threw down the shots, sucked limes, licked the salt, intermittently tapped his hand on the table to the music, and felt vaguely melancholy. Smoke drifted around him, almost as thick as the special-effects fog in a bad horror movie. The inn's dance floor was in a dim, domed room lined with rough pine.

He suddenly stared, puzzled by a flash of near-recognition. He had been watching one dancer in particular, a tall woman with curly raven hair, who had danced with a succession of cowboys. When he looked at her face, he thought he saw someone familiar. When he looked at her body, he wondered whether she wore underwear beneath the wide-weave red knit dress.

The Great Falls Dead launched into "Good-hearted Woman" and the floor was instantly filled with dancers. Across the room, someone squealed, "Willieee!" This time the woman in red danced very close to Steve's table. Her high cheekbones looked hauntingly familiar. Her hair, he thought. If it were longer—She met his eyes and smiled at him.

The set ended, her partner drifted off toward the bar, but she remained standing beside his table. "Carroll?" he said. "*Carroll?*"

She stood there smiling, with right hand on hip. "I wondered when you'd figure it out."

Steve shoved his chair back and got up from the table. She moved very easily into his arms for a hug. "It's been a long time."

"It has."

"Fourteen years? Fifteen?"

"Something like that."

He asked her to sit at his table, and she did. She sipped a Campari-and-tonic as they talked. He switched to beer. The years unreeled. The Great Falls Dead pounded out a medley of country standards behind them.

". . . I never should have married, Steve. I was wrong for Paul. He was wrong for me."

". . . *thought* about getting married. I met a lot of women in Hollywood, but nothing ever seemed . . ."

". . . all the wrong reasons . . ."

". . . did end up in a few made-for-TV movies. Bad stuff. I was always cast as the assistant manager in a hold-up scene, or got killed by the werewolf right near the beginning. I think there's something like ninety percent of all actors who are unemployed at any given moment, so I said . . ."

"You really came back here? How long ago?"

". . . to hell with it . . ."

"How long ago?"

". . . and sort of slunk back to Wyoming. I don't know. Several years ago. How long were you married, anyway?"

". . . a year, more or less. What do you do here?"

". . . beer's getting warm. Think I'll get a pitcher . . ."

"What do you do here?"

"... better cold. Not much. I get along. You ..."

"... lived in Taos for a time. Then Santa Fe. Bummed around the Southwest a lot. A friend got me into photography. Then I was sick for a while and that's when I tried painting ..."

"... landscapes of the Tetons to sell to tourists?"

"Hardly. A lot of landscapes, but trailer camps and oil fields and perspective vistas of I–80 across the Red Desert ..."

"I tried taking pictures once ... kept forgetting to load the camera."

"... and then I ended up half-owner of a gallery called Good Stuff. My partner throws pots."

"... must be dangerous ..."

"... located on Main Street in Lander ..."

"... going through. Think maybe I've seen it ..."

"What do you do here?"

The comparative silence seemed to echo as the band ended its set. "Very little," said Steve. "I worked awhile as a hand on the Two Bar. Spent some time being a roughneck in the fields up around Buffalo. I've got a pickup—do some short-hauling for local businessmen who don't want to hire a trucker. I ran a little pot. Basically I do whatever I can find. You know."

Carroll said, "Yes, I do know." The silence lengthened between them. Finally she said, "Why did you come back here? Was it because—"

"—because I'd failed?" Steve said, answering her hesitation. He looked at her steadily. "I thought about that a long time. I decided that I could fail anywhere, so I came back here." He shrugged. "I love it. I love the space."

"A lot of us have come back," Carroll said. "Ginger and Paul are here."

Steve was startled. He looked at the tables around them.

"Not tonight," said Carroll. "We'll see them tomorrow. They want to see you."

"Are you and Paul back—" he started to say.

She held up her palm. "Hardly. We're not exactly on the same wavelength. That's one thing that hasn't changed. He ended up being the sort of thing you thought you'd become."

Steve didn't remember what that was.

"Paul went to the School of Mines in Colorado. Now he's the chief exploratory geologist for Enerco."

"Not bad," said Steve.

"Not good," said Carroll. "He spent a decade in South America and the Middle East. Now he's come back home. He wants to gut the state like a fish."

"Coal?"

"And oil. And uranium. And gas. Enerco's got its thumb in a lot of holes." Her voice had lowered, sounded angry. "Anyway, we *are* having a reunion tomorrow, of sorts. And Ginger will be there."

Steve poured out the last of the beer. "I thought for sure she'd be in California."

"Never made it," said Carroll. "Scholarships fell through. Parents said they wouldn't support her if she went back to the West Coast—you know how one hundred and five percent converted immigrants are. So Ginger went to school in Laramie and ended up with a degree in elementary education. She did marry a grad student in journalism. After the divorce five or six years later, she let him keep the kid."

Steve said, "So Ginger never got to be an ace reporter."

"Oh, she did. Now she's the best writer the *Salt Creek Gazette*'s got. Ginger's the darling of the environmental groups and the bane of the energy corporations."

"I'll be damned," he said. He accidentally knocked his glass off the table with his forearm. Reaching to retrieve the glass, he knocked over the empty pitcher.

"I think you're tired," Carroll said.

"I think you're right."

"You ought to go home and sack out." He nodded. "I don't

want to drive all the way back to Lander tonight," Carroll said. "Have you got room for me?"

When they reached the small house Steve rented off Highway 170, Carroll grimaced at the heaps of dirty clothes making soft moraines in the living room. "I'll clear off the couch," she said. "I've got a sleeping bag in my car."

Steve hesitated a long several seconds and lightly touched her shoulders. "You don't have to sleep on the couch unless you want to. All those years ago . . . You know, all through high school I had a crush on you? I was too shy to say anything."

She smiled and allowed his hands to remain. "I thought you were pretty nice too. A little shy, but cute. Definitely an under-achiever."

They remained standing, faces a few inches apart, for a while longer. "Well?" he said.

"It's been a lot of years," Carroll said. "I'll sleep on the couch."

Steve said disappointedly, "Not even out of charity?"

"Especially not for charity." She smiled. "But don't discount the future." She kissed him gently on the lips.

Steve slept soundly that night. He dreamed of sliding endlessly through a warm, fluid current. It was not a nightmare. Not even when he realized he had fins rather than hands and feet.

Morning brought rain.

When he awoke, the first thing Steve heard was the drumming of steady drizzle on the roof. The daylight outside the window was filtered gray by the sheets of water running down the pane. Steve leaned off the bed, picked up his watch from the floor, but it had stopped. He heard the sounds of someone moving in the living room and called, "Carroll? You up?"

Her voice was a soft contralto. "I am."

"What time is it?"

"Just after eight."

Steve started to get out of bed, but groaned and clasped the crown of his head with both hands. Carroll stood framed in the doorway and looked sympathetic. "What time's the reunion?" he said.

"When we get there. I called Paul a little earlier. He's tied up with some sort of meeting in Casper until late afternoon. He wants us to meet him in Shoshoni."

"What about Ginger?"

They both heard the knock on the front door. Carroll turned her head away from the bedroom, then looked back at Steve. "Right on cue," she said. "Ginger didn't want to wait until tonight." She started for the door, said back over her shoulder, "You might want to put on some clothes."

Steve pulled on his least filthy jeans and a sweatshirt labeled AMAX TOWN-LEAGUE VOLLEYBALL across the chest. He heard the front door open and close, and words murmured in his living room. When he exited the bedroom he found Carroll talking on the couch with a short blonde stranger who only slightly resembled the long-ago image he'd packed in his mind. Her hair was long and tied in a braid. Her gaze was direct and more inquisitive than he remembered.

She looked up at him and said, "I like the mustache. You look a hell of a lot better now than you ever did then."

"Except for the mustache," Steve said, "I could say the same."

The two women seemed amazed when Steve negotiated the disaster area that was the kitchen and extracted eggs and Chinese vegetables from the refrigerator. He served the huge omelet with toast and freshly brewed coffee in the living room. They all balanced plates on laps.

"Do you ever read the *Gazoo?*" said Ginger.

"*Gazoo?*"

"The *Salt Creek Gazette*," said Carroll.

Steve said, "I don't read any papers."

"I just finished a piece on Paul's company," said Ginger.

"Enerco?" Steve refilled all their cups.

Ginger shook her head. "A wholly owned subsidiary called Native American Resources. Pretty clever, huh?" Steve looked blank. "Not a poor damned Indian in the whole operation. The name's strictly sham while the company's been picking up an incredible number of mineral leases on the reservation. Paul's been concentrating on an enormous new coal field his teams have mapped out. It makes up a substantial proportion of the reservation's best lands."

"Including some sacred sites," said Carroll.

"Nearly a million acres," said Ginger. "That's more than a thousand square miles."

"The land's never the same," said Carroll, "no matter how much goes into reclamation, no matter how tight the EPA says they are."

Steve looked from one to the other. "I may not read the papers," he said, "but no one's holding a gun to anyone else's head."

"Might as well be," said Ginger. "If the Native American Resources deal goes through, the mineral royalty payments to the tribes'll go up precipitously."

Steve spread his palms. "Isn't that good?"

Ginger shook her head vehemently. "It's economic blackmail to keep the tribes from developing their own resources at their own pace."

"Slogans," said Steve. "The country needs the energy. If the tribes don't have the investment capital—"

"They *would* if they weren't bought off with individual royalty payments."

"The tribes have a choice—"

"—with the prospect of immediate gain dangled in front of them by NAR."

"I can tell it's Sunday," said Steve, "even if I haven't been inside a church door in fifteen years. I'm being preached at."

"If you'd get off your ass and think," said Ginger, "nobody'd have to lecture you."

Steve grinned. "I don't think with my ass."

"Look," said Carroll. "It's stopped raining."

Ginger glared at Steve. He took advantage of Carroll's diversion and said, "Anyone for a walk?"

The air outside was cool and rain-washed. It soothed tempers. The trio walked through the fresh morning along the cottonwood-lined creek. Meadowlarks sang. The rain front had moved far to the east; the rest of the sky was bright blue.

"Hell of a country, isn't it?" said Steve.

"Not for much longer if—" Ginger began.

"Gin," Carroll said warningly.

They strolled for another hour, angling south where they could see the hills as soft as blanket folds. The tree-lined draws snaked like green veins down the hillsides. The earth, Steve thought, seemed gathered, somehow expectant.

"How's Danny?" Carroll said to Ginger.

"He's terrific. Kid wants to become an astronaut." A grin split her face. "Bob's letting me have him for August."

"Look at that," said Steve, pointing.

The women looked. "I don't see anything," said Ginger.

"Southeast," Steve said. "Right above the head of the canyon."

"There—I'm not sure." Carroll shaded her eyes. "I thought I saw something, but it was just a shadow."

"Nothing there," said Ginger.

"Are you both blind?" said Steve, astonished. "There was something in the air. It was dark and cigar-shaped. It was there when I pointed."

"Sorry," said Ginger, "didn't see a thing."

"Well, it *was* there," Steve said, disgruntled.

Carroll continued to stare off toward the pass. "I saw it too, but just for a second. I didn't see where it went."

"Damnedest thing. I don't think it was a plane. It just sort of cruised along, and then it was gone."

"All I saw was something blurry," Carroll said. "Maybe it was a UFO."

"Oh, you guys," Ginger said with an air of dawning comprehension. "Just like prom night, right? Just a joke."

Steve slowly shook his head. "I really saw something then, and I saw this now. This time Carroll saw it too." She nodded in agreement. He tasted salt.

The wind started to rise from the north, kicking up early spring weeds that had already died and begun to dry.

"I'm getting cold," said Ginger. "Let's go back to the house."

"Steve," said Carroll, "you're shaking."

They hurried him back across the land.

PHOSPHORIC FORMATION
PERMIAN
225–270 MILLION YEARS

They rested for a while at the house; drank coffee and talked of the past, of what had happened and what had not. Then Carroll suggested they leave for the reunion. After a small confusion, Ginger rolled up the windows and locked her Saab and Carroll locked her Pinto.

"I hate having to do this," said Carroll.

"There's no choice anymore," Steve said. "Too many people around now who don't know the rules."

The three of them got into Steve's pickup. In fifteen minutes they had traversed the doglegs of U.S. 20 through Thermopolis and crossed the Big Horn River. They passed the massive mobile-home park with its trailers and RVs sprawling in carapaced glitter.

The flood of hot June sunshine washed over them as they passed between the twin bluffs, red with iron, and descended into the miles and years of canyon.

TENSLEEP FORMATION
PENNSYLVANIAN
270–310 MILLION YEARS

On both sides of the canyon, the rock layers lay stacked like sections from a giant meat slicer. In the pickup cab, the passengers had been listening to the news on KTWO. As the canyon deepened, the reception faded until only a trickle of static came from the speaker. Carroll clicked the radio off.

"They're screwed," said Ginger.

"Not necessarily." Carroll, riding shotgun, stared out the window at the slopes of flowers the same color as the bluffs. "The BIA's still got hearings. There'll be another tribal vote."

Ginger said again, "They're screwed. Money doesn't just talk— it makes obscene phone calls, you know? Paul's got this one bagged. You know Paul—I know him just about as well. Son of a bitch."

"Sorry there's no music," said Steve. "Tape player busted a while back and I've never fixed it."

They ignored him. "Damn it," said Ginger. "It took almost fifteen years, but I've learned to love this country."

"I know that," said Carroll.

No one said anything for a while. Steve glanced to his right and saw tears running down Ginger's cheeks. She glared back at him defiantly. "There's Kleenexes in the glove box," he said.

MADISON FORMATION
MISSISSIPPIAN
310–350 MILLION YEARS

The slopes of the canyon became more heavily forested. The walls were all shades of green, deeper green where the runoff had found channels. Steve felt time collect in the great gash in the earth, press inward.

"I don't feel so hot," said Ginger.

"Want to stop for a minute?"

She nodded and put her hand over her mouth.

Steve pulled the pickup over across both lanes. The Chevy skidded slightly as it stopped on the graveled turnout. Steve turned off the key and in the sudden silence they heard only the light wind and the tickings as the Chevy's engine cooled.

"Excuse me," said Ginger. They all got out of the cab. Ginger quickly moved through the Canadian thistle and the currant bushes and into the trees beyond. Steve and Carroll heard her throwing up.

"She had an affair with Paul," Carroll said casually. "Not too long ago. He's an extremely attractive man." Steve said nothing. "Ginger ended it. She still feels the tension." Carroll strolled over to the side of the thistle patch and hunkered down. "Look at this."

Steve realized how complex the ground cover was. Like the rock cliffs, it was layered. At first he saw among the sunflowers and dead dandelions only the wild sweet peas with their blue blossoms like spades with the edges curled inward.

"Look closer," said Carroll.

Steve saw the hundreds of tiny purple moths swooping and swarming only inches from the earth. The creatures were the same color as the low purple blooms he couldn't identify. Intermixed were white, bell-shaped blossoms with leaves that looked like primeval ferns.

"It's like going back in time," said Carroll. "It's a whole nearly invisible world we never see."

The shadow crossed them with an almost subliminal flash, but they both looked up. Between them and the sun had been the wings of a large bird. It circled in a tight orbit, banking steeply when it approached the canyon wall. The creature's belly was dirty white, muting to an almost-black on its back. It seemed to Steve that the bird's eye was fixed on them. The eye was a dull black, like unpolished obsidian.

"That's one I've never seen," said Carroll. "What is it?"

"I don't know. The wingspread's got to be close to ten feet. The markings are strange. Maybe it's a hawk? An eagle?"

The bird's beak was heavy and blunt, curved slightly. As it circled, wings barely flexing to ride the thermals, the bird was eerily silent, pelagic, fishlike.

"What's it doing?" said Carroll.

"Watching us?" said Steve. He jumped as a hand touched his shoulder.

"Sorry," said Ginger. "I feel better now." She tilted her head back at the great circling bird. "I have a feeling our friend wants us to leave."

They left. The highway wound around a massive curtain of stone in which red splashed down through the strata like dinosaur blood. Around the curve, Steve swerved to miss a deer dead on the pavement—half a deer, rather. The animal's body had been truncated cleanly just in front of its haunches.

"Jesus," said Ginger. "What did that?"

"Must have been a truck," said Steve. "An eighteen-wheeler can really tear things up when it's barreling."

Carroll looked back toward the carcass and the sky beyond. "Maybe that's what our friend was protecting."

GROS VENTRE FORMATION
CAMBRIAN
500–600 MILLION YEARS

"You know, this was all under water once," said Steve. He was answered only with silence. "Just about all of Wyoming was covered with an ancient sea. That accounts for a lot of the coal." No one said anything. "I think it was called the Sundance Sea. You know, like in the Sundance Kid. Some Exxon geologist told me that in a bar."

He turned and looked at the two women. And stared. And turned back to the road blindly. And then stared at them again. It seemed to Steve that he was looking at a double exposure, or a triple exposure, or—he couldn't count all the overlays. He started to say something, but could not. He existed in a silence that was also stasis, the death of all motion. He could only see.

Carroll and Ginger faced straight ahead. They looked as they had earlier in the afternoon. They also looked as they had fifteen years before. Steve saw them *in process*, lines blurred. And Steve saw skin merge with feathers, and then scales. He saw gill openings appear, vanish, reappear on textured necks.

And then both of them turned to look at him. Their heads swiveled slowly, smoothly. Four reptilian eyes watched him, unblinking and incurious.

Steve wanted to look away.

The Chevy's tires whined on the level blacktop. The sign read:

SPEED ZONE AHEAD
35 MPH

"Are you awake?" said Ginger.

Steve shook his head to clear it. "Sure," he said. "You know that reverie you sometimes get into when you're driving? When you can drive miles without consciously thinking about it, and then suddenly you realize what's happened?"

Ginger nodded.

"That's what happened."

The highway passed between modest frame houses, gas stations, motels. They entered Shoshoni.

There was a brand-new WELCOME TO SHOSHONI sign, as yet without bullet holes. The population figure had again been revised upward. "Want to bet on when they break another thousand?" said Carroll.

Ginger shook her head silently.

Steve pulled up to the stop sign. "Which way?"

Carroll said, "Go left."

"I think I've got it." Steve saw the half-ton truck with the Enerco decal and NATIVE AMERICAN RESOURCES DIVISION labeled below that on the door. It was parked in front of the Yellowstone Drugstore. "Home of the world's greatest shakes and malts," said Steve. "Let's go."

The interior of the Yellowstone had always reminded him of nothing so much as an old-fashioned pharmacy blended with the interior of the cafe in *Bad Day at Black Rock*. They found Paul at a table near the fountain counter in the back. He was nursing a chocolate malted.

He looked up, smiled, said, "I've gained four pounds this afternoon. If you'd been any later, I'd probably have become diabetic."

Paul looked far older than Steve had expected. Ginger and Carroll both appeared older than they had been a decade and a half before, but Paul seemed to have aged thirty years in fifteen. The star quarterback's physique had gone a bit to pot. His face was creased with lines emphasized by the leathery curing of skin that has been exposed years to wind and hot sun. Paul's hair, black as coal, was streaked with firn lines of glacial white. His eyes, Steve thought, looked tremendously old.

He greeted Steve with a warm handclasp. Carroll received a gentle hug and a kiss on the cheek. Ginger got a warm smile and a hello. The four of them sat down and the fountain man came over. "Chocolate all around?" Paul said.

"Vanilla shake," said Ginger.

Steve sensed a tension at the table that seemed to go beyond dissolved marriages and terminated affairs. He wasn't sure what to say after all the years, but Paul saved him the trouble. Smiling and soft-spoken, Paul gently interrogated him.

So what have you been doing with yourself?

Really?

How did that work out?

That's too bad; then what?

What about afterward?

And you came back?

How about since?

What do you do now?

Paul sat back in the scrolled-wire ice-cream parlor chair, still smiling, playing with the plastic straw. He tied knots in the straw and then untied them.

"Do you know," said Paul, "that this whole complicated reunion of the four of us is not a matter of chance?"

Steve studied the other man. Paul's smile faded to impassivity. "I'm not that paranoid," Steve said. "It didn't occur to me."

"It's a setup."

Steve considered that silently.

"It didn't take place until after I had tossed the yarrow stalks a considerable number of times," said Paul. His voice was wry. "I don't know what the official company policy on such irrational behavior is, but it all seemed right under extraordinary circumstances. I told Carroll where she could likely find you and left the means of contact up to her."

The two women waited and watched silently. Carroll's expression was, Steve thought, one of concern. Ginger looked apprehensive. "So what is it?" he said. "What kind of game am I in?"

"It's no game," said Carroll quickly. "We need you."

"You know what I thought ever since I met you in Miss Gorman's class?" said Paul. "You're not a loser. You've just needed some—direction."

Steve said impatiently, "Come on."

"It's true." Paul set down the straw. "Why we need you is because you seem to see things most others can't see."

Time's predator hunts.

Years scatter before her like a school of minnows surprised. The rush of her passage causes eons to eddy. Wind sweeps down the canyon with the roar of combers breaking on the sand. The moon, full and newly risen, exerts its tidal force.

Moonlight flashes on the slash of teeth.

She drives for the surface not out of rational decision. All blunt power embodied in smooth motion, she simply is what she is.

Steve sat without speaking. Finally he said vaguely, "Things."

"That's right. You see things. It's an ability."

"I don't know . . ."

"We think *we* do. We all remember that night after prom. And there were other times, back in school. None of us has seen you since we all played scatter-geese, but I've had the resources, through the corporation, to do some checking. The issue didn't come up until recently. In the last month, I've read your school records, Steve. I've read your psychiatric history."

"That must have taken some trouble," said Steve. "Should I feel flattered?"

"Tell him," said Ginger. "Tell him what this is all about."

"Yeah," said Steve. "Tell me."

For the first time in the conversation, Paul hesitated. "Okay," he finally said. "We're hunting a ghost in the Wind River Canyon."

"Say again?"

"That's perhaps poor terminology." Paul looked uncomfortable. "But what we're looking for is a presence, some sort of extranatural phenomenon."

" 'Ghost' is a perfectly good word," said Carroll.

"Better start from the beginning," said Steve.

When Paul didn't answer immediately, Carroll said, "I know you don't read the papers. Ever listen to the radio?"

Steve shook his head. "Not much."

"About a month ago, an Enerco mineral survey party on the Wind River got the living daylights scared out of them."

"Leave out what they saw," said Paul. "I'd like to include a control factor."

"It wasn't just the Enerco people. Others have seen it, both Indians and Anglos. The consistency of the witnesses has been remarkable. If you haven't heard about this at the bars, Steve, you must have been asleep."

"I haven't been all that social for a while," said Steve. "I did hear that someone's trying to scare the oil and coal people off the reservation."

"Not someone," said Paul. "Some *thing.* I'm convinced of that now."

"A ghost," said Steve.

"A presence."

"There're rumors," said Carroll, "that the tribes have revived the Ghost Dance—"

"Just a few extremists," said Paul.

"—to conjure back an avenger from the past who will drive every white out of the county."

Steve knew of the Ghost Dance, had read of the Paiute mystic Wovoka who, in 1888, had claimed that in a vision the spirits had promised the return of the buffalo and the restoration to the Indians of their ancestral lands. The Plains tribes had danced the Ghost Dance assiduously to insure this. Then in 1890 the U.S. government suppressed the final Sioux uprising and, except for a few scattered incidents, that was that. Discredited, Wovoka survived to die in the midst of the Great Depression.

"I have it on good authority," said Paul, "that the Ghost Dance was revived *after* the presence terrified the survey crew."

"That really doesn't matter," Carroll said. "Remember prom night? I've checked the newspaper morgues in Fremont and Lander and Riverton. There've been strange sightings for more than a century."

"That was then," said Paul. "The problem now is that the tribes are infinitely more restive, and my people are actually getting frightened to go out into the field." His voice took on a bemused tone. "Arab terrorists couldn't do it, civil wars didn't bother them, but a damned ghost is scaring the wits out of them—literally."

"Too bad," said Ginger. She did not sound regretful.

Steve looked at the three gathered around the table. He knew he did not understand all the details and nuances of the love and hate and trust and broken affections. "I can understand Paul's concern," he said. "But why the rest of you?"

The women exchanged glances. "One way or another," said Carroll, "we're all tied together. I think it includes you, Steve."

"Maybe," said Ginger soberly. "Maybe not. She's an artist. I'm a journalist. We've all got our reasons for wanting to know more about what's up there."

"In the past few years," said Carroll, "I've caught a tremendous amount of Wyoming in my paintings. Now I want to capture this too."

Conversation languished. The soda-fountain man looked as though he were unsure whether to solicit a new round of malteds.

"What now?" Steve said.

"If you'll agree," said Paul, "we're going to go back up into the Wind River Canyon to search."

"So what am I? Some sort of damned occult Geiger counter?"

Ginger said, "It's a nicer phrase than calling yourself bait."

"Jesus," Steve said. "That doesn't reassure me much." He looked from one to the next. "Control factor or not, give me some clue to what we're going to look for."

Everyone looked at Paul. Eventually he shrugged and said, "You know the Highway Department signs in the canyon? The geological time chart you travel when you're driving U.S. 20?"

Steve nodded.

"We're looking for a relic of the ancient, inland sea."

After the sun sank in blood in the west, they drove north and watched dusk unfold into the splendor of the night sky.

"I'll always marvel at that," said Paul. "Do you know, you can see three times as many stars in the sky here as you can from any city?"

"It scares the tourists sometimes," said Carroll.

Ginger said, "It won't after a few more of those coal-fired generating plants are built."

Paul chuckled humorlessly. "I thought they were preferable to your nemesis, the nukes."

Ginger was sitting with Steve in the back seat of the Enerco truck. Her words were controlled and even. "There are alternatives to both those."

"Try supplying power to the rest of the country with them before the next century," Paul said. He braked suddenly as a jackrabbit darted into the bright cones of light. The rabbit made it across the road.

"Nobody actually *needs* air conditioners," said Ginger.

"I won't argue that point," Paul said. "You'll just have to argue with the reality of all the people who think they do."

Ginger lapsed into silence. Carroll said, "I suppose you should be congratulated for the tribal council vote today. We heard about it on the news."

"It's not binding," said Paul. "When it finally goes through, we hope it will whittle the fifty percent jobless rate on the reservation."

"It sure as hell won't!" Ginger burst out. "Higher mineral royalties mean more incentive not to have a career."

Paul laughed. "Are you blaming me for being the chicken, or the egg?"

No one answered him.

"I'm not a monster," he said.

"I don't think you are," said Steve.

"I know it puts me in a logical trap, but I think I'm doing the right thing."

"All right," said Ginger. "I won't take any easy shots. At least, I'll try."

From the back seat, Steve looked around his uneasy allies and hoped to hell that someone had brought aspirin. Carroll had aspirin in her handbag and Steve washed it down with beer from Paul's cooler.

GRANITE
PRECAMBRIAN
600+ MILLION YEARS

The moon had risen by now, a full, icy disc. The highway curved around a formation that looked like a vast, layered birthday cake. Cedar provided spectral candles.

"I've never believed in ghosts," said Steve. He caught the flicker of Paul's eyes in the rearview mirror and knew the geologist was looking at him.

"There are ghosts," said Paul, "and there are ghosts. In spectroscopy, ghosts are false readings. In television, ghost images—"

"What about the kind that haunt houses?"

"In television," Paul continued, "a ghost is a reflected electronic image arriving at the antenna some interval after the desired wave."

"And are they into groans and chains?"

"Some people are better antennas than others, Steve."

Steve fell silent.

"There is a theory," said Paul, "that molecular structures, no matter how altered by process, still retain some sort of 'memory' of their original form."

"Ghosts."

"If you like." He stared ahead at the highway and said, as if musing, "When an ancient organism becomes fossilized, even the DNA patterns that determine its structure are preserved in the stone."

GALLATIN FORMATION
CAMBRIAN
500–600 MILLION YEARS

Paul shifted into a lower gear as the half-ton began to climb one of the long, gradual grades. Streaming black smoke and bellowing like a great saurian lumbering into extinction, an eighteen-wheel semi with oil-field gear on its back passed them, forcing Paul part of the way onto the right shoulder. Trailing a dopplered call from its airhorn, the rig disappeared into the first of three short highway tunnels quarried out of the rock.

"One of yours?" said Ginger.

"Nope."

"Maybe he'll crash and burn."

"I'm sure he's just trying to make a living," said Paul mildly.

"Raping the land's a living?" said Ginger. "Cannibalizing the past is a living?"

"Shut up, Gin." Quietly, Carroll said, "Wyoming didn't do anything to your family, Paul. Whatever was done, people did it."

"The land gets into the people," said Paul.

"That isn't the only thing that defines them."

"This always has been a fruitless argument," said Paul. "It's a dead past.

"If the past is dead," Steve said, "then why are we driving up this cockamamie canyon?"

AMSDEN FORMATION
PENNSYLVANIAN
270–310 MILLION YEARS

Boysen Reservoir spread to their left, rippled surface glittering in the moonlight. The road hugged the eastern edge. Once the crimson taillights of the oil-field truck had disappeared in the distance, they encountered no other vehicle.

"Are we just going to drive up and down Twenty all night?" said Steve. "Who brought the plan?" He did not feel flippant, but he had to say something. He felt the burden of time.

"We'll go where the survey crew saw the presence," Paul said. "It's just a few more miles."

"And then?"

"Then we walk. It should be at least as interesting as our hike prom night."

Steve sensed that a lot of things were almost said by each of them at that point.

I didn't know then . . .

Nor do I know for sure yet.

I'm seeking . . .

What?

Time's flowed. I want to know where now, finally, to direct it.

"Who would have thought . . ." said Ginger.

Whatever was thought, nothing more was said.

The headlights picked out the reflective green-and-white Highway Department sign. "We're there," said Paul. "Somewhere on the right there ought to be a dirt access road."

SHARKTOOTH FORMATION
CRETACEOUS
100 MILLION YEARS

"Are we going to use a net?" said Steve. "Tranquilizer darts? What?"

"I don't think we can catch a ghost in a net," said Carroll. "You catch a ghost in your soul."

A small smile curved Paul's lips. "Think of this as the Old West. We're only a scouting party. Once we observe whatever's up here, we'll figure out how to get rid of it."

"That won't be possible," said Carroll.

"Why do you say that?"

"I don't know," she said. "I just feel it."

"Women's intuition?" He said it lightly.

"*My* intuition."

"Anything's possible," said Paul.

"If we really thought you could destroy it," said Ginger, "I doubt either of us would be up here with you."

Paul had stopped the truck to lock the front hubs into four-wheel drive. Now the vehicle clanked and lurched over rocks and across potholes eroded by the spring rain. The road twisted tortuously around series of barely graded switchbacks. Already they had climbed hundreds of feet above the canyon floor. They could see no lights anywhere below.

"Very scenic," said Steve. If he had wanted to, he could have reached out the right passenger's side window and touched the porous rock. Pine branches whispered along the paint on the left side.

"Thanks to Native American Resources," said Ginger, "this is the sort of country that'll go."

"For Christ's sake," said Paul, finally sounding angry. "I'm *not* the Antichrist."

"I know that." Ginger's voice softened. "I've loved you, remember? Probably I still do. Is there no way?"

The geologist didn't answer.

"Paul?"

"We're just about there," he said. The grade moderated and he shifted to a higher gear.

"Paul—" Steve wasn't sure whether he actually said the word or not. He closed his eyes and saw glowing fires, opened them again and wasn't sure what he saw. He felt the past, vast and primeval, rush over him like a tide. It filled his nose and mouth, his lungs, his brain. It—

"Oh, my God!"

Someone screamed.

"Let go!"

The headlight beams twitched crazily as the truck skidded toward the edge of a sheer dark drop. Both Paul and Carroll wrestled for the wheel. For an instant, Steve wondered whether both of them or, indeed, either of them was trying to turn the truck back from the dark.

Then he saw the great, bulky, streamlined form coasting over the slope toward them. He had the impression of smooth power, immense and inexorable. The dead stare from flat black eyes, each one inches across, fixed them like insects in amber.

"Paul!" Steve heard his own voice. He heard the word echo and then it was swallowed up by the crashing waves. He felt unreasoning terror, but more than that, he felt—awe. What he beheld was juxtaposed on this western canyon, but yet it was not out of place. *Genius loci*, guardian, the words hissed like the surf.

It swam toward them, impossibly gliding on powerful gray-black fins.

Brakes screamed. A tire blew out like a gunshot.

Steve watched its jaws open in front of the windshield; the snout pulling up and back, the lower jaw thrusting forward. The maw could have taken in a heifer. The teeth glared white in reflected light, white with serrated razor edges. Its teeth were as large as shovel blades.

"Paul!"

The Enerco truck fishtailed a final time, then toppled sideways into the dark. It fell, caromed off something massive and unseen, and began to roll.

Steve had time for one thought. *Is it going to hurt?*

When the truck came to rest, it was upright. Steve groped toward the window and felt rough bark rather than glass. They were wedged against a pine.

The silence astonished him. That there was no fire astonished him. That he was alive—"Carroll?" he said. "Ginger? Paul?" For a moment, no one spoke.

"I'm here," said Carroll, muffled, from the front of the truck. "Paul's on top of me. Or somebody is. I can't tell."

"Oh, God, I hurt," said Ginger from beside Steve. "My shoulder hurts."

"Can you move your arm?" said Steve.

"A little, but it hurts."

"Okay." Steve leaned forward across the front seat. He didn't feel anything like grating, broken bone ends in himself. His fingers touched flesh. Some of it was sticky with fluid. Gently he pulled someone he assumed was Paul away from Carroll. She moaned and struggled upright.

"There should be a flashlight in the glove box," he said.

The darkness was almost complete. Steve could see only vague shapes inside the truck. When Carroll switched on the flashlight, they realized the truck was buried in thick, resilient brush. Carroll and Ginger stared back at him. Ginger looked as if she might be in shock. Paul slumped on the front seat. The angle of his neck was all wrong.

His eyes opened and he tried to focus. Then he said something. They couldn't understand him. Paul tried again. They made out "Good night, Irene." Then he said, "Do what you have . . ." His eyes remained open, but all the life went out of them.

Steve and the women stared at one another as though they were accomplices. The moment crystallized and shattered. He braced himself as best he could and kicked with both feet at the rear door. The brush allowed the door to swing open one foot, then another. Carroll had her door open at almost the same time. It took another few minutes to get Ginger out. They left Paul in the truck.

They huddled on a naturally terraced ledge about halfway between the summit and the canyon floor. There was a roar and bright lights for a few minutes when a Burlington Northern freight came down the tracks on the other side of the river. It would have done no good to shout and wave their arms, so they didn't.

No one seemed to have broken any bones. Ginger's shoulder

was apparently separated. Carroll had a nosebleed. Steve's head felt as though he'd been walloped with a two-by-four.

"It's not cold," he said. "If we have to, we can stay in the truck. No way we're going to get down at night. In the morning we can signal people on the road."

Ginger started to cry and they both held her. "I saw something," she said. "I couldn't tell—what was it?"

Steve hesitated. He had a hard time separating his dreams from Paul's theories. The two did not now seem mutually exclusive. He still heard the echoing thunder of ancient gulfs. "I'm guessing it's something that lived here a hundred million years ago," he finally said. "It lived in the inland sea and died here. The sea left, but it never did."

"A native . . ." Ginger said and trailed off. Steve touched her forehead; it felt feverish. "I finally saw," she said. "Now I'm a part of it." In a smaller voice, "Paul." Starting awake like a child from a nightmare, "Paul?"

"He's—all right now," said Carroll, her even tone plainly forced.

"No, he's not," said Ginger. "He's not." She was silent for a time. "He's dead." Tears streamed down her face. "It won't really stop the coal leases, will it?"

"Probably not."

"Politics," Ginger said wanly. "Politics and death. What the hell difference does any of it make now?"

No one answered her.

Steve turned toward the truck in the brush. He suddenly remembered from his childhood how he had hoped everyone he knew, everyone he loved, would live forever. He hadn't wanted change. He hadn't wanted to recognize time. He remembered the split-second image of Paul and Carroll struggling to control the wheel. "The land," he said, feeling the sorrow. "It doesn't forgive."

"That's not true." Carroll slowly shook her head. "The land just *is*. The land doesn't care."

"I care," said Steve.

Amazingly, Ginger started to go to sleep. They laid her down gently on the precipice, covered her with Steve's jacket, and cradled her head, stroking her hair. "Look," Carroll said. "Look." As the moon illuminated the glowing sea.

Far below them, a fin broke the dark surface of the forest.

GREEN BROTHER

HOWARD WALDROP

I am talking now about the time Red Cloud was fighting the Yellowlegs about the dirt road they put through our lands.

That started the last winter the Yellowlegs were beating the Grey White Men far to the east. We did not understand why they wanted to kill each other, but we did not mind so long as they left us alone.

I am Seldom Blanket. In those days I was a big medicine chief of my people. I would not have been down there in all the fighting with the soldiers if it had not been that my two sons-in-law wanted to go with the others. I don't give much of a damn for most of the rest of my people, but I did like my two daughters and the men who married them.

So early that spring we moved our lodges up to the places where the rest of the Lakota were camped, and we did the medicine dances and the younger men went off to fight the soldiers in their fort on the great dirt road.

I was in camp most of the time, though I would occasionally go up and watch the shooting and killing. Sometimes the war parties brought back one of our men, and we sang the death songs and wept. Sometimes we heard they caught a few of the soldiers and

117

had fun with them and then killed them. It wasn't really a war at that time. We were just showing them how annoyed we were.

They had had a big meeting some years before, with representatives of the Great White Father, and we had all touched the pen, and got nice gifts and had a big supper. Then they brought us a lot of blankets and hardtack and beads. Then they built a road through our best hunting lands.

The road had filled up with wagons and the people who came through let us know they did not like us. They were afraid, too, so soon the soldiers came out while we were in the winter hunting grounds to the south and built a big wooden fort. It was there when our first scouts came back north. Also the soldiers were shooting the buffalo for their livers.

Red Cloud, the big talker for our people, went to the big fort and asked the main soldier there if they were going to move before it got cold again. The man said no.

They sent a man from the East who told Red Cloud that he had agreed to the building of the fort and the road.

Red Cloud said he didn't remember the subject ever coming up.

So they sent more white people to see Red Cloud.

"We ate real good for a week," he said to the Council, "but I don't think any one of them ever spoke from his heart the whole time." He said the white men complained that they were fighting with each other now over the Black White Men and needed the big dirt road.

Red Cloud told them the big wooden building was an eyesore in the Great Mystery's vision, and the dirt road was making the buffalo skittish and could they please move them both.

They said no, and waved the piece of paper around.

So Red Cloud and a few hundred warriors went out one night and burned the fort down.

*   *   *

Then the white men rebuilt it two winters ago. Now everybody was in on the fight. My sons-in-law were gone most of the time, except when they brought food back, and I was much in the company of older men, and women and children. It is pleasant occasionally to do this. It gives a man perspective.

The favorite of my grandchildren was then called Fall Colt, but that would change soon, as he was nearing his thirteenth birthday. He was a fast learner and picked up on the wisdom that I gave him very quickly. I could tell he wanted to be out there with the men fighting around the fort, but he was as yet too young.

I was smoking outside my lodge one day when he came to see me. I puffed on my pipe after offering some smoke to the winds. Then I sat facing the open end of the circled teepees. The sun had been up a few hours.

"Grandfather!" he said, all out of breath. He was thin and his hair was as black as night. He wore deerskin leggings even in the summer. It was all the fashion among young boys that year, as I remember.

"Yes? Something excites you?"

"Onion Boy is no longer Onion Boy. He went off three days ago and came back, and now he is Falcon Foot."

"Ah, that is good. I shall try to remember his new name. Is he changed much?"

"No, except that he now has a medicine bundle with a falcon foot in it. He said the hawk must have been shot, because as it flew over him, it lurched in the air and its foot dropped to the ground before him."

"Ah, a good sign. Did he dream of flying? Usually people who take bird's names have visions of flying while on their quest."

"I forgot to ask him."

"Not important," I said.

"Grandfather?"

"Yes?"

"What was your vision quest like?"

I saw before me in my mind's eye the river valley, the wavering of my sight and my tiredness, felt the ache in my lids and the cuts between my toes where I had wedged the sharp rocks. I experienced again my shakes and sweats, and the heat of the day. Then I saw again the man who was me walking through snow without a blanket, walking and walking, not cold, not tired, not sick or fevered. It would be forever on my brain.

"Oh, that was a long time ago," I said. "I saw a man who did not need a blanket in the winter."

"Did you see a spirit animal?" he asked.

The great beast reared up before me, huge and terrible, its eyes afire, its shaggy coat rippling with power, its claws large as knives, its teeth the size of bullets, its head wide as a hide shield, its breath rancid, its smell stifling, its charge unstoppable. I had evacuated my bowels.

"A bear," I said. "Go and play now."

One of my sons-in-law was brought in with a bullet in his leg. I did the medicine and took out the bullet and chewed tobacco and invoked the Great Mystery to wrestle with death for him. He was up and about in no time.

I decided to ride up to the big dirt road where the fighting was going on and see it for myself.

"Can I go with you, Grandfather?" asked Fall Colt.

I looked at his mother. She shrugged her shoulders.

"Yippppeeee!" he said, running to get his pony.

"You must remember we will not be able to see much," I said after him.

"I don't care!" he said. "I don't care!"

*   *   *

There were three small hills before you got to the big wooden fort. Our people stayed on the third hill, just outside rifle range from the walls.

Between the first and second hills, woods used to grow, but the soldiers had cut those down to build the forts, and they had to come between the second and third hills for their firewood. That was still in sight of the fort, and occasionally they would send men out to get logs in a wagon. They would also send men out to shoot at us while the others gathered wood. That was when we would try to kill them and they would try to kill us.

We did not like fighting this way, but other methods had failed. Early on, some of the warriors had attacked during the night and had been shot. Others had tried getting close during the day but the soldiers had used them for target practice. They seemed to have plenty of food and ammunition, but no firewood. So we waited till they came out.

It was boring work. Most of the time our men lay around and watched from the warm grass on the hills, polishing their coup sticks or sharpening their knives. Others would go hunting or fishing. They always cooked the game on the hills where the soldiers could see. The soldiers always shot at them when they did. That is how my son-in-law got the bullet in his leg.

Fall Colt and I walked up the hill where his father, Terrible Wolf, was dozing in the sun.

"Ho, Father," he said, waking, as he saw us come up the draw. He sat up.

"Don't get up on our account," I said.

Fall Colt ran to his father and hugged him. "You embarrass me," said Terrible Wolf. The boy let go of him.

"How are things in camp?"

"Dull," I said. "Your brother is fine. He will come back this week." We sat down. Terrible Wolf and I started to talk.

It was a few minutes before I noticed that Fall Colt had not said anything. He was back down the draw toward the horses. But he kept looking toward the top of the hill behind me. He appeared nervous.

"Hey-A! Hey-A!" yelled someone from the top of the hill. Instantly Terrible Wolf and all the other men were up, rifles in hand and onto their horses. They swept up over the hill in a cloud of dust.

From the direction of the fort we could hear rifle fire. I went to my horse and pulled my shotgun from its holder and Fall Colt got his boy's bow and arrows from his mount. Then we went to the ridgetop.

Below us the ground swelled downward to the fort. Soldiers were on the walls, others milled around in the open gateway. Halfway between us and them, a wagon and several dozen mounted soldiers were on the near side of the first hill.

The warriors swept down toward them from all sides, yelling and raising a great bother. The soldiers came determinedly on, until they reached the timber on the near side of the second hill. Then the wagon stopped and the horsemen dismounted and began to shoot while others with axes started cutting up dead trees.

The braves rode toward them and stopped and dismounted and began firing. The soldiers all fired at once, the warriors whenever they wanted. The sound of axes could be heard intermittently.

Then came the formal charge from the fort, with another two dozen soldiers on horses riding out toward the braves. The warriors mounted and turned back up the third hill. Then they stopped and fired back at the blue-clad soldiers.

Then our second bunch of braves charged from the draw near the third rise, and the soldiers in the fort went wild. Smoke rose up everywhere on the walls as they shot. The wave of troops rushing the hill turned. Everywhere was motion and gunshots. A lot of dust was raised.

Some of the first braves had run back up the hill beside us and were yelling and taunting the soldiers. An occasional bullet whistled by. One man dropped his breechclout and danced ribaldly with his buttocks toward the fort. Then he held his ankles and hopped backwards down the hill toward the firing.

Many bullets began to hit around us.

The second wave of soldiers would never come up the third rise. Some started to, but the man with the sword and the two bars on his hat stopped them. They are usually more cautious than the ones with one bar on their hats.

Dust obscured everything. The warriors on the hill fired down into the woodchopping party, holding their rifles high. The soldiers there and in the fort were firing as fast as they could. The troops between them and us flitted in and out of the smoke and dust.

Then everything was quiet. The dust began to settle.

The wagon and the soldiers were going back into the fort, only a few logs bouncing in the back. The mounted soldiers kept a wary eye backward on the hills. Some of our people put their thumbs in their ears and stuck out their tongues, an old white man's insult.

The doors to the fort closed. We went back over the hill.

No one had been hurt.

I looked around, then up. Fall Colt was standing against the skyline, looking down at the fort. He was shaking and pale.

"Come down," I said. "They might hit you by mistake."

He shook himself, looked around.

"What is it?"

He looked down at the bow in his hand. "I don't know, Grandfather ... I ... I ..."

"Was the excitement too much for you?"

"No ... I ... I didn't pay much attention."

His eyes were troubled. I said no more to him, and we rode back to our camp.

*   *   *

It did not surprise me when I saw him calling his friends together two days later. He handed one his bow, another his arrows and knife. Then he passed out his leggings, his moccasins, his breech-clout. Naked, he turned his back on the lodges and fires of our people and walked toward the distant mountains.

His mother came to me. "Father, did you see . . ."

I took my pipe from my mouth so her shadow wouldn't fall across it and harm the tobacco. "It is time," I said. "This has been coming on for days. He will be fine."

We watched him until he was lost in the evening sun.

Then we got busy for a few days, and I thought of Fall Colt rarely.

What we got busy doing was killing soldiers. It happened this way:

I accompanied my other son-in-law when he went back to the big dirt road. We got there when the sun stood straight up. The heat was already oppressive, the air still. Sound traveled a long way. We heard the gates of the fort open from up on our hill. The brave on watch let out his cry then. I looked up into the sky. A lone flycatcher chased a winged insect. I drew my shotgun from its scabbard and mounted up.

We did the same things we did the other day. The wagon came out, and we harassed it. Then the other soldiers charged out. Then our reserves came out of their places. Then our warriors mounted up and came back up the hill.

I saw what was happening before the others did. I let out a cry and began my death chant.

Because the second wave of soldiers had not stopped at the near side of the second hill. They kept coming. They were led by a soldier with one bar on his hat. He pointed his sword at us and spurred his horse. I could see each of his horse's hoofbeats raise dust. His eyes locked on mine.

Supposing the ritual to be the same, some of our people had dismounted and were prancing on top of the hill.

"Yah-Yah-Yah!" they said, turning somersaults. "Yah-Yah-Can't catch us!" Then they noticed the mounted soldiers had not stopped but were bearing down on them. They fell all over each other for a second, then jumped on their horses.

Bullets whipped around me as the oncoming soldiers flew up the hill. As I jumped on my horse, I could see the man in charge of the wagon party shaking his fist at the man leading the charge up the hill. It was a very foolish thing for the man with one bar to do.

For a few seconds, it seemed like a marvelous thing, but only because we did not expect it. But even as they neared the top of the hill and we spurred down into the open flat beyond, I saw that our reserves which had already made their ritual charge had turned and were heading up around the draw. Spotted Bull was in charge and he was a good man.

So we kicked our ponies and made them run. We could tell when the white men reached the top of the hill, because they started shooting everything in sight. Bullets hit all around us. Somebody on my left went down. The man to my right turned and fired, and we circled to the right so the white men would come sooner between us and the reserves. We turned on the soldiers as soon as their fire became scattered.

This was because Spotted Bull had gotten between them and the top of the hill. I turned to see the soldiers milling around as his bunch came down on them.

There were twenty or so mounted soldiers. There were a hundred of us.

I sent Terrible Wolf back up to the top of the hill. "Tell us when the whole fort is coming," I said.

Then we turned back into battle.

I had no coup stick with me, so I leaned down next to my mount and swung up and out when I neared a soldier. He fired at me with his pistol. Powder burned my face and arms. I came up and hit him under the chin with the butt of my shotgun. He went limp and slid off his horse.

Then I saw the man with one bar and shot him in the face with both barrels. He died quickly.

A few of the soldiers had killed their horses and were shooting at us from behind them. We dismounted and began walking toward them, firing as we went. Smoke hung over everything.

"The whole fort is coming," yelled Terrible Wolf.

"Keep killing!" I said. "Keep killing!"

"They're on the second hill," yelled Terrible Wolf, but he hadn't mounted up yet.

We killed the last soldier just as the world filled with the sound of hooves. Terrible Wolf jumped on his mount and took off across the ridge.

I got on mine and did the same. We divided up, half going east, half west.

Seventy soldiers came over the hill in brown and blue waves. Bullets went by like bees. Then we all turned and went over the same hill back down toward the fort. We caught the wagon party unprepared.

We killed most of them and looted and set the wagon afire.

Somebody got off his horse and pissed on the face of a dead man. Then we rode as fast as we could away from there with everything we had taken from the wagon. They chased us until it was too dark to see.

We moved the camp some miles away from where it had been. Things calmed down in a few days, and our warriors were back on the hill and the soldiers were back in the fort.

It was evening. I sat smoking in front of my lodge. Then I saw a naked boy coming towards camp from a long way off. It was my grandson.

He paused often. He was limping. He kept turning to stare back toward the near mountains, in the direction the fort lay.

"Hello, Grandson," I said. "Did you follow our travois trail?"

He stared at me a moment.

"Grandfather," he said.

"Yes?"

"Can I sleep now? I will tell you about it later."

"Here," I said, moving over and giving him half my buffalo robe. He lay down slowly and then he was asleep. I patted his head while he dreamed.

He woke up late the next night.

"Could you help me with my new name?" asked my grandson.

"Most people do not need help with theirs," I said.

"That is because they have seen a totem animal spirit and know its name," he said.

"You saw no animal?"

"I saw an animal, Grandfather, but I do not know its name."

"That *is* a problem. Perhaps I can help."

He began to tell me what he remembered of his vision quest. It was disjointed, like most are up until a vision comes. He had roamed the hills, chanted, he did not sleep. He put rocks between his toes and scoured his eyes with brambles to keep himself awake. He heard voices, but it was always the wind when he listened closer. He lay over a rock with his head down to help get a vision. One did not come until the third day.

"I turned in the direction of the big dirt road," he said. "And I saw it. I saw everything. There was water out there, much water. It was shining in the sun. The ground steamed and all was green and growing. Many small animals I did not know moved through the growths. In the water, things with long necks waded thick as buffalo on the plains. Animals like bats with long noses wheeled through the skies and dipped into the water for fish. All was large and out of proportion. All was cries and calls and roars like cougars. I did not understand."

"Visions are sometimes not meant to be understood, only acted upon," I said. "What was your animal like?"

"Then I *was* an animal, moving through the reeds. The wading animals that had seemed large were small to me now, my size. I brushed aside ferns. I chased one of the long-necked things which was trying to run from me. Its eyes were filled with terror. I caught it in a jump. I bit into its head and it crushed like pecans. I felt blood and bone. I bit off the head and swallowed it, while the rest of the thing stumbled and staggered around, bleeding in great gouts. I waited and then I pushed it over and began eating while it flopped and heaved on the ground, mashing a place flat with its tail and legs. I threw my head back to eat and swallowed whole chunks without chewing.

"I was near the water and I saw my reflection. I was huge and green. I stood on two legs and had tiny claws where my arms were. My eyes were at the sides of a great head. I had a long mouth full of sharp teeth, and a long thick tail which I used to balance.

"I stood up from my prey and roared a challenge to all the world around me. The earth was silent for a moment, then all resumed as it was before."

My grandson looked at me. "I feel great kinship with that beast, Grandfather. I do not know what it is. It is a beast of terror and strength, and it had skin like a snake."

"There is no doubt it is a powerful animal."

"Grandfather, there is something else."

"What is it?"

"It is still here. Near the white man's fort."

*   *   *

My grandson looked around him, saw some of the booty from the attack on the wagon a few days before. "I will need that," he said, picking up a tool.

"There is no great magic in a shovel," I said.

"There is no great water near the white man's fort, either," he said. "But I saw it there."

He said he would choose a new name after he was done with his work. The shovel was taller than he was. He strapped it on his pony and rode off toward the big dirt road.

"Where is Fall Colt going?" asked his mother.

"His name is not Fall Colt anymore."

"What is it, then?"

"He is going to find that out," I said.

"Aren't you going with him, Father?" she asked.

"I was just leaving," I said.

When I arrived, Terrible Wolf was standing on top of the hill scratching his head. He held his rifle across the crook of his left arm.

"He has been on his vision quest, hasn't he?" asked my son-in-law.

"Yes. He is troubled. It was inconclusive."

"I can . . . wait . . . what's he doing?"

We looked down the hill toward the fort. I saw that my grandson had been keeping to cover behind a clump of small trees, but now, shovel in hand, he took off running toward the fortress.

We saw puffs of smoke from the walls, then heard the crack of Army rifles. My grandson zigged and zagged like the woodpecker in flight. Puffs of dirt went up around him.

Some others had joined us on the hill, curious since they heard shots but no one had raised a cry. They watched the lone figure darting over the ground.

"Has he lost his wits?" asked someone.

"Great Mystery problems," I said.

"Oh."

Then he stopped. He looked around back and forth. Dust went up all around him, and the fire from the fort became heavy. I saw one of his braids whip in the air behind him.

He dropped down. I thought he was dead. He was obscured by a small bush barely big enough to hide a dog. Then we saw the flash of his shovel moving, the handle end sticking back up in the air like a great tongue.

"Yayyy!" we all yelled.

A few more shots came from the fort, then it was quiet.

Faintly we could hear the sound of the shovel, digging.

By nightfall he had disappeared behind a mound of dirt.

"I'm going down there soon to see if he is all right," said Terrible Wolf.

"Better take him some food and his bow," I said. "The white man might send someone out to try to hurt him."

My grandson was about two bowshots out from the fort but that seemed to worry the soldiers. The white men do not understand things dealing with the Great Mystery. I am sure they thought his digging had something to do with their fort. They were deathly afraid a thirteen-year-old was going to tunnel up under their buildings and kill them all in their sleep. So there was no telling what the soldiers would do.

After pitch dark, Terrible Wolf made his way out toward the sound of the shovel.

"I kept my eyes turned away," said Terrible Wolf later. "When I saw what he was doing."

"Oh," I said, smoking my pipe on the side of the hill away from the fort.

"There were parts of Storm Beasts around there. He was digging among them."

"That *is* bad," I said. We believe Storm Beasts dash themselves from the sky during rains. They are monsters who live in the heavens with the Thunderbird. They kill themselves with roars which is the thunder, and fall with a flash which is the lightning.

We believe this because you can always find their remains after storms, as they are exposed when the rains carry the earth away. Their bones litter our hunting grounds for miles after the spring rainstorms. We usually go around them, as they are unlucky animals.

"Did he mention Storm Beasts in his vision?" asked Terrible Wolf.

"There was no thunder and lightning in his story," I said.

"Do you think the Great Mystery has driven my son mad?" he asked.

"Let me get a reading on that," I said.

I was beginning to have a few doubts myself.

I performed three ceremonies, each more taxing than the one before it. I was sweating and tired, and my medicine bundle was oily and smelled bad when I finished.

"The Great Mystery is not punishing your son," I said to Terrible Wolf. "But there is magic at work out there, and it's so great I'd rather not be around when it happens."

"But you will."

"Of course I will."

The mound had grown. He was piling it up on the side toward the big dirt road. Occasionally a shovelful of dirt would clear the place he dug. Otherwise, the days were serene.

We could see men moving in the fort. Sometimes one would

fire at the place where my grandson dug. Then they even quit doing that.

We settled into a routine. Terrible Wolf would take food and water out to his son at night, and we would watch and wait during the day, in case the soldiers came out for firewood or to harm my grandson. It was not the kind of thing we liked to do.

Terrible Wolf came back one night. He sat down tiredly, put his head between his knees and stared at the ground. I noticed in the moonlight that his moccasins had already started wearing out this early in the summer.

"I did not know one person could move so much dirt," he said.

"Grandfather," someone said, shaking me awake.

"Yes," I said, sitting up on my robe where I had fallen asleep. I rubbed my eyes and sat up. It was some hours before dawn. There was a dull boom far away.

"I need some great medicine worked."

He was streaked with dirt, haggard. His eyes were clouded over with fatigue, barely reflecting the fires on the hill. He was as naked as he had been when he left on his vision quest.

In the distance, I heard another rumble of thunder, and the sky flashed light.

"If a storm is coming, and you are working among Storm Beasts, you are going to need more power than I can ask for. But I will see what I can do."

The first thing I did was to strip off naked and do a protection dance for myself. I am no fool. Then I did a small one for him, because he is so small. I didn't think that would stop the lightning from killing us, anyway. Then I picked up my medicine bundle.

"Have you thought of a name yet, Grandson?" I asked as we walked down the hill. The eastern horizon talked to itself in flashes of light. Great clouds walked toward us across the sky, their tops reaching far out in our direction.

"I am going to be called Green Brother," he said.

"Green Brother is a good name."

The small trees were being whipped about in the rising wind. Dust blew from the big dirt road. I was getting afraid, though my grandson did not know it.

Lightning slammed to the ground behind the white man's fort. Men moved on the walls. Possibly lightning would hit it and burn it to the ground and end all our troubles. I could not be concerned with the soldiers just now.

The pit was before us. Green Brother had dug a rampway down into the place he had scooped out of the ground. It started a long way back, the hole was so deep.

I did not know one person could move so much dirt, either.

"Guide me," I said, closing my eyes. I moved my lips in the death chant. If I saw the spirit animal all at once, it would be easier on me. I would either live or die in that instant.

I felt us go downward into the earthworks. The whistling wind stopped, only dust was blown onto my face from above. I felt my heart pound within my chest. I could not breathe right.

Green Brother turned to me. "It is before you, Grandfather."

"Is it terrible, Grandson?"

"Not after you get used to it."

My nerve failed then.

"Turn me away from it," I said. "The magic will be better if I am not used to it."

"There," he said, turning me.

I opened my eyes. The sides of the hole slanted down around me. The rampway went up from where I stood. A flash of lightning threw a horrible shadow on the ground before me. I felt the dead presence of the thing behind me.

"Make magic with it, Grandfather," said Green Brother.

"Is it upright? Are its legs and arms free? Will it step on us?"

"It is only bones, but they are iron. It is upright though curled toward us as if falling. Its body is stuck in the rock beneath us. I could not cut it away with the shovel."

"It is well you didn't. It might have fallen on you, and I would not know your new name." I wiped my brow. "This is going to be tough. What do you wish it to do?"

Green Brother looked up behind me. He smiled. "I want it to walk up this ramp and then across the big dirt road and into the fort."

"That would *probably* impress the white men," I said.

Thunder smashed outside the pit with a white flash. It unsettled me mightily. A few drops of rain hit my head. Soon the storm would open up. Perhaps more of the Storm Beasts would fall on us and kill us.

"Stand back," I said. "I need lots of room."

"Is there anything I can do?" asked my grandson Green Brother. "I feel kinship with this beast. I *was* this beast in my vision."

"If it moves," I said, "you can do *anything* you want."

I spread the things from my medicine bundle before me. It would take them all. I wished I had more sacred things. I had never tried anything so powerful before.

I called on the Great Mystery and reminded him that I was small before the storm, as are all men and women. I asked that he remember the things our people had done in gratitude for his blessings, and thanked him for the many times he had wrestled death for me.

When I had worked up his enthusiasm for me, I began to speak of specific things the soldiers had done to us, then asked him to intercede through the Storm Beast behind me.

As I paused for breath I heard the first gunshot. Then the warning cry from our people that meant the soldiers were coming from the fort.

"Sing your death song, Green Brother," I said. "I will try to finish this."

I had left my shotgun up on the hill because I did not like to carry it in a storm. Years ago I had seen a man melted to his rifle where he sat. It had not been pretty.

The storm crashed about us. There was a sound of firing, and hooves drummed near.

"Hurry, Grandfather!" said Green Brother. "Hurry!"

I was calling on the spirit of the Storm Beast to help us. I was really inspired, since it was no longer just my people, it was Green Brother and I who were in trouble. A gun fired from the dirt up near the mound from the pit, and voices called. The wind howled and roared. The sky danced with light and noise.

A bullet whipped into the ground near me. I closed my eyes tight. I heard men at the top of the ramp, nervous laughter.

"Thing!" I yelled, opening my eyes and dancing around. "Thing! Come alive! Come alive!"

A great bolt of lightning hit just outside the pit.

I saw many things at once:

I saw six soldiers on foot halfway down the ramp. Some were crouched down, rifles ahead of them. Two were upright, guns pointing toward me.

I saw Green Brother near me, head up, the shovel drawn back in his arms, ready to swing at the soldiers on the ramp.

I saw the shadow of the thing behind me on the ground.

It moved. It may have been only shadows from a different lightning flash.

I saw two of the soldiers jerk. I saw their hearts stop working in their chests. I saw six sets of eyes go wide as the doorknobs on the white man's houses. The eyes of the two men who died fell away to each side. The others disappeared backwards up the ramp.

Thunder crashed on top of us.

I turned and looked up at the thing behind me.

I wet myself all over my legs and fell forward into the soft ground.

* * *

Rain was falling in torrents, pushing at my face and eyes. I sat up. Water was running down into the pit. Green Brother lay sprawled across from me, his head bleeding where he had fallen against the shovel.

I went to him after retrieving my medicine bag. Strangely there was no more thunder and lightning, just the rain.

I took the rifles from the two dead men and put them over one shoulder. I picked up Green Brother and walked up the muddy ramp. I did not look back. I did not care if the other soldiers were still there or not.

It was very calm under the cold rain.

Soon after, the white men left and we burned down the fort again. After the snows melted the next spring, we signed another treaty, and a Doctor of Bones came out from the Great River Potomac to see the field of Storm Beasts.

He and Green Brother spent much time at the pit and all around there. Then men and a wagon came and took all the Storm Beasts away. The Doctor of Bones said Green Brother's vision animal was called in the white man's language *Tyrannosaurus rex*. He said this one was splendid.

Green Brother asked to go back East with the doctor and to learn more about all the spirit animals he had seen.

So he is at the university, and I miss him greatly. We are peaceful here now, and get our coffee and cattle and flour every month, and things are very boring.

Before he left, Green Brother said his spirit animal had been like the long-tailed yellow and brown lizard, only much bigger and much more fierce.

I am a simple man, and I am ignorant of many white men's

things. But I do know one truth, and as long as there is a blue sky above me, and the Great Mystery smiles, I know this. That thing I saw that night in the pit was no lizard.

Please turn me toward the sun so I can smoke.

WILDCAT

POUL ANDERSON

It was raining again, hot and heavy out of a hidden sky, and the air stank with swamp. Herries could just see the tall derricks a mile away, under a floodlight glare, and hear their engines mutter. Farther away, a bull brontosaur cried and thunder went through the night.

Herries's boots resounded hollowly on the dock. Beneath the slicker, his clothes lay sweat-soggy, the rain spilled off his hat and down his collar. He swore in a tired voice and stepped onto his gangplank.

Light from the shack on the barge glimmered off drenched wood. He saw the snaky neck just in time, as it reared over the gangplank rail and struck at him. He sprang back, grabbing for the Magnum carbine slung over one shoulder. The plesiosaur hissed monstrously and flipper-slapped the water. It was like a cannon going off.

Herries threw the gun to his shoulder and fired. The long sleek form took the bullet—somewhere—and screamed. The raw noise hurt the man's eardrums.

Feet thudded over the wharf. Two guards reached Herries and began to shoot into the dark water. The door of the shack opened and a figure stood black against its yellow oblong, a tommy gun stammering idiotically in its hands.

"Cut it out!" bawled Herries. "That's enough! Hold your fire!"

Silence fell. For a moment only the ponderous rainfall had voice. Then the brontosaur bellowed again, remotely, and there were seethings and croakings in the water.

"He got away," said Herries. "Or more likely his pals are now stripping him clean. Blood smell." A dull anger lifted in him. He turned and grabbed the lapel of the nearest guard. "How often do I have to tell you characters, every gangway has to have a man near it with grenades?"

"Yes, sir. Sorry, sir." Herries was a large man, and the other face looked up at him, white and scared in the wan electric radiance. "I just went off to the head—"

"You'll stay here," said Herries. "I don't care if you explode. Our presence draws these critters, and you ought to know that by now. They've already snatched two men off this dock. They nearly got a third tonight—me. At the first suspicion of anything out there, you're to pull the pin on a grenade and drop it in the water, understand? One more dereliction like this, and you're fired— No." He stopped, grinning humorlessly. "That's not much of a punishment, is it? A week in hack on bread."

The other guard bristled. "Look here, Mr. Herries, we got our rights. The union—"

"Your precious union is a hundred million years in the future," snapped the engineer. "It was understood that this is a dangerous job, that we're subject to martial law, and that I can discipline anyone who steps out of line. Okay—remember."

He turned his back and tramped across the gangplank to the barge deck. It boomed underfoot. With the excitement over, the shack had been closed again. He opened the door and stepped through, peeling off his slicker.

Four men were playing poker beneath an unshaded bulb. The

room was small and cluttered, hazy with tobacco smoke and the Jurassic mist. A fifth man lay on one of the bunks, reading. The walls were gaudy with pinups.

Olson riffled the cards and looked up. "Close call, Boss," he remarked, almost casually. "Want to sit in?"

"Not now," said Herries. He felt his big square face sagging with weariness. "I'm bushed." He nodded at Carver, who had just returned from a prospecting trip farther north. "We lost one more derrick today."

"Huh?" said Carver. "What happened this time?"

"It turns out this is the mating season." Herries found a chair, sat down, and began to pull off his boots. "How they tell one season from another, I don't know . . . length of day, maybe . . . but anyhow the brontosaurs aren't shy of us any more—they're going nuts. Now they go gallyhooting around and trample down charged fences or anything else that happens to be in the way. They've smashed three rigs to date, and one man."

Carver raised an eyebrow in his chocolate-colored face. It was a rather sour standing joke here, how much better the Negroes looked than anyone else. A white man could be outdoors all his life in this clouded age and remain pasty. "Haven't you tried shooting them?" he asked.

"Ever try to kill a brontosaur with a rifle?" snorted Herries. "We can mess 'em up a little with .50-caliber machine guns or a bazooka—just enough so they decide to get out of the neighborhood—but being less intelligent than a chicken, they take off in any old direction. Makes as much havoc as the original rampage." His left boot hit the floor with a sullen thud. "I've been begging for a couple of atomic howitzers, but it has to go through channels . . . Channels!" Fury spurted in him. "Five hundred human beings stuck in this nightmare world, and our requisitions have to go through channels!"

Olson began to deal the cards. Polansky gave the man in the bunk a chill glance. "You're the wheel, Symonds," he said. "Why the devil don't you goose the great Transtemporal Oil Company?"

"Nuts," said Carver. "The great benevolent all-wise United States Government is what counts. How about it, Symonds?"

You never got a rise out of Symonds, the human tape recorder, just a playback of the latest official line. Now he laid his book aside and sat up in his bunk. Herries noticed that the volume was Marcus Aurelius, in Latin yet.

Symonds looked at Carver through steel-rimmed glasses and said in a dusty tone: "I am only the comptroller and supply supervisor. In effect, a chief clerk. Mr. Herries is in charge of operations."

He was a small shriveled man, with thin gray hair above a thin gray face. Even here, he wore a stiff-collared shirt and sober tie. One of the hardest things to take about him was the way his long nose waggled when he talked.

"In charge!" Herries spat expertly into a gobboon. "Sure, I direct the prospectors and the drillers and everybody else on down through the bull cook. But who handles the paperwork—all our reports and receipts and requests? You." He tossed his right boot on the floor. "I don't want the name of boss if I can't get the stuff to defend my own men."

Something bumped against the supervisors' barge; it quivered and the chips on the table rattled. Since there was no outcry from the dock guards, Herries ignored the matter. Some swimming giant. And except for the plesiosaurs and the nonmalicious bumbling bronties, all the big dinosaurs encountered so far were fairly safe. They might step on you in an absentminded way, but most of them were peaceful and you could outrun those that weren't. It was the smaller carnivores, about the size of a man, leaping out of brush or muck with a skullful of teeth, that had taken most of the personnel lost. Their reptile life was too diffuse: even mortally wounded by elephant gun or grenade launcher, they could rave about for hours. They were the reason for sleeping on barges tied up by this sodden coast, along the gulf that would someday be Oklahoma.

Symonds spoke in his tight little voice: "I send your recommendations in, of course. The project office passes on them."

"I'll say it does," muttered young Greenstein irreverently.

"Please do not blame me," insisted Symonds.

I wonder. Herries glowered at him. Symonds had an in of some kind. That was obvious. A man who was simply a glorified clerk would not be called to Washington for unspecified conferences with unspecified people as often as this one was. But what was he, then?

A favorite relative? No . . . in spite of high pay, this operation was no political plum. FBI? Scarcely . . . the security checks were all run in the future. A hack in the bureaucracy? That was more probable. Symonds was here to see that oil was pumped and dinosaurs chased away and the hideously fecund jungle kept beyond the fence according to the least comma in the latest directive from headquarters.

The small man continued: "It has been explained to you officially that the heavier weapons are all needed at home. The international situation is critical. You ought to be thankful you are safely back in the past."

"Heat, large economy-size alligators, and not a woman for a hundred million years," grunted Olson. "I'd rather be blown up. Who dealt this mess?"

"You did," said Polansky. "Gimme two, and make 'em good."

Herries stripped the clothes off his thick hairy body, went to the rear of the cabin, and entered the shower cubby. He left the door open, to listen in. A boss was always lonely. Maybe he should have married when he had the chance. But then he wouldn't be here. Except for Symonds, who was a widower and in any case more a government than company man, Transoco had been hiring only young bachelors for operations in the field.

"It seems kinda funny to talk about the international situation," remarked Carver. "Hell, there won't be any international situation for several geological periods."

"The inertial effect makes simultaneity a valid approximational concept," declared Symonds pedantically. His habit of lecturing scientists and engineers on their professions had not endeared him to them. "If we spend a year in the past, we must necessarily return to our own era to find a year gone, since the main projector operates only at the point of its own existence which—"

"Oh, stow it," said Greenstein. "I read the orientation manual too." He waited until everyone had cards, then shoved a few chips forward and added: "Druther spend my time a little nearer home. Say with Cleopatra."

"Impossible," Symonds told him. "Inertial effect again. In order to send a body into the past at all, the projector must energize it so much that the minimal time-distance we can cover becomes precisely the one we have covered to arrive here, one hundred and one million, three hundred twenty-seven thousand, et cetera, years."

"But why not time-hop into the future? You don't buck entropy in that direction. I mean, I suppose there is an inertial effect there, too, but it would be much smaller, so you could go into the future—"

"—about a hundred years at a hop, according to the handbook," supplied Polansky.

"So why don't they look at the twenty-first century?" asked Greenstein.

"I understand that that is classified information," Symonds said. His tone implied that Greenstein had skirted some unimaginably gross obscenity.

Herries put his head out of the shower. "Sure it's classified," he said. "They'd classify the wheel if they could. But use your reason and you'll see why travel into the future isn't practical. Suppose you jump a hundred years ahead. How do you get

143

home to report what you've seen? The projector will yank you a hundred million years into the past, less the distance you went forward."

Symonds dove back into his book. Somehow he gave an impression of lying there rigid with shock that men dared think after he had spoken the phrase of taboo.

"Uh . . . yes. I get it." Greenstein nodded. He had been recruited only a month ago, to replace a man drowned in a moss-veiled bog. Before then, like nearly all the world, he had had no idea time travel existed. So far he had been too busy to examine its implications.

To Herries it was an old, worn-thin story.

"I daresay they did send an expedition a hundred million years up, so it could come back to the same week as it left," he said. "Don't ask me what was found. Classified: Tip-top Secret, Burn Before Reading."

"You know, though," said Polansky in a reflective tone, "I been thinking some myself. Why are we here at all? I mean, oil is necessary to defense and so forth, but it seems to me it'd make more sense for the U.S. Army to come through, cross the ocean, and establish itself where the enemy nations are going to be. Then we'd have a gun pointed at their heads!"

"Nice theory," said Herries. "I've daydreamed myself. But there's only one main projector, to energize all the subsidiary ones. Building it took almost the whole world supply of certain rare earths. Its capacity is limited. If we started sending military units into the past, it'd be a slow and cumbersome operation—and not being a security officer, I'm not required to kid myself that Moscow doesn't know we have time travel. They've probably even given Washington a secret ultimatum: 'Start sending back war material in any quantity, and we'll hit you with everything we've got.' But evidently they don't feel strongly enough about our pumping oil on our own territory—or what will one day be our own territory—to make it a, uh, *casus belli*."

"Just as we don't feel their satellite base in the twentieth century is dangerous enough for us to fight about," said Greenstein. "But I suspect we're the reason they agreed to make the moon a neutral zone. Same old standoff."

"I wonder how long it can last?" murmured Polansky.

"Not much longer," said Olson. "Read your history. I'll see you, Greenstein, boy, and raise you two."

Herries let the shower run about him. At least there was no shortage of hot water. Transoco had sent back a complete nuclear reactor. But civilization and war still ran on oil, he thought, and oil was desperately short up there.

Time, he reflected, was a paradoxical thing. The scientists had told him it was utterly rigid. Perhaps, though of course it would be a graveyard secret, the cloak-and-dagger boys had tested that theory the hard way, going back into the historical past (it could be done after all, Herries suspected, by a roundabout route that consumed fabulous amounts of energy) in an attempt to head off the Bolshevik revolution. It would have failed. Neither past nor future could be changed; they could only be discovered. Some of Transoco's men had discovered death, an eon before they were born . . . But there would not be such a shortage of oil in the future if Transoco had not gone back and drained it in the past. A self-causing future . . .

Primordial stuff, petroleum. Hoyle's idea seemed to be right; it had not been formed by rotting dinosaurs but was present from the beginning. It was the stuff that had stuck the planets together.

And, Herries thought, was sticking to him now. He reached for the soap.

Earth spun gloomily through hours, and morning crept over wide brown water. There was no real day as men understood day; the heavens were a leaden sheet with dirty black rainclouds scudding below the permanent fog layers.

Herries was up early, for a shipment was scheduled. He came out of the bosses' messhall and stood for a moment looking over the mud beach and the few square miles of cleared land, sleazy buildings, and gaunt derricks inside an electric mesh fence. Automation replaced thousands of workers, so that five hundred men were enough to handle everything, but still the compound was the merest scratch, and the jungle remained a terrifying black wall. Not that the trees were so utterly alien. Besides the archaic grotesqueries, like ferns and mosses of gruesome size, he saw cycad, redwood, and gingko, scattered prototypes of oak and willow and birch. But Herries missed wildflowers.

A working party with its machines was repairing the fence the brontosaur had smashed through yesterday, the well it had wrecked, the inroads of brush and vine. A caterpillar tractor hauled a string of loaded wagons across raw red earth. A helicopter buzzed overhead, on watch for dinosaurs. It was the only flying thing. There had been a nearby pterodactyl rookery, but the men had cleaned that out months ago. When you got right down to facts, the most sinister animal of all was man.

Greenstein joined Herries. The new assistant was tall, slender, with curly brown hair and the defenseless face of youth. Above boots and dungarees he wore a blue sports shirt; it offered a kind of defiance to this sullen world. "Smoke?" he invited.

"Thanks." Herries accepted the cigarette. His eyes still dwelt on the drills. Their walking beams went up and down, up and down, like a joyless copulation. Perhaps a man could get used to the Jurassic rain forest and eventually see some dark beauty there, for it was at least life; but this field would always remain hideous, being dead and pumping up the death of men.

"How's it going, Sam?" he asked when the tobacco had soothed his palate.

"All right," said Greenstein. "I'm shaking down. But God, it's good to know today is mail call!"

They stepped off the porch and walked toward the transceiving station. Mud squelched under their feet. A tuft of something, too pale and fleshy to be grass, stood near Herries's path. The yard crew had better uproot that soon, or in a week it might claim the entire compound.

"Girlfriend, I suppose," said the chief. "That does make a month into a hell of a long drought between letters."

Greenstein flushed and nodded earnestly. "We're going to get married when my two years here are up," he said.

"That's what most of 'em plan on. A lot of saved-up pay and valuable experience—sure, you're fixed for life." It was on Herries's tongue to add that the life might be a short one, but he suppressed the impulse.

Loneliness dragged at his nerves. No one waited in the future for him. It was just as well, he told himself during the endless nights. Hard enough to sleep without worrying about some woman in the same age as the cobalt bomb.

"I've got her picture here, if you'd like to see it," offered Greenstein shyly.

His hand was already on his wallet. A tired grin slid up Herries's mouth. "Right next to your . . . er . . . heart, eh?" he murmured.

Greenstein blinked, threw back his head, and laughed. The field had not heard so merry a sound in a long while. Nevertheless, he showed the other man a pleasant-faced, unspectacular girl.

Out in the swamp, something hooted and threshed about.

Impulsively, Herries asked: "How do you feel about this operation, Sam?"

"Huh? Why, it's . . . interesting work. And a good bunch of guys."

"Even Symonds?"

"Oh, he means well."

"We could have more fun if he didn't bunk with us."

"He can't help being . . . old," said Greenstein.

Herries glanced at the boy. "You know," he said, "you're the first man in the Jurassic Period who's had a good word for Ephraim

Symonds. I appreciate that. I'd better not say whether or not I share the sentiment, but I appreciate it."

His boots sludged ahead, growing heavier with each step. "You still haven't answered my first question," he resumed after a while. "I didn't ask if you enjoyed the work, I asked how you feel about it. Its purpose. We have the answers here to questions which science has been asking—will be asking—for centuries. And yet, except for a couple of underequipped paleobiologists, who aren't allowed to publish their findings, we're doing nothing but rape the Earth in an age before it has ever conceived us."

Greenstein hesitated. Then, with a surprise dryness: "You're getting too psychoanalytic for me, I'm afreud."

Herries chuckled. The day seemed a little more alive, all at once. "*Touché!* Well, I'll rephrase Joe Polansky's question of last night. Do you think the atomic standoff in our home era—to which this operation is potentially rather important—is stable?"

Greenstein considered for a moment. "No," he admitted. "Deterrence is a stopgap till something better can be worked out."

"They've said as much since it first began. Nothing has been done. It's improbable that anything will be. Ole Olson describes the international situation as a case of the irresistibly evil force colliding with the immovably stupid object."

"Ole likes to use extreme language," said Greenstein. "So tell me, what else could our side do?"

"I wish to God I had an answer." Herries sighed. "Pardon me. We avoid politics here as much as possible; we're escapists in several senses of the word. But frankly, I sound out new men. I was doing it to you. Because in spite of what Washington thinks, a Q clearance isn't all that a man needs to work here."

"Did I pass?" asked Greenstein, a bit too lightly.

"Sure. So far. You may wish you hadn't. The burning issue today is not whether to tolerate 'privileged neutralism,' or whatever the latest catchword is up there. It's: Did I get the armament I've been asking for?"

The transceiving station bulked ahead. It was a long corrugated-iron shed, but dwarfed by the tanks that gleamed behind it. Every one of those was filled, Herries knew. Today they would pump their crude oil into the future. Or rather, if you wanted to be exact, their small temporal unit would establish a contact and the gigantic main projector in the twentieth century would then "suck" the liquid toward itself. And in return the compound would get food, tools, weapons, supplies, and mail. Herries prayed for at least one howitzer . . . and no VIPs. That senator a few months ago!

For a moment, contemplating the naked ugliness of tanks and pumps and shed, Herries had a vision of this one place stretching through time. It would be abandoned someday, when the wells were exhausted, and rain and jungle would rapidly eat the last thin traces of man. Later would come the sea, and then it would be dry land again, a cold prairie scoured by glacial winds, and then it would grow warm and . . . on and on, a waste of years until the time projector was invented and the great machine stood on this spot. And afterward? Herries didn't like to think what might be here after that.

Symonds was already present. He popped rabbitlike out of the building, a coded manifest in one hand, a pencil behind his ear. "Good morning, Mr. Herries," he said. His tone gave its usual impression of stiff self-importance.

"Morning. All set in there?" Herries went in to see for himself. A spatter of rain began to fall, noisy on the metal roof. The technicians were at their posts and reported clear. Outside, one by one, the rest of the men were drifting up. This was mail day, and little work would be done for the remainder of it.

Herries laid the sack of letters to the future inside the shed in its proper spot. His chronometer said one minute to go. "Stand by!" At the precise time, there was a dim whistle in the air and an obscure pulsing glow. Meters came to life. The pumps began to throb, driving crude oil through a pipe that faced open-ended into the shed. Nothing emerged that Herries could see. Good. Everything in order. The other end of the pipe was a hundred million years in the future. The mail sack vanished with a small puff, as air rushed in where it had waited. Herries went back outside.

"Ah . . . excuse me."

He turned around, with a jerkiness that told him his nerves were half unraveled. "Yes?" he snapped.

"May I see you a moment?" asked Symonds. "Alone?" And the pale eyes behind the glasses said it was not a request but an order.

Herries nodded curtly, swore at the men for hanging around idle when the return shipment wasn't due for hours, and led the way to a porch tacked onto one side of the transceiving station. There were some camp stools beneath it. Symonds hitched up his khakis as if they were a business suit and sat primly down, his hands flat on his knees.

"A special shipment is due today," he said. "I was not permitted to discuss it until the last moment."

Herries curled his mouth. "Go tell Security that the Kremlin won't be built for a hundred million years. Maybe they haven't heard."

"What no one knew, no one could put into a letter home."

"The mail is censored anyway. Our friends and relatives think we're working somewhere in Asia." Herries spat into the mud and said: "And in another year the first lot of recruits are due home. Plan to shoot them as they emerge, so they can't possibly talk in their sleep?"

Symonds seemed too humorless even to recognize sarcasm. He pursed his lips and declared: "Some secrets need be kept for a few months only; but within that period, they *must* be kept."

"Okay, okay. Let's hear what's coming today."

"I am not allowed to tell you that. But about half the total tonnage will be crates marked top secret. These are to remain in the shed, guarded night and day by armed men." Symonds pulled a slip of paper from his jacket. "These men will be assigned to that duty, each one taking eight hours a week."

Herries glanced at the names. He did not know everyone here by sight, though he came close, but he recognized several of these. "Brave, discreet, and charter subscribers to *National Review*," he murmured. "Teacher's pets. All right. Though I'll have to curtail exploration correspondingly—either that, or else cut down on escorts and sacrifice a few extra lives."

"I think not. Let me continue. You will get these orders in the mail today, but I will prepare you for them now. A special house must be built for the crates, as rapidly as possible, and they must be moved there immediately upon its completion. I have the specifications in my office safe; essentially, it must be air conditioned, burglar-proof, and strong enough to withstand all natural hazards."

"Whoa, there!" Herries stepped forward. "That's going to take reinforced concrete and—"

"Materials will be made available," said Symonds. He did not look at the other man but stared straight ahead of him, across the rain-smoky compound to the jungle. He had no expression on his pinched face, and the reflection of light off his glasses gave him a strangely blind look.

"But—Judas priest!" Herries threw his cigarette to the ground; it was swallowed in mud and running water. He felt the heat enfold him like a blanket. "There's the labor too, the machinery, and—How the devil am I expected to expand this operation if—"

"Expansion will be temporarily halted," cut in Symonds. "You will simply maintain current operations with skeleton crews. The majority of the labor force is to be reassigned to construction."

"*What?*"

"The compound fence must be extended and reinforced. A number of new storehouses are to be erected to hold certain supplies which will presently be sent to us. Bunkhouse barges for an additional five hundred are required. This, of course, entails more sick bay, recreational, mess, laundry, and other facilities."

Herries stood dumbly, staring at him. Pale lightning flickered in the sky.

The worst of it was, Symonds didn't even bother to be arrogant. He spoke like a schoolmaster.

"Oh, no!" whispered Herries after a long while. "They're not going to try to establish that Jurassic military base after all!"

"The purpose is classified."

"Yeah. Sure. Classified. Arise, ye duly cleared citizens of democracy, and cast your ballot on issues whose nature is classified, that your leaders whose names and duties are classified may— Great. Hopping. Balls. Of. Muck." Herries swallowed. Vaguely, through his pulse, he felt his fingers tighten into fists.

"I'm going up," he said. "I'm going to protest personally in Washington."

"That is not permitted," Symonds said in a dry, clipped tone. "Read your contract. You are under martial law. Of course," and his tone was neither softer nor harder, "you may file a written recommendation."

Herries stood for a while. Out beyond the fence stood a bulldozer, wrecked and abandoned. The vines had almost buried it and a few scuttering little marsupials lived there. Perhaps they were his own remote ancestors. He could take a .22 and go potshooting at them someday.

"I'm not permitted to know anything," he said at last. "But is curiosity allowed? An extra five hundred men aren't much. I suppose, given a few airplanes and so on, a thousand of us could plant atomic bombs where enemy cities will be. Or could we? Can't locate them without astronomical studies first, and it's always clouded here. So it would be practical to boobytrap only with mass action weapons. A few husky cobalt bombs, say. But there are missiles available to deliver those in the twentieth century. So . . . what is the purpose?"

"You will learn the facts in due course," answered Symonds. "At present, the government has certain military necessities."

"Haw!" said Herries. He folded his arms and leaned against the roofpost. It sagged a bit—shoddy work, shoddy world, shoddy destiny. "Military horses' necks! I'd like to get one of those prawn-eyed brass hats down here, just for a week, to run his precious security check on a lovesick brontosaur. But I'll probably get another visit from Senator Lardhead, the one who took up two days of my time walking around asking about the possibilities of farming. *Farming!*"

"Senator Wien is from an agricultural state. Naturally he would be interested—"

"—in making sure that nobody here starts raising food and shipping it back home to bring grocery prices down to where people can afford an occasional steak. Sure. I'll bet it cost us a thousand man-hours to make his soil tests and tell him, yes, given the proper machinery this land could be farmed. Of course, maybe I do him an injustice. Senator Wien is also on the Military Affairs Committee, isn't he? He may have visited us in that capacity, and soon we'll get a directive to start our own little victory gardens."

"Your language is close to being subversive," declared Symonds out of prune-wrinkled lips. "Senator Wien is a famous statesman."

For a moment the legislator's face rose in Herries's memory; it had been the oldest and most weary face he had ever known. Something had burned out in the man who fought a decade for honorable peace; the knowledge that there was no peace and could be none became a kind of death, and Senator Wien dropped out of his Free World Union organization to arm his land for Ragnarok. Briefly, his anger fading, Herries pitied Senator Wien. And the President, and the Chief of Staff, and the Secretary of State, for their work must be like a nightmare where you strangled your mother and could not stop your hands. It was easier to fight dinosaurs.

He even pitied Symonds, until he asked if his request for an atomic weapon had finally been okayed, and Symonds replied, "Certainly not." Then he spat at the clerk's feet and walked out into the rain.

After the shipment and guards were seen to, Herries dismissed his men. There was an uneasy buzz among them at the abnormality of what had arrived; but today was mail day, after all, and they did not ponder it long. He would not make the announcement about the new orders until tomorrow. He got the magazines and news-papers to which he subscribed (no one up there "now" cared enough to write to him, though his parents had existed in a section of space-time that ended only a year before he took this job) and wandered off to the boss's barge to read a little.

The twentieth century looked still uglier than it had last month. The nations felt their pride and saw no way of retreat. The Middle Eastern war was taking a decisive turn which none of the great powers could afford. Herries wondered if he might not be cut off in the Jurassic. A single explosion could destroy the main projector. Five hundred womanless men in a world of reptiles—He'd take the future, cobalt bomb and all.

After lunch there fell a quiet, Sunday kind of atmosphere. Men lay on their bunks reading their letters over and over. Herries made his rounds, machines and kitchen and sick bay, inspecting.

"I guess we'll discharge O'Connor tomorrow," said Dr. Yama-guchi. "He can do light work with that Stader on his arm. Next time tell him to duck when a power shovel comes down."

"What kind of sick calls have you been getting?" asked the chief.

Yamaguchi shrugged. "Usual things, very minor. I'd never have

154

thought this swamp country could be so healthful. I guess disease germs that can live on placental mammals haven't evolved yet."

Father Gonzales, one of the camp's three chaplains, buttonholed Herries as he came out. "Can you spare me a minute?" he said.

"Sure, padre. What is it?"

"About organizing some baseball teams. We need more recreation. This is not a good place for men to live."

"Sawbones was just telling me—"

"I know. No flu, no malaria, oh, yes. But man is more than a body."

"Sometimes I wonder," said Herries. "I've seen the latest headlines. The dinosaurs have more sense than we do."

"We have the capacity to do nearly all things," said Father Gonzales. "At present, I mean in the twentieth century, we seem to do evil very well. We can do as much good, given the chance."

"Who's denying us the chance?" asked Herries. "Just ourselves, H. Sapiens. Therefore I wonder if we really are able to do good."

"Don't confuse sinfulness with damnation," said the priest. "We have perhaps been unfortunate in our successes. And yet even our most menacing accomplishments have a kind of sublimity. The time projector, for example. If the minds able to shape such a thing in metal were only turned toward human problems, what could we not hope to do?"

"But that's my point," said Herries. "We don't do the high things. We do what's trivial and evil so consistently that I wonder if it isn't in our nature. Even this time travel business . . . more and more I'm coming to think there's something fundamentally unhealthy about it. As if it's an invention that only an ingrown mind would have made first."

"First?"

Herries looked up into the steaming sky. A foul wind met his face. "There are stars above those clouds," he said, "and most stars must have planets. I've not been told how the time projector works, but elementary differential calculus will show that travel into the past is equivalent to attaining, momentarily, an infinite velocity. In other words, the basic natural law that the projector uses is one that somehow goes beyond relativity theory. If a time projector is possible, so is a spaceship that can reach the stars in a matter of days, maybe of minutes or seconds. If we were sane, padre, we wouldn't have been so anxious for a little organic grease and the little military advantage involved that the first thing we did was go back into the dead past after it. No, we'd have invented that spaceship first, and gone out to the stars where there's room to be free and to grow. The time projector would have come afterward, as a scientific research tool."

He stopped, embarrassed at himself and trying awkwardly to grin. "Excuse me. Sermons are more your province than mine."

"It was interesting," said Father Gonzales. "But you brood too much. So do a number of men. Even if they have no close ties at home—it was wise to pick them for that—they are all of above-average intelligence, and aware of what the future is becoming. I'd like to shake them out of their depression. If we could get some more sports equipment . . ."

"Sure. I'll see what I can do."

"Of course," said the priest, "the problem is basically philosophical. Don't laugh. You too were indulging in philosophy, and doubtless you think of yourself as an ordinary, unimaginative man. Your wildcatters may not have heard of Aristotle, but they are also thinking men in their way. My personal belief is that this heresy of a fixed, rigid time line lies at the root of their growing sorrowfulness, whether they know it or not."

"Heresy?" The engineer lifted thick sandy brows. "It's been proved. It's the basis of the theory which showed how to build a projector; that much I do know. How could we be here, if the Mesozoic were not just as real as the Cenozoic? But if all time is coexistent, then all time must be fixed—unalterable—because every instant is the unchanging past of some other instant."

"Perhaps so, from God's viewpoint," said Father Gonzales. "But we are mortal men. And we have free will. The fixed-time concept need not, logically, produce fatalism. Remember, Herries, man's will is an important reason why twentieth-century civilization is approaching suicide. If we think we know our future is unchangeable, if our every action is foreordained, if we are doomed already, what's the use of trying? Why go through the pain of thought, of seeking an answer and struggling to make others accept it? But if we really believed in ourselves, we would look for a solution, and find one."

"Maybe," said Herries uncomfortably. "Well, give me a list of the equipment you want, and I'll put in an order for it the next time the mail goes out."

As he walked off, he wondered if the mail would ever go out again.

Passing the rec hall, he noticed a small crowd before it and veered to see what was happening. He could not let men gather to trade doubts and terrors, or the entire operation was threatened. *In plain English*, he told himself with a growing bitter honesty, *I can't permit them to think.*

But the sound which met him, under the subtly alien rustle of forest leaves and the distant bawl of a thunder lizard, was only a guitar. Chords danced forth beneath expert fingers, and a young voice lilted:

> . . . I traveled this wide world over,
> A hundred miles or more,
> But a saddle on a milk cow,
> I never seen before! . . .

Looking over shoulders, Herries made out Greenstein, sprawled on a bench and singing. He heard chuckles from the listeners. Well deserved: the kid was good; Herries wished he could relax and simply enjoy the performance. Instead, he must note that they were finding it pleasant, and that swamp and war were alike forgotten for a valuable few minutes.

The song ended. Greenstein stood up and stretched. "Hi, Boss," he said.

Hard, wind-beaten faces turned to Herries and a mumble of greeting went around the circle. He was well enough liked, he knew, insofar as a chief can be liked. But that is not much. A leader can inspire trust, loyalty, what have you, but he cannot be humanly liked, or he is no leader.

"That was good," said Herries. "I didn't know you played."

"I didn't bring this whangbox with me, since I had no idea where I was going till I got here," answered Greenstein. "Wrote home for it and it arrived today."

A heavy-muscled crew-cut man said, "You ought to be on the entertainment committee." Herries recognized Worth, one of the professional patriots who would be standing guard on Symonds's crates; but not a bad sort, really, after you learned to ignore his rather tedious opinions.

Greenstein said an indelicate word. "I'm sick of committees," he went on. "We've gotten so much into the habit of being herded around—everybody in the twentieth century has—that we can't even have a little fun without first setting up a committee."

Worth looked offended but made no answer. It began to rain again, just a little.

"Go on now, anyway," said Joe Eagle Wing. "Let's not take ourselves so goddam serious. How about another song?"

"Not in the wet." Greenstein returned his guitar to its case. The group began to break up, some to the hall and some back toward their barges.

Herries lingered, unwilling to be left alone with himself. "About that committee," he said. "You might reconsider. It's probably true what you claim, but we're stuck with a situation. We've simply got to tell most of the boys, 'Now is the time to be happy,' or they never will be."

Greenstein frowned. "Maybe so. But hasn't anyone ever thought of making a fresh start? Of unlearning those bad habits?"

"You can't do that within the context of an entire society's vices," said Herries. "And how're you going to get away?"

Greenstein gave him a long look. "How the devil did you ever get this job?" he asked. "You don't sound like a man who'd be cleared for a dishwashing assistantship."

Herries shrugged. "All my life I've liked totalitarianism even less than what passes for democracy. I served in a couple of the minor wars and—No matter. Possibly I might not be given the post if I applied now. I've been here more than a year, and it's changed me some."

"It must," said Greenstein, flickering a glance at the jungle.

"How's things at home?" asked Herries, anxious for another subject.

The boy kindled. "Oh, terrific!" he said eagerly. "Miriam, my girl, you know, she's an artist, and she's gotten a commission to—"

The loudspeaker coughed and blared across the compound, into the strengthening rain: "Attention! Copter to ground, attention! Large biped dinosaur, about two miles away north-northeast, coming fast."

Herries cursed and broke into a run.

Greenstein paced him. Water sheeted where their boots struck. "What is it?" he called.

"I don't know . . . yet . . . but it might be . . . a really big . . . carnivore." Herries reached the headquarters shack and flung the door open. A panel of levers was set near his personal desk. He slapped one down and the "combat stations" siren skirled above the field. Herries went on, "I don't know why anything biped should make a beeline for us unless the smell of blood from the critter we drove off yesterday is attracting it. The smaller carnivores are sure as hell drawn. The charged fence keeps them away, but I doubt if it would do much more than enrage a dinosaur—Follow me!"

Jeeps were already leaving their garage when Herries and Greenstein came out. Mud leaped up from their wheels and dripped back off the fenders. The rain fell harder, until the forest beyond the fence blurred and the earth smoked with vapors. The helicopter hung above the derricks, like a skeleton vulture watching a skeleton army, and the alarm sirens filled the brown air with screaming.

"Can you drive one of these buggies?" asked Herries.

"I did in the Army," said Greenstein.

"Okay, we'll take the lead one. The main thing is to stop that beast before it gets in among the wells." Herries vaulted the right-hand door and planted himself on sopping plastic cushions. A .50-caliber machine gun was mounted on the hood before him, and the microphone of a police car radio hung at the dash. Five jeeps followed as Greenstein swung into motion. The rest of the crew, ludicrous ants across these wide wet distances, went scurrying to defend the most vital installations.

The north gate opened and the cars splashed out beyond the fence. There was a strip several yards across, also kept cleared; then the jungle wall rose, black, brown, dull red, and green and yellow. Here and there along the fence an occasional bone gleamed up out of the muck, some animal shot by a guard or killed by the voltage. Oddly enough, Herries irrelevantly remembered, such a corpse drew enough scavenging insects to clean it in a day, but it was usually ignored by the nasty man-sized hunter dinosaurs that still slunk and hopped and slithered in this neighborhood. Reptiles just did not go in for carrion. However, they followed the odor of blood . . .

"Farther east," said the helicopter pilot's radio voice. "There. Stop. Face the woods. He's coming out in a minute. Good luck,

Boss. Next time gimme some bombs and I'll handle the bugger myself."

"We haven't been granted any heavy weapons." Herries licked lips that seemed rough. His pulse was thick. No one had ever faced a tyrannosaur before.

The jeeps drew into line, and for a moment only their windshield wipers had motion. Then undergrowth crashed, and the monster was upon them.

It was indeed a tyrannosaur, thought Herries in a blurred way. A close relative, at least—he remembered vaguely that the *Tyrannosaurus rex*, belonged in the Cretaceous period, but never mind, this fellow was some kind of early cousin, unknown to science until this moment—It blundered ahead with the overweighted, underwitted stiffness which paleontologists had predicted, and which had led some of them to believe that it must have been a gigantic, carrion-eating hyena.* They forgot that, like the Cenozoic snake or crocodile, it was too dull to recognize dead meat as food; that the brontosaurs it preyed on were even more clumsy; and that sheer length of stride would carry it over the earth at a respectable rate.

Herries saw a blunt head three man-heights above ground, and a tail ending fifteen yards away. Scales of an unfairly beautiful steel gray shimmered in the rain, which made small waterfalls off flanks and wrinkled neck and tiny useless forepaws. Teeth clashed in a mindless reflex, the ponderous belly wagged with each step, and Herries felt the vibration of tons coming down claw-footed. The beast paid no attention to the jeeps, but moved jerkily toward the fence. Sheer weight would drive it through the mesh.

"Get in front of him, Sam!" yelled the engineer.

*Eds. note: For evidence relating to this possibility of undiscovered carnosaurs, see L. Sprague de Camp and Catherine Crook de Camp, *The Day of the Dinosaur* (Garden City, New York: Doubleday and Company, Inc., 1968), 132–133.

He gripped the machine gun. It snarled on his behalf, and a sleet of bullets stitched a bloody seam across the white stomach. The tyrannosaur halted, weaving its head about. It made a hollow, coughing roar. Greenstein edged the jeep closer.

The others attacked from the sides. Tracer streams hosed across alligator tail and bird legs. A launched grenade burst with a little puff on the right thigh. It opened a red ulcerlike crater. The tyrannosaur swung slowly about toward one of the cars.

That jeep dodged aside. "Get in on him!" shouted Herries. Greenstein shifted gears and darted through a fountain of mud. Herries stole a glance. The boy was grinning. Well, it would be something to tell the grandchildren, all right!

His jeep fled past the tyrannosaur, whipped about on two wheels, and crouched under a hammer of rain. The reptile halted. Herries cut loose with his machine gun. The monster standing there, swaying a little, roaring and bleeding, was not entirely real. This had happened a hundred million years ago. Rain struck the hot gun barrel and sizzled off.

"From the sides again," rapped Herries into his microphone. "Two and Three on his right, Four and Five on his left. Six, go behind him and lob a grenade at the base of his tail."

The tyrannosaur began another awkward about-face. The water in which it stood was tinged red.

"Aim for his eyes!" yelled Greenstein, and dashed recklessly toward the profile now presented him.

The grenade from behind exploded. With a sudden incredible speed, the tyrannosaur turned clear around. Herries had an instant's glimpse of the tail like a snake before him, then it struck.

He threw up an arm and felt glass bounce off it as the windshield shattered. The noise when metal gave way did not seem loud, but it went through his entire body. The jeep reeled on ahead. Instinct sent Herries to the floorboards. He felt a brutal impact as his car struck the dinosaur's left leg. It hooted far above him. He looked up and saw a foot with talons, raised and filling

162

the sky. It came down. The hood crumpled at his back and the engine was ripped from the frame.

Then the tyrannosaur had gone on. Herries crawled up into the bucket seat. It was canted at a lunatic angle. "Sam," he croaked. "Sam, Sam."

Greenstein's head was brains and splinters, with half the lower jaw on his lap and a burst-out eyeball staring up from the seat beside him.

Herries climbed erect. He saw his torn-off machine gun lying in the mud. A hundred yards off, at the jungle edge, the tyrannosaur fought the jeeps. It made clumsy rushes, which they sideswerved, and they spat at it and gnawed at it. Herries thought in a dull, remote fashion: *This can go on forever. A man is easy to kill, one swipe of a tail and all his songs are a red smear in the rain. But a reptile dies hard, being less alive to start with. I can't see an end to this fight.*

The Number Four jeep rushed in. A man sprang from it and it darted back in reverse from the monster's charge. The man— "Stop that, you idiot," whispered Herries into a dead microphone, "stop it, you fool"—plunged between the huge legs. He moved sluggishly enough with clay on his boots, but he was impossibly fleet and beautiful under that jerking bulk. Herries recognized Worth. He carried a grenade in his hand. He pulled the pin and dodged claws for a moment. The flabby, bleeding stomach made a roof over his head. Jaws searched blindly above him. He hurled the grenade and ran. It exploded against the tyrannosaur's belly. The monster screamed. One foot rose and came down. The talons merely clipped Worth, but he went spinning, fell in the gumbo ten feet away and tried weakly to rise but couldn't.

The tyrannosaur staggered in the other direction, spilling its entrails. Its screams took on a ghastly human note. Somebody stopped and picked up Worth. Somebody else came to Herries and gabbled at him. The tyrannosaur stumbled in yards of gut, fell slowly, and struggled, entangling itself.

Even so, it was hard to kill. The cars battered it for half an hour as it lay there, and it hissed at them and beat the ground with its tail. Herries was not sure it had died when he and his men finally left. But the insects had long been busy, and a few of the bones already stood forth clean white.

The phone jangled on Herries's desk. He picked it up. "Yeh?"

"Yamaguchi in sick bay," said the voice. "Thought you'd want to know about Worth."

"Well?"

"Broken lumbar vertebra. He'll live, possibly without permanent paralysis, but he'll have to go back for treatment."

"And be held incommunicado a year, till his contract's up. I wonder how much of a patriot he'll be by that time."

"What?"

"Nothing. Can it wait till tomorrow? Everything's so disorganized right now, I'd hate to activate the projector."

"Oh, yes. He's under sedation anyway." Yamaguchi paused. "And the man who died—"

"Sure. We'll ship him back too. The government will even supply a nice coffin. I'm sure his girlfriend will appreciate that."

"Do you feel well?" asked Yamaguchi sharply.

"They were going to be married," said Herries. He took another pull from the fifth of bourbon on his desk. It was getting almost too dark to see the bottle. "Since patriotism nowadays . . . in the future, I mean . . . in our own home, sweet home . . . since patriotism is necessarily equated with necrophilia, in that the loyal citizen is expected to rejoice every time his government comes up with a newer gadget for mass-producing corpses . . . I am sure the young lady will just love to have a pretty coffin. So much nicer than a mere husband. I'm sure the coffin will be chrome plated."

"Wait a minute—"

"With tail fins."

"Look here," said the doctor, "you're acting like a case of combat fatigue. I know you've had a shock today. Come see me and I'll give you a tranquilizer."

"Thanks," said Herries, "I've got one." He took another swig and forced briskness into his tone. "We'll send 'em back tomorrow morning, then. Now don't bother me. I'm composing a letter to explain to the great white father that this wouldn't have happened if we'd been allowed one stinking little atomic howitzer. Not that I expect to get any results. It's policy that we aren't allowed heavy weapons down here, and who ever heard of facts affecting a policy? Why, facts might be un-American."

He hung up, put the bottle on his lap and his feet on the desk, lit a cigarette and stared out the window. Darkness came sneaking across the compound like smoke. The rain had stopped for a while, and lamps and windows threw broken yellow gleams off puddles, but somehow the gathering night was so thick that each light seemed quite alone. There was no one else in the headquarters shack at this hour. Herries had not turned on his own lights.

To hell with it, he thought. *To hell with it.*

His cigarette tip waxed and waned as he puffed, like a small dying star. But the smoke didn't taste right when invisible. Or had he put away so many toasts to dead men that his tongue was numbed? He wasn't sure. It hardly mattered.

The phone shrilled again. He picked it up, fumble-handed in the murk. "Chief of operations," he said pleasantly. "To hell with you."

"What?" Symonds's voice rattled a bare bit. Then: "I have been trying to find you. What are you doing there this late?"

"I'll give you three guesses. Playing pinochle? No. Carrying on a sordid affair with a lady *Iguanodon*? No. None of your business? Right! *Give* that gentleman a box of see-gars."

"Look here, Mr. Herries," stated Symonds, "this is no time for

levity. I understand that Matthew Worth was seriously injured today. He was supposed to be on guard duty tonight—the secret
shipment. This has disarranged all my plans."

"Tsk-tsk-tsk. My nose bleeds for you."

"The schedule of duties must be revised. According to my
notes, Worth would have been on guard from midnight until four
A.M. Since I do not know precisely what other jobs his fellows are
assigned to, I cannot single any one of them out to replace him.
Will you do so? Select a man who can then sleep later tomorrow
morning?"

"Why?" asked Herries.

"Why? Because . . . because—"

"I know. Because Washington said so. Washington is afraid
some nasty dinosaur from what is going to be Russia will sneak in
and look at an unguarded crate and hurry home with the information. Sure, I'll do it. I just wanted to hear you sputter."

Herries thought he made out an indignant breath sucked past
an upper plate. "Very good," said the clerk. "Make the necessary
arrangements for tonight, and we will work out a new rotation of
watches tomorrow."

Herries put the receiver back.

The list of tight-lipped, tight-minded types was somewhere in
his desk, he knew vaguely. A copy, rather. Symonds had a copy,
and no doubt copies would be going to the Pentagon and the FBI
and the Transoco personnel office and—Well, look at the list,
compare it with the work schedule, see who wouldn't be doing
anything of critical importance tomorrow forenoon, and put him
on a bit of sentry-go. Simple.

Herries took another swig. He could resign, he thought. He
could back out of the whole fantastically stupid, fantastically mean-
ingless operation. He wasn't compelled to work. Of course, they
could hold him for the rest of his contract. It would be a lonesome
year. Or maybe not; maybe a few others would trickle in to keep

him company. To be sure, he'd then be under surveillance the rest of his life. But who wasn't, in a century divided between two garrisons?

The trouble was, he thought, there was nothing a man could do about the situation. You could become a peace-at-any-cost pacifist and thereby, effectively, league yourself with the enemy; and the enemy had carried out too many cold massacres for any halfway sane man to stomach. Or you could fight back (thus becoming more and more like what you fought) and hazard planetary incineration against the possibility of a tolerable outcome. It only took one to make a quarrel, and the enemy had long ago elected himself that one. Now, it was probably too late to patch up the quarrel. Even if important men on both sides wished for a disengagement, what could they do against their own fanatics, vested interests, terrified common people . . . against the whole momentum of history?

Hell take it, thought Herries, *we may be damned but why must we be fools into the bargain?*

Somewhere a brontosaur hooted, witlessly plowing through a night swamp.

Well, I'd better—No!

Herries stared at the end of his cigarette. It was almost scorching his fingers. At least, he thought, at least he could find out what he was supposed to condone. A look into those crates, which should have held the guns he had begged for, and perhaps some orchestral and scientific instruments . . . and instead held God knew what piece of Pentagonal-brained idiocy . . . a look would be more than a blow in Symonds's smug eye. It would be an assertion that he was Herries, a free man, whose existence had not yet been pointlessly spilled from a splintered skull. He, the individual, would know what the Team planned; and if it turned out to be a crime against reason, he could at the very least resign and sit out whatever followed.

Yes. By the dubious existence of divine mercy, yes.

*   *   *

Again a bit of rain, a small warm touch on his face, like tears. Herries splashed to the transceiver building and stood quietly in the sudden flashlight glare. At last, out of blackness, the sentry's voice came: "Oh, it's you, sir."

"Uh-huh. You know Worth got hurt today? I'm taking his watch."

"What? But I thought—"

"Policy," said Herries.

The incantation seemed to suffice. The other man shuffled forth and laid his rifle in the engineer's hands. "And here's the glim," he added. "Nobody came by while I was on duty."

"What would you have done if somebody'd tried to get in?"

"Why, stopped them, of course."

"And if they didn't stop?"

The dim face under the dripping hat turned puzzledly toward Herries. The engineer sighed. "I'm sorry, Thornton. It's too late to raise philosophical questions. Run along to bed."

He stood in front of the door, smoking a damp cigarette, and watched the man trudge away. All the lights were out now, except overhead lamps here and there. They were brilliant, but remote; he stood in a pit of shadow and wondered what the phase of the moon was and what kind of constellations the stars made nowadays.

He waited. There was time enough for his rebellion. Too much time, really. A man stood in rain, fog about his feet and a reptile smell in his nose, and he remembered anemones in springtime, strewn under trees still cold and leafless, with here and there a little snow between the roots. Or he remembered drinking beer in a New England country inn one fall day, when the door stood open to red sumac and yellow beech and a far blue wandering sky. Or he remembered a man snatched under black Jurassic quagmires, a man stepped into red ruin, a man sitting in a jeep and bleeding brains down onto the picture of the girl he had planned to marry. And then he started wondering what the point of it all was, and decided that it was either without any point whatsoever or else had the purpose of obliterating anemones and quiet country inns, and he was forced to dissent somehow.

When Thornton's wet footsteps were lost in the dark, Herries unlocked the shed door and went through. It was smotheringly hot inside. Sweat sprang forth under his raincoat as he closed the door again and turned on his flashlight. Rain tapped loudly on the roof. The crates loomed over him, box upon box, many of them large enough to hold a dinosaur. It had taken a lot of power to ship that tonnage into the past. No wonder taxes were high. And what might the stuff be? A herd of tanks, possibly . . . some knocked-down bombers . . . Lord knew what concept the men who lived in offices, insulated from the sky, would come up with. And Symonds had implied it was a mere beginning; more shipments would come when this had been stored out of the way, and more, and more.

Herries found a workbench and helped himself to tools. He would have to be careful; no sense in going to jail. He laid the flashlight on a handy barrel and stooped down by one of the crates. It was of strong wood, securely screwed together. But while that would make it harder to dismantle, it could be reassembled without leaving a trace. Maybe. Of course, it might be booby-trapped. No telling how far the religion of secrecy could lead the office men.

Oh, well, if I'm blown up I haven't lost much. Herries peeled off his slicker. His shirt clung to his body. He squatted and began to work.

It went slowly. After taking off several boards, he saw a regular manufacturer's crate, open-slatted. Something within was wrapped in burlap. A single curved metal surface projected slightly. What the devil? Herries got a crowbar and pried one slat loose. The nails shreiked. He stooped rigid for a while, listening, but heard only the rain, grown more noisy. He reached in and fumbled with the padding. . . . God, it was hot!

Only when he had freed the entire blade did he recognize what it was. And then his mind would not quite function; he gaped a long while before the word registered.

A plowshare.

"But they don't know what to do with the farm surpluses at home," he said aloud, inanely.

Like a stranger's, his hands began to repair what he had torn apart. He couldn't understand it. Nothing seemed altogether real any more. Of course, he thought in a dim way, theoretically anything might be in the other boxes, but he suspected more plows, tractors, discs, combines . . . why not bags of seeds? . . . *What were they planning to do?*

"Ah."

Herries whirled. The flashlight beam caught him like a spear.

He grabbed blindly for his rifle. A dry little voice behind the blaze said: "I would not recommend violence." Herries let the rifle fall. It thudded.

Symonds closed the shed door behind him and stepped forward in his mincing fashion, another shadow among bobbing misshapen shadows. He had simply flung on shirt and pants, but bands of night across them suggested necktie, vest, and coat.

"You see," he explained without passion, "all the guards were instructed *sub rosa* to notify me of anything unusual, even when it did not seem to warrant action on their part." He gestured at the crate. "Please continue reassembling it."

Herries crouched down again. Hollowness filled him; his sole wonder was how best to die. For if he were sent back to the twentieth century, surely, surely they would lock him up and lose the key, and the sunlessness of death was better than that. It was strange, he thought, how his fingers used the tools with untrembling skill.

Symonds stood behind him and held his light on the work. At last he asked primly, "Why did you break in like this?"

I could kill him, thought Herries. *He's unarmed. I could wring his scrawny neck between these two hands, and take a gun, and go into the swamp to live a few days . . . But it might be easier just to turn the rifle on myself.*

He sought words with care, for he must decide what to do, though it seemed remote and scarcely important. "That's not an easy question to answer," he said.

"The significant ones never are."

Astonished, Herries jerked a glance upward and back. (And was the more surprised that he could still know surprise.) But the little man's face was in darkness. Herries saw a blank glitter off the glasses.

He said, "Let's put it this way. There are limits even to the rights of self-defense. If a killer attacked me, I could fight back with anything I've got. But I wouldn't be justified in grabbing some passing child for a shield."

"So you wished to make sure that nothing you would consider illegitimate was in those boxes?" asked Symonds academically.

"I don't know. What is illegitimate, these days? I was . . . I was disgusted. I liked Greenstein, and he died because Washington had decided we couldn't have bombs or atomic shells. I didn't know how much more I could consent to. I had to find out."

"I see." The clerk nodded. "For your information, it is agricultural equipment. Later shipments will include industrial and scientific material, a large reserve of canned food, and as much of the world's culture as it proves possible to microfilm."

Herries stopped working, turned around and rose. His knees would not hold him. He leaned against the crate and it was a minute before he could get out: "Why?"

Symonds did not respond at once. He reached forth a precise hand and took up the flashlight Herries had left on the barrel.

Then he sat down there himself, with the two glowing tubes in his lap. The light from below ridged his face in shadows, and his glasses made blind circles. He said, as if ticking off the points of an agenda:

"You would have been informed of the facts in due course, when the next five hundred people arrive. Now you have brought on yourself the burden of knowing what you would otherwise have been ignorant of for months yet. I think it may safely be assumed that you will keep the secret and not be broken by it. At least, the assumption is necessary."

Herries heard his own breath harsh in his throat. "Who are these people?"

The papery half-seen countenance did not look at him, but into the pitlike reaches of the shed. "You have committed a common error," said Symonds, as if to a student. "You have assumed that because men are constrained by circumstances to act in certain ways, they must be evil or stupid. I assure you, Senator Wien and the few others responsible for this are neither. They must keep the truth even from those officials within the project whose reaction would be rage or panic instead of a sober attempt at salvage. Nor do they have unlimited powers. Therefore, rather than indulge in tantrums about the existing situation, they use it. The very compartmentalization of effort and knowledge enforced by Security helps conceal their purposes and mislead those who must be given some information."

Symonds paused. A slight frown crossed his forehead, and he tapped an impatient fingernail on a flashlight casing. "Do not misunderstand," he went on. "Senator Wien and his associates have not forgotten their oaths of office, nor are they trying to play God. Their primary effort goes, as it must, to a straightforward dealing with the problems of the twentieth century. It is not they who are withholding the one significant datum—a datum which, incidentally, any informed person could reason out for himself if he cared to. It is properly constituted authority, using powers legally granted to stamp certain reports top secret. Of course, the senator has used his considerable influence to bring about the present eventuality, but that is normal politics."

Herries growled: "Get to the point, damn you! What are you talking about?"

Symonds shook his thin gray head. "You are afraid to know, are you not?" he asked quietly.

"I—" Herries turned about, faced the crate and beat it with his fist. The parched voice in the night continued to punish him:

"You know that a time-projector can go into the future about a hundred years at a jump, but can only go pastward in jumps of approximately one hundred megayears. We all realize there is a way to explore certain sections of the historical past, in spite of this handicap, by making enough century hops forward before the one long hop backward. But can you tell me how to predict the historical future? Say, a century hence? Come, come, you are an intelligent man. Answer me."

"Yeah," said Herries. "I get the idea. Leave me alone."

"Team A, a group of well-equipped volunteers, went into the twenty-first century," pursued Symonds. "They recorded what they observed and placed the data in a chemically inert box within a large block of reinforced concrete erected at an agreed-on location: one which a previous expedition to circa one hundred million A.D. had confirmed would remain stable. I presume they also mixed radioactive materials of long half-life into the concrete, to aid in finding the site. Of course, the bracketing of time jumps is such that they cannot now get back to the twentieth century. But Team B went a full hundred-megayear jump into the future, excavated the data, and returned home."

Herries squared his body and faced back to the other man. He was drained, so weary that it was all he could do to keep on his feet. "What did they find?" he asked. There was no tone in his voice or in him.

"Actually, several expeditions have been made to the year one hundred million," said Symonds. "Energy requirements for a visit to two hundred million—A.D. or B.C.—were considered prohibitive. In one hundred million, life is re-evolving on Earth. However, as yet the plants have not liberated sufficient oxygen for the atmosphere to be breathable. You see, oxygen reacts with exposed rock, so that if no biological processes exist to replace it continuously— But you have a better technical education than I."

"Okay," said Herries, flat and hard. "Earth was sterile for a long time in the future. Including the twenty-first century?"

"Yes. The radioactivity had died down enough so that Team A reported no danger to itself, but some of the longer-lived isotopes were still measurably present. By making differential measurements of abundance, Team A was able to estimate rather closely when the bombs had gone off."

"And?"

"Approximately one year from the twentieth-century base date we are presently using."

"One year . . . from now." Herries stared upward. Blackness met him. He heard the Jurassic rain on the iron roof, like drums.

"Possibly less," Symonds told him. "There is a factor of uncertainty. This project must be completed well within the safety margin before the war comes."

"The war comes," Herries repeated. "Does it have to come? Fixed time line or not, does it have to come? Couldn't the enemy leaders be shown the facts . . . couldn't our side, even, capitulate—"

"Every effort is being made," said Symonds like a machine. "Quite apart from the theory of rigid time, it seems unlikely that they will succeed. The situation is too unstable. One man, losing his head and pressing the wrong button, can write the end; and there are so many buttons. The very revelation of the truth, to a few chosen leaders or to the world public, would make some of them panicky. Who can tell what a man in panic will do? That is what I meant when I said that Senator Wien and his coworkers have not forgotten their oaths of office. They have no thought of

174

taking refuge, they know they are old men. To the end, they will try to save the twentieth century. But they do not expect it; so they are also trying to save the human race."

Herries pushed up from the crate he had been leaning against. "Those five hundred who're coming," he whispered. "Women?"

"Yes. If time remains to rescue a few more, after the ones you are preparing for have gone through, it will be done. But there will be at least a thousand young, healthy adults here, in the Jurassic. You face a difficult time, when the truth must be told them; you can see why the secret must be kept until then. It is quite possible that someone here will lose his head. That is why no heavy weapons have been sent: a single deranged person must not be able to destroy everyone. But you will recover. You must."

Herries jerked the door open and stared out into the roaring darkness. "No traces of us . . . in the future," he said, hearing his voice high and hurt like a child's.

"How much trace do you expect would remain after geological eras?" answered Symonds. He was still the reproving schoolmaster; but he sat on the barrel and faced the great moving shadows in a corner. "It is assumed that you will remain here for several generations, until your numbers and resources have been expanded sufficiently. The Team A I spoke of will join you a century hence. It is also, I might add, composed of young men and women in equal numbers. But this planet in this age is not a good home. We trust that your descendants will perfect the spaceships we know to be possible, and take possession of the stars instead."

Herries leaned in the doorway, sagging with tiredness and the monstrous duty to survive. A gust of wind threw rain into his eyes. He heard dragons calling in the night.

"And you?" he said, for no good reason.

"I shall convey any final messages you may wish to send home," said the dried-out voice.

Neat little footsteps clicked across the floor until the clerk paused beside the engineer. Silence followed, except for the rain.

175

"Surely I will deserve to go home," said Symonds.

And the breath whistled inward between teeth which had snapped together. He raised his hands, claw-fingered, and screamed aloud: "You can let me go home *then*!"

He began running toward the supervisors' barge. The sound of him was soon lost. Herries stood for a time yet in the door.

JUST LIKE OLD TIMES

ROBERT J. SAWYER

The transference went smoothly, like a scalpel slicing into skin.

Cohen was simultaneously excited and disappointed. He was thrilled to be here—perhaps the judge was right, perhaps this was where he really belonged. But the gleaming edge was taken off that thrill because it wasn't accompanied by the usual physiological signs of excitement: no sweaty palms, no racing heart, no rapid breathing. Oh, there was a heartbeat, to be sure, thundering in the background, but it wasn't Cohen's.

It was the dinosaur's.

Everything was the dinosaur's: Cohen saw the world now through tyrannosaur eyes.

The colors seemed all wrong. Surely plant leaves must be the same chlorophyll green here in the Mesozoic, but the dinosaur saw them as navy blue. The sky was lavender; the dirt underfoot ash gray.

Old bones had different cones, thought Cohen. Well, he could get used to it. After all, he had no choice. He would finish his life as an observer inside this tyrannosaur's mind. He'd see what the beast saw, hear what it heard, feel what it felt. He wouldn't be able to control its movements, they had said, but he would be able to experience every sensation.

The rex was marching forward.

Cohen hoped blood would still look red.

It wouldn't be the same if it wasn't red.

"And what, Ms. Cohen, did your husband say before he left your house on the night in question?"

"He said he was going out to hunt humans. But I thought he was making a joke."

"No interpretations, please, Ms. Cohen. Just repeat for the court as precisely as you remember it, exactly what your husband said."

"He said, 'I'm going out to hunt humans.'"

"Thank you, Ms. Cohen. That concludes the Crown's case, my lady."

The needlepoint on the wall of the Honorable Madam Justice Amanda Hoskins's chambers had been made for her by her husband. It was one of her favorite verses from *The Mikado*, and as she was preparing sentencing she would often look up and reread the words:

> *My object all sublime*
> *I shall achieve in time—*
> *To let the punishment fit the crime—*
> *The punishment fit the crime.*

This was a difficult case, a horrible case. Judge Hoskins continued to think.

It wasn't just colors that were wrong. The view from inside the tyrannosaur's skull was different in other ways, too.

The tyrannosaur had only partial stereoscopic vision. There was an area in the center of Cohen's field of view that showed true depth perception. But because the beast was somewhat walleyed, it had a much wider panorama than normal for a human, a kind of saurian Cinemascope covering 270 degrees.

The wide-angle view panned back and forth as the tyrannosaur scanned along the horizon.

Scanning for prey.

Scanning for something to kill.

The Calgary Herald, Thursday, October 16, 2042, hard copy edition: "Serial killer Rudolph Cohen, 43, was sentenced to death yesterday.

"Formerly a prominent member of the Alberta College of Physicians and Surgeons, Dr. Cohen was convicted in August of thirty-seven counts of first-degree murder.

"In chilling testimony, Cohen had admitted, without any signs of remorse, to having terrorized each of his victims for hours before slitting their throats with surgical implements.

"This is the first time in eighty years that the death penalty has been ordered in this country.

"In passing sentence, Madam Justice Amanda Hoskins observed that Cohen was 'the most cold-blooded and brutal killer to have stalked Canada's prairies since *Tyrannosaurus rex* . . . ' "

From behind a stand of dawn redwoods about ten meters away, a second tyrannosaur appeared. Cohen suspected tyrannosaurs might be fiercely territorial, since each animal would require huge amounts of meat. He wondered if the beast he was in would attack the other individual.

His dinosaur tilted its head to look at the second rex, which was standing in profile. But as it did so, almost all of the dino's mental picture dissolved into a white void, as if when concentrating on details the beast's tiny brain simply lost track of the big picture.

At first Cohen thought his rex was looking at the other dinosaur's head, but soon the top of the other's skull, the tip of its muzzle and the back of its powerful neck faded away into snowy nothingness. All that was left was a picture of the throat. Good, thought Cohen. One shearing bite there could kill the animal.

The skin of the other's throat appeared gray-green and the throat itself was smooth. Maddeningly, Cohen's rex did not attack; rather, it simply swiveled its head and looked out at the horizon again.

In a flash of insight, Cohen realized what had happened. Other kids in his neighborhood had had pet dogs or cats. He'd had lizards and snakes—cold-blooded carnivores, a fact to which expert psychological witnesses had attached great weight. Some kinds of male lizards had dewlap sacs hanging from their necks. The rex he was in—a male, the Tyrrell paleontologists had believed—had looked at this other one and seen that she was smooth-throated and therefore a female. Something to be mated with, perhaps, rather than to attack.

Perhaps they would mate soon. Cohen had never orgasmed except during the act of killing. He wondered what it would feel like.

"We spent a billion dollars developing time travel, and now you tell me the system is useless?"

"Well—"

"That is what you're saying, isn't it, Professor? That chrono-transference has no practical applications?"

"Not exactly, Minister. The system *does* work. We can project a human being's consciousness back in time, superimposing his or her mind over that of someone who lived in the past."

"With no way to sever the link. *Wonderful.*"

"That's not true. The link severs automatically."

"Right. When the historical person you've transferred consciousness into dies, the link is broken."

"Precisely."

"And then the person from our time whose consciousness you've transferred back dies as well."

"I admit that's an unfortunate consequence of linking two brains so closely."

"So I'm right! This whole damn chronotransference thing is useless."

"Oh, not at all, Minister. In fact, I think I've got the perfect application for it."

The rex marched along. Although Cohen's attention had first been arrested by the beast's vision, he slowly became aware of its other senses, too. He could hear the sounds of the rex's footfalls, of twigs and vegetation being crushed, of birds or pterosaurs singing, and, underneath it all, the relentless drone of insects. Still, all the sounds were dull and low; the rex's simple ears were incapable of picking up high-pitched noises, and what sounds they did detect were discerned without richness. Cohen knew the late Cretaceous must have been a symphony of varied tones, but it was as if he was listening to it through earmuffs.

The rex continued along, still searching. Cohen became aware of several more impressions of the world both inside and out, including hot afternoon sun beating down on him and a hungry gnawing in the beast's belly.

Food.

It was the closest thing to a coherent thought that he'd yet detected from the animal, a mental picture of bolts of meat going down its gullet.

Food.

* * *

The Social Services Preservation Act of 2022: Canada is built upon the principle of the Social Safety Net, a series of entitlements and programs designed to ensure a high standard of living for every citizen. However, ever-increasing life expectancies coupled with constant lowering of the mandatory retirement age have placed an untenable burden on our social-welfare system and, in particular, its cornerstone program of universal health care. With most taxpayers ceasing to work at the age of 45, and with average Canadians living to be 94 (males) or 97 (females), the system is in danger of complete collapse. Accordingly, all social programs will henceforth be available only to those below the age of 60, with one exception: all Canadians, regardless of age, may take advantage, at no charge to themselves, of government-sponsored euthanasia through chronotransference.

There! Up ahead! Something moving! Big, whatever it was: an indistinct outline only intermittently visible behind a small knot of fir trees.

A quadruped of some sort, its back to him/it/them.

Ah, there. Turning now. Peripheral vision dissolving into albino nothingness as the rex concentrated on the head.

Three horns.

Triceratops.

Glorious! Cohen had spent hours as a boy poring over books about dinosaurs, looking for scenes of carnage. No battles were better than those in which Tyrannosaurus rex squared off against Triceratops, a four-footed Mesozoic tank with a trio of horns projecting from its face and a shield of bone rising from the back of its skull to protect the neck.

And yet, the rex marched on.

No, thought Cohen. Turn, damn you! Turn and attack!

*　　*　　*

Cohen remembered when it had all begun, that fateful day so many years ago, so many years from now. It should have been a routine operation. The patient had supposedly been prepped properly. Cohen brought his scalpel down toward the abdomen, then, with a steady hand, sliced into the skin. The patient gasped. It had been a *wonderful* sound, a beautiful sound.

Not enough gas. The anesthetist hurried to make an adjustment. Cohen knew he had to hear that sound again. He had to.

The tyrannosaur continued forward. Cohen couldn't see its legs, but he could feel them moving. Left, right, up, down.

Attack, you bastard!

Left.

Attack!

Right.

Go after it!

Up.

Go after the triceratops.

Dow—

The beast hesitated, its left leg still in the air, balancing briefly on one foot.

Attack!

Attack!

And then, at last, the rex changed course. The triceratops appeared in the three-dimensional central part of the tyrannosaur's field of view, like a target at the end of a gun sight.

"Welcome to the Chronotransference Institute. If I can just see your government benefits card, please? Yup, there's always a last time for everything, heh heh. Now, I'm sure you want an exciting death. The problem is finding somebody interesting who hasn't been used yet. See, we can only ever superimpose one mind onto a given historical personage. All the really obvious ones have been done already, I'm afraid. We still get about a dozen calls a week asking for Jack Kennedy, but he was one of the first to go, so to speak. If I may make a suggestion, though, we've got thousands of Roman legion officers cataloged. Those tend to be very satisfying deaths. How about a nice something from the Gallic Wars?"

The triceratops looked up, its giant head lifting from the wide flat gunnera leaves it had been chewing on. Now that the rex had focused on the plant-eater, it seemed to commit itself.

The tyrannosaur charged.

The hornface was sideways to the rex. It began to turn, to bring its armored head to bear.

The horizon bounced wildly as the rex ran. Cohen could hear the thing's heart thundering loudly, rapidly, a barrage of muscular gunfire.

The triceratops, still completing its turn, opened its parrotlike beak, but no sound came out.

Giant strides closed the distance between the two animals. Cohen felt the rex's jaws opening wide, wider still, mandibles popping from their sockets.

The jaws slammed shut on the hornface's back, over the shoulders. Cohen saw two of the rex's own teeth fly into view, knocked out by the impact.

The taste of hot blood, surging out of the wound . . .

The rex pulled back for another bite.

The triceratops finally got its head swung around. It surged forward, the long spear over its left eye piercing the rex's leg . . .

Pain. Exquisite, beautiful pain.

The rex roared. Cohen heard it twice, once reverberating within the animal's own skull, a second time echoing back from distant hills. A flock of silver-furred pterosaurs took to the air. Cohen saw them fade from view as the dinosaur's simple mind shut them out of the display. Irrelevant distractions.

The triceratops pulled back, the horn withdrawing from the rex's flesh.

Blood, Cohen was delighted to see, still looked red.

"If Judge Hoskins had ordered the electric chair," said Axworthy, Cohen's lawyer, "we could have fought that on Charter grounds. Cruel and unusual punishment, and all that. But she's authorized full access to the chronotransference euthanasia program for you." Axworthy paused. "She said, bluntly, that she simply wants you dead."

"How thoughtful of her," said Cohen.

Axworthy ignored that. "I'm sure I can get you anything you want," he said. "Who would you like to be transferred into?"

"Not who," said Cohen. "What."

"I beg your pardon?"

"That damned judge said I was the most cold-blooded killer to stalk the Alberta landscape since *Tyrannosaurus rex.*" Cohen shook his head. "The idiot. Doesn't she know dinosaurs were warm-blooded? Anyway, that's what I want. I want to be transferred into a *T. rex.*"

"You're kidding."

"Kidding is not my forte, John. *Killing* is. I want to know which was better at it, me or the rex."

"I don't even know if they can do that kind of thing," said Axworthy.

"Find out, damn you. What the hell am I paying you for?"

The rex danced to the side, moving with surprising agility for a creature of its bulk, and once again it brought its terrible jaws down on the ceratopsian's shoulder. The plant-eater was hemorrhaging at an incredible rate, as though a thousand sacrifices had been performed on the altar of its back.

The triceratops tried to lunge forward, but it was weakening quickly. The tyrannosaur, crafty in its own way despite its trifling intellect, simply retreated a dozen giant paces. The hornface took one tentative step toward it, and then another, and, with great and ponderous effort, one more. But then the dinosaurian tank teetered and, eyelids slowly closing, collapsed on its side. Cohen was briefly startled, then thrilled, to hear it fall to the ground with a *splash*—he hadn't realized just how much blood had poured out of the great rent the rex had made in the beast's back.

The tyrannosaur moved in, lifting its left leg up and then smashing it down on the triceratops' belly, the three sharp toe claws tearing open the thing's abdomen, entrails spilling out into the harsh sunlight. Cohen thought the rex would let out a victorious roar, but it didn't. It simply dipped its muzzle into the body cavity, and methodically began yanking out chunks of flesh.

Cohen was disappointed. The battle of the dinosaurs had been fun, the killing had been well engineered, and there had certainly been enough blood, but there was no *terror*. No sense that the triceratops had been quivering with fear, no begging for mercy. No feeling of power, of control. Just dumb, mindless brutes moving in ways preprogrammed by their genes.

It wasn't enough. Not nearly enough.

Judge Hoskins looked across the desk in her chambers at the lawyer.

"A tyrannosaurus, Mr. Axworthy? I was speaking figuratively."

"I understand that, my lady, but it was an appropriate observation, don't you think? I've contacted the Chronotransference people, who say they can do it, if they have a rex specimen to work from. They have to back-propagate from actual physical material in order to get a temporal fix."

Judge Hoskins was as unimpressed by scientific babble as she was by legal jargon. "Make your point, Mr. Axworthy."

"I called the Royal Tyrrell Museum of Paleontology in Drumheller and asked them about the tyrannosaurus fossils available worldwide. Turns out there's only a handful of complete skeletons, but they were able to provide me with an annotated list, giving as much information as they could about the individual probable causes of death." He slid a thin plastic printout sheet across the judge's wide desk.

"Leave this with me, counsel. I'll get back to you."

Axworthy left, and Hoskins scanned the brief list. She then leaned back in her leather chair and began to read the needlepoint on her wall for the thousandth time:

My object all sublime
I shall achieve in time—

She read that line again, her lips moving slightly as she subvocalized the words: "I shall achieve *in time . . .*"

The judge turned back to the list of tyrannosaur finds. Ah, that one. Yes, that would be perfect. She pushed a button on her phone. "David, see if you can find Mr. Axworthy for me."

There had been a very unusual aspect to the triceratops kill—an aspect that intrigued Cohen. Chronotransference had been performed countless times; it was one of the most popular forms of euthanasia. Sometimes the transferee's original body would give an ongoing commentary about what was going on, as if talking during sleep. It was clear from what they said that transferees couldn't exert any control over the bodies they were transferred into.

Indeed, the physicists had claimed any control was impossible. Chronotransference worked precisely because the transferee could exert no influence, and therefore was simply observing things that had already been observed. Since no new observations were being made, no quantum-mechanical distortions occurred. After all, said the physicists, if one could exert control, one could change the past. And that was impossible.

And yet, when Cohen had willed the rex to alter its course, it eventually had done so.

Could it be that the rex had so little brains that Cohen's thoughts *could* control the beast?

Madness. The ramifications were incredible.

Still . . .

He had to know if it was true. The rex was torpid, flopped on its belly, gorged on ceratopsian meat. It seemed prepared to lie here for a long time to come, enjoying the early evening breeze.

Get up, thought Cohen. *Get up, damn you*!

Nothing. No response.

Get up!

The rex's lower jaw was resting on the ground. Its upper jaw was lifted high, its mouth wide open. Tiny pterosaurs were flitting in and out of the open maw, their long needlelike beaks apparently yanking gobbets of hornface flesh from between the rex's curved teeth.

Get up, thought Cohen again. *Get up!*

The rex stirred.

Up!

The tyrannosaur used its tiny forelimbs to keep its torso from sliding forward as it pushed with its powerful legs until it was standing.

Forward, thought Cohen. *Forward*!

The beast's body felt different. Its belly was full to bursting.

Forward!

With ponderous steps, the rex began to march.

It was wonderful. To be in control again! Cohen felt the old thrill of the hunt.

And he knew exactly what he was looking for.

*   *   *

"Judge Hoskins says okay," said Axworthy. "She's authorized for you to be transferred into that new T. rex they've got right here in Alberta at the Tyrrell. It's a young adult, they say. Judging by the way the skeleton was found, the rex died falling, probably into a fissure. Both legs and the back were broken, but the skeleton remained almost completely articulated, suggesting that scavengers couldn't get at it. Unfortunately, the chronotransference people say that back-propagating that far into the past they can only plug you in a few hours before the accident occurred. But you'll get your wish: you're going to die as a tyrannosaur. Oh, and here are the books you asked for: a complete library on Cretaceous flora and fauna. You should have time to get through it all; the chronotransference people will need a couple of weeks to set up."

As the prehistoric evening turned to night, Cohen found what he had been looking for, cowering in some underbrush: large brown eyes, long, drawn-out face, and a lithe body covered in fur that, to the tyrannosaur's eyes, looked blue-brown.

A mammal. But not just any mammal. *Purgatorius*, the very first primate, known from Montana and Alberta from right at the end of the Cretaceous. A little guy, only about ten centimeters long, excluding its ratlike tail. Rare creatures, these days. Only a precious few.

The little furball could run quickly for its size, but a single step by the tyrannosaur equaled more than a hundred of the mammal's. There was no way it could escape.

The rex leaned in close, and Cohen saw the furball's face, the nearest thing there would be to a human face for another sixty million years. The animal's eyes went wide in terror.

Naked, raw fear.

Mammalian fear.
Cohen saw the creature scream.
Heard it scream.
It was beautiful.

The rex moved its gaping jaws in toward the little mammal, drawing in breath with such force that it sucked the creature into its maw. Normally the rex would swallow its meals whole, but Cohen prevented the beast from doing that. Instead, he simply had it stand still, with the little primate running around, terrified, inside the great cavern of the dinosaur's mouth, banging into the giant teeth and great fleshy walls, and skittering over the massive, dry tongue.

Cohen savored the terrified squealing. He wallowed in the sensation of the animal, mad with fear, moving inside that living prison.

And at last, with a great, glorious release, Cohen put the animal out of its misery, allowing the rex to swallow it, the furball tickling as it slid down the giant's throat.

It was just like old times.

Just like hunting humans.

And then a wonderful thought occurred to Cohen. Why, if he killed enough of these little screaming balls of fur, they wouldn't have any descendants. There wouldn't ever be any *Homo sapiens.* In a very real sense, Cohen realized he *was* hunting humans— every single human being who would ever exist.

Of course, a few hours wouldn't be enough time to kill many of them. Judge Hoskins no doubt thought it was wonderfully poetic justice, or she wouldn't have allowed the transfer: sending him back to fall into the pit, damned.

Stupid judge. Why, now that he could control the beast, there was no way he was going to let it die young. He'd just—

There it was. The fissure, a long gash in the earth, with a crumbling edge. Damn, it *was* hard to see. The shadows cast by neighboring trees made a confusing gridwork on the ground that obscured the ragged opening. No wonder the dull-witted rex had missed seeing it until it was too late.

But not this time.

Turn left, thought Cohen.

Left.

His rex obeyed.

He'd avoid this particular area in future, just to be on the safe side. Besides, there was plenty of territory to cover. Fortunately, this was a young rex—a juvenile. There would be decades in which to continue his very special hunt. Cohen was sure that Axworthy knew his stuff: once it became apparent that the link had lasted longer than a few hours, he'd keep any attempt to pull the plug tied up in the courts for years.

Cohen felt the old pressure building in himself, and in the rex. The tyrannosaur marched on.

This was *better* than old times, he thought. Much better.

Hunting all of humanity.

The release would be *wonderful.*

He watched intently for any sign of movement in the underbrush.

THE LAST THUNDER HORSE WEST OF THE MISSISSIPPI

S. N. DYER

The evening-suited men moved into the lounge. "I have not seen any recent publications by you on fossils, Professor Leidy," a German-accented voice said. "Will you be on another collection trip to the West this year?"

"Hah!" another man commented. "Leidy's given up paleontology and gone back to microscopic studies—they're safer."

"Safer? Of course. You refer to your hostile savages . . ."

"No, not the Indians. I mean our battling paleontologists."

The German gazed in bewilderment at the smiling company.

A distinguished-looking older man said, "Please, gentlemen. I don't wish to cite personalities . . ."

"Come now, Leidy, we all know who has driven you from your field. The feuding fossil hunters. Marsh with his uncle Peabody's fortune—he would outbid you for your grandmother's skull."

"Have you heard the joke? Marsh is unmarried because he wouldn't be happy with one wife. He would want a collection."

The assemblage laughed. The angry scientist continued, "And

then there's Cope. Absolutely brilliant. He can stare over your shoulder at a bone, memorize its salient features, then rush into publication a description of *your* fossil."

Leidy smiled ruefully at the German. "Now you've heard two good reasons why I have abandoned vertebrate paleontology."

More scientists were entering the lounge as the Academy meeting concluded. Leidy withdrew an envelope from his inner coat pocket.

"Formerly every fossil discovered in the States was sent to me. Now people send to Marsh and Cope and let them bid. But I still receive the occasional letter." He read, " 'Dear Professor Leidy.' The spelling, gentlemen, is unique. My rendition cannot do it justice—'Dear Professor Leidy. I hear as you like strange animals. Well Johnny and Dave kilt all the big ones but me and Sairie caught a baby down the gulch out Watson Crick. Doc Watson says it looks to be a vertebrate'—I believe he intends vertebrate; the spelling is so creative I can't really be sure—'but he never seed a lizard tall as a horse before and said we should write you. If you want to see it you come to Coyote near Zak City and ask. Anyone knows me.' It's signed 'Charley Doppler.' ' "

The room had fallen silent while Leidy read the strange missive; a humming began as conversations resumed.

"Doppler. Surely no relation to Christian Doppler of Prague?"

"Probably not," a balding man said. "Have you heard how his formulae may be used to compute the distance to various stars by . . ."

Leidy returned the letter to his pocket.

Two men on opposite sides of the lounge separately checked their pocket watches, bid their companions hasty farewells, and rushed out to locate train schedules.

That same evening a less elegant social occasion took place some fifteen hundred miles to the west, at the Dopplers' ranch on the banks of the Foulwater. Dr. Watson, the local homeopath, had just completed his regular weekly examination of Ma Doppler.

"She gonna make it?" her oldest son asked solicitously. Johnny Doppler deserved his place on the wall of every frontier jail and post office, but he was second to none in filial devotion.

"Ma's all right, ain't she, Doc?" Young Charley's question tagged along behind his elder's. Both brothers had black hair and white faces which never tanned, leading to Johnny's prison-pallor and Charley's burnt redness.

"Hmmn," the doctor said, seating himself at the whitewashed table and pouring a mixed drink—half whiskey and half *Essence of Frankincense*. He sipped, then added another jolt of the patent medicine. "Well, I tell you, boys, I think she's got a number of years left amongst the earthly host. You know widows, they act touchy, that's all."

"Sure, look at Dave's wife."

"She's not technically a widow, Charley. Red-Eye Dave is still alive, you see, even if he does tend to avoid Kate's company." The doctor sloshed some *Essence of Frankincense* onto the table and watched the whitewash dissolve. "How is Dave?"

"Ain't here."

"Oh? Your mother tends to worry about you boys when you're away."

Johnny nodded slowly, eyes shifting back and forth as if he expected his doctor or his brother to draw on him. "Ma always had a fit when me and Dave'd go back to the war."

Doc shuddered. He'd served with Johnny Doppler and Red-Eye Dave Savage a good ten, twelve years earlier. Johnny had been the Missouri irregulars' most feared sniper. His cousin, though, had never been sober enough for the precision work of sniping. Dave's specialty had been demolitions, his enthusiasm for blowing things up helped by his willingness to work with short fuses.

War memories always made Doc uncomfortable. He rose, saying, "Thanks for the drink, friends. I'll send some more medicine over tomorrow; meantime, make sure she gets her *Essence of Frankincense* regular." He fingered the label with the smiling Indian Princess and the small type tributes, one from Mrs. Joseph Doppler herself. Then he left.

Charley called after him, "Say, Doc, I'll get the medicine. I'll be training my big lizard again tomorrow."

Johnny scowled. "You're a fool wastin' time over there, kid."

"I'll learn it to pull the plow, you'll see," Charley whined.

His brother sighed. Charley wanted to be a farmer. Charley could be very trying sometimes.

The tracks into Zak City were lined with the bleached bones of buffalo shot from train windows by bored passengers. Not a single living buffalo had been seen from the time the train left civilization to the time it pulled into Zak City and disgorged its passengers.

Two of those passengers caught sight of each other at opposite ends of the boardwalk station, and scowled. They looked very different from the evening-suited images they had presented at the scientific meeting the previous week. Both were five feet, ten inches, the pudgy man by virtue of the heels on his high hunting boots (guaranteed rattlesnake proof). Above the expensive footwear he presented an intentionally disreputable appearance, with slouch hat, corduroy suit, and a shooting jacket with the top button fastened and the sides flared out to either side of his substantial belly. A well-thumbed copy of *The Prairie Traveller* peeked out of one capacious pocket. He carried a pair of navy revolvers, a Sharps .50 caliber cavalry carbine, and a large hunting knife, and his small wide-set blue eyes were narrowed in advertisement of his toughness. He had a full reddish beard, a half-bald head, and a face with no apparent bone structure.

The other man presented a less western, less martial picture. He was a decade younger, in his early thirties, and unarmed. His conservative suit conveyed the image of a foreign scholar. He had an oval face, trimmed beard, and thick brown hair.

Each man stared at the other, distance diluting their malign expressions, then picked up their respective carpetbags and stalked off in different directions.

The pudgy man found his way to a busy saloon. The customers had spilled out into the street and were engaged in conversation with some women in the second story of the building opposite. The man stopped before a small cavalry private.

"I am Professor O. C. Marsh of Yale University, authorized by the Secretary of the Army to seek supplies and men from any government outpost." He patted the pocket in which he carried letters of introduction to the military, railroad officials, politicians, and sundry other frontier luminaries. "How do I locate the army?"

"Enlist."

"Where is your commanding officer?"

"Don't know. I deserted."

"I wish to hire a guide to take me to Coyote." He pronounced it carefully with two syllables, to show he was not a greenhorn.

The raucous crowd fell silent. Finally someone said, "You crazy? Coyote? There's easier ways underground."

"I need a guide to Coyote, where I must meet a Mr. Doppler."

The silence became a horrified mutter, and the crowd melted away until only Marsh and one other stood there. The stranger was over six feet tall, redolent of whiskey, and dressed like a Texas ranger—high-heeled boots with huge spurs, bright red sash with a brace of pistols, and broad-brimmed hat. He said, "*Who* yuh wanta meet?"

"A Mister Charles Doppler."

"Charley?" He shook his head incredulously. "Charley? He ain't much."

"You are acquainted with him?"

"Acquai—acquait—he's muh cousin! I stole Charley his first long pants."

"Will you take me to him?" Marsh held up a shiny dollar. "It is worth $3 per day. Mister . . . ?"

"Savage. Red-Eye Dave Savage. Maybe you seen a novel about me? You can call me Red-Eye." He grabbed at the coin.

"Fine, Red-Eye. Now let us see to procuring supplies." They began walking down the street, Marsh saying, "You know, I am a personal friend of Buffalo Bill Cody . . ."

Heading north of the tracks, the neatly dressed gentleman was presented with a vista of well-tended plank houses and empty streets. Two saddled horses nibbled the grass growing beside a church. A buckskinned, long-haired scout with hat over face leaned against a post. An Indian woman sat beside the scout, nursing a chubby baby which rather resembled a beardless President Grant. The man paused to admire the anthropologically interesting scene.

Without looking up, the squaw asked, "May I be of service?"

He jerked back in surprise. "Uh, yes. Do you know the way to Coyote?" His pronunciation had the three syllables used in the Southwest and Pacific Coast.

"Certainly I do."

He sighed. "What *is* the way to Coyote?"

The woman smiled sweetly. "The way *out* of Coyote is in a coffin. Horse in, hearse out."

He said, "Madam, a scientist is prepared to face the dangers of the unknown in order to acquire knowledge."

The scout stirred, and muttered a question in Lakota. The Indian woman listened, then asked, "Do you mean that you are a Natural Philosopher?"

"I have been elected fellow of the Academy of Natural Sciences of Philadelphia, the American Philosophical Society, the National Academy of Sciences, and the American Association for the Advancement of Science. Edward Drinker Cope, madam, at your

197

service." He bowed, freezing the moment in his mind so that he could send a humorous description of it to his daughter.

The scout again spoke Lakota into the hat. The woman translated. "Are you familiar with Man Who Picks Up Bones Running?"

"Frederick Hayden? I was on his survey."

More mumbling.

"Do you know Perfesser Leidy?"

"I studied under him. In fact, I am here because of a letter he received."

The scout sprung upright, revealing a tanned, scarred face with delicate female features. "I done scouted for Man Who Picks Up Bones Running in '68." She stuck out a hand for a vigorous shaking.

Cope said delightedly, "Then you must be Chokecherry Sairie, the Wilderness Philosopher." He had seen dime-novels devoted to her adventures. The petite, corseted women of the illustrations bore not the slightest resemblance to their inspiration.

The Indian also introduced herself. "I'm Jessie Crooked-Knife. My husband is a perfesser also—Perfesser Lancelot D'arcy Daid, manufacturer and proprietor of *Essence of Frankincense*, the Old Indian Princess' Authentic Miracle Cure for Whatever Ails You and Female Troubles As Well. I'm the Indian Princess."

Cope bowed once again.

Sairie was twisting the fringe on her left sleeve. "Y'come to see Charley's lizard? Let's go." She spoke rapidly to Jessie in Lakota, then lashed Cope's carpetbag behind the saddle of a Roman-nosed bay mare.

Jessie said, "Sairie was headed south to visit Frisco Flush and the Goodenough Kid, but she has changed her plans. She has always enjoyed scouting for scientific parties. You are borrowing my horse Boadicea; watch out, she puffs when you girth her. Sairie doesn't speak English very well; she was raised by wolves, you know."

On that surprising note Sairie leapt onto her small paint gelding, gestured for Cope to swing aboard the mare, and trotted off. Jessie Crooked-Knife switched her baby to her right arm, and waved goodbye.

As they trotted along the high prairie, Cope acquired the story of the giant lizard, monosyllable by monosyllable. The Doppler Gang had found a herd of the lizards, or "thunder horses" as Sairie called them, grazing peacefully in a deserted area near Foulwater. Johnny and Dave had left all but one for the buzzards.

Sairie tried to describe the beasts. "Big feet. Eyes like bird. Hips sort of like bird, but got four legs." She paused, frustrated, and waved her arms about.

"I think I understand," Cope said encouragingly. He didn't.

"Real big. Teeth like horse, not wolf."

"An herbivore—vegetarian—grass-eater?"

"Yeah. Like big bones all over, but smaller."

"Big . . . ?"

She held her arm up a good eight feet from the ground. "Bones, real big. All over. Get in way."

Cope's eyes lit up with something between avarice and glee.

They camped at dusk and ate a meal of pemmican. Cope stared at the spectacular sunset and began to talk of his rival.

"Marsh is curator of the museum at Yale only because his uncle built it and pays his allowance. The man won't stir into Indian territory without an army escort."

"You?"

"Yes, I have done so. I'm a Quaker; I don't bear arms. Once I pacified a war party with my false teeth . . ."

Sairie sat up happily. "Magic Tooth!"

Content that his reputation had preceded him, Cope continued. "Marsh purchases so many fossils that some have never been unpacked. He does not understand anatomy—an army of myrmidons studies his specimens and writes his papers. They are negligently paid and forbidden to carry on their own researches . . ." He did not include the fact that he had attempted to stir them to revolt.

"Marsh doesn't read the journals, leading him to duplicate others' work. Yet, with all this, they call him a scientist! In '72 Mudge intended to send me the 'bird with teeth' which has made Marsh's reputation. Marsh heard of the fossils and convinced Mudge to give them to him. At Bridger Basin his men took my bones. And he has instructed his collectors to smash duplicates and other bones—to actually *destroy fossils* to keep them from me!"

Sairie, listening to this tirade in the flickering of the dying campfire, muttered "hang him." As a consequence of that comment, after a sleep punctuated with nightmares in which the originals of his fossils tormented him, Cope greeted Sairie with "I wish *thee* a pleasant morning. Shall I name the giant lizard in thy honor, Miss Chokecherry?"

"Already named Joe. For Joe." She patted her pinto's neck.

Cope said, "Hmmn. *Josaurus.* Why not? It will send them scurrying to their Greek lexicons. I once named a species *Cophater*, and a friend, in desperation, asked me what it meant. I told him it was in honor of the Cope haters."

They rode on towards Coyote, comparing their knowledge of the animals they saw. Cope would furnish their genus and species as well as details of their evolutionary adaptations; Sairie would supply their personal habits, and a judgment on how they tasted.

Twenty-five miles nearer Zak City, Marsh was also enjoying his morning. The previous day had been spent in the purchase of supplies: a large wagon, harness and four-horse team, $520; provisions and camp utensils, $175; riding horse, $75. The new horse was tied behind the wagon with Red-Eye Dave Savage's chestnut Lightning. Red-Eye drove and his employer rode shotgun.

Marsh was an accomplished raconteur, with a fund of exciting anecdotes from his earlier western expeditions. Red-Eye, however, had spent his advance the night before, and was not the best of audiences. Every so often he took a swig of *Essence of Frankincense*, its herbs helping not so much as its alcoholic content.

". . . the colonel and his officers all complimented me on my feat. And I am now an army legend, the only man to shoot three buffalo from an ambulance. It happened in '70 but is still a topic of . . . Stop!"

Red-Eye pulled back on the reins and grabbed for a pistol. "Injuns? Rannies?"

"Sshh." Marsh pointed to a lone buffalo, grazing some distance away. Raising his carbine, he took careful aim and fired. The animal sank to its knees, mooed once, and died.

"Dang if you don't shoot like a Missouri bushwhacker!" Red-Eye crowed.

Marsh dissected out the buffalo's tongue, wrapping it in cloth. They enjoyed it that night at supper, while Marsh ran through an inventory of his friends. "Darwin, you've heard of Darwin? Well, he's quite important. He sent me congratulations on a paper. Huxley also greatly admires my work, especially my studies on the evolution of horses."

Red-Eye Dave was taken aback by that phrase. He looked over at Lightning, hobbled near the wagon, suspicious that at any second the beast might evolve, whatever that was. He was thankful for the security of the bottle of *Essence of Frankincense* clasped firmly in his hand.

"In fact, my elucidation of equine evolution has won me praise from all quarters, many unique. Brigham Young . . ."

"I hearda him," Red-Eye muttered.

". . . has named me a Defender of the Faith. It appears that *The Book of Mormon* mentioned horses in ancient America, and my fossil studies have inadvertently supported his religion. I had quite a friendly welcome in Salt Lake City . . ."

Red-Eye shuddered. Salt Lake made him think of polygamy, polygamy made him think of wives, and wives made him think of

Kate, who was waiting at their destination and who would, no doubt, have things to say to him. He chugged some more healing brew.

That sunset found Cope and Sairie at the Doppler ranch, a couple miles out of Coyote. The log cabin, Kate Savage's sod dugout, and the palatial barn were surrounded by a wooden palisade in moderate disrepair. The gate had fallen off the hinges and was pushed to one side.

Charley sat hunkered up to the table. He had never been so excited in his life; even killing his first (and so far only) man during the Hoedown Showdown had not been so thrilling as this conversation with a real live Natural Philosopher. Cope was discussing the wagon they would need to transport the lizard to the railroad. Charley broke in, "I c'n go, Ma, really, can't I?"

Ma Doppler, looking up from her dog-eared copy of *Beachs Home Eclectic Doctor*, said. "I don't know, Charley. You're young to go traipsing off to Philadelphy."

"But someone's gotta take care of Joe, and Doc here says he'll innerduce me to the Academy and I c'n go to college."

"Don't fret yore Ma, Charley." Johnny's voice was like a file scratching a notch in cold gun metal.

"I didn't mean no wrong," Charley whined.

Cope finished a sketch of the prehistoric sloth he had been describing, and passed it to the boy. He had drawn Charley, recognizable even without the label in Cope's illegible handwriting, beside the sloth to show the scale. Charley passed it around.

"I'd like t'hunt that," Johnny said. "Where'd I find him?"

"I fear the last died many, many years ago."

"Couldn't fit aboard the Ark in the Deluge," Ma Doppler said. "Remember your Bible, son." Cope smiled slightly. His own religious convictions had led him to discount Darwin for Lamarckian or "mechanical" evolution.

The door swung open and Johnny spun a pistol to cover it. Sairie entered carrying a child, age and sex indeterminate. She held it up for their inspection.

"That's little Johnny, or maybe Sue," Ma hazarded.

"I'm Li'l Kitty," the child howled in protest.

Sairie said, "Don't fool with horses." She dropped Kitty, who landed on her feet and scooted out of the cabin. Charley leaned towards the astonished Cope. "That's one of Red-Eye Dave and Kate's. There's round about twelve Savage kids."

"Dinopaed," the scholar muttered. Sairie snorted with laughter, startling Cope. "Thee understands Greek, Miss Chokecherry?"

"Jes' some."

Charley said with admiration, "Sairie attended Union Grammar School in Frisco for two years, right afore they stopped letting in girls."

Cope shook his head. The frontier was a fount of surprises.

At first light they rode over to Doc Watson's house. The homeopathic physician asked, "Long as you're here, need any medicine?"

"No, thank you," Cope answered. "I never travel without this." He held up a handy bottle of belladonna, quinine, and opium.

"Well, if you get to feeling poorly . . ." The doctor took a wakeup swallow of *Essence of Frankincense.*

Charley led the way along Watson Crick to a small valley. It was strewn with huge fossilized bones which had been used to build a fence and a hut. Charley dodged under a fence rung—a humerus suspended between heaped vertebrae—and walked towards the lean-to. "Here Joe, here Joe . . ."

A triangular head peeked out from the door of the hut, followed by a long cylindrical neck. It fixed one unblinking eye on Charley, turned its head and stared with the other. Then Joe exited the hut, revealing a barrel-like body, thick legs with flat feet, and a long, dragging tail, and lumbered towards the boy. An astonished Cope watched as the boy fed the animal a carrot.

"Grow 'em myself," he said proudly.

"It's . . . tall."

"Tall as me. The grownup ones were two, three times as big. Here, you feed him one. Mind your fingers."

Cope held the carrot gingerly. Joe's head snaked out, yanked the carrot from his fingers, and munched contentedly as Charley tied on a rope halter.

Sairie leaned against a fence post. "Gettin' thin." Charley ran one hand through the downy brown fuzz. "You're right. I can feel his ribs. I better feed him more."

Cope was examining the bones of the hut. "These fossils are clearly from creatures like Joe, only larger. His ancestors perhaps." The remainder of the morning was spent with Cope studying the bones, identifying them, pointing out similar ones in human construction, demonstrating muscle and tendon insertions, and then referring to Joe for confirmation. Finally, replete with anatomical speculations, the three turned toward Coyote for a cool drink.

Meanwhile, back at the Doppler ranch, the wagon had arrived. While Red-Eye Dave and his wife held a noisy and acrimonious reunion inside their sod dugout, Marsh held forth for the dozen or so Savage children.

"Indians believe fossilized bones to be the remnant of an extinct race of giants. They consider me a man of great wisdom, and call me 'Bone Medicine Man' and 'Big Bone Chief.' Chief Red Cloud is my personal friend, as is Buffalo Bill." He paused, waiting.

The oldest Savage daughter spoke. "Cousin Johnny says Buffalo Bill's a long-hair baby-face sissy."

"He does? Well . . ."

"I do," Johnny said, relishing the shiver which his voice brought.

"Of course, he only scouted for us for one day," Big Bone Chief added hastily. "I really didn't get to know him very well, and first impressions may be deceiving." *The Prairie Traveller* advised one to humor frontier roughs.

Dave Savage emerged, shaken, from his house. His wife, pregnant as usual, stood in the doorway and scowled after him. "Howdy, Johnny. Yuh met Perfesser Marsh here? He shoots like a bushwhacker. We coulda used him in the war. He wants that critter of Charley's."

"I'm sick of Charley's critter."

"I am prepared to purchase it."

Johnny smiled a thin-lipped, narrow smile that made the scientist feel like a goose in a store window. "That sounds more like it. That other feller didn't offer nothing."

"Other...? About so tall—beard—that blaggart! Gad! God damn it! (Begging your pardon, ma'am.) I wish the Lord would take him! He's insane, you know. I doubted his sanity the first time I met him. Berlin in '63; he was in Europe to escape the draft." After his diatribe had run its course, Marsh and Red-Eye Dave headed towards the valley, pausing at Doc Watson's for directions. As he rode, Marsh kept up a constant stream of comments and instructions for his horse, a habit which had earned him yet another Indian nickname, "Heap Whoa Man."

Doc Watson offered some medicine. Marsh replied, "*The Prairie Traveller* says the West's fresh air is the best medicine."

"Can't sell fresh air."

"On the other hand," Marsh decided, "it would be a fine addition to my collection of Western memorabilia," and he purchased two bottles at stiff prices. The pleased physician then pointed the way down the creek, to the paddock.

Joe was in his hut, but Dave shied him out with rocks. Marsh rubbed his hands. "It's better than I'd hoped. A class of beast unknown to modern man."

"Don't look like much to me." Red-Eye suspected that education destroyed a man's sense of values.

After a short gloat, Marsh and Red-Eye remounted. "I believe a celebration might be in order, Red-Eye."

Red-Eye held out an almost full bottle of *Essence of Frankincense.* "No thank you."

"There's the hotel in Coyote." Red-Eye led the way. The town of Coyote was, basically, the hotel. Cope and Charley were already standing at the bar of Lowland Larry's, alleviating their thirsts with draft beer. Chokecherry Sairie was seconding their toasts with the local whiskey. Johnny Doppler sat alone with his back to the wall; his hand hovered near his holster until he identified the newcomers as his cousin and the stocky greenhorn.

"Cope!" Marsh snarled.

Cope turned and graced the other with a winning smile. "Ah, the learned Professor of Copeology at Yale, Othniel Charles Marsh." From the other's flinch, it was evident that he was not fond of his Christian names. "Join us in a toast to *Josaurus dakotae* Cope, Othniel."

"Never!"

Cope glanced sideways at his friends. "You see? He is all I told ye."

Marsh said, "Did he tell you also how he'd spy on my diggers in '72? My men made a fake skull with parts of a dozen species, buried it, and dug it up while he spied. Then he snuck down that night, examined it, and wrote a paper on the fossil's significance. The brilliant genius Dr. Cope!"

The accused man shrugged. "To err is human. Of course, the telegraph man was in your pay."

Marsh hissed, "And did he tell you of this?" He reached into his jacket pocket and pulled out a thin, wrinkled copy of the *Transactions of the American Philosophical Society,* Vol. XIV. Cope stood, mouth and eyes wide, transfixed. Marsh advanced, brandishing the journal before him like a vampire-hunter brandishing a cross. Cope retreated before the journal, stopping only when he backed into the bar. The other halted before him, *Transactions* at arm's length, close enough that Cope could read the date.

" 'A report of a New Eralisaurian,' by Edward Drinker Cope," Marsh boomed. "The description of a fascinating creature which he named *Elasmosaurus* for its flexible neck and sturdy tail. He had to form an entire new order of creation to accommodate it. When he showed me his restoration, which he'd placed in the Academy Museum, I noticed that the articulations of the vertebrae were reversed."

"You fiend," Cope said through grated teeth.

"I gently suggested that he had the whole thing wrong and foremost. But it took Professor Leidy to prove to him that he'd made the neck the tail, and the tail the neck. By then he'd already described it to the American Association, restored it in the *American Naturalist*—not the most particular of journals—and the *Proceedings*, and had just published a long description in the *Transactions*."

"I tried to recall them to correct the error."

"Yes, and I gave you back one of my copies. But I still have two more." He almost thrust the journal in the pale man's face. On the sidelines, Johnny Doppler grinned in expectation of a fight.

Chokecherry Sairie interposed herself between the scientists. "Big talk, big belly."

Red-Eye Dave Savage said, "I wouldn't draw on her, Perfesser. Sairie's tough."

"Chokecherry Sairie?" Marsh was hard-pressed to maintain his usual pompous and chivalrous tone with such a female as she. "Uh, I believe you worked with General George Armstrong Custer? He's my very good friend."

"He ain't mine."

The man blushed. "Please, ma'am—you're a lady—a woman . . ."

She plucked the magazine from his hand and ripped it up, scattered the pieces onto the floor, took Cope by the elbow and left. Charley downed the last of both beers, and hurried after them.

Marsh said, "If she hadn't interfered, I believe he would have, as you westerners say, gone for me."

Red-Eye looked at the scientist's armaments. "Would you go for him?"

"Why not? I've done it in print often enough. Here, why shouldn't we make it fists, even pistols. God damn it, I want that lizard!"

Johnny Doppler's eyes narrowed in an expression of furtive thoughtfulness—in fact, had Aristotle chosen to envision a perfect form for furtive thoughtfulness, it could not have been one whit more furtive or more thoughtful than the expression Johnny Doppler wore.

Some sixty-six years later, in the penultimate chapter of a Republic Studios serial entitled *The Doppler Gang in the Big Range War*, Sheriff John Doppler walks down Main Street to a shootout with the hired thugs who have been harassing the Basque sheepherders. The actor's light-eyed, firm-jawed countenance is the very personification of nobility, determination, and self-sacrifice. The best way to visualize how Johnny looked, as he brooded on Marsh's desire to own Joe, is to remember that actor in his finest screen moment, and then rotate it 180 degrees.

Johnny rose and strode the three yards to where Marsh and Red-Eye stood. "How much you want the lizard?"

"Very much. I am prepared to pay $350."

Johnny answered, "Too bad. That Quaker slick's got first crack. Raw deal." He clapped Marsh on one beefy shoulder, winked at Red-Eye, and left the saloon.

The pudgy man said, "Hell and damnation. It is bad enough I cannot have the animal. But for Cope to . . . I would do anything to keep it from him!"

"Would you now?" Red-Eye asked. "Well well. Tell yuh what, Perfesser, you stay here at Lowlife Larry's tonight, they got better accom—accommer—beds than out the ranch, and I'll come by tomorrow morning with good news. Hey, Larry, set muh friend up." A bewildered Marsh watched his hireling lurch from the saloon. Then he ordered a slug of imported Missouri whiskey, and fell to conversing with the bartender about their mutual acquaintance General Custer.

Charley and Cope rode back towards the Foulwater. "Why has Miss Chokecherry gone? Have I offended her?"

"Shucks no, Doc. Sairie's just, well, she gets tired of folks real quick and goes off by herself. Ain't used to folks too much, bein' raised by wolves and all."

"Ah, I'm glad thee mentioned that. I have been wondering . . ." He tapered off as Charley spun his horse and slid his rifle from the saddle holster.

"Gitcher gun," Charley hissed.

"I do not own one."

The boy shot him a puzzled look, then pointed the rifle at a dust cloud coming up fast from the direction of Coyote.

Nearing gunshot range, the dust cloud was seen to be nucleated about a single horse and a rider who yelled, "Hey, Charley!" The boy relaxed. "It's my brother."

Johnny pulled up beside them, and they fell into step towards the Doppler ranch. "Good boy, Charley. Time was you wouldn't't've pulled the rifle so fast. You're learning." While Charley basked in his elder's praise, Johnny turned to Cope. "That's a nice suit of clothes y'got there, Perfesser."

"Thank you."

"Expensive like . . . I got bad news for you. I know you got here first and all, but I done sold the critter to the fat bone sharp. For $500."

"But Johnny!"

"No words from you, kid. I been like a daddy to you, and I'spect

respect and obedience like in Ma's Bible. Five hundred bucks'll
buy shoes for Dave's kids and medicine for Ma. You want your
Ma to get lumbago? So don't sass me." He wheeled off, highly
pleased with himself.

"I'm sorry, Doc Cope . . ."

"Do not trouble thyself, Charley. I see what is happening.
Marsh has cited the authority he knows best, cold cash. Your
brother hopes I will raise a better offer, and I will. In fact, I will
inflate the price as high as it will go, knowing Marsh will not be
able to resist outbidding me." He fell into a gloomy study, the
only bright thought his plan to cost his foe—or rather, his foe's
rich uncle—as much as possible. That evening he informed
Johnny that he was prepared to offer $700. Johnny accepted, and
went to bed with expectations of a healthy auction the next day.

Around midnight Cope was awakened by a nightmare. He lay abed
awhile, regarding the nearly full moon through an unchinked spot
between two logs, then leaned down and touched Charley, rolled
up in a blanket on the floor. The lad bolted upright, and as a
second thought grabbed his Smith and Wesson .45.

"Hist, it's me, Charley. Hast thou two lanterns?"

Cope saddled their horses by moonlight. Charley joined him in
the stable. "I couldn't find t'other lantern. Will one do?"

The other lantern was sitting on a fossilized pelvis, as Red-Eye
Dave Savage worked rapidly. "Yep, that dude Cope won't git
nothing." He hummed, visions of a grateful Marsh's reward dancing like sugarplums over his head.

Johnny Doppler heard Cope and Charley ride out; he woke rifle
in hand. The facts that the dogs weren't barking and the hoofbeats

were receding calmed him, but he was unable to return to sleep. "Might as well go into town now and tell the fat guy about Cope's bid." He reached for his boots.

Marsh removed his reading glasses and put down the journal. He had been plowing through an involved discussion of seal anatomy; his contempt for knowledge that did not apply directly to his needs rendered the article uninteresting. The piano player downstairs in the saloon was still pounding away. Shooting seemed too lenient a fate for the musician. Thinking of such bold, vigorous, and decisive action stimulated Marsh's mind to make an unaccustomed imaginative leap.

He chuckled, then rose and dressed.

Red-Eye reached into his pocket for a match, and found a hole instead. He muttered some uncomplimentary phrases about his wife, and then sighed. Swinging into Lightning's saddle, he headed up along the creek towards the doctor's cabin. Doc Watson hated to be awakened for anything less than a blessed event or a slow death, but this was also an emergency of sorts . . .

Red-Eye was nearing the homeopath's cabin when a silent figure stepped into his path. Lightning snorted and stopped.

"Need Doc?" the shadow asked with Chokecherry Sairie's voice.

"Naw, everybody's fine and dandy, Sairie. Yuh gotta match?"

Sairie handed him a box and faded back into the brush. Red-Eye turned Lightning about and set off humming a song from his service days. After all, it had been in those halcyon days of war that he had first learned about explosives.

*   *   *

Finding Marsh's hotel room empty, Johnny Doppler stalked back downstairs and started toward the piano player. The musician had survived thus far by developing preternatural instincts; as the man in black took his first step, the pianist leapt up and behind the upright piano.

"It's me," Johnny said reassuringly.

The piano player peeked over the top, decided it was safe, and came back around. He was a gangling twelve-year-old with a creditable mustache, and bloodshot eyes exactly like those of his father, Red-Eye Dave Savage. "Howdy Cousin Johnny sir."

"You seen the fat greenie? He off with a gal?"

"Took his horse. North. 'Bout five songs ago."

Johnny nodded, and gave his cousin's son a bared-tooth grimace. The boy felt proud. He'd never seen Johnny smile before.

Charley held the lantern and the halter while Cope measured Joe. He wrote the figure beside his sketch of the beast.

Charley yawned. "Can't we do this tomorrow?"

Cope shook his head. "I told thee, Charley, that Marsh can outbid me, and will never let me, or any other scientist, near Joe again. But we shall laugh last. While Marsh is still transporting Joe to New Haven, I will be reading my report to the Academy, and my article will be in press."

"Will you send me a copy?"

"Send—Charley, I shall enroll thee as a subscriber to the *Naturalist*. I shall give thee two subscriptions if thee will only hold the lantern steady—what?"

Charley had snapped the lid down to shut off the light. "Horse. Shh." He motioned the scientist to duck behind an immense shoulder blade. Released, Joe wandered towards his pile of hay.

A bulky silhouette paused on the valley's rim, turning slowly as it surveyed the location.

"See the belly?" Cope whispered. "It's Marsh."

Standing on the rim, Marsh observed the salient features of the approach into the valley, and calculated that a determined group of well-paid men could rush in and whisk away the lizard. "A guerilla raid," he muttered. He would be able to keep the prize from Cope after all.

"He's here to gloat over his acquisition," Cope whispered to Charley.

Marsh had just realized that the lizard might be too young to walk all the way to the railroad in Zak City. They would have to build a large wagon to carry it. A wagon could not be brought into the valley itself without a crew to dig a road, and there was no time for that. Thus, the lizard would have to be herded up to the road. Marsh began to pace off the distance down to the bone hut, shining gray in the moonlight.

Cope sprung up before his unaware foe. "Admiring the moon?" he asked bitterly.

Marsh snarled. "Couldn't wait to examine the beast at leisure? Hasty work and hasty bad judgment are your hallmarks, Cope."

The slim man shook his fist. "My feelings towards you were not hastily developed. They were nurtured slowly by your treacheries."

"By Gad, I've had enough of you," Marsh said. "You're a vile rascal and a faulty reasoner and a . . ."

Cope planted a right in the other's eye, then stared at his hand in amazement. Marsh staggered back, and began to reach for his navy revolvers. "I've borne enough from you," he hissed.

A steel finger graced his back. Charley Doppler reached around with his left hand and took the revolvers and knife. Then he holstered his own pistol and stepped back.

Bellowing with frustration, Marsh charged his rival. At last he had the chance to put to use *The Prairie Traveller's* hints on hand-to-hand combat. Soon the scientists were rolling in the dust, like small boys scuffling in a schoolyard. Charley stood, astounded, on the sidelines.

Joe had been happily munching away during the conversation. As the fight began he stiffened, turned tail, and loped into the comforting shelter of the hut.

Johnny Doppler met Sairie as he dismounted beside Marsh's horse. The pale man wore his most cheerful grimace; he was pleased that his mark was unable to stay away from the merchandise. It boded well for the bidding. "Good evening, or whatever, Sairie."

"Huh." She felt strangely worried as she rode Shaggy Joe beside the walking gunslinger, the pony giving her only a slight advantage in height. Her worries centered on the matches she'd given Red-Eye, and went beyond the obvious fact that, in his usual inebriated condition, Dave Savage was probably flammable.

The two paused on the path into the valley, and widened their eyes. The surface was littered with the shadowy masses of the fence and hut, and amongst those indistinct objects was a black shape that rolled about emitting grunts and curses.

Johnny drew his gun. "That you, Perfesser?"

Two voices gasped, "Yes."

Standing on a massive lumbar vertebra for a better view, Charley called, "Hey Johnny, it's a fracas." Natural tact kept him from adding that it was a funnier sight than Custer's military band.

Sairie bellowed a tentative, "Dave?" Far off, from the opposite rim of the valley, they heard, "Jest a minute, Sair." Red-Eye Dave, celebrating his brilliant scheme with red-eye whiskey, finally managed to light his fuse.

The valley erupted as the trail of powder ignited clump after clump of explosives lining the fence, with a final godawful boom as the hut—with Joe inside—was blasted into bits. A cloud of dust almost obscured the flying rock, topsoil, fossils, and scraps of giant lizard. Marsh's horse, reins looped around a small bush, took off towards the Black Hills with bush in tow.

Marsh and Cope, already on the ground, covered their heads against the dust and debris. Charley was less lucky; he'd been standing on a mined fence post. Sairie jumped from her pinto and ran to the boy, sprawled beside the creek bed.

Red-Eye stumbled across the valley, waving a bottle and shouting, "Wahoo! Hey, Johnny, jest like old times!"

"What the hell were you doing?"

Red-Eye stopped beside his cousin, eager as a hound dog showing his master a ripe carcass. "The fat guy said he'd give anything to keep t'other dude from getting Charley's critter. So I blew the critter up. Smart, huh?"

"You drunken son of a bitch, I was just making 'em worry so's to get more money. Now you've done it." He scowled and took aim into the valley. "Well, I'll just have to settle for the money they got on 'em."

It was a long shot in poor light. The bullet scudded into the dirt inches to the left of Marsh.

The scientists, who had dazedly picked themselves up and had been taking stock of personal damages, hit the dirt.

"Don't take no offense; it's business," Red-Eye called. He sat down and reassured himself with a swig of the Indian Princess' restorative elixir.

Sairie shouted, "Magic Tooth! Head down!" Cope obliged by almost inhaling the topsoil.

"Get me out of this," Marsh screamed. "I'll pay! Don't shoot!"

"Over here, idiot," Cope hissed, and began squirming for cover. The nation's foremost reptile expert, he did a fair snake imitation. Marsh was less adept, but an eager learner.

Behind the minimal shelter afforded by a fossilized scapula, Cope whispered, "Only one of them is shooting. If we wait until right after a shot, then both run in opposite directions, one of us may escape." Marsh nodded agreement.

Meanwhile, the explosion had roused Doc Watson. He arrived in nightgown and boots, and carrying shotgun and medical kit. "Over here, Doc," Sairie called. The man examined Charley. "Concussion, a few broken bones—Doppler, are you through taking potshots yet?"

Johnny squeezed off another. "Not quite, Doc. They ain't dead yet."

"Look to your brother. He's not doing too good."

Johnny said loudly, "Don't you fellers go anywhere," and prodded Red-Eye Dave into a position of watchfulness. Sairie snuck towards where Cope and Charley's horses were grazing—it would take more than an explosion to keep a Doppler Gang horse from eating—and whistled. Her pinto pony trotted to her.

The homeopath was telling Johnny to ride home and fetch a wagon. "Soon as I'm finished," Johnny promised. "He's gonna be all right, ain't he?" He gazed at his younger brother. "Ma'll have a fit," he mumbled, and his pale face grew even paler.

Cope observed Red-Eye wobbling with the breeze. "It's now or never. Run," he urged Marsh, who gave him a twenty second start, either from slow reactions or to give Cope more opportunity to shine as a solitary target. Sairie nudged Shaggy Joe into a gallop, leading the other horses. She dropped one off by the running Marsh and the other by the running Cope. In seconds all three were galloping east, revolver slugs flying ineffectually in their wake.

It was a silent, hard ride to Zak City, but Sairie got them there a little before sundown, just as a train was pulling into the station.

Sairie took the reins of the beat horses and began walking them in a slow circle. "Train to Denver. Go now." Marsh thrust a random handful of coins and bills into her hand—counting later revealed it as less than $50—and ran for the train.

"I cannot thank thee enough, Miss Chokecherry," Cope said.

"I will pray for Charley's recovery; tell him I will get him the job as fossil collector if he still wishes. If thee is ever in Philadelphia, please visit me." Chokecherry Sairie was not exactly the ideal person to introduce to one's wife and daughter, but Red Cloud and Buffalo Bill had made headlines visiting Marsh's New Haven home.

Sairie stared at the scientist, dusty, bloody, tattered. She shrugged, dropped the reins, grabbed Cope and kissed him. Then she picked the reins back up. The man began backing towards the train.

"Uh . . . I only wish we had been able to have *Josaurus* with us. I lost, Miss Chokecherry, but at least Marsh lost as well."

Sairie shook her head. "When Dave blew up Joe you lost, Big Bone Chief lost, science, all lost." Cope blushed, started as if to tip his hat, realized it was long gone, and hurried aboard the train.

Sairie walked the horses south of the tracks and found Jessie Crooked-Knife. The sounds of the *Essence of Frankincense* medicine show covered the whistle as the train left for Denver.

HATCHING SEASON

HARRY TURTLEDOVE

The Montana Rockies reared against the western horizon, a pur-
ple-black jumble of stone. The breeze came from the east. It carried a spicy, resinous conifer tang and, more faintly, the smell of
the sea.

From her blind in the center of a clump of cycads, Paula Shaffer
watched the hadrosaurs foraging by the river. Not many people,
she thought with a touch of pique, remembered the big, ungainly
duckbills when they heard the word "dinosaur." The bizarrely
horned ceratopsians and savage tyrannosaurs were the ones that
sprang to mind, just as "mammal" was more likely to call up the
image of a tiger or a giraffe than that of a cow.

Yet there are a lot more cows than tigers or giraffes, and the
hadrosaurs were among the most successful dinosaurs of the Cretaceous. And so they would remain for another ten million years,
until the asteroid strike that would turn the world's climate upside
down and bring all the dinosaurs to an end.

Besides which, Paula's dissertation was on hadrosaur behavior.
The beasts were not dramatic, but she found them fascinating. A
good thing, too; her grant only gave her two weeks of fieldwork.
She was just thankful she had arrived in the middle of hatching

season. That was pure luck. The time probe couldn't pick out a specific season, or a specific year either.

Something bit her on the ankle: a dinosaur tick. She exclaimed in disgust and popped the tick into an ampule of formaldehyde so she could take it uptime with her. It had already begun letting go when she grabbed it. The warm blood she shared with its usual hosts had drawn it, but she did not taste right. An eon of evolution saw to that.

"And I'm not one damn bit sorry, either," Paula muttered, slapping a Band-aid on the oozing puncture.

While she was taking care of herself, a hadrosaur ambled over to browse on the palmlike leaves of one of the cycads around her. Even though it walked—waddled, really—with a pronounced forward stoop, it still stood a meter and a half taller than she did; it was about seven meters long. If it decided to go through the stand of cycads instead of around, all she could do was dodge.

It showed no intention of that, though, as it happily munched away. The small, flat teeth inside the duckbill made a grinding noise rather like that of an enormous peppermill. Paula giggled. " 'It's rumblings abdominal are simply phenomenal,' " she said into the recorder, quoting the only limerick both funny and clean ever written.

The hadrosaur had a cool, almost pleasant odor, not quite like any she knew in her own time—strange plants in the diet and strange pheromones, she thought. The beast did a good job of denuding the cycads before it moved on to look for more food. Like an elephant, it spent a lot of time eating.

It paused, grunted, and lifted its tail, leaving a large dropping behind as it waddled on. Only a specialist could have told the flies buzzing around the turd from their modern equivalents. Along with roaches, they had found their niche early and prospered in it.

That was depressing to dwell on. Only time-travelers, Paula thought, really realized what a mayfly man was on the face of the

Earth . . . and no one came back from the Cretaceous without a new perspective on the permanence of his works.

With an effort of will, she put aside her gloom. Before she started this fieldwork, her chairman had warned her she would be her own worst enemy here. "It always happens that way," he said. "You'll be the only thinking being on the planet. Sometimes I think that's too large a burden to put on anyone."

"Yes, Professor Musson," she had said dutifully, wishing he wouldn't turn mystical like that. Now she saw he had been speaking from experience.

The hadrosaur grunted again, a welcome distraction. It bent to uproot a large fern, and then another close by. Instead of eating them, though, it left them in its mouth as it walked purposefully downstream.

Excitement ran through Paula. She rolled up the green nylon mesh under which she had hidden, stuffed it into her backpack. Then she emerged from the cycads to follow the dinosaur.

It looked back at her suspiciously. It had no innate fear of man, of course, but many small, carnivorous dinosaurs were bipeds; it might have perceived her as one of those. She ducked behind the trunk of a cypress. Being without any memory to speak of, the hadrosaur forgot her as soon as she was no longer visible.

She trotted after it; even the waddle of a seven-meter beast is a long way from slow. From time to time her hadrosaur exchanged moans and hoots with others of the herd it was passing. She recognized the calls as mere acknowledgment signals, but kept her recorder going nonetheless. Someone had recently done work on hadrosaur calls in New Mexico; it might be worthwhile finding out if the "dialects" differed from North to South.

A hypsilophodont flashed by her, squeaking in terror. The little dinosaur ran on its hind legs, but it was a vegetarian; speed was its only defense. It was going flat out, its long tail stiff behind it to serve as a counterpoise to the weight of its trunk.

It needed all the speed it could muster, too, for on its heels was one of the horrors that made even the bulky hadrosaurs nervous: a *Deinonychus*. The predator was about two and a half meters long, and built along the same general lines as the beast it was pursuing. But its long forearms ended in clawed, grasping hands, and the third toe of each foot in a vicious twelve-centimeter talon made for slashing.

The *Deinonychus* ran the hypsilophodont down about a hundred meters from Paula. It seized its thrashing victim with those clutching forefeet, held it away from its own body so it could bring a hind foot into play for a disemboweling stroke. Its tail balanced it and kept it upright while it stood on one leg for the kill. When the hypsilophodont was dead, its slayer stooped over the carcass and greedily began to feed.

Shuddering, Paula slapped the .45 on her hip. The *Deinonychus* could as easily have chosen her to attack, but a slug or two would have gone a long way toward changing its mind. She wished for a grenade-launcher, in case one of the bigger carnivores deigned to notice her. She was glad they were uncommon.

She hurried after the hadrosaur, which had built up quite a lead. She was sweating hard by the time it reached the nesting ground, both from the exercise and from the muggy subtropical climate.

The nesting ground reminded her of nothing so much as a seabird colony at breeding time. That was fitting enough, she thought, for what were birds but the feathered survivors of the dinosaur clan?

Here, though, the scale was vastly larger. Each bowl-shaped mud nest was a good two meters across and more than a meter high. The musty odor of rotting vegetation overpowered the dinosaur smell in the area. The hadrosaurs did not sit on their clutches of eggs, but, like crocodiles, used the heat generated by the decaying plants they put in their nests to help hatch them.

Not all the clutches had hatched yet; some still had parent dinosaurs hanging about to protect them from predators, as penguins guard their eggs against skuas. Paula saw one hadrosaur grunt threateningly and lower its head as if to charge at a *Troodon*, a small flesh-eating dinosaur of a type that often raided unguarded nests. The *Troodon* hissed but drew back.

The hadrosaurs were not perfect guardians. A lizard scrambled off the side of a nest and scurried away, still licking yolk from its jaws with methodical flicks of its black, forked tongue. The parent dinosaur was only a couple of meters away, but made no response. To an adult hadrosaur, a lizard was so small as not to exist.

Paula's hadrosaur pressed through the crowd of its fellows; she followed more circumspectly. Fragments of old eggshell crunched under her boots. The hadrosaurs of this herd had been returning to their breeding site for uncounted generations. Again she was reminded of seabirds.

And so, despite its minuscule brain, her beast knew where it was going. As it approached the nest it had built, she shifted her video camera to telephoto. If she tried to get closer herself, the hadrosaur would drive her off as the other had the *Troodon*.

Her hadrosaur leaned into its nest, dropped the load of ferns it had been carrying for so long. Instantly a couple of dozen hatchlings swarmed onto the food, eating as if there were no tomorrow. Their squeals of excitement were a soprano mimicry of their elders' deep-toned calls.

Watching the babies, Paula could not help smiling. A seven-meter hadrosaur was a staid, serious beast, foraging with single-minded intensity. A thirty-centimeter, newly hatched hadrosaur was something else again. The hatchlings hopped about, falling over one another and leaping back in alarm from imaginary dangers. They squabbled over leaves and branches and bit each other's feet and tails.

When one of the hatchlings tried to scramble out of the nest, the adult hadrosaur used its duckbill to bunt the little beast back. Another baby did succeed in getting out, and started to wander away. The full-grown animal gave a snorting call. The youngster obediently turned around and climbed back into the nest.

Paula wished she knew whether the adult was male or female; the sexes had no obvious differences. One school held that both parents cared for the young, the other that only the mother did. One day a team would stay in the Cretaceous for a whole year, and find out the truth. When the funding for that kind of project would come through, though, was anyone's guess. No time soon, Paula thought sadly.

Another fully grown hadrosaur was leading an older brood, just out of the nest, on a foraging expedition. The juveniles were almost as long as Paula was tall, and were beginning to lose their immature blotching for the solid green-brown of the adults' hides.

When her hadrosaur left to gather more food for its young, Paula cautiously approached the nest to learn exactly what plants it fed them. The hatchlings scrambled back in fear as she pawed through the remains of their feast.

She was surprised to see one egg still standing upright, unhatched. A bit more than half of its twenty-centimeter length was visible above the rotting vegetation in which it had been laid. The gray-green shell was ridged, to give it more surface area to release the carbon dioxide the developing embryo produced.

She thought for a moment that this egg was infertile, but then she noticed the crack running along one of the vertical striations. The baby hadrosaur was about to hatch; perhaps it had been delayed because its egg was not as well covered as the rest of the clutch and therefore incubated more slowly.

She focused the video camera on the egg; as far as she could remember, no one had ever recorded a hadrosaur hatching. It was a shame the parent was not around, she thought, so she could see how it reacted to the new arrival.

The emergence was a struggle—dinosaur eggshells were a couple of millimeters thick. At last the baby hadrosaur lay gasping in the nest, still wet with fluid from the inside of the egg. One of its brothers or sisters, utterly indifferent, walked on its head. It paid the sibling no more attention than it had been given.

Paula, however, was big enough to notice. The baby hadrosaur opened its mouth and waited expectantly.

Paula burst out laughing. She could not help it; the little animal looked just like one of the stuffed toys the university bookstore sold. "All right, pal, you've earned it," she said. She found some tender fern leaves the other hatchlings had missed, fed them to the youngest one. It chewed rapturously.

A grunt from one of the adult hadrosaurs nearby made Paula jump away from the nest in a hurry. She did not want the beast mistaking her for a predator. It was too stupid to listen to explanations, and too big to argue with.

Another grunt came from behind her, this one treble rather than bass. The newest hatchling had struggled up to the rim of the nest and was peeping about. When it saw Paula, it leaped down, landing in a heap at the base of the nest. It staggered to its feet and came after her.

"Oh, for heaven's sake," she said in exasperation. She picked up the little hadrosaur. It wriggled and batted her wrist with its tail. As gently as she could, she set it back in the nest.

She drew away before she upset any of the adults again. That same high-pitched grunt came from behind her. She turned and saw the hatchling land even more clumsily than it had before.

"Stay where you are, would you please?" she told it. "I'm not your mama . . . Or am I?" she added as it got to its hind legs and walked toward her.

Her eyes widened. "You little son of a lizard, I think I've imprinted you!" Birds worked that way, she knew; they accepted the first thing they saw after hatching as their mother, which sometimes gave rise to such ludicrous spectacles as a long line of ducklings happily following a chicken.

The scientific community had realized since the late twentieth century that birds were a modern offshoot of dinosaurs. Paula did not think anyone, though, had recorded an instant of imprinting among dinosaurs—or looked for one, for that matter. "Sometimes you'd rather be lucky than good," she breathed, and started talking into her recorder.

She replaced the baby hadrosaur in its nest once more. "Third time's the charm," she muttered. She felt like shouting when the small beast again clambered to the top of the nest and looked about for her. To celebrate, she pulled up a newly sprouted fern too tiny for an adult hadrosaur to notice and gave it to the infant.

If anything, the second feeding strengthened the bond the little dinosaur had formed with her. "You think I'm the horn of plenty, don't you?" she said. As often as she returned it to the nest, it scrambled out again.

She was surprised how low the sun had sunk in the west. Soon it would fall behind the Rockies, peaks taller and more jagged than they would be eighty million years from now. She grimaced. The baby hadrosaur, now coming up to her for the umpteenth time, had eaten up a big chunk of one of her precious days in the Cretaceous. No, that wasn't fair, she decided—what she was learning from it was worth the time.

She picked up the hatchling and was about to replace it yet again when she heard the distress cries from the east. The adult hadrosaurs heard them too. Heads went up; eyes widened. Though they had seen nothing dangerous themselves, the adults echoed the distress call, alerting the whole herd for flight.

A hadrosaur burst from among the shrubs and tall ferns at the eastern edge of the nesting ground. Its waddling trot was desperately urgent. Alarm shot through Paula. Not many beasts were big enough to panic a dinosaur that weighed as much as a small elephant.

Paula shifted the hatchling to her left hand and drew her pistol, wishing again for something with more punch. Sure, big carnivores were rare, but she should have realized that a concentration of large herbivores like a nesting ground would draw them if anything would. Even the grenade-launcher she had thought about before might not stop a tyrannosaur.

The undergrowth shook again as the flesh-eater on the trail of the hadrosaur came crashing through. Paula's mouth went dry. It was not a tyrannosaur, but it was the next worst thing: the *Gorgosaurus* was nine meters long, three meters high, and armed with an enormous mouthful of ten-centimeter teeth. Paula wondered insanely whether a zebra cared if it was eaten by a lion or a leopard.

No such abstractions burdened the hadrosaurs in the nesting ground. They fled the moment they set eyes on the gorgosaur, and woe betide the nests or hatchlings that got in their way. Paula ran with them, praying she would not stumble. None of her training had dealt with being part of a dinosaur stampede. The only thing she was sure of was that going with the tide was smarter than trying to stem it. She had always thought King Canute was a damned fool.

The roar of the gorgosaur sounded like a steam engine with horrible indigestion. Paula could hear that the beast was gaining on the herd; she did not dare look back to see how quickly. Her breath sobbed in her lungs, but she kept running. In her undergrad days she had run a pretty fair 3,000 meters until the pressure of study made her quit the track team. Now she wished she had been a marathoner.

Something bucked against her left wrist. She realized she was still holding the baby hadrosaur. It squirmed and writhed, trying to get away. She hung onto it. It was not interfering with her running, and if she let go it would be crushed in an instant.

A whistling hiss came from behind her and to her right, signaling the arrival of another gorgosaur. That wasn't fair, she thought—the big carnivores were solitary killers. They did not hunt in packs as *Deinonychus* and other small meat-eaters often did. The furious bellow of the first gorgosaur declared how little it welcomed its fellow.

Paula heard a shriek that reminded her of the scream of a wounded horse: one of the monsters had killed. Then the steam whistles started again, at double the volume, as the other gorgosaur disputed ownership of the corpse.

As the two great carnivores quarreled with each other, Paula drew in a shuddering gasp of relief. It was over now; the rest of the herd was safe. Soon the hadrosaurs would stop, and she could get out from among them.

Only they did not stop. Once begun, a stampede gains a momentum of its own, one with nothing to do with what had touched it off. Swaying with exhaustion, Paula loped a couple of paces to the side and rear of a fat hadrosaur with a limp. There was nothing else she could do, except give up and get trampled. The couple of times she tried drifting across the current toward the edge of the herd, she was almost run down. The same thing happened when she slowed. Gritting her teeth, she ran on.

Then the hadrosaurs were in among the trees and ferns south of the nesting ground. Up ahead, the leaders of the herd swerved this way and that, sometimes on account of the terrain, sometimes for no reason at all. In the forest half-light, Paula soon had no idea in which direction she was going.

She spotted a tree—a magnolia, of all things—that looked sturdy enough to hide behind while the herd streamed past. But as she swerved to make for it, one of the hadrosaurs caught her, quite by accident, with the very tip of its tail. She smashed against the trunk of the magnolia and remembered nothing more.

It was dark when she returned to her senses. She groaned as she sat up. Pain thudded behind her eyes with every heartbeat, held her ribs in a vise, dwelt like fire in her right wrist. She cautiously took a deep breath. The ache in her chest did not get worse. No broken ribs, anyway, she thought.

That wrist was something else. She could feel bone grate when she moved. As carefully as she could, she eased off her backpack. She fumbled in it left-handed for her flashlight.

Something by her left knee twisted in surprise as the light went on. "Are you still here?" she said, turning the beam away from the baby hadrosaur. After a moment's reflection, she decided the little beast had nowhere else to go. Away from its nest, what else could it do but stay by the one being that represented safety to it? There were dangers in the Mesozoic night: not only small marauding mammals, but also—and more to be feared—nocturnal cousins of *Deinonychus* that hunted the mammals and anything else they could find.

Such musing was only a small concern as Paula dug through the pack for a vial of pain pills. She dry-swallowed one and then, a few seconds later, another one. While she was waiting for them to kick in, she pulled out a bandage-roll and found a couple of sticks to use in a splint.

Her hurts began to recede. She undid the wrist strap that held her compass and the homer for the time probe. "Oh, Jesus Christ," she said. The drug made her sound detached and conversational but she could feel the scream behind her words. Both devices were smashed to worthless junk.

She sat perfectly still, trying to will them back to life. When that did not work, she nodded bitterly, as if the failure were a petition a dean had rejected. She fought down panic. "First things first," she said, and went to work splinting her wrist.

Even as she tightened the bandage, though, her mind kept yammering at her. If she was not at the time probe when it left the Cretaceous, she was stuck here-and-now for as long as she lived, which wouldn't be long. They had drilled that into her during her training. The releases she had had to sign would have made a small book by themselves.

Perhaps it was the fear of being stranded, perhaps the blow to the head she had taken, but she made a bad mistake. Instead of waiting until morning and backtracking along the trail the hadrosaur stampede had left, she decided she had to know *at once* where she was and in which direction she should go. She got to her feet to look for a clearing so she could see the stars.

The baby hadrosaur trustingly scuttled along behind her, as it might have after a real parent on the way to a patch of berry bushes. After a while, she stopped and picked it up. "We've come this far; we may as well stick together," she told it, as if it understood.

The forest canopy kept all but the occasional star from peeping through. Paula kept walking—there had to be an open patch somewhere. Her flashlight beam drew insects, just as it would have in her own time. She drenched herself with repellant. Cretaceous biting bugs had mouthparts like drill-presses. They had to, to penetrate dinosaur hide.

Two or three times, she saw pairs of eyes reflecting her light in yellow or red. As long as the eyes were close to the ground and close together, she did not let them worry her.

"At last!" she exclaimed some weary time later. A forest giant had toppled, and in its fall taken several smaller trees with it. Ferns and weeds were already filling the gap, but as yet the new growth was no higher than Paula's knees.

She went into the middle of the clearing and turned off her flashlight to let her eyes adjust to the dark. She was no great shakes at astronomy, but she was confident she knew enough of the major constellations to figure out which way was which.

Or so she thought, but when she looked up to the heavens, none of the patterns she saw meant anything to her. A red star stood almost directly overhead; it was bright as Venus. Several others here and there were nearly its match. The cluster close to horizon put the Pleiades to shame.

"Shit," she said as the realization washed over her. To her, the stars were the stars, and pretty much unchanging. Over eighty million years, though, that wasn't so; the Earth was almost halfway round the galaxy from where it would be. They had talked about

229

this in training, but she had only listened with half an ear: what they were saying hadn't seemed useful, not when she had simpler, more accurate ways of finding direction. Now she didn't.

That old saw about moss growing on the north side of trees did not mean anything here, either. In this climate, moss grew everywhere.

About then, she figured out what she should have done. If she could retrace her path to the clearing . . . her laugh held desperation. She had got so turned around looking at the stars that she wasn't even sure from which direction she had entered.

"Stupid, Paula, stupid," she said. Before, being stupid had meant getting marked down in a seminar or having to do an experiment over. Now it was liable to kill her.

She was grateful for the pain pills. They took the edge off her fear, left her able to think straight, if slowly. When the sun rose, she would be able to tell directions from the shadows it cast, well enough to go roughly north. That would get her to the river, and give her an even-money chance of heading back toward familiar territory.

"Unless you have a better idea?" she asked the baby hadrosaur. If it did, it wasn't letting on.

Until morning, she decided, the best thing to do was rest. She intended to be as clearheaded as she could when day came. "No more screwups," she said firmly, getting out her bedroll. She set the hatchling down beside it. "If you want to go, go. Otherwise, I'll see you in the morning."

She thought she would be too keyed-up to sleep, but the next thing she knew, the sun was blasting full in her face. "East," she said: progress. She looked around for the baby hadrosaur. It was right where she'd left it, still sleeping, with its tail curled over its eyes.

"Wish I could do that," she said, and this time her chuckle was only one of honest amusement. The foolish little creature was good for her morale, and she needed all the help she could get.

She picked up the hatchling—it let out a hiss at being disturbed, but quickly calmed—and started off.

Knowing which way she should go did not make the trip easy. Paula squelched into marshes (and discovered the hard way that there were leeches in the Cretaceous), scrambled around tangles of undergrowth too thick to walk through. A couple of times the leaves overhead hid the sun altogether and kept her from gauging shadows. Once she emerged to discover she was going east instead of north. Shaking her head, she turned left.

Her cheer when she saw the river frightened the baby hadrosaur, which curled its tail round her wrist, painfully tight. She felt like one of Xenophon's men spying the Black Sea.

She cautiously approached the water and drank, always keeping one eye—and part of the other—peeled for trouble. Crocodiles and worse things infested Cretaceous rivers.

She peered upstream and down. As she had feared, the two directions looked equally unfamiliar. She set the baby hadrosaur down, fed it a leaf. "You don't know which way to go either, do you?" she said accusingly.

She stopped and gave it another look, a good long one. "Or do you?" The hadrosaurs of the herd always came back to the same nesting ground to breed. Were they biologically programmed to do so, as salmon always returned to the same stream or birds to the same island?

Nobody knew. Even after years of time travel, there was so much nobody knew about dinosaurs. If Paula had some reason to think the hatchling could find its way home, she would feel vastly better about picking a direction. As things stood, choosing which way to go was like playing Russian roulette with half the chambers loaded.

Her mouth tightened. Maybe she could find out. She set the baby hadrosaur down. It didn't go anywhere at all. It stood there looking at her. "I wish you didn't think I was your mama," she told it.

She picked it up again while she thought. After a while, she got out several feet of light cord and tied a cord of harness around the hatchling's forelimbs and back. She tied the other end of the cord to a stout chunk of wood that she anchored firmly in the ground.

Then she went back into the forest, making sure she stayed downwind so the hadrosaur could neither see nor smell her. The tape she was looking for was labeled *Nesting Ground—I.* She put on her headphones and skipped through the tape until she found the section she needed.

She played the snorting call at top volume. The baby hadrosaur's head came up. It started confidently upstream—toward its nest, she hoped, for that was what the call meant. The harness brought the hatchling up short. It did not understand about ropes, and kept marching in place at the end of its tether.

When Paula showed herself again, the hadrosaur turned toward her. She picked it up, still in its harness, and carried it and the anchoring chunk of wood a couple of hundred meters upstream. She put it down there, went back into the woods, and repeated the experiment. The direction the baby went the first time, she reasoned, might well have been chosen randomly.

It started upstream again.

She went another couple of hundred meters and tried it again, with identical results. The baby hadrosaur did the same thing on the next three repetitions. Paula threw her hands in the air. She untied the beast. "All right, I'm convinced. Upstream it is."

After less than an hour, she began encountering hadrosaurs browsing near the river. She did a silly jig when she first came across country she recognized, and was amazed to discover how beautiful a stretch of two-meter mud nests could be. From the nesting ground, she knew exactly how to return to the time probe.

For the last time, she put down the baby hadrosaur. She played the return-to-the-nest call, softly now so as not to disturb other dinosaurs. As it had all along, the hatchling knew where it was going. It had no trouble finding its own nest among the hundreds around it. Climbing in was harder, but the little dinosaur managed.

Paula never doubted it would. Though she would never know for sure, she was irrationally certain it would escape every Cretaceous predator and grow up big and fat and stupid, so that in the long run the beast's sad confusion about its relationship to her would not matter at all.

As she left the nesting ground, she felt a trifle sad just the same. After all, she had never been a mother before.

A GUN FOR DINOSAUR

L. SPRAGUE DE CAMP

No, Mr. Seligman, I won't take you hunting late-Mesozoic dinosaur.

Why not? How much d'you weigh? A hundred and thirty? Let's
see, that's under ten stone, which is my lower limit.

I'll take you to any period in the Cenozoic. I'll get you a shot
at an entelodont or a titanothere or a uintathere. They've all got
fine heads.

I'll even stretch a point and take you to the Pleistocene, where
you can try for one of the mammoths or the mastodon.

I'll take you back to the Triassic, where you can shoot one of
the smaller ancestral dinosaur.

But I will not—will jolly well not—take you to the Jurassic or
Cretaceous. You're just too small.

No offense, of course.

What's your weight got to do with it?

Look here, old boy, what did you think you were going to shoot
them with?

You hadn't thought, eh?

Well, sit there a minute . . .

Here you are, my own private gun for that work, a Continental
.600. Does look like a shotgun, doesn't it? But it's rifled, as you

can see by looking through the barrels. Shoots a pair of .600 nitro express cartridges the size of bananas; weighs fourteen and a half pounds and has a muzzle energy of over seven thousand foot-pounds. Costs fourteen hundred and fifty dollars. Lot of money for a gun, what?

I have some spares I rent to the sahibs. Designed for knocking down elephant. Not just wounding them, knocking them base-over-apex. That's why they don't make guns like this in America, though I suppose they will if hunting parties keep going back in time through Prochaska's machine.

I've been guiding hunting parties for twenty years. Guided 'em in Africa until the game gave out there except on the preserves. That just about ended the world's real big-game hunting.

My point is, all that time I've never known a man your size who could handle the six-nought-nought. It knocks 'em over. Even when they stay on their feet, they get so scared of the bloody cannon after a few shots that they flinch. Can't hit an elephant at spitting range. And they find the gun too heavy to drag around rough Mesozoic country. Wears 'em out.

It's true, lots of people have killed elephant with lighter guns: the .500, .475, and .465 doubles, for instances, or even .375 magnum repeaters. The difference is that with a .375 you have to hit something vital, preferably the heart, and can't depend on simple shock power.

An elephant weighs—let's see—four to six tons. You're planning to shoot reptiles weighing two or three times as much as an elephant and with much greater tenacity of life. That's why the syndicate decided to take no more people dinosaur-hunting unless they could handle the .600. We learned the hard way, as you Americans say. There were some unfortunate incidents ...

I'll tell you, Mr. Seligman. It's after seventeen hundred. Time I closed the office. Why don't we stop at the bar on our way out while I tell you the story?

*   *   *

It was about the Raja's and my fifth safari. The Raja? Oh, he's the Aiyar half of Rivers & Aiyar. I call him the Raja because he's the hereditary monarch of Janpur. Means nothing nowadays, of course. Knew him in India and ran into him in New York running the Indian tourist agency. That dark chap in the photograph on my office wall, the one with his foot on the dead saber-tooth.

Well, the Raja was fed up with handing out brochures about the Taj Mahal and wanted to do a bit of hunting again. I was at loose ends when we heard of Professor Prochaska's time machine at Washington University.

Where is the Raja? Out on safari in the early Oligocene, after titanothere, while I run the office. We take turns about now, but the first few times we went out together.

Anyhow, we caught the next plane to St. Louis. To our mortification, we found we weren't the first.

Lord, no! There were other hunting guides and no end of scientists, each with his own idea of the right use for the machine.

We scraped off the historians and archeologists right at the start.

Seems the bloody machine won't work for periods more recent than a hundred thousand years ago. From there, up to about a billion years.

Why? Oh, I'm no four-dimensional thinker, but as I understand it, if people could go back to a more recent time, their actions would affect our own history, which would be a paradox or contradiction of facts. Can't have that in a well-run universe. But before one hundred thousand B.C., more or less, the actions of the expeditions are lost in the stream of time before human history begins. At that, once a stretch of past time has been used, say the month of January, one million B.C., you can't use that stretch over again by sending another party into it. Paradoxes again.

But the professor isn't worried; with a billion years to exploit, he won't soon run out of eras.

Another limitation of the machine is the matter of size. For technical reasons, Prochaska had to build the transition chamber just big enough to hold four men with their personal gear, plus the chamber-wallah. Larger parties have to be sent through in relays. That means, you see, it's not practical to take jeeps, boats, aircraft, or other powered vehicles.

On the other hand, since you're going to periods without human beings, there's no whistling up a hundred native bearers to trot along with your gear on their heads. So we usually take a train of asses—burros, they call them here. Most periods have enough natural forage to get you where you want to go.

As I say, everybody had his own idea for using the machine. The scientists looked down their noses at us hunters and said it would be a crime to waste the machine's time pandering to our sadistic amusements.

We brought up another angle. The machine cost a cool thirty million. I understand this came from the Rockefeller Board and such people, but that only accounted for the original cost, not the cost of operation. And the thing uses fantastic amounts of power. Most of the scientists' projects, while worthy as worthy could be, were run on a shoestring, financially speaking.

Now we guides catered to people with money, a species with which America seems overstocked. No offense, old boy. Most of these could afford a substantial fee for passing through the machine to the past. Thus we could help finance the operation of the machine for scientific purposes, provided we got a fair share of its time.

Won't go into the details, but in the end the guides formed a syndicate of eight members, one member being the partnership of Rivers & Aiyar, to apportion the machine's time.

We had rush business from the start. Our wives—the Raja's and mine—raised bloody hell with us. They'd hoped when the big game gave out they'd never have to share us with lions and things again, but you know how women are. Can't realize hunt-

237

ing's not really dangerous if you keep your head and take precautions.

On the fifth expedition, we had two sahibs to wet-nurse: both Americans and in their thirties, both physically sound, and both solvent. Otherwise they were as different as different can be.

Courtney James was what you chaps call a playboy: a rich young man from New York who'd always had his own way and didn't see why that agreeable condition shouldn't continue. A big bloke, almost as big as I am; handsome in a florid way, but beginning to run to fat. He was on his fourth wife, and when he showed up at the office with a blonde with "model" written all over her, I assumed this was the fourth Mrs. James.

"Miss Bartram," she corrected me, with an embarrassed giggle.

"She's not my wife," James explained. "My wife is in Mexico, I think, getting a divorce. But Bunny here would like to go along—"

"Sorry," I said, "we don't take ladies. At least not to the late Mesozoic."

This wasn't strictly true, but I felt we were running enough risks, going after a little-known fauna, without dragging in people's domestic entanglements. Nothing against sex, you understand. Marvelous institution and all that, but not where it interferes with my living.

"Oh, nonsense," said James. "If she wants to go, she'll go. She skis and flies my airplane, so why shouldn't she—"

"Against the firm's policy."

"She can keep out of the way when we run up against the dangerous ones."

"No, sorry."

"Damn it," said he, getting red. "After all, I'm paying you a goodly sum and I'm entitled to take who I please."

"You can't hire me to do anything against my best judgment," I said. "If that's how you feel, get another guide."

238

"All right, I will. And I'll tell all my friends you're a goddamn—" Well, he said a lot of things I won't repeat. It ended with my telling him to get out of the office or I'd throw him out.

I was sitting in the office thinking sadly of all that lovely money James would have paid me if I hadn't been so stiff-necked, when in came my other lamb, one August Holtzinger. This was a little slim pale chap with glasses, polite and formal where the other had been breezily self-confident to the point of obnoxiousness.

Holtzinger sat on the edge of his chair and said: "Uh—Mr. Rivers, I don't want you to think I'm here under false pretenses. I'm really not much of an outdoorsman and I'll probably be scared to death when I see a real dinosaur. But I'm determined to hang a dinosaur head over my fireplace or die in the attempt."

"Most of us are frightened at first," I soothed him, and little by little I got the story out of him.

While James had always been wallowing in money, Holtzinger was a local product who'd only lately come into the real thing. He'd had a little business here in St. Louis and just about made ends meet when an uncle cashed in his chips somewhere and left little Augie the pile.

He'd never been married but had a fiancée. He was building a big house, and when it was finished, they'd be married and move into it. And one furnishing he demanded was a ceratopsian head over the fireplace. Those are the ones with the big horned heads with a parrot-beak and frill over the neck, you know. You have to think twice about collecting them, because if you put a seven-foot triceratops head into a small living room, there's apt to be no room left for anything else.

We were talking about this when in came a girl, a small girl in her twenties, quite ordinary-looking, and crying.

"Augie!" she wept. "You can't! You mustn't! You'll be killed!" She grabbed him round and said to me: "Mr. Rivers, you mustn't take him! He's all I've got! He'll never stand the hardships!"

"My dear young lady," I said, "I should hate to cause you distress, but it's up to Mr. Holtzinger to decide whether he wishes to retain my services."

"It's no use, Claire," said Holtzinger. "I'm going, though I'll probably hate every minute of it."

"What's that, old boy?" I asked. "If you hate it, why go? Did you lose a bet or something?"

"No," said Holtzinger. "It's this way. Uh—I'm a completely undistinguished kind of guy. I'm just an ordinary Midwestern small-businessman. You never even notice me at Rotary luncheons, I fit in so perfectly. But that doesn't say I'm satisfied. I've always hankered to go to far places and do big things. I'd like to be a glamorous, adventurous sort of guy. Like you, Mr. Rivers."

"Oh, come," I protested. "Professional hunting may seem glamorous to you, but to me it's just a living."

He shook his head. "Nope. You know what I mean. Well, now I've got this legacy, I could settle down to play bridge and golf the rest of my life and try to act like I wasn't bored. But I'm determined to do something big for once. Since there's no more real big-game hunting, I'm gonna shoot a dinosaur and hang his head over my mantel. I'll never be happy otherwise."

Well, Holtzinger and his girl, whose name was Roche, argued, but he wouldn't give in. She made me swear to take the best care of her Augie and departed, sniffling.

When Holtzinger had left, who should come in but my vile-tempered friend Courtney James. He apologized for insulting me, though you could hardly say he groveled.

"I don't actually have a bad temper," he said, "except when people won't cooperate with me. Then I sometimes get mad. But so long as they're cooperative, I'm not hard to get along with."

I knew that by "cooperate" he meant to do whatever Courtney James wanted, but I didn't press the point. "How about Miss Bartram?" I asked.

"We had a row," he said. "I'm through with women. So if there's no hard feelings, let's go on from where we left off."

"Absolutely," I agreed, business being business.

The Raja and I decided to make it a joint safari to eighty-five million years ago: the early upper Cretaceous, or the middle Cretaceous, as some American geologists call it. It's about the best period for dinosaur in Missouri. You'll find some individual species a little larger in the late upper Cretaceous, but the period we were going to gives a wider variety.

Now, as to our equipment, the Raja and I each had a Continental .600 like the one I showed you and a few smaller guns. At this time, we hadn't worked up much capital and had no spare .600s to rent.

August Holtzinger said he would rent a gun, as he expected this to be his only safari and there was no point in spending over a thousand dollars for a gun he'd shoot only a few times. But since we had no spare .600s, his choice was between buying one of those and renting one of our smaller pieces.

We drove into the country to let him try the .600. We set up a target. Holtzinger heaved up the gun as if it weighed a ton and let fly. He missed completely and the kick knocked him flat on his back with his legs in the air.

He got up, looking paler than ever, and handed me back the gun, saying: "Uh—I think I'd better try something smaller."

When his shoulder stopped being sore, I tried him out on the smaller rifles. He took a fancy to my Winchester 70, chambered for the .375 magnum cartridge. It's an excellent all-round gun—

What's it like? A conventional magazine rifle with a Mauser-type bolt action. It's perfect for the big cats and bears, but a little light for elephant and very definitely light for dinosaur. I should never have given in, but I was in a hurry and it might have taken months to get him a new .600. They're made to order, you know, and James was getting impatient. James already had a gun, a Holland

& Holland .500 double express. With 5700 foot-pounds of muzzle energy, it's almost in a class with the .600.

Both sahibs had done a bit of shooting so I didn't worry about their accuracy. Shooting dinosaur is not a matter of extreme accuracy but of sound judgment and smooth coordination so you shan't catch twigs in the mechanism of your gun, or fall into holes, or climb a small tree the dinosaur can pluck you out of, or blow your guide's head off.

People used to hunting mammals sometimes try to shoot a dinosaur in the brain. That's the silliest thing you can do, because dinosaur haven't got any. To be exact, they have a little lump of tissue about the size of a tennis ball on the front end of their spines, and how are you going to hit that when it's imbedded in a moving six-foot skull?

The only safe rule with dinosaur is—always try for a heart shot. They have big hearts, over a hundred pounds in the largest species, and a couple of .600 slugs through the heart will kill them just as dead as a smaller beast. The problem is to get the slugs through that mountain of muscle and armor around it.

Well, we appeared at Prochaska's laboratory one rainy morning: James and Holtzinger, the Raja and I, our herder Beauregard Black, three helpers, a cook, and twelve jacks. Burros, that is.

The transition chamber is a little cubbyhole the size of a small lift. My routine is for the men with the guns to go first in case a hungry theropod might be standing in front of the machine when it arrived. So the two sahibs, the Raja and I crowded into the chamber with our guns and packs. The operator squeezed in after us, closed the door, and fiddled with his dials. He set the thing for April twenty-fourth, eighty-five million B.C., and pressed the red button.

The lights went out, leaving the chamber lit by a little battery-operated lamp. James and Holtzinger looked pretty green, but that may have been the dim lighting. The Raja and I had been through all this before, so the vibration and vertigo didn't bother us.

I could see the little black hands of the dials spinning round, some slowly and some so fast they were a blur. Then they slowed down and stopped. The operator looked at his ground-level gauge and turned a handwheel that raised the chamber so it shouldn't materialize underground. Then he pressed another button and the door slid open.

No matter how often I do it, I get a frightful thrill out of stepping into a bygone era. The operator had raised the chamber a foot above ground level, so I jumped down, my gun ready. The others came after. We looked back at the chamber, a big shiny cube hanging in midair a foot off the ground, with this little lift-door in front.

"Right-ho," I told the chamber-wallah, and he closed the door. The chamber disappeared and we looked around. The scene hadn't changed from my last expedition to this era, which had ended, in Cretaceous time, five days before this one began. There weren't any dinosaur in sight, nothing but lizards.

In this period, the chamber materializes on top of a rocky rise from which you can see in all directions as far as the haze will let you.

To the west, you see the arm of the Kansas Sea that reaches across Missouri and the big swamp around the bayhead where the sauropods live. It used to be thought the sauropods became extinct before the Cretaceous, but that's not so. They were more limited in range because swamps and lagoons didn't cover so much of the world, but there were plenty of them if you knew where to look.

To the north is a low range that the Raja named the Janpur Hills after the little Indian kingdom his forebears had ruled. To the east, the land slopes up to a plateau, good for ceratopsians, while to the south is flat country with more sauropod swamps and lots of ornithopods: duckbills and iguanodonts.

The finest thing about the Cretaceous is the climate: balmy, like the South Sea Islands, with little seasonal change, but not so muggy as most Jurassic climates. We happened to be there in spring, with dwarf magnolias in bloom all over, but the air feels like spring almost any time of year.

A thing about this landscape is that it combines a fairly high rainfall with an open type of vegetation cover. That is, the grasses hadn't yet evolved to the point of forming solid carpets over all open ground, so the ground is thick with laurel, sassafras and other shrubs, with bare ground between. There are big thickets of palmettos and ferns. The trees round the hill are mostly cycads, standing singly and in copses. Most people call them palms, though my scientific friends tell me they're not true palms.

Down toward the Kansas Sea are more cycads and willows, while the uplands are covered with screw pine and gingkos.

Now I'm no bloody poet—the Raja writes the stuff, not me— but I can appreciate a beautiful scene. One of the helpers had come through the machine with two of the jacks and was pegging them out, and I was looking through the haze and sniffing the air, when a gun went off behind me—bang! bang!

I turned round and there was Courtney James with his .500 and an ornithomime legging it for cover fifty yards away. The ornithomimes are medium-sized running dinosaurs, slender things with long necks and legs, like a cross between a lizard and an ostrich. This kind is about seven feet tall and weighs as much as a man. The beggar had wandered out of the nearest copse and James gave him both barrels. Missed.

I was a bit upset, as trigger-happy sahibs are as much a menace as those who get panicky and freeze or bolt. I yelled:

"Damn it, you idiot, I thought you weren't to shoot without a word from me!"

"And who the hell are you to tell me when I'll shoot my own gun?" he demanded.

We had a rare old row until Holtzinger and the Raja got us calmed down.

I explained: "Look here, Mr. James, I've got reasons. If you shoot off all your ammunition before the trip's over, your gun won't be available in a pinch and it's the only one of its caliber. Second, if you empty both barrels at an unimportant target, what would happen if a big theropod charged before you could reload? Finally, it's not sporting to shoot everything in sight. I'll shoot for meat, or for trophies, or to defend myself, but not just to hear the gun go off. If more people had exercised moderation in killing, there'd still be decent sport in our own era. Understand?"

"Yeah, I guess so," he said. Mercurial sort of bloke.

The rest of the party came through the machine and we pitched our camp a safe distance from the materializing place. Our first task was to get fresh meat. For a twenty-one-day safari like this, we calculate our food requirements closely so we can make out on tinned stuff and concentrates if we must, but we count on killing at least one piece of meat. When that's butchered, we go on a short tour, stopping at four or five camping places to hunt and arriving back at base a few days before the chamber is due to appear.

Holtzinger, as I said, wanted a ceratopsian head, any kind. James insisted on just one head: a tyrannosaur. Then everybody'd think he'd shot the most dangerous game of all time.

Fact is, the tyrannosaur's overrated. He's more a carrion-eater than an active predator, though he'll snap you up if he gets the chance. He's less dangerous than some of the other theropods— the flesh eaters—such as the big saurophagus of the Jurassic, or even the smaller gorgosaurus from the period we were in. But everybody's read about the tyrant lizard and he does have the biggest head of the theropods.

The one in our period isn't the rex, which is later and a little bigger and more specialized. It's the trionyches with the forelimbs not reduced to quite such little vestiges, though they're too small for anything but picking the brute's teeth after a meal.

When camp was pitched, we still had the afternoon, so the Raja and I took our sahibs on their first hunt. We already had a map of the local terrain from previous trips. The Raja and I have worked out a system for dinosaur hunting. We split into two groups of two men and walk parallel from twenty to forty yards apart. Each group consists of one sahib in front and one guide following and telling the sahib where to go.

We tell the sahibs we put them in front so they shall have first shot, which is true, but another reason is they're always tripping and falling with their guns cocked, and if the guide were in front, he'd get shot.

The reason for two groups is that if a dinosaur starts for one, the other gets a good heart shot from the side.

As we walked, there was the usual rustle of lizards scuttling out of the way: little fellows, quick as a flash and colored like all the jewels in Tiffany's, and big gray ones that hiss and plod off. There were tortoises and a few little snakes. Birds with beaks full of teeth flapped off squawking. And always that marvelous mild Cretacean air. Makes a chap want to take his clothes off and dance with vine leaves in his hair, if you know what I mean. Not that I'd ever do such a thing, you understand.

Our sahibs soon found that Mesozoic country is cut up into millions of nullahs—gullies, you'd call them. Walking is one long scramble, up and down, up and down.

We'd been scrambling for an hour and the sahibs were soaked with sweat and had their tongues hanging out, when the Raja whistled. He'd spotted a group of bonehead feeding on cycad shoots.

These are the troödonts, small ornithopods about the size of men with a bulge on top of their heads that makes them look quite intelligent. Means nothing, because the bulge is solid bone and the brain is as small as in other dinosaur, hence the name. The males butt each other with these heads in fighting over the females. They would drop down to all fours, munch a shoot, then stand up and look round. They're warier than most dinosaur because they're the favorite food of the big theropods.

People sometimes assume that because dinosaur are so stupid, their senses must be dim, but it's not so. Some, like the sauropods, are pretty dim-sensed, but most have good smell and eyesight and fair hearing. Their weakness is that, having no minds, they have no memories; hence, out of sight, out of mind. When a big theropod comes slavering after you, your best defense is to hide in a nullah or behind a bush, and if he can neither see nor smell you, he'll just forget all about you and wander off.

We sneaked up behind a patch of palmetto downwind from the bonehead. I whispered to James: "You've had a shot already today. Hold your fire until Holtzinger shoots and then shoot only if he misses or if the beast is getting away wounded."

"Uh-huh," said James and we separated, he with the Raja and Holtzinger with me. This got to be our regular arrangement. James and I got on each other's nerves, but the Raja, once you forget that Oriental-potentate rot, is a friendly, sentimental sort of bloke nobody can help liking.

Well, we crawled round the palmetto patch on opposite sides and Holtzinger got up to shoot. You daren't shoot a heavy-caliber rifle prone. There's not enough give and the kick can break your shoulder.

Holtzinger sighted round the last few fronds of palmetto. I saw his barrel wobbling and weaving and then off went James's gun, both barrels again. The biggest bonehead went down, rolling and thrashing, and the others ran on their hindlegs in great leaps, their heads jerking and their tails sticking up behind.

"Put your gun on safety," I said to Holtzinger, who'd started forward. By the time we got to the bonehead, James was standing over it, breaking open his gun and blowing out the barrels. He looked as smug as if he'd inherited another million and he was asking the Raja to take his picture with his foot on the game. His first shot had been excellent, right through the heart. His second had missed because the first knocked the beast down. James couldn't resist that second shot even when there was nothing to shoot at.

I said: "I thought you were to give Holtzinger first shot."

"Hell, I waited," he said, "and he took so long, I thought something must have gone wrong. If we stood around long enough, they'd see us or smell us."

There was something in what he said, but his way of saying it got me angry. I said: "If that sort of thing happens just once more, we'll leave you in camp the next time we go out."

"Now, gentlemen," said the Raja. "After all, Reggie, these aren't experienced hunters."

"What now?" asked Holtzinger. "Haul the beast back ourselves or send out the men?"

"I think we can sling him under the pole," I said. "He weighs under two hundred." The pole was a telescoping aluminum carrying pole I had in my pack, with yokes on the ends with sponge-rubber padding. I brought it along because in such eras you can't always count on finding saplings strong enough for proper poles on the spot.

The Raja and I cleaned our bonehead, to lighten him, and tied him to the pole. The flies began to light on the offal by the thousands. Scientists say they're not true flies in the modern sense, but they look and act like them. There's one conspicuous kind of carrion fly, a big four-winged insect with a distinctive deep note as it flies.

The rest of the afternoon, we sweated under that pole. We took turns about, one pair carrying the beast while the other two carried the guns. The lizards scuttled out of the way and the flies buzzed round the carcass.

When we got to camp, it was nearly sunset. We felt as if we

could eat the whole bonehead at one meal. The boys had the camp running smoothly, so we sat down for our tot of whiskey feeling like lords of creation while the cook broiled bonehead steaks.

Holtzinger said: "Uh—if I kill a ceratopsian, how do we get his head back?"

I explained: "If the ground permits, we lash it to the patent aluminum roller-frame and sled it in."

"How much does a head like that weigh?" he asked.

"Depends on the age and the species," I told him. "The biggest weigh over a ton, but most run between five hundred and a thousand pounds."

"And all the ground's rough like today?"

"Most of it. You see, it's the combination of the open vegetation cover and the high rainfall. Erosion is frightfully rapid."

"And who hauls the head on its little sled?"

"Everybody with a hand. A big head would need every ounce of muscle in this party and even then we might not succeed. On such a job, there's no place for sides."

"Oh," said Holtzinger. I could see him wondering whether a ceratopsian head would be worth the effort.

The next couple of days, we trekked round the neighborhood. Nothing worth shooting; only a herd of fifty-odd ornithomimes who went bounding off like a lot of bloody ballet dancers. Otherwise there were only the usual lizards and pterosaurs and birds and insects. There's a big lace-winged fly that bites dinosaurs, so you can imagine its beak makes nothing of a human skin. One made Holtzinger leap into the air when it bit through his shirt. James joshed him about it, saying: "What's all this fuss over one little bug?"

The second night, during the Raja's watch, James gave a yell that brought us all out of our tents with rifles. All that had happened was that a dinosaur tick had crawled in with him and started drilling into his armpit. Since it's as big as your thumb even when it hasn't fed, he was understandably startled. Luckily he got it before it had taken its pint of blood. He'd pulled Holtzinger's leg pretty hard about the fly bite, so now Holtzinger repeated: "What's all the fuss over one little bug, buddy?"

James squashed the tick underfoot and grunted. He didn't like being twitted with his own words.

We packed up and started on our circuit. We meant to take them first to the borders of the sauropod swamp, more to see the wildlife than to collect anything.

From where the transition chamber materializes, the sauropod swamp looks like a couple of hours' walk, but it's an all-day scramble. The first part is easy, as it's downhill and the brush isn't heavy. But as you get near the swamp, the cycads and willows grow so thickly, you have to worm your way among them.

There was a sandy ridge on the border of the swamp that I led the party to, for it's pretty bare of vegetation and affords a fine view. When we got to the ridge, the sun was about to go down. A couple of crocs slipped off into the water. The sahibs were so exhausted, being soft yet, that they flopped down in the sand as if dead.

The haze is thick round the swamp, so the sun was deep red and distorted by the atmospheric layers—pinched in at various levels. There was a high layer of clouds reflecting the red and gold, too, so altogether it was something for the Raja to write one of his poems about. Only your modern poet prefers to write about a rainy day in a garbage dump. A few little pterosaur were wheeling overhead like bats, only they don't flutter like bats. They swoop and soar after the big night-flying insects.

Beauregard Black collected firewood and lit a fire. We'd started on our steaks, and that pagoda-shaped sun was just slipping below the horizon, and something back in the trees was making a noise like a rusty hinge, when a sauropod breathed out in the water. If

Mother Earth were to sigh over the misdeeds of her children, it would sound just about like that.

The sahibs jumped up, waving and shouting: "Where is he? Where is he?"

I said: "That black spot in the water, just to the left and this side of that point."

They yammered while the sauropod filled its lungs and disappeared. "Is that all?" yelped James. "Won't we see any more of him?"

Holtzinger said: "I read they never come out of the water because they're too heavy."

"No," I explained. "They can walk perfectly well and often do, for egg-laying and moving from one swamp to another. But most of the time they spend in the water, like hippopotamus. They eat eight hundred pounds of soft swamp plants a day, all with those little heads. So they wander about the bottoms of lakes and swamps, chomping away, and stick their heads up to breathe every quarter-hour or so. It's getting dark, so this fellow will soon come out and lie down in the shallows to sleep."

"Can we shoot one?" demanded James.

"I wouldn't," said I.

"Why not?"

I said: "There's no point in it and it's not sporting. First, they're even harder to hit in the brain than other dinosaurs because of the way they sway their heads about on those long necks and their hearts are too deeply buried in tissue to reach unless you're awfully lucky. Then, if you kill one in the water, he sinks and can't be recovered. If you kill one on land, the only trophy is that little head. You can't bring the whole beast back because he weighs thirty tons or more. We don't need thirty tons of meat."

Holtzinger said: "That museum in New York got one."

"Yes," I agreed. "The American Museum of Natural History sent a party of forty-eight to the early Cretaceous, with a fifty-caliber machine gun. They assembled the gun on the edge of a swamp, killed a sauropod—and spent two solid months skinning it and hacking the carcass apart and dragging it to the time machine. I know the chap in charge of that project and he still has nightmares in which he smells decomposing dinosaur. They also had to kill a dozen big theropods who were attracted by the stench and refused to be frightened off, so they had *them* lying round and rotting, too. And the theropods ate three men of the party despite the big gun."

Next morning, we were finishing breakfast when one of the helpers called: "Look, Mr. Rivers! Up there!"

He pointed along the shoreline. There were six big duckbill feeding in the shallows. They were the kind called parasaurolophus, with a crest consisting of a long spike of bone sticking out the back of their heads, like the horn of an oryx, and a web of skin connecting this with the back of their neck.

"Keep your voices down," I said. The duckbill, like the other ornithopods, are wary beasts because they have no armor or weapons against the theropods. The duckbill feed on the margins of lakes and swamps, and when a gorgosaur rushes out of the trees, they plunge into deep water and swim off. Then when phobosuchus, the super-crocodile, goes for them in the water, they flee to the land. A hectic sort of life, what?

Holtzinger said: "Uh—Reggie, I've been thinking over what you said about ceratopsian heads. If I could get one of those yonder, I'd be satisfied. It would look big enough in my house, wouldn't it?"

"I'm sure of it, old boy," I said. "Now look here. I could take you on a detour to come out on the shore near there, but we should have to plow through half a mile of muck and brush, up to our knees in water, and they'd hear us coming. Or we can creep up to the north end of this sand spit, from which it's four or five hundred yards—a long shot, but not impossible. Think you could do it?"

"With my 'scope sight and a sitting position—yes, I'll try it."

"You stay here," I said to James. "This is Augie's head and I don't want any argument over your having fired first."

James grunted while Holtzinger clamped his 'scope to his rifle. We crouched our way up the spit, keeping the sand ridge between us and the duckbills. When we got to the end where there was no more cover, we crept along on hands and knees, moving slowly. If you move slowly directly toward or away from a dinosaur, it probably won't notice you.

The duckbills continued to grub about on all fours, every few seconds rising to look round. Holtzinger eased himself into the sitting position, cocked his piece, and aimed through the 'scope. And then—

Bang! bang! went a big rifle back at the camp.

Holtzinger jumped. The duckbills jerked up their heads and leaped for the deep water, splashing like mad. Holtzinger fired once and missed. I took a shot at the last duckbill before it disappeared. I missed, too: the .600 isn't designed for long ranges.

Holtzinger and I started back toward the camp, for it had struck us that our party might be in theropod trouble and need reinforcements.

What happened was that a big sauropod, probably the one we'd heard the night before, had wandered down past the camp under water, feeding as it went. Now the water shoaled about a hundred yards offshore from our spit, halfway over to the edge of the swamp on the other side. The sauropod had ambled up the slope until its body was almost all out of water, weaving its head from side to side and looking for anything green to gobble. This kind looks like the well-known brontosaurus, but a little bigger. Scientists argue whether it ought to be included in the genus camarasaurus or a separate genus with an even longer name.

When I came in sight of the camp, the sauropod was turning round to go back the way it had come, making horrid groans. It disappeared into deep water, all but its head and ten or twenty feet of neck, which wove about for some time before they vanished into the haze.

When we came up to the camp, James was arguing with the Raja. Holtzinger burst out: "You bastard! That's the second time you've spoiled my shots!" Strong language for little August.

"Don't be a fool," said James. "I couldn't let him wander into camp and stamp everything flat."

"There was no danger of that," objected the Raja politely. "You can see the water is deep offshore. It is just that our trigger-happee Mr. James cannot see any animal without shooting."

I said: "If it did get close, all you needed to do was throw a stick of firewood at it. They're perfectly harmless." This wasn't strictly true. When the Comte de Lautre ran after one for a close shot, the sauropod looked back at him, gave a flick of its tail, and took off the Comte's head as neatly as if he'd been axed in the Tower.

"How was I to know?" yelled James, getting purple. "You're all against me. What the hell are we on this goddamn trip for except to shoot things? You call yourselves hunters, but I'm the only one who's hit anything!"

I got pretty wrothy and said he was just an excitable young skite with more money than brains, whom I should never have brought along.

"If that's how you feel," he said, "give me a burro and some food and I'll go back to the base by myself. I won't pollute your air with my loathsome presence!"

"Don't be a bigger ass than you can help," I snapped. "That's quite impossible."

"Then I'll go all alone!" He grabbed his knapsack, thrust a couple of tins of beans and an opener into it, and started off with his rifle.

Beauregard Black spoke up: "Mr. Rivers, we cain't let him go off like that by hisself. He'll git lost and starve or be et by a theropod."

"I'll fetch him back," said the Raja and started after the runaway. He caught up as James was disappearing into the cycads. We could see them arguing and waving their hands, but couldn't make out what they said. After a while, they started back with arms around each other's necks like old school pals. I simply don't know how the Raja does it.

This shows the trouble we get into if we make mistakes in planning such a do. Having once got back into the past, we had to make the best of our bargain. We always must, you see.

I don't want to give the impression Courtney James was only a pain in the rump. He had his good points. He got over these rows quickly and next day would be as cheerful as ever. He was helpful with the general work of the camp—when he felt like it, at any rate. He sang well and had an endless fund of dirty stories to keep us amused.

We stayed two more days at the camp. We saw crocodiles, the small kind, and plenty of sauropod—as many as five at once—but no more duckbill. Nor any of those fifty-foot super-crocodiles.

So on the first of May, we broke camp and headed north toward the Janpur Hills. My sahibs were beginning to harden up and were getting impatient. We'd been in the Cretaceous a week and no trophies.

I won't go into details of the next leg. Nothing in the way of a trophy, save a glimpse of a gorgosaur out of range and some tracks indicating a whooping big iguanodont, twenty-five or thirty feet high. We pitched camp at the base of the hills.

We'd finished off the bonehead, so the first thing was to shoot fresh meat. With an eye to trophies, too, of course. We got ready the morning of the third.

I told James: "See here, old boy, no more of your tricks. The Raja will tell you when to shoot."

"Uh-huh, I get you," he said, meek as Moses. Never could tell how the chap would act.

We marched off, the four of us, into the foothills. We were looking for bonehead, but we'd take an ornithomime. There was also a good chance of getting Holtzinger his ceratopsian. We'd seen a couple on the way up, but mere calves without decent horns.

It was hot and sticky and we were soon panting and sweating like horses. We'd hiked and scrambled all morning without seeing a thing except lizards, when I picked up the smell of carrion. I stopped the party and sniffed. We were in an open glade cut up by these little dry nullahs. The nullahs ran together into a couple of deeper gorges that cut through a slight depression choked with a denser growth, cycad and screw pine. When I listened, I heard the thrum of carrion flies.

"This way," I said. "Something ought to be dead—ah, here it is!"

And there it was: the remains of a huge ceratopsian lying in a little hollow on the edge of the copse. Must have weighed six or eight tons alive; a three-horned variety, perhaps the penultimate species of Triceratops. It was hard to tell because most of the hide on the upper surface had been ripped off and many bones had been pulled loose and lay scattered about.

Holtzinger said: "Oh, hell! Why couldn't I have gotten to him before he died? That would have been a darn fine head." Associating with us rough types had made little August profane, you'll observe.

I said: "On your toes, chaps. A theropod's been at this carcass and is probably nearby."

"How d'you know?" James challenged, with the sweat running off his round red face. He spoke in what was for him a low voice, because a nearby theropod is a sobering thought even to the flightiest.

I sniffed again and thought I could detect the distinctive rank odor of theropod. But I couldn't be sure because the stench of the carcass was so strong. My sahibs were turning green at the sight and smell of the cadaver.

I told James: "It's seldom even the biggest theropod will attack a full-grown ceratopsian. Those horns are too much for them. But they love a dead or dying one. They'll hang round a dead ceratopsian for weeks, gorging and then sleeping their meals off for days at a time. They usually take cover in the heat of the day anyhow, because they can't stand much direct hot sunlight. You'll find them lying in copses like this or in hollows, anywhere there's shade."

"What'll we do?" asked Holtzinger.

"We'll make our first cast through this copse, in two pairs as usual. Whatever you do, don't get impulsive or panicky." I looked at Courtney James, but he looked right back and then merely checked his gun.

"Should I still carry this broken?" he wanted to know.

"No; close it, but keep the safety on till you're ready to shoot," I said. It's risky carrying a double closed like that, especially in brush, but with a theropod nearby, it would have been a greater risk to carry it open and perhaps catch a twig in it when one tried to close it.

"We'll keep closer than usual, to be in sight of each other," I said. "Start off at that angle, Raja. Go slowly and stop to listen between steps."

We pushed through the edge of the copse, leaving the carcass but not its stink behind us. For a few feet, we couldn't see a thing. It opened out as we got in under the trees, which shaded out some of the brush. The sun slanted down through the trees. I could hear nothing but the hum of insects and the scuttle of lizards and the squawks of toothed birds in a treetop. I thought I could be sure of the theropod smell, but told myself that might be imagination. The theropod might be any of several species, large or small, and the beast itself might be anywhere within a half-mile radius.

"Go on," I whispered to Holtzinger, for I could hear James and the Raja pushing ahead on my right and see the palm fronds and ferns lashing about as they disturbed them. I suppose they were trying to move quietly, but to me they sounded like an earthquake in a crockery shop.

"A little closer," I called, and presently they appeared slanting in toward me.

We dropped into a gully filled with ferns and clambered up the other side, then found our way blocked by a big clump of palmetto.

"You go round that side: we'll go round this," I said, and we started off, stopping to listen and smell. Our positions were exactly the same as on that first day when James killed the bonehead.

I judge we'd gone two-thirds of the way round our half of the palmetto when I heard a noise ahead on our left. Holtzinger heard it and pushed off his safety. I put my thumb on mine and stepped to one side to have a clear field.

The clatter grew louder. I raised my gun to aim at about the height a big theropod's heart would be at the distance it would appear to us out of the greenery. There was a movement in the foliage—and a six-foot-high bonehead stepped into view, walking solemnly across our front from left to right, jerking its head with each step like a giant pigeon.

I heard Holtzinger let out a breath and had to keep myself from laughing. Holtzinger said: "Uh—"

"Quiet," I whispered. "The theropod might still—"

That was as far as I got when that damned gun of James's went off, bang! bang! I had a glimpse of the bonehead knocked arsy-varsy with its tail and hindlegs flying.

"Got him!" yelled James, and I heard him run forward.

"My God, if he hasn't done it again!" I groaned. Then there was a great swishing, not made by the dying bonehead, and a wild yell from James. Something heaved up and out of the shrubbery and I saw the head of the biggest of the local flesh-eaters, tyrannosaurus trionyches himself.

The scientists can insist that rex is bigger than trionyches, but I'll swear this tyrannosaur was bigger than any rex ever hatched. It must have stood twenty feet high and been fifty feet long. I could see its bright eye and six-inch teeth and the big dewlap that hangs down from its chin to its chest.

The second of the nullahs that cut through the copse ran athwart our path on the far side of the palmetto clump. Perhaps six feet deep. The tyrannosaur had been lying in this, sleeping off its last meal. Where its back struck up above ground level, the ferns on the edge of the nullah masked it. James had fired both barrels over the theropod's head and woke it up. Then James, to compound his folly, ran forward without reloading. Another twenty feet and he'd have stepped on the tyrannosaur's back.

James understandably stopped when this thing popped up in front of him. He remembered his gun was empty and he'd left the Raja too far behind to get a clear shot.

James kept his nerve at first. He broke open his gun, took two rounds from his belt and plugged them into the barrels. But in his haste to snap the gun shut, he caught his right hand between the barrels and the action—the fleshy part between his thumb and palm. It was a painful pinch and so startled James that he dropped his gun. That made him go to pieces and he bolted.

His timing couldn't have been worse. The Raja was running up with his gun at high port, ready to snap it to his shoulder the instant he got a clear view of the tyrannosaur. When he saw James running headlong toward him, it made him hesitate, as he didn't want to shoot James. The latter plunged ahead and, before the Raja could jump aside, blundered into him and sent them both sprawling among the ferns. The tyrannosaur collected what little wits it had and crashed after to snap them up.

And how about Holtzinger and me on the other side of the

palmettos? Well, the instant James yelled and the tyrannosaur's head appeared, Holtzinger darted forward like a rabbit. I'd brought my gun up for a shot at the tyrannosaur's head, in hope of getting at least an eye, but before I could find it in my sights, the head was out of sight behind the palmettos. Perhaps I should have shot at where I thought it was, but all my experience is against wild shots.

When I looked back in front of me, Holtzinger had already disappeared round the curve of the palmetto clump. I'm pretty heavily built, as you can see, but I started after him with a good turn of speed, when I heard his rifle and the click of the bolt between shots: bang—click-click—bang—click-click, like that.

He'd come up on the tyrannosaur's quarter as the brute started to stoop for James and the Raja. With his muzzle twenty feet from the tyrannosaur's hide, he began pumping .375s into the beast's body. He got off three shots when the tyrannosaur gave a tremendous booming grunt and wheeled round to see what was stinging it. The jaws came open and the head swung round and down again.

Holtzinger got off one more shot and tried to leap to one side. He was standing on a narrow place between the palmetto clump and the nullah. So he fell into the nullah. The tyrannosaur continued its lunge and caught him, either as he was falling or after he struck bottom. The jaws went chomp and up came the head with poor Holtzinger in them, screaming like a damned soul.

I came up just then and aimed at the brute's face. Then I realized its jaws were full of my friend and I'd be shooting him. As the head went up, like the business end of a big power shovel, I fired a shot at the heart. But the tyrannosaur was already turning away and I suspect the ball just glanced along the ribs.

The beast took a couple of steps away when I gave it the other barrel in the back. It staggered on its next step but kept on. Another step and it was nearly out of sight among the trees, when the Raja fired twice. The stout fellow had untangled himself from James, got up, picked up his gun and let the tyranno-saur have it.

The double wallop knocked the brute over with a tremendous smash. It fell into a dwarf magnolia and I saw one of its hindlegs waving in the midst of a shower of incongruously pretty pink-and-white petals.

Can you imagine the leg of a bird of prey enlarged and thick-ened until it's as big round as the leg of an elephant?

But the tyrannosaur got up again and blundered off without even dropping its victim. The last I saw of it was Holtzinger's legs dangling out one side of its jaws (by now he'd stopped screaming) and its big tail banging against the tree trunks as it swung from side to side.

The Raja and I reloaded and ran after the brute for all we were worth. I tripped and fell once, but jumped up again and didn't notice my skinned elbow till later. When we burst out of the copse, the tyrannosaur was already at the far end of the glade. I took a quick shot, but probably missed, and it was out of sight before I could fire another.

We ran on, following the tracks and spatters of blood, until we had to stop from exhaustion. Their movements look slow and pon-derous, but with those tremendous legs, they don't have to step very fast to work up considerable speed.

When we'd finished gasping and mopping our foreheads, we tried to track the tyrannosaur, on the theory that it might be dying and we should come up to it. But the spoor faded out and left us at a loss. We circled round hoping to pick it up, but no luck.

Hours later, we gave up and went back to the glade, feeling very dismal.

Courtney James was sitting with his back against a tree, holding his rifle and Holtzinger's. His right hand was swollen and blue where he'd pinched it, but still usable.

His first words were: "Where the hell have you been? You shouldn't have gone off and left me; another of those things might have come along. Isn't it bad enough to lose one hunter through your stupidity without risking another one?"

I'd been preparing a pretty warm wigging for James, but his attack so astonished me, I could only bleat: "We lost—?"

"Sure," he said. "You put us in front of you, so if anybody gets eaten it's us. You send a guy up against these animals undergunned. You—"

"You stinking little swine," I began and went on from there. I learned later he'd spent his time working out an elaborate theory according to which this disaster was all our fault—Holtzinger's, the Raja's and mine. Nothing about James's firing out of turn or panicking or Holtzinger's saving his worthless life. Oh, dear, no. It was the Raja's fault for not jumping out of his way, et cetera.

Well, I've led a rough life and can express myself quite eloquently. The Raja tried to keep up with me, but ran out of English and was reduced to cursing James in Hindustani.

I could see by the purple color on James's face that I was getting home. If I'd stopped to think, I should have known better than to revile a man with a gun. Presently James put down Holtzinger's rifle and raised his own, saying: "Nobody calls me things like that and gets away with it. I'll just say the tyrannosaur ate you, too."

The Raja and I were standing with our guns broken open, under our arms, so it would take a good part of a second to snap them shut and bring them up to fire. Moreover, you don't shoot a .600 holding it loosely in your hands, not if you know what's good for you. Next thing, James was setting the butt of his .500 against his shoulder, with the barrels pointed at my face. Looked like a pair of blooming vehicular tunnels.

The Raja saw what was happening before I did. As the beggar brought his gun up, he stepped forward with a tremendous kick. Used to play football as a young chap, you see. He knocked the

262

.500 up and it went off so the bullet missed my head by an inch and the explosion jolly well near broke my eardrums.

The butt had been punted away from James's shoulder when the gun went off, so it came back like the kick of a horse. It spun him half round.

The Raja dropped his own gun, grabbed the barrels and twisted it out of James's hands, nearly breaking the bloke's trigger finger. He meant to hit James with the butt, but I rapped James across the head with my own barrels, then bowled him over and began punching the stuffing out of him. He was a good-sized lad, but with my sixteen stone, he had no chance.

When his face was properly discolored, I stopped. We turned him over, took a strap out of his knapsack and tied his wrists behind him. We agreed there was no safety for us unless we kept him under guard every minute until we got him back to our time. Once a man has tried to kill you, don't give him another opportunity. Of course he might never try again, but why risk it?

We marched James back to camp and told the crew what we were up against. James cursed everybody and dared us to kill him.

"You'd better, you sons of bitches, or I'll kill you someday," he said. "Why don't you? Because you know somebody'd give you away, don't you? Ha-ha!"

The rest of that safari was dismal. We spent three days combing the country for that tyrannosaur. No luck. It might have been lying in any of those nullahs, dead or convalescing, and we should never see it unless we blundered on top of it. But we felt it wouldn't have been cricket not to make a good try at recovering Holtzinger's remains, if any.

After we got back to our main camp, it rained. When it wasn't raining, we collected small reptiles and things for our scientific friends. When the transition chamber materialized, we fell over one another getting into it.

The Raja and I had discussed the question of legal proceedings by or against Courtney James. We decided there was no precedent for punishing crimes committed eighty-five million years before, which would presumably be outlawed by the statute of limitations. We therefore untied him and pushed him into the chamber after all the others but us had gone through.

When we came out in the present, we handed him his gun—empty—and his other effects. As we expected, he walked off without a word, his arms full of gear. At that point, Holtzinger's girl, Claire Roche, rushed up crying: "Where is he? Where's August?"

I won't go over the painful scene except to say it was distressing in spite of the Raja's skill at that sort of thing.

We took our men and beasts down to the old laboratory building that Washington University has fitted up as a serai for expeditions to the past. We paid everybody off and found we were nearly broke. The advance payments from Holtzinger and James didn't cover our expenses and we should have damned little chance of collecting the rest of our fees from James or from Holtzinger's estate.

And speaking of James, d'you know what the blighter was doing all this time? He went home, got more ammunition and came back to the university. He hunted up Professor Prochaska and asked him:

"Professor, I'd like you to send me back to the Cretaceous for a quick trip. If you can work me into your schedule right now, you can just about name your own price. I'll offer five thousand to begin with. I want to go to April twenty-third, eighty-five million B.C."

Prochaska answered: "Vot do you vant to go back again so soon so badly for?"

"I lost my wallet in the Cretaceous," said James. "I figure if I go back to the day before I arrived in that era on my last trip, I'll watch myself when I arrived on that trip and follow myself till I see myself lose the wallet."

"Five thousand is a lot for a valet."

"It's got some things in it I can't replace. Suppose you let me worry about whether it's worth my while."

"Vell," said Prochaska, thinking, "the party that vas supposed to go out this morning has phoned that they vould be late, so maybe I can vork you in. I have alvays vondered vot vould happen vhen the same man occupied the same time tvice."

So James wrote out a check and Prochaska took him to the chamber and saw him off. James's idea, it seems, was to sit behind a bush a few yards from where the transition chamber would appear and pot the Raja and me as we emerged.

Hours later, we'd changed into our street clothes and phoned our wives to come get us. We were standing on Forsythe Boulevard waiting for them when there was a loud crack, like an explosion or a close-by clap of thunder, and a flash of light not fifty feet from us. The shock wave staggered us and broke windows in quite a number of buildings.

We ran toward the place and got there just as a policeman and several citizens came up. On the boulevard, just off the curb, lay a human body. At least it had been that, but it looked as if every bone in it had been pulverized and every blood vessel burst. The clothes it had been wearing were shredded, but I recognized an H. & H. .500 double-barreled express rifle. The wood was scorched and the metal pitted, but it was Courtney James's gun. No doubt whatever.

Skipping the investigations and the milling about, what had happened was this: Nobody had shot us as we emerged on the twenty-fourth and that, of course, couldn't be changed. For that matter, the instant James started to do anything that would make a visible change in the world of eighty-five million B.C., the space-time forces would snap him forward to the present to prevent a paradox.

Now that this is better understood, the professor won't send anybody to a period less than five hundred years prior to the time that some time traveler has already explored, because it would be too easy to do some act, like chopping down a tree or losing some durable artifact, that would affect the later world. Over long periods, he tells me, such changes average out and are lost in the stream of time.

We had a bloody rough time after that, with the bad publicity and all, though we did collect a fee from James's estate. The disaster hadn't been entirely James's fault. I shouldn't have taken him when I knew what a spoiled, unstable sort he was. And if Holtzinger could have used a heavy gun, he'd probably have knocked the tyrannosaur down, even if he didn't kill it, and so given the rest of us a chance to finish it.

So that's why I won't take you to that period to hunt. There are plenty of other eras, and if you think them over, I'm sure you'll find—

Good Lord, look at the time! Must run, old boy; my wife'll skin me. Good night!

OUR LADY OF THE SAUROPODS

ROBERT SILVERBERG

21 August. 0750 hours. Ten minutes since the module meltdown. I can't see the wreckage from here, but I can smell it, bitter and sour against the moist tropical air. I've found a cleft in the rocks, a kind of shallow cavern, where I'll be safe from the dinosaurs for a while. It's shielded by thick clumps of cycads, and in any case it's too small for the big predators to enter. But sooner or later I'm going to need food, and then what? I have no weapons. How long can one woman last, stranded and more or less helpless, aboard a habitat unit not quite five hundred meters in diameter that she's sharing with a bunch of active, hungry dinosaurs?

I keep telling myself that none of this is really happening. Only I can't quite convince myself of that.

My escape still has me shaky. I can't get out of my mind the funny little bubbling sound the tiny powerpak made as it began to overheat. In something like fourteen seconds my lovely mobile module became a charred heap of fused-together junk, taking with

267

it my communicator unit, my food supply, my laser gun, and just about everything else. And but for the warning that funny little sound gave me, I'd be so much charred junk now too. Better off that way, most likely.

When I close my eyes I imagine I can see Habitat Vronsky floating serenely in orbit a mere 120 kilometers away. What a beautiful sight! The walls gleaming like platinum, the great mirror collecting sunlight and flashing it into the windows, the agricultural satellites wheeling around it like a dozen tiny moons. I could almost reach out and touch it. Tap on the shielding and murmur, "Help me, come for me, rescue me." But I might just as well be out beyond Neptune as sitting here in the adjoining Lagrange slot. No way I can call for help. The moment I move outside this cleft in the rock I'm at the mercy of my saurians, and their mercy is not likely to be tender.

Now it's beginning to rain—artificial, like practically everything else on Dino Island. But it gets you just as wet as the natural kind. And clammy. Pfaugh.

Jesus, what am I going to do?

0815 hours. The rain is over for now. It'll come again in six hours. Astonishing how muggy, dank, thick the air is. Simply breathing is hard work, and I feel as though mildew is forming on my lungs. I miss Vronsky's clear, crisp, everlasting springtime air. On previous trips to Dino Island I never cared about the climate. But of course I was snugly englobed in my mobile unit, a world within a world, self-contained, self-sufficient, isolated from all contact with this place and its creatures. Merely a roving eye, traveling as I pleased, invisible, invulnerable.

Can they sniff me in here?

We don't think their sense of smell is very acute. Sharper than a crocodile's, not as good as a cat's. And the stink of the burned wreckage dominates the place at the moment. But I must reek with fear-signals. I feel calm now, but it was different as I went desperately scrambling out of the module during the meltdown. Scattering pheromones all over the place, I bet.

Commotion in the cycads. *Something's coming in here!*

Long neck, small birdlike feet, delicate grasping hands. Not to worry. *Struthiomimus,* is all—dainty dino, fragile, birdlike critter barely two meters high. Liquid golden eyes staring solemnly at me. It swivels its head from side to side, ostrichlike, click-click, as if trying to make up its mind about coming closer to me. *Scat!* Go peck a stegosaur. Let me alone.

The *Struthiomimus* withdraws, making little clucking sounds.

Closest I've ever been to a live dinosaur. Glad it was one of the little ones.

0900 hours. Getting hungry. What am I going to eat?

They say roasted cycad cones aren't too bad. How about raw ones? So many plants are edible when cooked and poisonous otherwise. I never studied such things in detail. Living in our antiseptic little L5 habitats we're not required to be outdoors-wise, after all. Anyway, there's a fleshy-looking cone on the cycad just in front of the cleft, and it's got an edible look. Might as well try it raw, because there's no other way. Rubbing sticks together will get me nowhere.

Getting the cone off takes some work. Wiggle, twist, snap, tear—*there.* Not as fleshy as it looks. Chewy, in fact. Like munching on rubber. Decent flavor, though. And maybe some useful carbohydrate.

The shuttle isn't due to pick me up for thirty days. Nobody's apt to come looking for me, or even to think about me, before then. I'm on my own. Nice irony there: I was desperate to get out of Vronsky and escape from all the bickering and maneuvering, the endless meetings and memoranda, the feinting and counterfeinting, all the ugly political crap that scientists indulge

269

in when they turn into administrators. Thirty days of blessed isolation on Dino Island! An end to that constant dull throbbing in my head from the daily infighting with Director Sarber. Pure research again! And then the meltdown, and here I am cowering in the bushes wondering which comes first, starving or getting gobbled.

0930 hours. Funny thought just now. Could it have been sabotage?

Consider. Sarber and I, feuding for weeks over the issue of opening Dino Island to tourists. Crucial staff vote coming up next month. Sarber says we can raise millions a year for expanded studies with a program of guided tours and perhaps some rental of the island to film companies. I say that's risky both for the dinos and the tourists, destructive of scientific values, a distraction, a sell-out. Emotionally the staff's with me, but Sarber waves figures around, shows fancy income projections, and generally shouts and blusters. Tempers running high, Sarber in lethal fury at being opposed, barely able to hide his loathing for me. Circulating rumors—designed to get back to me—that if I persist in blocking him he'll abort my career. Which is malarkey, of course. He may outrank me, but he has no real authority over me. And then his politeness yesterday. (*Yesterday?* An eon ago.) Smiling smarmily, telling me he hopes I'll rethink my position during my observation tour on the island. Wishing me well. Had he gimmicked my powerpak? I guess it isn't hard, if you know a little engineering, and Sarber does. Some kind of timer set to withdraw the insulator rods? Wouldn't be any harm to Dino Island itself, just a quick compact localized disaster that implodes and melts the unit and its passenger, so sorry, terrible scientific tragedy, what a great loss. And even if by some fluke I got out of the unit in time, my chances of surviving here as a pedestrian for thirty days would be pretty skimpy, right? Right.

It makes me boil to think that someone's willing to murder you over a mere policy disagreement. It's barbaric. Worse than that: it's tacky.

1130 hours. I can't stay crouched in this cleft forever. I'm going to explore the island and see if I can find a better hideout. This one simply isn't adequate for anything more than short-term huddling. Besides, I'm not as spooked as I was right after the meltdown. I realize now that I'm not going to find a tyrannosaur hiding behind every tree. And tyrannosaurs aren't going to be much interested in scrawny stuff like me.

Anyway I'm a quick-witted higher primate. If my humble mammalian ancestors seventy million years ago were able to elude dinosaurs well enough to survive and inherit the earth, I should be able to keep from getting eaten for the next thirty days. And, with or without my cozy little mobile module, I want to get out into this place, whatever the risks. Nobody's ever had a chance to interact this closely with the dinos before.

Good thing I kept this pocket recorder when I jumped from the module. Whether I'm a dino's dinner or not, I ought to be able to set down some useful observations.

Here I go.

1830 hours. Twilight is descending now. I am camped near the equator in a lean-to flung together out of tree-fern fronds—a flimsy shelter, but the huge fronds conceal me and with luck I'll make it through the morning. That cycad cone doesn't seem to have poisoned me yet, and I ate another one just now, along with some tender new fiddleheads uncoiling from the heart of a tree-fern. Spartan fare, but it gives me the illusion of being fed.

In the evening mists I observe a brachiosaur, half grown but already colossal, munching in the treetops. A gloomy-looking *Tri-*

ceratops stands nearby, and several of the ostrichlike struthiom-imids scamper busily in the underbrush, hunting I know not what. No sign of tyrannosaurs all day. There aren't many of them here, anyway, and I hope they're all sleeping off huge feasts somewhere in the other hemisphere.

What a fantastic place this is!

I don't feel tired. I don't even feel frightened—just a little wary. I feel exhilarated, as a matter of fact.

Here I sit peering out between fern fronds at a scene out of the dawn of time. All that's missing is a pterosaur or two flapping overhead, but we haven't brought those back yet. The mournful snufflings of the huge brachiosaur carry clearly even in the heavy air. The struthiomimids are making sweet honking sounds. Night is falling swiftly, and the great shapes out there take on dreamlike primordial wonder.

What a brilliant idea it was to put all the Olsen-process dinosaur reconstructs aboard a little L5 habitat of their very own and turn them loose to re-create the Mesozoic! After that unfortunate San Diego event with the tyrannosaur it became politically unfeasible to keep them anywhere on earth, I know, but even so this is a better scheme. In just a little more than seven years, Dino Island has taken on an altogether convincing illusion of reality. Things grow so fast in this lush, steamy, high-CO_2 tropical atmosphere! Of course we haven't been able to duplicate the real Mesozoic flora, but we've done all right using botanical survivors, cycads and tree-ferns and horsetails and palms and gingkos and auracarias, and thick carpets of mosses and selaginellas and liverworts covering the ground. Everything has blended and merged and run amok: it's hard now to recall the bare and unnatural look of the island when we first laid it out. Now it's a seamless tapestry in green and brown, a dense jungle broken only by streams, lakes, and mead-ows, encapsulated in spherical metal walls some two kilometers in circumference.

And the animals, the wonderful fantastic grotesque animals! We don't pretend that the real Mesozoic ever held any such mix of fauna as I've seen today, stegosaurs and corythosaurs side by side, a *Triceratops* sourly glaring at a brachiosaur, *Struthiomimus* contemporary with *Iguanodon*, a wild unscientific jumble of Triassic, Jurassic, and Cretaceous, a hundred million years of the dinosaur reign scrambled together. We take what we can get. Olsen-process reconstructs require sufficient fossil DNA to permit the computer synthesis, and we've been able to find that in only some twenty species so far. The wonder is that we've accomplished even that much: to replicate the complete DNA molecule from battered and sketchy genetic information millions of years old, to carry out the intricate implants in reptilian host ova, to see the embryos through to self-sustaining levels. The only word that applies is *miraculous.* If our dinos come from eras millions of years apart, so be it: we do our best. If we have no pterosaur and no allosaur and no *Archaeopteryx*, so be it: we may have them yet. What we already have is plenty to work with. Someday there may be separate Triassic, Jurassic, and Cretaceous satellite habitats, but none of us will live to see that, I suspect.

Total darkness now. Mysterious screechings and hissings out there. This afternoon, as I moved cautiously but in delight from the wreckage site up near the rotation axis to my present equatorial camp, sometimes coming within fifty or a hundred meters of living dinos, I felt a kind of ecstasy. Now my fears are returning, and my anger at this stupid marooning. I imagine clutching claws reaching for me, terrible jaws yawning above me.

I don't think I'll get much sleep tonight.

22 August. 0600 hours. Rosy-fingered dawn comes to Dino Island, and I'm still alive. Not a great night's sleep, but I must have had some, because I can remember fragments of dreams. About dinosaurs, naturally. Sitting in little groups, some playing pinochle and some knitting sweaters. And choral singing, a dinosaur rendition of the *Messiah* or maybe Beethoven's Ninth.

I feel alert, inquisitive, and hungry. Especially hungry. I know we've stocked this place with frogs and turtles and other small-size anachronisms to provide a balanced diet for the big critters. Today I'll have to snare some for myself, grisly though I find the prospect of eating raw frog's legs.

I don't bother getting dressed. With rainshowers programmed to fall four times a day it's better to go naked anyway. Mother Eve of the Mesozoic, that's me! And without my soggy tunic I find that I don't mind the greenhouse atmosphere half as much.

Out to see what I can find.

The dinosaurs are up and about already, the big herbivores munching away, the carnivores doing their stalking. All of them have such huge appetites that they can't wait for the sun to come up. In the bad old days when the dinos were thought to be reptiles, of course, we'd have expected them to sit there like lumps until daylight got their body temperatures up to functional levels. But one of the great joys of the reconstruct project was the vindication of the notion that dinosaurs were warm-blooded animals, active and quick and pretty damned intelligent. No sluggardly crocodilians these! Would that they were, if only for my survival's sake.

1130 hours. A busy morning. My first encounter with a major predator.

There are nine tyrannosaurs on the island, including three born in the past eighteen months. (That gives us an optimum predator-to-prey ratio. If the tyrannosaurs keep reproducing and don't start eating each other we'll have to begin thinning them out. One of the problems with a closed ecology: natural checks and balances

274

don't fully apply.) Sooner or later I was bound to encounter one, but I had hoped it would be later.

I was hunting frogs at the edge of Cope Lake. A ticklish business; calls for agility, cunning, quick reflexes. I remember the technique from my girlhood—the cupped hand, the lightning pounce—but somehow it's become a lot harder in the last twenty years. Superior frogs these days, I suppose. There I was, kneeling in the mud, swooping, missing, swooping, missing; some vast sauropod snoozing in the lake, probably our *Diplodocus*: a corythosaur browsing in a stand of gingko trees, quite delicately nipping off the foul-smelling yellow fruits. Swoop. Miss. Swoop. Miss. Such intense concentration on my task that old *T. rex* could have tiptoed right up behind me and I'd never have noticed. But then I felt a subtle something, a change in the air, maybe, a barely perceptible shift in dynamics. I glanced up and saw the corythosaur rearing on its hind legs, looking around uneasily, pulling deep sniffs into that fantastically elaborate bony crest that houses its early-warning system. *Carnivore alert*! The corythosaur obviously smelled something wicked this way coming, for it swung around between two big gingkos and started to go galumphing away. Too late. The treetops parted, giant boughs toppled, and out of the forest came our original tyrannosaur, the pigeon-toed one we call Belshazzar, moving in its heavy clumsy waddle, ponderous legs working hard, tail absurdly swinging from side to side. I slithered into the lake and scrunched down as deep as I could go in the warm oozing mud. The corythosaur had no place to slither. Unarmed, unarmored, it could only make great bleating sounds, terror mingled with defiance, as the killer bore down on it.

I had to watch. I had never seen a kill.

In a graceless but wondrously effective way the tyrannosaur dug its hind claws into the ground, pivoted astonishingly, and, using its massive tail as a counterweight, moved in a 90-degree arc to knock the corythosaur down with a stupendous sidewise swat of its huge head. I hadn't been expecting that. The corythosaur dropped and lay on its side, snorting in pain and feebly waving its limbs. Now came the *coup de grâce* with hind legs, and then the rending and tearing, the jaws and the tiny arms at last coming into play. Burrowing chin-deep in the mud, I watched in awe and weird fascination. There are those among us who argue that the carnivores ought to be segregated into their own island, that it is folly to allow reconstructs created with such effort to be casually butchered this way. Perhaps in the beginning that made sense, but not now, not when natural increase is rapidly filling the island with young dinos. If we are to learn anything about these animals, it will only be by reproducing as closely as possible their original living conditions. Besides, would it not be a cruel mockery to feed our tyrannosaurs on hamburger and herring?

The killer fed for more than an hour. At the end came a scary moment. Belshazzar, blood-smeared and bloated, hauled himself ponderously down to the edge of the lake for a drink. He stood no more than ten meters from me. I did my most convincing imitation of a rotting log; but the tyrannosaur, although it did seem to study me with a beady eye, had no further appetite. For a long while after he departed, I stayed buried in the mud, fearing he might come back for dessert. And eventually there was another crashing and bashing in the forest—not Belshazzar this time, though, but a younger one with a gimpy arm. It uttered a sort of whinnying sound and went to work on the corythosaur carcass. No surprise: we already knew that tyrannosaurs had no prejudices against carrion.

Nor, I found, did I.

When the coast was clear I crept out and saw that the two tyrannosaurs had left hundreds of kilos of meat. Starvation knoweth no pride and also few qualms. Using a clamshell for my blade, I started chopping away.

Corythosaur meat has a curiously sweet flavor—nutmeg and cloves, dash of cinnamon. The first chunk would not go down. You are a pioneer, I told myself, retching. You are the first human ever to eat dinosaur meat. *Yes, but why does it have to be raw?* No choice about that. Be dispassionate, love. Conquer your gag reflex or die trying. I pretended I was eating oysters. This time the meat went down. It didn't stay down. The alternative, I told myself grimly, is a diet of fern fronds and frogs, and you haven't been much good at catching the frogs. I tried again. Success!

I'd have to call corythosaur meat an acquired taste. But the wilderness is no place for picky eaters.

23 August. 1300 hours. At midday I found myself in the southern hemisphere, along the fringes of Marsh Marsh about a hundred meters below the equator. Observing herd behavior in sauropods: five brachiosaurs, two adult and three young, moving in formation, the small ones in the center. By "small" I mean only some ten meters from nose to tail-tip. Sauropod appetites being what they are, we'll have to thin that herd soon too, especially if we want to introduce a female *Diplodocus* into the colony. *Two* species of sauropods breeding and eating like that could devastate the island in three years. Nobody ever expected dinosaurs to reproduce like rabbits—another dividend of their being warm-blooded, I suppose. We might have guessed it, though, from the vast quantity of fossils. If that many bones survived the catastrophes of a hundred-odd million years, how enormous the living Mesozoic population must have been! An awesome race in more ways than mere physical mass.

I had a chance to do a little herd-thinning myself just now. Mysterious stirring in the spongy soil right at my feet, and I looked down to see *Triceratops* eggs hatching! Seven brave little critters, already horny and beaky, scrabbling out of a nest, staring around defiantly. No bigger than kittens, but active and sturdy from the moment of birth.

The corythosaur meat has probably spoiled by now. A more

pragmatic soul very likely would have augmented her diet with one or two little ceratopsians. I couldn't do it.

They scuttled off in seven different directions. I thought briefly of catching one and making a pet out of it. Silly idea.

25 August. 0700 hours. Start of the fifth day. I've done three complete circumambulations of the island. Slinking around on foot is fifty times as risky as cruising around in a module, and fifty thousand times as rewarding. I make camp in a different place every night. I don't mind the humidity any longer. And despite my skimpy diet I feel pretty healthy. Raw dinosaur, I know now, is a lot tastier than raw frog. I've become an expert scavenger—the sound of a tyrannosaur in the forest now stimulates my salivary glands instead of my adrenals. Going naked is fun, too. And I appreciate my body much more, since the bulges that civilization puts there have begun to melt away.

Nevertheless, I keep trying to figure out some way of signaling Habitat Vronsky for help. Changing the position of the reflecting mirrors, maybe, so I can beam an SOS? Sounds nice, but I don't even know where the island's controls are located, let alone how to run them. Let's hope my luck holds out another three and a half weeks.

27 August. 1700 hours. The dinosaurs know that I'm here and that I'm some extraordinary kind of animal. Does that sound weird? How can great dumb beasts *know* anything? They have such tiny brains. And my own brain must be softening on this protein-and-cellulose diet. Even so, I'm starting to have peculiar feelings about these animals. I see them *watching* me. An odd knowing look in their eyes, not stupid at all. They stare, and I imagine them nodding, smiling, exchanging glances with each other, discussing me.

278

I'm supposed to be observing them, but I think they're observing me too, somehow.

This is crazy. I'm tempted to erase the entry. But I'll leave it as a record of my changing psychological state, if nothing else.

28 August. 1200 hours. More fantasies about the dinosaurs. I've decided that the big brachiosaur—Bertha—plays a key role here. She doesn't move around much, but there are always lesser dinosaurs in orbit around her. Much eye contact. *Eye contact between dinosaurs?* Let it stand. That's my perception of what they're doing. I get a definite sense that there's communication going on here, modulating over some wave that I'm not capable of detecting. And Bertha seems to be a central nexus, a grand totem of some sort, a—a switchboard? What am I talking about? What's happening to me?

30 August. 0945 hours. What a damned fool I am! Serves me right for being a filthy voyeur. Climbed a tree to watch *Iguanodons* mating at the foot of Bakker Falls. At climactic moment the branch broke. I dropped twenty meters. Grabbed a lower limb or I'd be dead now. As it is, pretty badly smashed around. I don't think anything's broken, but my left leg won't support me and my back's in bad shape. Internal injuries too? Not sure. I've crawled into a little rock-shelter near the falls. Exhausted and maybe feverish. Shock, most likely. I suppose I'll starve now. It would have been an honor to be eaten by a tyrannosaur, but to die from falling out of a tree is just plain humiliating.

The mating of *Iguanodons* is a spectacular sight, by the way. But I hurt too much to describe it now.

*　　*　　*

31 August. 1700 hours. Stiff, sore, hungry, hideously thirsty. Leg still useless, and when I try to crawl even a few meters I feel as if I'm going to crack in half at the waist. High fever.

How long does it take to starve to death?

1 Sep. 0700 hours. Three broken eggs lying near me when I awoke. Embryos still alive—probably stegosaur—but not for long. First food in 48 hours. Did the eggs fall out of a nest somewhere overhead? Do stegosaurs make their nests in trees, dummy?

Fever diminishing. Body aches all over. Crawled to the stream and managed to scoop up a little water.

1330 hours. Dozed off. Awakened to find haunch of fresh meat within crawling distance. *Struthiomimus* drumstick, I think. Nasty sour taste, but it's edible. Nibbled a little, slept again, ate some more. Pair of stegosaurs grazing not far away, tiny eyes fastened on me. Smaller dinosaurs holding a kind of conference by some big cycads. And Bertha Brachiosaur is munching away in Ostrom Meadow, benignly supervising the whole scene.

This is absolutely crazy.

I think the dinosaurs are taking care of me.

2 Sep. 0900 hours. No doubt of it at all. They bring me eggs, meat, even cycad cones and tree-fern fronds. At first they delivered things only when I slept, but now they come hopping right up to me and dump things at my feet. The struthiomimids are the bearers—they're the smallest, most agile, quickest hands. They bring their offerings, stare me right in the eye, pause as if waiting for a tip. Other dinosaurs watching from the distance. This is a coordinated effort. I am the center of all activity on the island, it seems. I imagine that even the tyrannosaurs are saving choice cuts for me. Hallucination? Fantasy? Delirium of fever? I feel lucid. The fever is abating. I'm still too stiff and weak to move very far, but I think I'm recovering from the effects of my fall. With a little help from my friends.

1000 hours. Played back the last entry. Thinking it over. I don't *think* I've gone insane. If I'm sane enough to be worried about my sanity, how crazy can I be? Or am I just fooling myself? There's a terrible conflict between what I think I perceive going on here and what I know I ought to be perceiving.

1500 hours. A long strange dream this afternoon. I saw all the dinosaurs standing in the meadow, and they were connected to one another by gleaming threads, like the telephone lines of olden times, and all the threads centered on Bertha. As if she's the switchboard, yes. And telepathic messages were traveling. An extrasensory hookup, powerful pulses moving along the lines. I dreamed that a small dinosaur came to me and offered me a line, and in pantomime showed me how to hook it up, and a great flood of delight went through me as I made the connection. And when I plugged it in I could feel the deep and heavy thoughts of the dinosaurs, the slow rapturous philosophical interchanges.

When I woke the dream seemed bizarrely vivid, strangely real, the dream-ideas lingering as they sometimes do. I saw the animals about me in a new way. As if this is not just a zoological research station, but a community, a settlement, the sole outpost of an alien civilization—an alien civilization native to earth.

Come off it. These animals have minute brains. They spend

their days chomping on greenery, except for the ones that chomp on other dinosaurs. Compared with dinosaurs, cows and sheep are downright geniuses.

I can hobble a little now.

3 Sep. 0600 hours. The same dream again last night, the universal telepathic linkage. Sense of warmth and love flowing from dinosaurs to me.

Fresh tyrannosaur eggs for breakfast.

5 Sep. 1100 hours. I'm making a fast recovery. Up and about, still creaky but not much pain left. They still feed me. Though the struthiomimids remain the bearers of food the bigger dinosaurs now come close too. A stegosaur nuzzled up to me like some Goliath-sized pony, and I petted its rough scaly flank. The *Diplodocus* stretched out flat and seemed to beg me to stroke its immense neck.

If this is madness, so be it. There's a community here, loving and temperate. Even the predatory carnivores are part of it: eaters and eaten are aspects of the whole, yin and yang. Riding around in our sealed modules, we could never have suspected any of this.

They are gradually drawing me into their communion. I feel the pulses that pass between them. My entire soul throbs with that strange new sensation. My skin tingles.

They bring me food of their own bodies, their flesh and their unborn young, and they watch over me and silently urge me back to health. Why? For sweet charity's sake? I don't think so. I think they want something from me. I think they need something from me.

What could they need from me?

*　　*　　*

6 Sep. 0600 hours. All this night I have moved slowly through the forest in what I can only term an ecstatic state. Vast shapes, humped monstrous forms barely visible by dim glimmer, came and went about me. Hour after hour I walked unharmed, feeling the communion intensify. Until at last, exhausted, I have come to rest here on this mossy carpet, and in the first light of dawn I see the giant form of the great brachiosaur standing like a mountain on the far side of Owen River.

I am drawn to her. I could worship her. Through her vast body surge powerful currents. She is the amplifier. By her are we all connected. The holy mother of us all. From the enormous mass of her body emanate potent healing impulses.

I'll rest a little while. Then I'll cross the river to her.

0900 hours. We stand face to face. Her head is fifteen meters above mine. Her small eyes are unreadable. I trust her and I love her.

Lesser brachiosaurs have gathered behind her on the riverbank. Farther away are dinosaurs of half a dozen other species, immobile, silent.

I am humble in their presence. They are representatives of a dynamic, superior race, which but for a cruel cosmic accident would rule the earth to this day, and I am coming to revere them.

Consider: they endured for a hundred forty million years in ever-renewing vigor. They met all evolutionary challenges, except the one of sudden and catastrophic climatic change, against which nothing could have protected them. They multiplied and proliferated and adapted, dominating land and sea and air, covering the globe. Our own trifling contemptible ancestors were nothing next to them. Who knows what these dinosaurs might have achieved, if that crashing asteroid had not blotted out their light? What a vast irony: millions of years of supremacy ended in a single generation by a chilling cloud of dust. But until then—the wonder, the grandeur!

Only beasts, you say? How can you be sure? We know just a shred of what the Mesozoic was really like, just a slice, literally the bare bones. The passage of a hundred million years can obliterate all traces of civilization. Suppose they had language, poetry, mythology, philosophy? Love, dreams, aspirations? No, you say, they were beasts, ponderous and stupid, that lived mindless bestial lives. And I reply that we puny hairy ones have no right to impose our own values on them. The only kind of civilization we can understand is the one we have built. We imagine that our own trivial accomplishments are the determining case, that computers and spaceships and broiled sausages are such miracles that they place us at evolution's pinnacle. But now I know otherwise. Humanity has done marvelous things, yes. But we would not have existed at all, had this greatest of races been allowed to live to fulfill its destiny.

I feel the intense love radiating from the titan that looms above me. I feel the contact between our souls steadily strengthening and deepening.

The last barriers dissolve.

And I understand at last.

I am the chosen one. I am the vehicle. I am the bringer of rebirth, the beloved one, the necessary one. Our Lady of the Sauropods am I, the holy one, the prophetess, the priestess.

Is this madness? Then it is madness.

Why have we small hairy creatures existed at all? I know now. It is so that through our technology we could make possible the return of the great ones. They perished unfairly. Through us, they are resurrected abroad this tiny globe in space.

I tremble in the force of the need that pours from them.

I will not fail you, I tell the great sauropods before me, and the sauropods send my thoughts reverberating to all the others.

284

*   *   *

20 September. 0600 hours. The thirtieth day. The shuttle comes from Habitat Vronsky today to pick me up and deliver the next researcher.

I wait at the transit lock. Hundreds of dinosaurs wait with me, each close beside the next, both the lions and the lambs, gathered quietly, their attention focused entirely on me.

Now the shuttle arrives, right on time, gliding in for a perfect docking. The airlocks open. A figure appears, Sarber himself! Coming to make sure I didn't survive the meltdown, or else to finish me off.

He stands blinking in the entry passage, gaping at the throngs of placid dinosaurs arrayed in a huge semicircle around the naked woman who stands beside the wreckage of the mobile module. For a moment he is unable to speak.

"Anne?" he says finally. "What in God's name—"

"You'll never understand," I tell him. I give the signal. Belshazzar rumbles forward. Sarber screams and whirls and sprints for the airlock, but a stegosaur blocks the way.

"No!" Sarber cries, as the tyrannosaur's mighty head swoops down. It is all over in a moment.

Revenge! How sweet!

And this is only the beginning. Habitat Vronsky lies just 120 kilometers away. Elsewhere in the Lagrange belt are hundreds of other habitats ripe for conquest. The earth itself is within easy reach. I have no idea yet how it will be accomplished, but I know it will be done and done successfully, and I will be the instrument by which it is done.

I stretch forth my arms to the mighty creatures that surround me. I feel their strength, their power, their harmony. I am one with them, and they with me.

The Great Race has returned, and I am its priestess. Let the hairy ones tremble!

PERMISSIONS